THE
BLACK
UNICORN

HEATHER E. F. CARTER

Praise for *The Black Unicorn*

"Emotionally evocative. Historically authentic. And Irresistibly sensuous. The Black Unicorn, a captivating historical romance novel from gifted writer Heather E. F. Carter, explores the deeply sensual and conflict-ridden relationship between a notorious, highborn rakehell and the elegantly willful woman who challenges him at every turn. A riveting tale of betrayal, duplicity and intoxicating passion, this beautifully written novel will delight readers. 5 stars!"

LAURA TAYLOR
6-TIME ROMANTIC TIMES AWARD WINNER

"A love story with adventure and intrigue. Heather E. F. Carter is an exciting new voice."

JULIA BENNET,
AUTHOR OF THE RUIN OF EVANGELINE JONES

"Rampant with pulsating passion, gallant heroism, and lascivious treachery!"

InD'TALE MAGAZINE

For Terry

PROLOGUE

I'D MADE AN ENEMY.

I knew it as I watched Sebastian Throckmorton, the young Earl of Delemere, stalk away from me.

It would be for the last time.

I tracked Sebastian's progress across the ballroom until the sea of shimmering silks and laced velvets enveloped him. The sound of the orchestra faded into the background along with the drawling accents, inane laughter, and the odor of wilting hothouse orchids.

A soft rustle of silks sounded from my side. "You did what you had to do."

I nodded to my sister. I had just informed my former stepson that the three months I'd spent mourning his father were three months longer than the monster had deserved.

"He was away at school, Sophie," I murmured. "He had no idea the things that happened under his father's roof."

"The boy left you no choice, Elina," Charlotte pronounced from my other side.

I sighed, suddenly feeling very old for five and twenty. "He is a good boy. His father does not deserve him. Not in life, and not in death."

Charlotte nearly choked. "Elina! How on earth can you say that?"

"Sebastian is just young. And very proud."

In time to the music, my friend had been beating her closed fan in a sharp tattoo against her inner wrist. Now Charlotte stopped, and laid her fan on my sleeve. "But more importantly," she said, "why did you choose to come out of mourning in such a ghastly shade of yellow? I cannot think of a worse color for your ginger curls. You look seasick."

"*Auburn* curls," I corrected. It was an old argument, originating from the simpler days of our girlhood. "It was the only fabric the modiste could acquire on such short notice."

"The Throckmortons would never have allowed you any peace, my love. Not until you remarried," Sophie said.

I pressed my lips together and nodded. "I am sorry he forced me to cut ties with him and his family so publicly."

"Still, to threaten him . . ." Sophie said.

I nodded. "I know."

The threat, though only implied, had been significant. After all, my family's connections were the reason his father had married me in the first place. Still, I should never have reminded Sebastian of such things in public. The boy's pale eyes had widened while he listened to my words. He stood a moment in silence, swaying on legs still spindly from his sudden growth spurt last summer. Then he'd rallied some of the famous Throckmorton arrogance.

"Devil hang you, madam!" he'd hissed.

Sophie gently touched my arm, jolting me back to the present. "Do not worry, Elina. This has been a week for the gossips, what with three more robberies on the road to Bath."

From the corner of my eye, I saw Charlotte brush her fingers over the little jewel on her velvet choker, a small unicorn of black onyx and enamel. I had noticed several other ladies with similar jewels this evening.

"Indeed, the Black Unicorn has been busy of late," I replied.

"What we need now is a distraction," Charlotte declared, closing her fan with an emphatic snap. "Elina, do you not hear the music?"

A flute had added its light thread to the music's tapestry, followed by the darker, more sonorous timbre of the oboe's rapid countermelody. In and out they weaved, wrapping the sustained voices of the strings in their metrical pattern, anchored by the tinkling chords of the harpsichord.

Sophie arched a gilded brow, a slow smile spreading across her face. "A courante."

"But not just any courante . . . A *French* courante. Which means . . ." Charlotte allowed her voice to trail off significantly.

"The Duchess must have a new light o' love," I finished.

"Come, Dearest . . ." Charlotte grasped my hand and began to pull me towards the crowd of spectators. " . . . let us have a look at her new pet. At the very least, he will be handsome enough to distract you for a few moments from Lord Delemere."

I shook my head as I allowed her to tow me along. "I find that Her Grace's preferences tend to run too far into the nursery for my tastes."

Once we reached the front of the crowd of spectators, the Dowager Duchess of Surrey and her partner had their backs to us as they moved side by side away from the Presence—supplied this evening by Prinny, His Royal Highness the Prince of Wales—watching from just a short distance away to our right. As usual, he stood flanked by Sir Percy and Lady Marguerite Blakeney, the Beau Monde's acknowledged king and queen of fashion.

Turning my attention to the duchess's partner, I noted that

he was dark, with thick locks of softly waving hair, free from any powder or pomade, pulled back into the traditional queue at the nape of his neck with a black satin ribbon. He was tall, but not excessively so, and built along sleek, graceful lines, broad in the shoulders and narrow at the hip.

But it was his attire that first caused me to pay him any notice. In the radiant glow from the hundreds of lights in the cut-glass chandeliers and rows of girandoles mounted along the walls, the heavy gold embroidery encrusting every inch of his dress coat positively glittered as he moved, its sparks and incandescent flashes like the mingled elements of gold and fire in a Chinese dragon's scales.

This gentleman could be no new light o' love. He surely did not number among the aristocracy's second or third sons, cast adrift by the vicissitudes of primogeniture to beg temporary shelter in the dowager duchess's chilly harbor. The confident set of his shoulders clearly belonged to a man long habituated to being his own master, and nothing in his movements suggested the puppyish awkwardness normally favored by the dowager.

Having reached the opposite wall, the dancers executed a quarter turn to face each other and proceeded through a short advance and then a lengthier, intricately choreographed retreat. Then they moved through another quarter turn to face the Presence, and my breath caught in my throat as I caught my first glimpse of his face.

Damnation.

He was not English, at least not entirely. His dark coloring did not harken back to the raiders from Normandy, but rather to blood whispering of heat-scorched mornings, afternoon siestas, and the lazy currents of warm bluish-green waters. His eyes, though I knew from long experience to be blue, appeared now as dark as his hair, and were fringed with sooty lashes so impossibly thick and long they cast permanent shadows beneath them, lending him a thoroughly debauched air.

In fact, his beauty was staggering; the sort a Michelangelo or a Raphael might have found in some Mediterranean brothel; an incubus to be immortalized by lending a face to divinity.

He advanced towards us, the light shimmering around him like the gentle waves of the flautist's *vibrato* as he moved through the intricate series of steps.

"Who is he?" Charlotte queried from my other side. "I do not think I have ever seen him before."

"That is Ashby Harcourt," I said. "Earl of Ashenhurst up in Northumberland and whoring companion to my late husband."

"Tristan has spoken of him," murmured Charlotte. "They were schoolfellows, though my brother thinks very poorly of him. He is just as attractive as they say."

"But why does he keep looking at you, Elina?" Sophie asked.

"It is just a game he plays," I said through gritted teeth.

The dowager duchess and Lord Ashenhurst, having passed one another in a diagonal that left them at opposite corners of the polished parquetry floor, turned to face one another and followed a circuitous path in a broad, clockwise spiral that brought them together in the center. Their hands touched briefly before they turned again to move counterclockwise in a tighter spiral that brought them back to their original stance side by side before the Presence in the center of the floor.

But as the last notes of the music reverberated throughout the ballroom, and Her Grace dipped low in a surprisingly graceful curtsy, her partner shifted the angle of his hips and executed his bow with an old-fashioned Continental flourish towards my general direction rather than the future King of England's. A collective gasp erupted from the spectators, followed immediately by an uproar of agitated whispering as the Prince loosed a peal of silly, high-pitched laughter. The dark Adonis righted himself, and this time there was no mistaking the fact that he was looking directly at me, one corner of his beautiful mouth kicked up into a smirk.

"And who is the lady who has caught your eye this time, you scoundrel?" Prinny demanded as he leaned forward to gaze down our line of spectators through his quizzing glass. Once he reached us, he lowered his glass and an indolent smile spread across his face. "Ah, one of Hertford's daughters, is it? But which one, my dear fellow? The pretty blonde or the tall redhead?"

I felt the heat rush to my face as I glanced around the room. Everyone looked at us, their faces blending together into a mass of scorn and outrage.

"The blonde is betrothed, I am afraid," Prinny continued through a stifled yawn. "Though the redhead is recently widowed. *Too* recently, I should think, for her to be appearing amongst such gay company," he added, magnifying a lazy blue eye with his quizzing glass as he favored me with a critical stare. "But that might be good news for you, dear chap. I find that unconventional women do have a certain *joie de vivre* that often makes their pursuit a very pleasant distraction."

"Elina!" Sophie hissed as she grabbed my arm. Mortified, I immediately followed her lead and dropped into a curtsy so deep my knees nearly grazed the floor. "Your Highness," I murmured, keeping my head bowed to hide the spectacular blush burning from my hairline down to my collarbone.

But thankfully, the Prince had already tired of us and directed his attention back to Lady Blakeney. Sophie and I quickly made our escape, pushing rudely through the crowd in our haste. Charlotte awaited us near the doors leading to the supper room, her face anxious. I could not blame her for abandoning us; Sophie's betrothal and my widowhood bolstered us somewhat from the harsher aspects of public opinion, as did the fact that we were the daughters of the fifth marquess of Hertford. Had Prinny's careless comments been directed at Charlotte, the unmarried sister of a baronet, it could have cost her far more dearly than a few moments of embarrassment.

Charlotte reached out to take both my hands and gave them a little squeeze. "I am sorry, Elina. It is my fault, since I am the one who dragged you over to watch the dance."

"It is nothing, my love." I breezily waved my hand, hoping she did not notice my forced smile. "Everyone will surely have forgotten it by the end of the evening, I promise you."

Charlotte did not look convinced.

Quickly, I leaned forward and kissed her on the cheek. "Come, I would like to find Papa and sit down for supper. It has suddenly become too hot in here for my tastes."

Charlotte had been correct about one thing at least: I had forgotten completely my troubles with Sebastian and the Throckmorton clan.

CHAPTER 1

L ONG AGO, PAPA TOLD me that there are essentially four
types of men.

The first two are easy to tell apart: good men who do
good things, and bad men who do bad things. But life is rarely so
simple, which is why the latter two types are far more common in
this world: good men who do bad things, and bad men who do
good things. I knew from experience that a woman's only chance
to maintain control over her own life was to develop a talent
for figuring out what type of man she was dealing with. But six
months after the death of my husband, and three months after
the Foreign Secretary's Ball, it was still a skill I had yet to acquire.

"Ready, my girls?" Papa murmured, snapping me out of
my reverie.

I took a deep breath. "Ready."

Phosey, my fifteen-year-old half-sister, sounded less sure.

"I think so," came her small voice from behind us.

Papa nodded. "We've got our story straight?"

"Yes, Papa," Phosey and I said together.

9

"Very well," he said grimly. "Let's get this evening over with."

As the clock chimed for ten o'clock, I stepped into the crowded drawing room of Scarcliff Towers on Papa's arm. Despite our arrival at the prodigy house up in the North Yorkshire Moors only an hour earlier, my maid Edith had done her best with me. Nevertheless, I could still feel the exhausted set of my expression.

We'd had trouble on the road, making us the last to arrive for Lord Rydale's shooting party.

Barely had we made our appearance when a buxom brunette with bright green eyes like a tabby cat's descended upon us.

"There you are at last," she cried, her voice warmed by the rolling burr of a common Yorkshire brogue. "I was beginning to worry, wasn't I, Eleazer? Wasn't I just telling you that I was beginning to worry?"

Eleazer was a portly gentleman with the complexion of a man who spent too much time out of doors. Not one to be embarrassed by his handsome wife's easy manners, Lord Rydale, our host for the next month, ambled over to take his place beside her. They were a remarkable couple, their union a rare example of a love match—love at first sight, in fact. Papa had told us at breakfast the morning of our departure: many years ago, the earl happened to be passing through Pickering on his way to Scarborough when he stopped at the tavern owned by Lady Rydale's father. There he first encountered Cathy, as she was known in those days, and found himself captivated by her pretty eyes and purity of spirit. Six months later he married her, the love match sealed forever by the fact that she brought nothing with her in the way of a trousseau.

"Just herself," Papa had said, "which is enough for any happy marriage."

"Lady Tryphosia," Lady Rydale addressed my sister hiding timidly behind us, "bless me, but you look more and more like your mama every day. But where is Lady Sophronia? Has she taken ill?"

Papa and I glanced at each other. "Er, yes," he said. "She was feeling a bit poorly when we left London, perhaps from a little overindulgence at a soiree the night before. We hope she will be feeling fit by tomorrow."

"Oh, the poor dear!" Lady Rydale exclaimed. "If only I'd known sooner, I would have sent some tea and broth to her. I've heard all about those London soirees," she added with a wink to me. "I'll ring the maid straight away."

Papa bowed. "You are very kind."

Meanwhile, I took the opportunity to glance around the room for any familiar faces. The more people I knew, the quicker this evening would pass.

The woman in the corner, with jowly cheeks and pendulous flesh at her throat lending her the look of a plucked turkey, was likely the earl's sister, Lady Mildred.

The gentleman and young lady with matching platinum curls must be Lord and Lady Rydale's two adult children, the Viscount and Lady Dorothea.

I could not imagine who the homely little fellow dressed in an old-fashioned suit of plain brown broadcloth could be, and I could not see the face of the dark-haired cavalier engaging all of Lady Dorothea's attention, though his sumptuous suit of gray velvet laced in silver was certainly arresting.

Lady Rydale, having sent the housemaid in search of broth for Sophie, now appeared at my side.

"Come with me, dear, there is someone I would like you to meet," she said, taking me by the hand and pulling me across the room.

At first I thought with a sinking feeling that she was taking me toward the professional man, but we passed him and moved on towards Dorothea and her beautifully-dressed companion.

Then *Le Monsieur De L'Habit Gris* shifted position, leaning one elegant shoulder against the gilded cabinet next to him, allowing me my first glimpse of his face.

My pulse leapt, accelerating my heart into a thudding rhythm against my chest. Damning myself for a ginger, I immediately felt the telltale flush spreading up my throat.

What the devil was *he* doing here?

"Dorothea!" Lady Rydale announced as we arrived. "You have monopolized Lord Ashenhurst's attention for long enough. Your poor cousin has been standing alone for twenty minutes. Go tend to him at once." The girl's shoulders hunched at the rebuke; she whirled around to face her mother, rebellion writ clearly on her face.

But seeing me standing next to her mama, she seemed to think better of it. In a remarkable display of spoiled manners, she turned back to Lord Ashenhurst, bobbed a quick curtsey, then sailed off towards the professional man without the slightest acknowledgment of my presence.

But I was too preoccupied to take any real offence to the girl's rudeness. It had been three months since I'd last seen Lord Ashenhurst.

Meanwhile, Lady Rydale had begun the introductions. "Lord Ashenhurst," she said, "the lady about whom I spoke to you earlier has taken ill this evening, but this is her charming sister—"

"—Lady Delemere," he finished smoothly. His voice was almost as lovely as he was, deep and musical, and shaped by the hint of an exotic cadence I never could place. "As always, it is a pleasure."

He bowed over my hand, sending a small shiver up my arm as he brought my fingers to his lips.

I snatched my hand away. "Lord Ashenhurst was quite close to my late husband," I explained to Lady Rydale. "We have crossed paths before, though we've never been properly introduced."

In fact, Lord Ashenhurst had spent weeks at a time with us, sometimes months, though he and William had always been so drunk and besotted with dancing girls, I'd made it a point to spend as little time in their company as possible.

"Wonderful!" Lady Rydale clapped her hands in delight. "I'll just leave you two to become better acquainted."

And off she went, abandoning me to the attentions of this confounded libertine, her duties as hostess and mama discharged with admirable efficiency.

Dorothea, I noted enviously, was safely across the room engaged in sulky conversation with her cousin. I turned back to glower at the pretty creature now watching me.

"I dare say," he said after we'd stared at each other awhile in silence, "I think this dreadful evening will pass by more quickly if we speak to each other. We have been properly introduced now, so engaging in conversation with me is perfectly respectable. I intend to play the part of the gentleman this evening, so you may as well play the part of the lady. It can be our own private game."

I gasped before I could catch myself. "And what is that supposed to mean?"

A corner of his mouth kicked up raffishly. "I think you know what it means. And you know it to be true, so do not pretend to be offended. Now," he waved the matter aside, "at this point, we are supposed to figure out whether we have any acquaintances in common."

"How dare you!" I hissed. "In what manner do you suppose I am not a lady?"

"Come now, Lady Delemere. Back to the question of our acquaintances—"

"You are a cad," I cut in. "A lecher! A debaucher! A miserable—"

"I did not think so either," he replied. "At least none that we could admit to in Society, anyway. Though for propriety's sake, I had to ask. Now we shall ask each other about our families, and we can discuss them for a while. I will ask first—"

"Does Beelzebub have a family?"

"He does," he rejoined with a smile. "A lovely family—"

"I find that hard to believe."

"But now you are cheating. I am supposed to ask you first. How is your family, Lady Delemere? Somewhat smaller, I suppose, since you sorted out that young reprobate Sebastian Throckmorton at the Foreign Secretary's Ball last Spring? Bravo, by the way. It takes courage to come out of mourning so publically after only three months. But since young Delemere is not the sort to cultivate forgiveness in his black heart, I assume that you're now effectively cut off from the rest of the Throckmorton clan?"

"You are in no moral position to call anyone else a reprobate!" I exclaimed. "He is just a boy with a boy's youthful pride, nothing more."

His expression suddenly turned serious. "Since I am indeed a reprobate myself, I am in the perfect moral position to recognize the qualities of degeneracy in others. And Delemere *is* a reprobate. My brother Chrysander is schoolfellows with him at Westminster—an attachment I regret—and his reports home regarding Delemere demonstrate beyond a doubt that the young earl is following perfectly in his father's footsteps."

I snapped open my fan. It had suddenly become too warm. "You are wrong. The boy takes after his mother. He is a good boy. He will not become like his father."

"No, Elina—do you mind if I call you that? I hate using such a dreadful surname to address a beautiful woman. I am afraid that, in this case, you are the one who is wrong. The boy already is like his father. If he is like his mother, then she must have been a whore. And since a man can withstand the reputation for being a whore much more readily than a woman, I think it best if we just agree that the boy takes after his father."

I opened my mouth, then snapped it shut, finding myself at a loss for words.

Suddenly he leaned in close, and for a horrified moment I thought he intended to kiss me. Instead, his lips grazed my cheekbone, and I felt the warmth of his breath stirring the tiny hairs in my ear.

"Elina," he murmured. "Judge carefully what you say next. The World is now listening."

Glancing around, I saw all eyes fixed on us with varying degrees of surprise.

And triumph, in the case of Dorothea.

Then the large double doors to the dining room swung open, and the butler and a footman came to stand on either side of the doorway. Lord Ashenhurst silently offered me his arm, and I took it, allowing him to guide me into place behind Papa and Lady Rydale.

"No," I said as we proceeded into the dining room.

"No, what? I have forgotten what we were talking about."

"No, you may not call me Elina."

"Very well," he replied. "I am and will always remain your most humble servant. Elina."

CHAPTER 2

INNER PROGRESSED AS DINNERS usually do.

Lord Ashenhurst behaved himself, so I took stock of my surroundings. I found Lord Rydale's dining room to be highly unusual for the standards of the day, bearing none of the features currently in vogue throughout the rest of England.

Most Palladian dining rooms were light and airy, pastel and plush, with delicate painted plasterwork and the room's dramatic *pièce de résistance*: a French chandelier of cut glass glittering as it refracted candlelight off its prisms, drops, and faceted lustres.

But this room was dark.

Ancient oak paneling and threadbare carpets in faded Oriental designs absorbed light like a sponge, and the two-tiered chandelier with its twelve branches of lights reflecting off the highly polished brass looked heavy and old. The massive carved mantle dwarfed a fireplace large enough to roast a sheep or a pig, and the size of the room was colossal. At least twice the size of a modern dining room, it was so large that much of the ancient furnishings and tapestries remained totally obscured by shadow, lending our company the tenebrous mood of a Caravaggio, or perhaps a nocturne by de La Tour.

"Lady Delemere." Lord Rydale cleared his throat. "I, ah, see that you are favoring the room."

I turned to smile at my host. "Indeed."

"We are a family of antiquarians, you might say," he explained. "The only updates made to this house have been for comfort, not fashion. Except for my wife's saloon, that is. And the conservatory on the ground floor next to the gardens. Otherwise, this house is unique. And mysterious. Of course, you will have noticed the strange arrangement of the rooms—the humblest ones on the ground floor, the grandest up here on the third floor? Yes? Well, this house is also one of the first of this period to incorporate the use of corridors—"

"Oh, for heaven's sake!" Lady Rydale interrupted, her hands raised in mock surrender, "Not the corridors again, Eleazer! I keep telling you that no one cares about the corridors. Tell Lady Delemere about Bess's secret lover—or even the priest's hidey hole, but spare us from the corridors!"

"Bess Bewforest? The house's builder? She had a secret lover?" I winked at Lady Rydale before turning my attention back to her husband.

"She did," Lord Rydale answered before his wife could chime in again. "So secret that no one knew of his existence during her lifetime. But a few lines in her final Will and Testament indicate that she'd carried on a secret love affair with an unknown man for nearly two decades . . . assuming she waited to begin the relationship until after her husband died."

"But the first Earl of Rydale was a very old man at the time of his death," Lady Mildred's warbled voice cut in. "Who are we to assume that she waited? I would not wait."

A fine declaration coming from the virgin spinster, a fact not lost on Lord Ashenhurst, whom I glimpsed smiling into his napkin out of the corner of my eye.

"Either way, we have no idea who the fellow was. I assume,

Algernon, that you pointed out the parapets to your lovely daughters upon your arrival?"

"I beg your pardon, dear friend, but I did not," Papa replied. "We were already late for dinner, and I did not want to keep Lady Rydale waiting any longer than absolutely necessary."

"Then you are forgiven," Lady Rydale replied. "But the girls really must see the parapets—perhaps tomorrow if you walk in the garden after breakfast? I'd show you them myself, but Mildred and I will be in town for most of the day. Normally I couldn't be the least bit bothered over parapets myself, but our parapets are distinctive because they give us a clue to the mystery lover's identity."

I frowned. "The parapets? As in the *roof*?"

"The initials 'BH' are embedded in scrollwork at the top of each tower," the young Viscount drawled in a startling falsetto. "Nothing to become so worked up over. For all we know, they could be the initials of the house's architect or some other equally banal personage."

"Don't be ridiculous, Edwin," Lady Rydale admonished her son. "Of course the 'B' stands for Bewforest, so the 'H' must be the first letter of her lover's surname."

Lord Rydale held up his glass for the footman to refill. "Or the 'B' could stand for Bess, and the 'H' could be the first letter of her lover's Christian name."

"Eleezer," Papa said, "what is this about a priest hole? Scarcliff Towers truly has a priest hole?"

"It does. We found it about five years ago at the base of the southern tower," Lord Rydale said. "There was some flooding at the bases of the northern and southwestern towers, so we searched for water damage in the four remaining towers, and there it was—hidden beneath a storeroom."

"But a priest hole?" Papa pressed. "The Bewforests were among the first to convert to Protestantism."

"You are correct, Algernon, but it is a priest hole. Set up as a chapel actually, complete with altar, rood screen, statuary, and all the other papist paraphernalia. Even has an old, moldy copy of the Latin Vulgate."

"How bizarre!" Papa exclaimed.

"Indeed!" Lord Rydale motioned for the next course to be set. "And I left it as I found it. You are more than welcome to go have a look. We've had carpenters in, everything is structurally sound. Just try not to handle anything for too prolonged a period—some things, like the Missal, are disintegrating more and more with each passing day."

"Lady Rydale . . ." a timid voice suddenly cut into the conversation before Papa could reply. Everyone at the table turned in surprise to our party's youngest member.

"Yes, Lady Tryphosia?" our amiable hostess answered. "How may I assist you?"

"You'd said that the parapets were one of the only clues you had for the lover's identity."

"Yes, child," Lady Rydale replied. "Would you like to know what the others are?"

Phosey nodded.

"How about we just tell you about the second-best clue we have, and we will leave the others a mystery for you to discover on your own during your stay? It will give you something to do, young lady, to pass the time," suggested Lord Rydale.

"What a splendid idea!" Lady Rydale exclaimed. "Well. Eleazer, would you like to tell her? Or shall I?"

"I think I shall tell her, m'dear," he said. "As I mentioned, Bess's final Will and Testament makes mention of her lover, albeit obliquely. She left £100— a sum in those days—for an undisclosed number of masses to be performed in the memory of her lover, whom she refers to only as the Black Unicorn."

I gasped as my fork clattered down to my plate. "*What?*"

It happened in Lincolnshire just two days earlier, on a long, lonely stretch of the Great North Road.

✧

We had left London early in the morning, Papa seized by some curious inclination to put as much distance between us and the Home Counties as quickly as possible.

John the Driver set a challenging pace, requiring stops every twenty miles or so for a change of horse. We stopped in Huntingdon for a late breakfast, then again in Stamford for dinner at The George. Half-past three found us back on the road, and the next thing I remember was being startled awake sometime in the late afternoon, judging from the light filtering in through the coach's windows.

"What was that, Papa?" Phosey asked. Phosey's curly mop of hair was more rumpled than usual from leaning against the carriage wall, and both Sophie and Papa were rubbing the remnants of sleep from their eyes.

We heard shouts from outside and the coach began to slow down rapidly, lurching to a sudden stop.

"Something must be in the road, Phosey," Sophie said. "John will have it cleared quickly, I am sure." She patted the young girl's hand. "Is that not correct, Elina?"

I nodded at the sound of my name, but did not answer.

"Where are we, Papa?" I asked, watching his face. Something sounded off about the voices outside the coach.

"Lincolnshire," he said quietly. "We stopped for a change of horse at Thistleton about an hour ago."

Suddenly, we heard a rough voice very close to the coach. "Ger down off there, ye gormless bastards."

I looked out my window, searching for any other vehicles. There were none.

"Papa," I said, "I do not think there is an obstacle in the road."

He nodded, then leaned forward to reach under his seat. He pulled out a long pistol richly inlaid with silver and gold in Turkish designs, and laid it down on the seat next to him, piling his traveling cloak on top of it.

"Keep calm, my girls." As he spoke, the coach shifted from side to side as John and Cliff the footman both climbed down off the box.

Abruptly the coach door wrenched open. For a moment, it just stood ajar while we all held our breath to see what horrors awaited us, then a dirty man with greasy red hair popped his head into the carriage.

"Afternoon," he cheerfully greeted Papa, touching his forelock. "Everybody out of th'coach."

"You may treat with me, sir," Papa said. "But my daughters will remain in the coach. They are unmarried, and own nothing of value."

The red-headed man scratched at a facial sore with the hook in place of his right hand. "With all due respect to right clever dick such as yerself," he said in a thick Northern accent, "that there is for us to say. And since we're th'ones with th'pistols, ye'd best do what we ask. Otherwise, we'll cut th'driver's throat." He stepped back so that we could see John and an evil looking little man holding a nasty-looking blade pressed above his neckstock.

Papa sighed, looked at the three of us, and nodded. Without another word, Sophie stepped out of the coach. I rose to follow her so that Phosey would not have to be next, then came Papa, who, once alighted, turned his back bravely to the highwaymen so that he could hand poor Phosey out.

"It's all right, lass," the ring leader said to the trembling girl, "this'll all be over soon." He winked at me, then exclaimed, "But where are me manners? Let me first introduce misself. I'm Red Jack, and we're th' Northern Gang.

A massive ogre of a man had come to stand next to Red Jack, positioning himself in front of Sophie. He gave her a frank assessment from head to toe, then honored her with a nasty, gap-toothed grin. His broad, ugly face bore the marks of corporal punishment, marred down the left side by an angry red rope of scar tissue running the length from his piggy eye down to the corner of his mouth. Both nostrils of his broad, flat nose had been slit.

I quickly glanced around at the rest of the thieves. There were indeed far too many of them for us to think of struggling.

Two barefoot youths held the agitated horses, dancing beneath the hooves while carrying on a conversation in some bastardized form of English.

And then there were two more with John, the one still holding a knife to John's throat, using the threat to control Cliff and the postilion, who both sat quietly in the grass with their heads down.

"I can't abide any more bluthering from th' gawly lass," the man with the knife snarled, pointing his blade towards Phosey. "Shut her up, or I'll do it misself."

This only caused Phosey to wail louder. Putting my arm around her shoulders, I pulled her in close and began stroking her back the way I used to when she was small.

"It is all right, Phosey," I murmured into her hair. "They are just frightening us now, but everything will be okay."

Problem was, Papa looked worried.

Red Jack, who clearly viewed himself as something of showman, moved over to Papa and indicated for him to hold out his arms. "Right then," he said, "I'll just search yer pockets while Oliver searches th' coach. Th' wee lad has a knack fer finding clever hiding spots," he added with a grin.

As Papa submitted to the indignity of a personal search, one of the boys left the horses and hopped up into the coach. Meanwhile, the ogre had slowly begun to inch towards Sophie, a calculating look in his eyes.

With some difficulty, I wrenched free of Phosey's grasp so that I could transfer the girl to my other side. Then I sidled up close to Sophie and linked my arm through hers. I glared at the ogre, calling upon every ounce of silent threat within me, but his eyes never left my sister.

"*Right then,*" *Red Jack said once he'd counted out the £25 in Papa's coin purse and seen that Oliver had found only the Turkish pistol in the coach,* "*where is th' rest of th' brass then?*"

Papa remained calm. "*That is all I have.*"

A slow, evil smile spread across the ogre's face.

"*Yer telling me that a fine gentleman such as yerself wi' fine horses such as these is traveling from th' Capital wi' only £25?*"

"*Yes.*"

"*I don't believe it.*"

"*You must believe it, sir, because it is true. I sent our servants and baggage ahead yesterday and my brass, as you call it, was packed in the luggage.*"

Red Jack spat on the ground at Papa's feet. "*Buford!*"

The ogre's hand shot out and gripped Sophie's arm like a vice. She shrieked from surprise, and Buford's evil little smile graduated into a grin.

"*Take her into th' wood,*" *Red Jack ordered.* "*Strip 'er and search 'er thoroughly. But be quick about it; some feckless git is bound to come by sooner or later.*"

"*You will do no such thing!*" *Papa lunged towards Sophie, but found the Turkish pistol suddenly pressed into his chest. Red Jack pushed Papa back to his place beside me, then transferred the barrel to my breast. All traces of humor had vanished from his eyes.*

Sophie continued to shriek and struggle while Buford dragged her toward the trees.

"*That lass is gone to ye,*" *Red Jack said, his voice low and flat.* "*But there are two more to worry about. If ye don't tell me where th' brass is hidden, Reuben will cut th' driver's throat, and then I'll send him into th' woods with th' tall lass, and then I'll take th' wee boddled lass for myself.*"

I stood there holding Phosey tightly, a pistol pressed between my breasts, watching Sophie's struggles in horror. I knew—as did we all—what Buford's "search" would entail, and the thought of that brute's hands on my poor sister left me feeling sick. All we could do now was hope he did not kill her.

They were at the tree line now. Suddenly she bit him and tore loose, desperately running away from the woods. But her skirts hindered her legs and the brute lurched after her, catching her easily and dragging her to the ground. Pinning her down with one hand, he began fumbling with her skirts with the other and it soon became evident that he meant to rape her right there in front of us. Jack removed the pistol from my chest and turned to watch the show with obvious enjoyment.

"What is he doing?" Phosey cried, and I quickly turned her away from the horrible scene, crushing her face into my bosom. Tears streamed down my face, but I forced myself to watch. I would stay with Sophie in what small way I could. Sophie continued to shriek and scream all the while with Buford laughing in enjoyment over her.

Then a sound like a crack of thunder erupted around us, followed by a second, identical sound, and a small explosion in the turf only a meter away from Sophie's struggles. Having never witnessed the firing of a firearm before, I had no idea what was happening, but followed Papa's lead when he whirled around to look behind us.

What I saw then seemed almost too fantastical to be true. A man clothed all in black, his face obscured behind a black scarf and what appeared to be black boot polish around his eyes, sat atop a black stallion wearing a strange medieval-looking black headpiece that ended in a long, twisted black horn protruding from the animal's forehead. With one hand, he held a pistol trained on Red Jack, and as we watched in stunned silence, he used his other to take another pistol out of a saddle holster and fire it towards the would-be rapist as he continued to struggle with Sophie's skirts.

But this shot got his attention.

Slowly, Buford rolled off Sophie, who yanked her skirts back into place and then scuttled backwards away from her attacker.

Meanwhile, the Black Unicorn—for who else could this eccentric figure possibly be —had pulled out yet another pistol which he kept trained on Buford who, with his hands up, took a few steps away from Sophie.

Once he reached about five yards, he lowered his hands to readjust his breeches, nonchalantly reaching towards his back as though to tuck in his shirt.

But just as I registered the crafty look in his eyes, a fourth shot tore through the air and Buford's chest burst in an explosion of blood and bone.

The force of the projectile knocked him off his feet and he landed with a thud, his hand still reaching behind him for the pistol tucked into the back of his breeches. Red Jack dropped Papa's pistol and took a few steps away from me.

Buford writhed and gurgled as he tried to breathe through ruined lungs, his lower limbs churning up the dirt around him. The struggle seemed to go on for ages, the sounds of his death becoming more and more horrible. Then abruptly it all stopped, his black soul cast forth from his body and launched ingloriously into eternity.

The Northern Gang troubled us no further.

Throughout Lord Rydale's final course, a dessert of sweetmeats and fruit, I feigned polite interest as our company chatted animatedly about black unicorns.

Lord Rydale told us of the black unicorns scattered throughout the estate's grounds, and Papa told him of the famous Black Unicorn, the highwayman plaguing the major arteries in and out of London, with a special preference for the road to Bath.

The Black Unicorn had become all anyone in London's Beau Monde could talk about. The elusive figure and his daring exploits inevitably became infused with an aura of romance, and his popularity began to compete even with that of the Scarlet Pimpernel among ladies of fashion, who sported jewels fashioned of onyx shaped into black unicorns at their throats and in their hair. Meanwhile, young bucks took to prowling the highways at night in the hopes of testing their mettle against this gentleman of the roads.

Papa reported all this and more to our company, as well as a rather succinct version of our personal experience with the highwayman. It was bound to come out sooner or later anyway, though he edited his account to keep it suitable for the ladies and to fulfill his part of the oath we had all sworn to Sophie.

As the Yorkshire ladies clapped their hands in delight and fell under the same spell as the ladies of London Society, I drank my wine in silence, hoping it would chase away my dark memories.

I could easily have fallen under the same spell as the rest of society, especially given his role in saving Sophie from Buford's attentions.

Instead, I felt only a deep abhorrence for the man.

But these feelings had not been automatic. When the Black Unicorn left us as abruptly as he'd arrived, I had thought him a hero.

After dinner, once our masculine company joined the ladies in the saloon, I made my excuses and bid everyone an early good night. Once back on the first floor, I walked down the dark corridor leading to our chambers and came to a stop before a door several down from mine.

It was the Black Unicorn's fault that we had been stopped.

It was the Black Unicorn's fault that Sophie had been attacked.

I didn't know how, but Sophie would have her vengeance. I would bring the Black Unicorn to justice—that much, I could do for her. No one had ever held my husband accountable for his crimes. I wouldn't allow Sophie to wind up like me.

I raised my hand, and knocked softly on the door.

"Come in, Elina."

CHAPTER 3

Inside, the room was dim.

Phosey had been sent down immediately following dessert, and now her rhythmic breathing came from the dark recesses of the massive bed in the center of the room.

Sophie sat at a dressing table *en chemisier*, brushing out her long flaxen hair, her dove gray eyes unfocused as she stared at her reflection in the mirror. An empty bowl and teapot with teacup sat on the table, waiting to be cleared away.

When I closed the door quietly behind me, Phosey snorted and the trance was broken. Sophie turned to me and smiled. She looked so young and delicate, so heartbreakingly fragile. I smiled back, seating myself lightly on the foot of the bed, not sure how to begin.

Sophie turned to look once more in the mirror. "Do you remember the story of Daphne and Apollo?"

I frowned, reaching back through old memories to our days in the schoolroom. "The one where she is turned into a tree to escape from Apollo's amorous advances?"

"Yes, but that is the end of the story. Do you remember the beginning?"

"Apollo ridicules Eros's use of a bow and arrow, saying that such weapons are for warriors, not children. So, Eros fashions two arrows: one of gold and the other of lead. He shoots Apollo with the golden arrow, causing him to fall in love with Daphne, and he shoots her with the lead arrow, causing her to abhor the romantic advances of all her suitors, including Apollo. She begs and pleads with her father, the river god Peneus, to allow her to remain unmarried like the virgin goddess Artemis, but her father refuses. Then, just as Apollo is about to catch her, Daphne begs her father to change her form, since it is her beauty that has brought her to this danger. He obliges and turns her into a bay laurel tree just as Apollo reaches her."

"Yes." Sophie twisted around to look at me, her eyes strangely intent. "That is the story exactly. I am worried about you, Elina. I am worried that Eros has shot you with an arrow of lead."

"You are worried about *me*? I am worried about you! After what transpired yesterday—"

"That was nothing, Elina." She waved her hand dismissively. "A moment's humiliation, nothing more. Far more troubling is your lead arrow. It turns you away from the attentions of your suitors and convinces you that a life of lonely solitude is preferable to one of marital harmony and motherhood."

"A moment's humiliation?" I repeated. "Sophie, I think it was more serious than that."

"I told you it was nothing," she said, an edge of warning in her voice. "I think it best if we all just forget it happened."

"Sophie—"

"Enough!" she snapped. "I do not wish to talk about it. I am fine. But what of your lead arrow, Elina?"

I paused, deciding whether I should press the issue. The last thing I wanted to do was upset her, but I did not believe for a moment that she was fine. I did not even know for sure whether Thad had yet kissed her, and I knew for certain he had not dared to take any liberties with her of the sort that her attacker had with such brutality. In the end, I took the cowardly route of least resistance, telling myself that she would come to me when she was ready to talk.

"Very well," I said. "If feeling that a life of independent spinsterhood is far more appealing than one of slavery means that I have been shot with a lead arrow, then I suppose I have. But please remember I have seven years' experience to guide me in this decision. And I have no suitors," I added.

"You have Sir Tristan."

"That was a very long time ago. He is certainly not my suitor any longer."

"He wants you, Elina. It is written clearly on his face every time he is near you."

I shook my head, using the movement to tear my eyes away from hers. "Men do not want broken things. But I did not come here to defend my choices to you, Sophie," I continued. "Just as I must accept your decision to marry Thaddeus, you must accept my decision to never remarry."

"You think you will never love again?"

"Love is a weakness; a means for one person to control the life of another. And men cannot help but abuse that control. I will never allow a man that kind of control over me again."

"Love is not a weakness, Elina," she said. "Not if it is unconditional."

"Love is always conditional."

"And what about motherhood?" she pressed quietly.

It was a cruel blow. The absence of any issue from my marriage to William Throckmorton probably had more to do with the incentives he gave me to refuse him access to my bed than any reproductive deficiencies on my part, though I could never be sure. The brute did occasionally manage to break through my defenses, and still I never experienced so much as a late visit of my monthlies to give me any hope.

"My decision has been informed by my experience," I said. "The day I buried William, I became the mistress of my own destiny, and so I shall remain. But Sophie," I continued more gently, "you skipped dinner, so I assume you must not be as recovered as you are pretending."

"I know, but I am fine. Really." She sighed, and I saw her shoulders release some of their tension. "I admit that at first I was not. Like Daphne, I prayed that my form might change so that I might never attract such brutal attentions again. But then I thought of my Thad, and I remembered that all men are not brutes. But God granted my wish nonetheless."

I could not help but smile. "He turned you into a tree, Sophie?"

The corners of her mouth twitched. "My outer form has remained the same, of course. But I have become something stronger—not unlike a bay laurel tree—on the inside. Heaven forbid anything like this should ever happen again; but if it should, it will not break me."

"And what about Thad? Are you going to tell him?"

In the mirror, I saw a shadow cloud her eyes.

"Of course," she replied. "A marriage should not begin with secrets. You would know that better than anyone, I suppose."

Indeed, I did. Secrets are poisonous things, and the bigger the secret, the deadlier its corrosive venom. My late husband had kept many secrets from me, and the experience was enough to instill in me a very healthy mistrust of men with secretive natures.

Sophie stifled a yawn, and I decided our talk had progressed as far as it could for now. I still sensed that she carried too heavy a burden, but she needed her rest. She'd not slept much the last two nights.

"Very well then," I said, catching her yawn as I rose from the bed. "I am greatly fatigued, so I will bid you good night. I will see you in the morning for breakfast?"

"You will," she agreed. "No doubt with quite an appetite by that time. Though not *too* early. I expect I shall sleep well tonight."

At the door, I turned to her and winked. "I imagine it will be Phosey waking you, not me."

"Elina?"

"Yes?"

"One of these days you will have to tell me."

"Tell you what?" I asked, though I already knew what she would say.

"What happened the night Lord Delemere died."

I nodded. "Good night, Sophie."

Once back in the corridor, I walked slowly down to my own chamber, lost in thought. I knew Sophie to be possessed of a nature too tender to allow her such easy peace.

At my door, I reached for the handle and suddenly chuckled as I remembered the lead arrow. Where on earth did Sophie come up with these things?

"*Elina!*"

I startled violently, dropping my chamberstick.

As the acrid plume of smoke from the snuffed-out flame reached my nose, I turned and found *him* standing in the doorway just across from mine.

Lord Ashenhurst.

He was haloed by the glow from the fire burning behind him in his chamber's hearth, softening the angles of his face with shadow. He crossed his arms and shifted position, leaning one shoulder against the doorframe and angling his head so that the dancing light gilded a cheekbone, the sweep of his jaw, the tips of his eyelashes.

All thoughts of Sophie abruptly vanished.

"Devil hang you!" I said harshly. "You nearly frightened me to death!"

"I beg your pardon, Elina," he said. "But I only raised my

voice when you did not respond to my first two hails. I wonder, what were you thinking of just now?"

"I told you not to call me that," I snapped. "And I certainly was not thinking of you if that is what you are implying."

"No," he replied. "You were frowning. And when women think of me, they generally do not frown."

"Well, I suppose I must be the exception then."

"So you *were* thinking of me just now?"

"Good night."

"Wait, Elina—"

Reluctantly, I turned back, one hand still resting on the door handle. "Yes?"

"How is your sister?"

"Why?"

"Lady Sophronia. She did not come up for dinner. Is she ill?"

"And why would you care about that?" I demanded. "She is engaged, you know. I will not tolerate it if you assault her with the same vulgar attentions with which you enjoy harassing me."

"I would never dream of it," he said, his tone almost solicitous. "Though I would like to know how she fares. Is she ill?"

"No, she is not ill. Fatigued from the journey, that is all. You will have the opportunity to make her acquaintance tomorrow, though I warn you—"

"You warn me, Lady Delemere?" The soft curve of his mouth twitched at the corners.

I closed my eyes and pressed my fingers to my temples. "I am not in the mood for your games tonight, Lord Ashenhurst."

"He was mad, you know," he said. "Not all men are like him."

I glanced up at him. "Sorry?"

"It wasn't your fault," he said.

Then Lord Ashenhurst closed his door.

CHAPTER 4

THE FOLLOWING MORNING, I found Sophie, Phosey, and Dorothea sitting at the large mahogany table in the breakfast parlor, their heads bent together.

My eyes naturally went to Sophie. She looked relaxed. She was smiling even.

Phosey saw me first and called out a cheerful haloo, causing Sophie and Dorothea to straighten up with guilty looks on their faces.

"Good morning, Phosey," I replied, taking a seat next to Sophie. "What was it you were all talking about just now?"

"Nothing!" Dorothea answered.

"Lord Ashenhurst," Sophie and Phosey said together.

I raised my eyebrows as a housemaid placed a cup of steaming chocolate in front of me. "Really? And what have you been saying about him?"

"Dorothea told us he is the most handsome cavalier she has ever seen—" Phosey began.

"I said no such thing!" Dorothea exclaimed. "You are telling lies, Phosey!"

"I am not lying," Phosey answered with dignity. "Sophie was here. She heard you say that, too." Then, turning back to me, she

HEATHER E. F. CARTER

continued, "And then Dorothea was telling Sophie about your argument with Lord Ashenhurst last night."

"And I am sorry I missed it," Sophie declared. "It is not every day that someone manages to ruffle the feathers of the great Elinamifia Brinkley Throckmorton!"

"True," I conceded. "But if you had been there, it would have been you shouting at him, not me. I would have spent the evening in boring, yet civil conversation with Lady Rydale's toady-looking nephew."

Dorothea pulled a face. "Count yourself lucky that you were not. Phineas Froggenhall *is* a toad. Though he prefers it if you call him *Doctor* Froggenhall."

"I beg your pardon, Dorothea," I said. Of course, Lady Rydale's toady-looking nephew would also be Dorothea's toady-looking cousin.

"So *I* was to be partnered with him?" Sophie exclaimed.

I nodded. "You would have been the one shouting at that confounded libertine."

"Lord Ashenhurst is *not* a libertine!" Dorothea declared.

"Indeed," I replied. "He is a devil."

The girl fixed me with a haughty stare. I noticed her eyes were brown rather than blue, rather an unusual combination with her platinum hair. "You must have provoked him last night," she said. "He has only behaved like a perfect gentleman to me."

"I did not provoke him." I virtuously sipped my chocolate.

Sophie looked incredulous.

"He does have something of a reputation," Dorothea admitted. "But that is only because he needs a wife. Once he is married, he will no longer have the desire to entertain so many ladies."

"Well, if it is a wife he wants, it seems strange that he only favors the ladies who already have husbands," I pointed out.

"Because he cannot just marry *anyone*," Dorothea countered. "His wife must be very rich."

"Why?" I turned my attention to the sideboard, where a tempting spread of hot and cold breads, and cakes of all colors awaited my perusal. "Does his dissolute lifestyle extend to his finances as well? Is he a gambler as well as a lecher?"

"What is a lecher?" Phosey asked.

Sophie gave me a warning look.

"Certainly not!" Dorothea rejoined. "It was not Lord Ashenhurst, but his reckless, spendthrift father, who ruined the family by squandering their fortune. Now it is up to Ashby to marry a rich wife so that he can restore the Harcourts back to their place of honor."

"And I suppose you are just the wife he is looking for," I said.

"Of course!" came her immediate reply. "Why else would he be here?"

"To shoot grouse?" I offered.

"Edwin will never marry, so it is up to me to continue the family line, if not the family name," Dorothea explained. "I have told Papa that I choose Lord Ashenhurst, and I am sure that he will settle as large a portion on me as is needed. Papa favors me, you know," she added in conspiratorial tones. "He always gives me whatever I want."

Sophie smiled gently at the girl. "But if he favors you so much, will he not be sad to send you away to Lord Ashenhurst's estate in Northumberland? That is where you said it was, yes? Would he not prefer to marry you to someone established more locally?"

"Papa will give me what I want. And I want Lord Ashenhurst. And Lord Ashenhurst wants me."

"He has said so?" I asked. "He has made his intentions clear?"

"Well, no," Dorothea admitted. "Though gentlemen never like to say such things. And since he is not here to shoot grouse—he can do that on his own estate in Northumberland—why else would he be here?"

"Elina!" Phosey cut in, her small voice stern. "You never told me what a lecher is. And why will Viscount Bewforest not ever get married?"

⤚

After breakfast Sophie and I decided to take a walk in the gardens. The guns were out on the moor for the day, so we had the whole estate to ourselves to explore.

Dorothea had taken Phosey to the library. At first I'd some misgivings about leaving the girl with Dorothea, but as Sophie pointed out, Phosey's character was too strong to be so easily influenced by the nitwit.

The gardens located behind the house proved lovely. Separated into four compartments by gravel paths lined alternately with cherry trees and rose bushes, they included a labyrinth, a flower garden, an orchard, and an old-fashioned heraldic garden. Beyond these central compartments stood a mount covered in more cherry trees to the north, a beautiful terrace crowned with a small banqueting house to the east, and the acreage of the great wooded park spreading out to the south.

Sophie and I first did a turn around the pleasure garden, admiring its marble fountain and late-blooming gillyflowers and tulips. I continued to observe her closely, watchful for any signs of stress or anxiety. But she seemed very much at peace.

"Sophie," I began as she stooped to finger the golden peach petals of a blossom.

"Yes?" She turned to me as she straightened up. "Your tone sounds serious. You are not still worried about me, are you?"

"Oh, no," I lied. "And it is nothing serious. Dorothea just said something at breakfast that made me think."

She laughed as she moved down the path to the crimson roses. "What on earth could she have said to set you thinking?"

"It is not so much what she said, but something she reminded me of."

"And that is?"

"Have you guessed yet why we are here? It is clear that Papa and Lord Rydale are old friends, but do you not think it rather out of character for Papa to choose to visit him during a shooting party? And does it not seem strange that Papa should decide to bring us along to accompany him?"

"You are not worried that Papa brought you here for Lord Ashenhurst's benefit, are you?" she teased.

"You do not know what you are saying," I told her as I quickly moved past her. "He is horrible. You will see that for yourself soon enough. Only he better treat you with more respect than he does me. Which he will," I added, "because you are an angel and everyone cannot help but love you."

"I do know why we are here," she said. "Thad told me before we left. We are here for political reasons."

"*Thad* told you?"

"He is really not as awful as you think, Elina," she said. "Eventually you will be forced to spend more than a few moments with him, and you will see that he is wonderful, intelligent, and sensitive—"

"Yes, yes." I cut in. "So why then does Thad say we are here?"

"Papa has left the Whig party, along with most of his political followers, to join Mr. Pitt. No one knows exactly what made him leave, but many guess it has something to do with Mr. Fox's radical views in support of the Revolutionaries in France. Mr. Pitt's views are the opposite, and even now he is preparing Britain for war with France. A formal declaration could be made any day now."

"And Thad told you all of this?"

"Yes!" she exclaimed, suddenly angry. "But if it will make this information more credible to you, I will tell you that Thad heard all of this from Sir Tristan. Surely you will respect *Sir Tristan's* opinions regarding the matter!"

"Tristan is Papa's confidant," I pointed out. "You cannot be angry at me for that."

"I am not angry at you only for that."

I felt my temper beginning to rise, but I did my best to be diplomatic. "Be angry with me, if you must. I am making a very great effort to accept Sir Thaddeus as your future husband. It is difficult for me, you must understand."

"You think he is not good enough for me"

I turned to face her. "No one is good enough for you, Sophie. As I said, you are an angel."

"Thad is good enough for me."

My diplomacy failed. "I do not think he is."

"And how could you possibly know that?" she demanded. "You do not know him at all!"

I shrugged and resumed my progress down the path. "I have much more experience in these matters than do you."

"Experience?" she called out from behind me. "You have more experience in love, Elina? I believe that in the case of love, it is *I* who have the greater experience."

I did not respond, but continued to walk in silence. Her naïveté pained me.

And Thad was so young. It could not help matters that his naiveté likely matched her own.

I stopped to wait for her at the foot of the steps leading up to the banquet house, then began to climb once she'd caught up. Picking up the threads of our conversation before it devolved into an argument, I said "So Papa has left his party then. To the great upset of the rest of the party, I would imagine. But that does not explain why we are hiding up in the north. We could just as easily be hiding in Hertfordshire, and Papa would not have to pretend to enjoy shooting small birds and I would not have to endure Lord Ashenhurst."

"I do not believe we are hiding," Sophie said as climbed behind me. "I believe Papa just needs a respite. It is a three-day journey to Scarcliff Towers from the Home Counties; a man would have to be very determined to make that journey just for the purpose of coaxing Papa back into the fold. Writing a long letter would be far more convenient, and Papa can just choose not to open his mail."

"Does—*Thad*—feel that Papa is in any danger from political reprisals from the rest of the party?" I'd come to a stop at the top of the stairs and turned to hand Sophie up the final few steps.

"He does not know."

I sighed. "Papa a Pittite."

We paused then to admire the stone edifice standing before us. The banqueting house, like others of its kind, was shaped in an octagon and appeared to be only one story, though it most likely had steps leading up to the roof. Carved into the stone above the door, were the initials "BH" embedded in scrollwork just like the parapets on the house's six towers. Only these initials had an additional ornament: they were flanked on each side by unicorns rampant.

Sophie tried the door, and it swung open on well-oiled hinges.

Once inside, we found ourselves in a dark little space, the sunlight straining through the thick leaded glass with its tiny diamond-shaped panes. Fortunately, there was plenty of glass with canted bay windows and padded window seats on six sides of the octagon. On the seventh side, there was a fireplace with a carved stone mantle, and the door behind us took up the eighth. In the center of the room stood a large octagonal stone table.

"It looks as though it is still kept up for use," I said. "There is hardly any dust."

Sophie nodded. "It is very small. It must have been used only for intimate entertaining."

"Intimate banquets for a lady and her Unicorn, I suppose. Lord and Lady Rydale must maintain it for similar reasons."

Sophie moved over to one of the window seats. "The views are lovely," she remarked. "At least what I can see of them through this old glass. I think I can see the fish pond from here."

"Yes, but not everything in here is old," I said as I studied the tapestry hanging over the fireplace. "This tapestry is new, though I am sure it was copied from an older textile."

Sophie came to stand beside me. "That is the Bewforest coat of arms. I remember seeing it in the hall when we first arrived."

"I recognize it, too," I said. "And flanking it—"

"Are two black unicorns rampant."

CHAPTER 5

THAT EVENING I ENTERED the drawing room on Papa's arm in high spirits.

Lord Ashenhurst had not yet arrived, though there was a new face amongst us. A handsome face, in fact, belonging to a gentleman looking to be somewhere in his forties with the tanned complexion and trim figure of a sportsman. Lady Rydale promptly brought him over to our little group, and proudly introduced him as Charles FitzWilliam, Marquess of Beverley, and Lord Lieutenant of Yorkshire. The appropriate honors were exchanged all round, and then Lady Rydale was on the move once more, pulling her guest across the room in a purposeful march towards Dorothea.

Ten minutes passed, and still no Lord Ashenhurst. I was just about to give up on him for the evening, when I felt a stir in the air behind me.

"Elina."

I rounded on him.

Ashby was not the right name for him. Lord Ashenhurst simply was not built along mortal lines. It was his mouth that had me. Sensual and expressive, his upper lip slightly fuller than the lower, and so perfectly shaped in the soft curve of a cupid's bow that it turned the corners of his mouth up just enough to hint at dimples and lend his natural expression a disarmingly playful quality. And he had a scar, just a tiny iridescent ribbon on his upper lip.

"Were you thinking of me just now?" Lord Ashenhurst asked. "You were scowling."

"I was," I snapped. "I was wondering where the devil you were. I believe we are about to go in for dinner."

A corner of his mouth kicked up appealingly. "I apologize for my tardiness. I was just finishing a letter to my sister, and I lost all track of time. And then I took some time trying to tie this damned cravat. Though I am certainly glad I made the effort," he continued as he stalked around me. "Good God, madam, but you are radiant."

I snorted. "It is common knowledge that you find a great number of ladies radiant."

Coming to stand before me, he leaned in close, his lips brushing my hair. "Indeed. But I find none so astonishingly beautiful as you."

I took another large step away from him. "Your attempts to make love to me are wasted. I am immune to your charms."

"Really?"

"Yes," I said. "Really."

He moved in close again. "Then why are you blushing?"

The room grew quiet around us, but his mouth continued to hold my attention. As though following the direction of my thoughts, the pink tip of his tongue flicked out and licked along the little scar's edge.

Oh, the things I could do to that lip.

"Elina?"

I dragged my gaze up to his eyes, but saw only that his eyebrows were raised in a question. I pressed my lips together, and took another fortifying breath through my nose.

"Little Mouse?"

"Why are you doing this?" I demanded.

"Doing what, Elina?"

"Making love to me."

"Do I need a reason?"

"You are here to court Dorothea. Yet you try me with your flirtation."

"Do you wish for me to stop?"

I drew in another long breath. "Yes."

"I do not think you do."

"I do not want you."

He raised an eloquent eyebrow, but said nothing.

I decided to try a different approach. "You are here for Dorothea. But you jeopardize your future with her by pursuing me so blatantly. Her father dotes on her; he will not take your romantic overtures towards me lightly."

He frowned. "Who told you I am here for Dorothea?"

I waved my hand dismissively. "That is not important. Are you telling me you are not here to court her?"

He shrugged. "Perhaps I am here for you."

"Impossible."

"Why are you so determined to resist me?"

"I will not be another one of your conquests."

"And if I told you I loved you, would that make any difference?"

"Impossible."

"Is it?" he asked softly.

"You do not even know me!"

"Mmmm," he murmured as his little smirk graduated into an alluring smile. "I know you better than you think, Elina."

"Stop calling me that!" I exclaimed. "Unless you wish for me to call you Ashby."

"Nothing would please me more," he replied. "But you are bluffing."

He paused a moment, his expression expectant as he waited for my answer. In truth, I *was* bluffing. Nothing on the face of this earth could induce me to such familiarity. At least not out loud.

"As I was saying," he continued once he realized I would not answer him. "I shall leave off making love to you. For now. But might I just ask you one question, Elina?"

"Fine."

His smile, still lingering around the corners of his mouth, deepened. "For whom did you put on that beautiful gown tonight?"

Dammit. He'd noticed. Back into the clothes press had gone the pretty muted plum satin Edith had selected for the evening, and I'd chosen instead my rose chiné-patterned silk taffeta, a gown whose bold color and daring neckline I normally reserved only for special occasions.

Praise Jupiter, the butler opened the doors to the Great Chamber. Lord Ashenhurst bowed before me and offered his arm.

Dinner proceeded along the same lines as the night before. But as the last of the second course was removed, Lord Rydale cleared his throat and stood up at the head of the table.

"Ladies and gentlemen," he said, "I beg your pardon for the intrusion, but I have planned a little surprise for you all tonight. If you would all be so good as to quit the table and follow me."

The gentlemen rose as one, and each followed the good earl's example by helping his lady out of her seat and offering his arm. We fell into line in the same order that we entered, and followed Lord Rydale and Lady Mildred out through the withdrawing room and into the corridor leading towards the winding staircase in the north tower.

Once on the roof, Lord Rydale and Lady Mildred led us along the parapets to a stone banqueting house crowning the eastern tower, much like the one in the garden. Creaking open the door, Lord Rydale stepped aside to allow us in before him.

"Oh, how lovely!" Sophie exclaimed, eyeing the marzipans, jellies, quince cakes, and meringues on the table.

"Is that ipocras?" Papa asked, indicating the large crystal bowl in the center.

"It certainly is!" Lord Rydale answered. "Of course *you* would know it, Algernon." To the rest of us, he explained, "A mulled wine steeped in sugar with cinnamon and a few other spices. It is a very old recipe, almost as old as this house."

Due to the close quarters of the tower, there were no servants to serve us, so the gentlemen attended first to the ladies and then to themselves. Lord Ashenhurst was behaving himself, so, with as little grace as possible, I allowed him to select a meringue and a small cake for me.

Once back out on the roof, I could not help but admire the view. Through the purple filter of twilight, the wild, haunted country of the north spread out for miles before us, clothed tonight in mist and shadow.

"It is beautiful country," I said to no one in particular.

"Indeed it is, Lady Delemere."

Startled, I turned to discover the strange little professional man standing next to me.

"Good evening, er, Dr. Froggenhall," I said.

"My cousin and milord are having conversation in the banquet room," he replied. "It seemed they might be awhile, so I took the liberty of following you out here so that you might not be alone."

I smiled. "So it would seem that Dorothea has orchestrated a little *coup*."

"Yes, though Lord Ashenhurst hardly seemed reluctant. I had read about men like him in my studies, though I confess that, until now, I've never had the opportunity to study such a specimen first hand."

"Such a specimen?" Nature had done Dr. Froggenhall no favors, endowing him with a grainy, pitted complexion; wide, thin lips that furthered the toady impression already suggested by his name; and a short, spare build with stooped shoulders whose boniness no amount of good tailoring could rectify.

Though he did have unusual yellow eyes, sharp as a fox's.

"I suppose Robert Burton explained such wanton men best in his treatise on melancholy," he replied. "According to him, such a man falls in love with every beauty he meets, but is so fickle that whomever is with him at the moment is the lady he loves best. Any woman who manages to keep him with her can have him, but she is sadly deluded if she thinks that he loves her especially."

I snorted. "I hope for the sake of his courtship that Lady Dorothea is more successful in keeping Lord Ashenhurst by her side."

"His courtship, milady?"

"Lady Dorothea seems to be under the impression that Lord Ashenhurst is here to court her."

"My cousin seems to be under the impression that all men of title exist only to court her," he said dryly. "She appears, in my humble opinion, to suffer from an exaggerated opinion of her own charms."

I could not help but smile. "But she is very pretty. You cannot deny that, Dr. Froggenhall."

"Beauty is in the eye of the beholder," he replied. "And in Lady Dorothea's case, her bright eyes, flaxen curls, and fine complexion are not enough to counterbalance her complete lack of womanly virtue."

"Womanly virtue?"

"Obedience, Godliness, and chastity."

My smile faded into something a shade darker. "You believe these to be lacking in Lady Dorothea?"

"Gentlemen are more accomplished in the arts of observation than ladies," he said. "So I am not surprised that you have not noticed these failings in Lady Dorothea. She is disobedient to her parents, and she is too slovenly to rise for the morning service on Sundays. She should be taught her proper place."

"But what about chastity? Are you claiming her to be unchaste?"

"Not by aristocratic standards," he allowed. "But I personally find that she speaks too freely to gentlemen, and lacks any semblance of modesty or diffidence."

"So you question her chastity because she speaks to gentlemen?"

He frowned at me. "Social intercourse outside a woman's immediate family inevitably leads to the more serious sins of adultery and fornication. And sin," he added, "is at the root of madness. I have seen it many times in my female patients."

"Your female patients?"

"Yes." His chest suddenly swelled with self-importance. "I am a physician at the York Asylum, and therefore consider myself an expert in the field of the human mind. The original cause of madness was the Fall of Man. Evil begets evil, mental and moral defect are synonymous, and so the activities of the devil are at the very root of a distracted mind. In order to effect a cure in the patient, one must root out their sinful predilections and replace them with Godly morality. Otherwise—"

"Am I on the road to madness, Dr. Froggenhall?" I interrupted. "You are not a member of my immediate family. And yet here we stand, engaging in sinful social intercourse."

"Possibly," he answered, his tone clinical as he studied my face, "though I have not yet had the opportunity to observe you long enough to make a formal diagnosis. I am concerned, however, that you might be suffering from melancholia. I often find melancholia most pronounced in widows, who suddenly find themselves prematurely and unnaturally deprived—"

"Deprived?" I exclaimed, not sure whether I was more amused or outraged. "You think I suffer because I am *deprived*?"

Spots of color tinged Dr. Froggenhall's sallow complexion. Phosey's voice filtering through the open door of the banquet room saved him from answering.

"Elina!" she called loudly in sing-song. "Where are you, Elina?"

"I am out here, Phosey," I called, then turned back to Dr. Froggenhall "If you will excuse me, Doctor, it would appear that my sister needs me."

The little man bowed awkwardly and seemed obliged to say something more, but Phosey promptly arrived to join us.

"There you are!" She heaved an exasperated sigh, ignoring Dr. Froggenhall. "I was looking all over for you!"

"Looking all over for me?" I smiled indulgently. "All over a single tiny room? Where did you think I had gone? Under the table, perhaps?"

"Well I did not know," she said, her expression serious. "Lord Ashenhurst was inside and so I thought you would be with him. But he is with Dorothea, and I could not find you."

I pulled out my handkerchief and wiped a smudge of strawberry jelly off the girl's cheek. "You have found me now, little love."

Phosey pouted. "Papa says that it is time for me to go to bed, and he told me to ask you to take me down to my room. Even though I do not feel tired at all, and I know exactly where my room is. I am not a child!"

"Well, I am envious of you, Phosey," I said, stifling a yawn. "I only wish I could go to bed now. And I am happy to escort you down—I feel in need of the exercise."

I turned back to Dr. Froggenhall. "Good evening, sir. Your conversation has been very . . . interesting."

The strange little man bowed, an odd look in his eye. I took Phosey by the hand, and pulled her away towards the tower steps.

∽

Once back in the room Phosey shared with Sophie, I sat at the dressing table while Phosey's maid Harriet helped the girl out of her dress and into her night shift.

"Elina?" Phosey asked as she bounced across the bed to her side and scooted under the covers.

"Are you all tucked in?" I asked.

"Yes. But may I ask you a question before you kiss me good night?"

"This better not be a ploy for you to stay up longer."

"It is not," she promised. "I was just wondering why you hate Lord Ashenhurst so much."

Surprised at her perceptiveness, I came over to take a seat next to her on the bed. "Why? Do you find him very handsome?"

"Yes," she said, her voice grave. "And he has been very kind to me. I do not understand why you do not like him"

"When has he been very kind to you, Phosey? How much time have you been spending with him?" I asked sharply.

"Just this morning at breakfast," she said.

"But you had breakfast with Sophie, Dorothea, and me," I reminded her.

"That was later. I came down much earlier and he was there by himself. So, I decided to keep him company.

"And what did you talk about?" I asked, relaxing a bit.

"He just wanted to know about the robbery, so I told him."

I stood up abruptly. "What? Why?"

"He just wanted to know how we fared," she answered calmly.

"And what did you tell him?"

"I told him that Sophie seemed well, but that I knew she was still frightened. And I told him that I was still frightened. But I told him that you were not. I told him that nothing frightens you ever."

"And what did he say?"

"He said that those horrible men were gone and that they would never hurt anyone ever again. He wanted me to know that."

"Humph." I sat back down on the bed. On the one hand, I was thankful to the scoundrel for alleviating Phosey's fears. But on the other hand, I did not like him lying to the girl.

"And did that help?" I asked finally, smoothing a stray lock of hair away from her eyes. "Did he ease your mind?"

"Yes. And I know that, if Red Jack or anyone else ever comes to hurt us again, Lord Ashenhurst will kill them first."

"He told you that?" I demanded.

"No," she replied softly. "He did not have to."

CHAPTER 6

L ATE THE FOLLOWING MORNING found me seated comfortably atop an amiable chestnut gelding named Rupert as
we ambled down a pretty country lane towards Black-
heath Moor.

We were to join the Guns for nuncheon. We were a small
party, just Sophie, Phosey, Dorothea, Lady Rydale, myself, and a
farm cart about half of an hour ahead of us carrying the refresh-
ments, the china, and two footmen to serve.

The day was milder than I expected, and I felt blissfully lazy
as the sunshine beat down upon my upturned face. This was
more like the summer weather I was used to: cloudless blue sky
stretching in every direction as far as the eye could see; butterflies fluttering amongst the wildflowers and dandelions in the
dry-stone wall lining the side of the road; the sound of birds and
other small animals ferreting around in the hawthorn hedgerow
on the other side.

After a while, the green and golden fields of the dale gave
way to hillier terrain, and the road narrowed as it began to grow
steeper. In the distance, the occasional crack of gunfire signaled
we were close to our destination.

The road wended its way around a rocky hill covered in

yellow-flowered gorse. We suddenly came upon the cart sent ahead of us, along with the two wagons that had carried out the Guns and their loaders, the dogs and their handlers, and the gamekeepers earlier this morning.

Two ponies for carrying the Guns' game bags and other supplies back to Scarcliff Towers stood tethered to a stunted tree, munching on what little grass they could find at its base.

"This is the end of the road for the horses," Lady Rydale announced as several grooms seemed to materialize from nowhere to take the reins and assist our dismount. "From here up to the cottage, we go on foot."

And so, we began to climb. After ten minutes, just about the point where the burning in my legs brought me dangerously close to requesting a quick stop to catch my breath, the grade of the terrain became less steep and soon began to even out to a broad plateau of spongy peat.

The prickly gorse that snagged our skirts for most of our climb gave way to a great expanse of purple heather undulating in the wind in full summer bloom.

The narrow footpath wound its way through the heath, bending a little here and there to skirt a large pile of rock or a boggy patch, until up ahead a tall formation of red sandstone came into view with a small cottage built up against it for shelter.

I deduced from the smoke puffing from the cottage's chimney, and the complete lack of any pavilions, that the cottage was our final destination.

"Isn't it lovely!" Sophie exclaimed. "Look at how the heather moves with the wind like waves in a great purple sea!"

"This is by far the prettiest time of year in these parts," Lady Rydale said. "I am so glad that you southerners can see it like this. I fear that our moorland suffers something of a bad reputation, propagated by those foolish enough to travel through here in the winter."

"And is this your cottage?" Sophie asked as we passed through its little gate into a garden long since grown wild.

"It used to belong to a gamekeeper in our employ. When he died about ten years ago, Eleezer came up with the idea of maintaining it for a refreshment place during the grouse season. It's cozy inside, as you'll see," she added.

As we shuffled inside, I saw that the cottage consisted of a single room with a very large fireplace, almost certainly expanded upon the original, taking up the northern wall and doing double duty by warming the place and boiling the water in the copper kettles hanging over the flames.

The furniture consisted only of a large, rustic wooden table with long benches running down either side, and a matching sideboard laden with the cold meats, cheeses, breads, fruit, and cakes that had been brought from the house.

Two matching tea sets of cobalt blue and white china sat ready on silver trays in the center of the table, and two footmen were laying out place settings.

"It appears as though we have arrived a bit early," I observed.

"We always do, dear," Lady Rydale said. "'Tis the nature of the shoot. There is no set time for nuncheon, though when they see the smoke coming from the chimney, they usually begin to make their way back in our direction. Then it just depends upon how many birds the dogs manage to flush on the way. Could be ten minutes, could be an hour."

As if to support this statement, the sound of gunfire crackled some little ways away.

"Sounds as though they are close," she continued. "If you like, you might go outside to have a look for them. Lud knows we've nothing to do in here until they arrive."

I thought about it a moment. It was so deliciously warm in the cottage, and the moor was so much chillier than it had been down in the dale for most of our ride.

But the moor was beautiful, quite unlike anything I'd experienced before. I was anxious to see more of it. So, I turned on my heel and walked back outside.

Standing in the garden, I could hear more gunfire and the sound of a voice carried on the wind, but I needed a higher vantage point if I was going to see anything in the distance. Glancing up at the rocky outcrop sheltering the cottage, I thought I might see if there was a way to climb up to its peak.

Sometimes I had a problem with heights, though it did not seem so very high from my current position.

As I quit the garden and circled around the mass of sandstone, I discovered a steep path leading up to the top. With some scrabbling and one or two missteps, I made it to the top and my breath caught in my throat as I took in the view.

It was very high.

"Lovely, isn't it?" came a disembodied voice from somewhere to my right.

I jumped, then swore under my breath. I would accuse him of following me, except that there was no denying that he was here first.

"Lord Ashenhurst, is that you?" I demanded unnecessarily.

"Of course, Elina," came the cool response. "Were you expecting someone else?"

"No," I grumbled. "Where are you? I cannot see you."

The wind carried his soft chuckle to my ears. "I am below you," he said, "and to your right. Inch forward a little and you will see the path leading down here."

From my current vantage point it looked like a few inches forward would bring me over the edge to a fall into the cottage's garden.

Still, I did not think he meant to kill me, and I was not about to admit any weakness to him. So forward I inched until I saw that just below the edge there was another shelf of rock—perfect for sitting—and easily accessible by the path I could now see to my right.

"Bloody fiend," I muttered as I inched cautiously down the path until he came into view, lounging back on his elbows with his legs dangling over the edge.

No sardonic looks or pithy commentary greeted my arrival; he just continued to gaze out onto the highland wilderness as though I was not there. I found this unusual silence refreshing, which made taking a seat next to him much easier than it might have been. And this was particularly good since I was going to need his assistance getting back up that path, and then, possibly, getting down the back of the rock again.

My corset prevented me from adopting his casual attitude of repose, so instead I scooted back against the rock face as far as I could with my legs crossed in front of me like I used to when I was a child.

Silence, however, has its pitfalls.

Without him distracting me with his arrogance, I found myself hypersensitive to his closeness. From where I sat, I could see the sleek, powerful muscles of his shoulders and upper arms pulled back to support his weight, the elegant curve of his jaw, the angle of a cheekbone, the soft tips of his dark eyelashes.

And then there was the long, lean line of his body stretched languorously out before him, his double-breasted shooting frock opened to display his waistcoat fitted snugly over his flat belly.

I swore again under my breath.

"I beg your pardon?" he inquired lazily.

"Why are you not down on the moor with the others?" I asked. "Not a very good shot?"

"I have already filled up my game bag. We shoot grouse in Northumberland," he added almost modestly.

"Then why bother with it here?" I demanded. "Do you lack the imagination to try something new?"

"Perhaps I am not here for the shooting."

"Oh?" This interested me more than I cared to admit. "Then why are you here?"

Suddenly, a cluster of gunshots crackled very close at hand.

"That was your father and Lord Rydale," Lord Ashenhurst observed from his vantage point. "Looks like Lord Rydale hit his bird, but your father did not."

"Papa hates shooting; he probably was not even aiming."

A strong gust of wind blew over us, bringing the scent of heather and discharged gunpowder to my nose. Softly, Lord Ashenhurst murmured, "I wonder then what it is *you* are doing here."

I did not answer, not sure whether the question was rhetorical. We sat together awhile in a silence I might have called companionable with anyone else, looking out over the moor.

There was something different about him, and I realized that for the first time in our acquaintance, I did not want to assault him. He lounged right on the edge of a deadly drop, and I had no desire whatsoever to shove him over.

Of course, he would probably grab me and take me over the edge with him, but it was not self-preservation that dampened my urge to murder him.

Could it be that, under the proper circumstances, Lord Ashenhurst might be decent company? It made sense really, since there had to be something more to him than just the carnal pleasures. Otherwise, someone would have killed him years ago.

I watched him closely, finding him more interesting than the breathtaking view spread out before me.

"What is it like?" I asked. "Northumberland?"

"It is a lot like this," he said at length, keeping his eyes trained on the view. "But darker, more savage. And more beautiful. Life can be difficult, but it can also be miraculous."

"But you love it," I said.

"I do. But it is not my home."

I frowned. "You are not from Northumberland?"

"My father was from Northumberland."

"You are speaking in riddles, Lord Ashenhurst."

"My mother was Portuguese."

"Oh. But your family—they live with you in Northumberland?"

"Three sisters and a brother. They are much younger than I, from my father's second marriage. They live with me at Castle Ashenhurst, when I am there. But it has been a while since I have been back," he added softly.

What a remarkably pensive mood he was in. I felt unaccountably special, rather like the singular person who has found a way to pet the vicious dog who bites everyone else.

"I cannot always play the rake, Elina," he said, his voice just loud enough to carry over the wind. "It grows tiresome. I have interests other than chasing ladies grown bored with their wedding vows."

"Then why do you continue doing it?"

"Perhaps someday I will tell you," he replied easily. "But not today. I think it time for us to go down to our repast. Lady Rydale will skin me alive if I am the last one in." As I puzzled over this strange remark, he sat up, pulled his knees to his chest, and rose in a smooth movement that left him standing so dangerously close to the edge that I gasped inadvertently. Turning, he fixed me with his customary sardonic look.

"Yes, Elina?"

I looked into his mocking eyes, glanced down to his boots flirting with the edge of the rock, then looked back into his face. I tried to stifle the sudden wave of nausea, as my vision blurred at the edges.

"Please, Lord Ashenhurst," I said through gritted teeth. "Away from the edge. Now."

He complied immediately. "Fear of heights?"

I nodded. "Comes and goes. Going up usually is not a problem, but getting down can be."

"Funny that," he replied easily. "I rather thought you would like to push me over the edge."

"I will find another way to murder you, Lord Ashenhurst," I promised with a weak smile. "But first, you must give me your hand, sir, and get me down off this bloody rock."

CHAPTER 7

ONCE BACK AT THE house, I changed into a light chemise dress and took a seat at the writing table in my room. Selecting a sheet of paper, I situated it onto the leather writing surface, and scratched in the date from Scarcliff Towers.

My Dear Charlotte, I began, *So much has happened since last I saw you . . .*

I stopped, the quill pen hovering over the empty page. What could I say? Condensing our encounter with the Black Unicorn to a single page seemed too daunting a task, and then there was this thing with Lord Ashenhurst.

I set the quill pen back into the inkstand.

I'd never before told anyone about him. As William's drinking and whoring companion, he had no place in polite conversation. And besides, he'd been nothing beyond a particularly trying nuisance.

Though he was just that: a nuisance.

Unlike some of the others William had brought back to the house, I'd never felt threatened by Lord Ashenhurst.

And today, as we sat together on the rock, he'd been different. Natural.

Who was the man behind 'the rake?'

Who was Ashby Harcourt?

I honestly did not know. Up until a few days ago, I'd made it my mission to know as little about him as possible.

Stifling a yawn, I glanced towards the bed. Perhaps a nice nap would cure me of this sudden lethargy. An hour at most. Then I would tackle this letter to Charlotte

A light scratching at the door woke me sometime later. Sitting bolt upright, I looked to the clock on the mantelpiece, then relaxed when I saw it was not so late as I feared.

Opening the door, I found a liveried footman waiting for me in the corridor, his features schooled into that look of impassive boredom trained into those in service. He bowed and handed me a note. I opened it and read an invitation to take tea with Lady Rydale in her dressing room.

Instructing the footman to wait for me, I ducked back inside to tidy myself and smooth out the wrinkles in my dress. Then I quit my chamber and fell into step behind him.

As I made my entrance following the footman's announcement, I was surprised to find only Dorothea and Lord Beverley in attendance. As usual, Dorothea did not look happy.

"There you are!" Lady Rydale exclaimed as she scooped tea leaves from a small strongbox into a teapot. "How do you take your tea, dear?"

"Milk and one sugar." I took the seat next to Lord Beverley on the *canapé*, then turned to him and remarked, "It seems a bit early for the guns to be back already. I hope that our little excursion did not interfere with your sport."

To my astonishment, Lord Beverley blushed under his tan. "Er, no, Lady Delemere," he said. "I returned alone. I wanted to take the opportunity to . . ."

"Why to have some private conversation with me, of course," Lady Rydale finished for him with a wink. Dorothea rolled her eyes and began to pick at a hangnail.

"Er, yes," Lord Beverley said, his eyes flashing over to Dorothea. "That is correct."

I nodded. "Ah. How nice."

So, Lord Ashenhurst was not Lady Rydale's first choice for Dorothea. Couldn't say I blamed the woman, though keeping the raffish earl under her roof while playing matchmaker for Lord Beverley seemed counterintuitive. Lord Beverley was certainly a handsome man, but he did not hold a candle to Lord Ashenhurst.

An awkward silence settled amongst us, and I began to wish that I was writing that letter to Charlotte. Witnessing Lord Beverley's unappreciated courtship of Dorothea was not my first choice for pleasant pastimes, and I began to wonder why I had been invited.

Fortunately, Lady Rydale was not one to waste time. "Lady Delemere," she began as she passed me my tea. "We were hoping you would tell us about your harrowing experience with the Black Unicorn—"

Of course.

"—Lord Hertford's rendition the night you arrived was a trifle *succinct*, and I've always found women to have a greater memory for detail. And a greater talent for the telling of a good story," she added with another wink to Lord Beverley. "And besides, Lord Beverley hasn't heard it yet, and as our *Lord Lieutenant*," she looked meaningfully at her daughter, "he is especially interested in the Black Unicorn."

Lord Beverley nodded. "Indeed."

I glanced over at the gentleman and caught the look of keen interest in his eyes.

And it was not difficult to realize why: The Black Unicorn's accomplices—the Northern Gang—were from Yorkshire, as we learned from the magistrate the evening after the robbery.

I accepted a scone from the plate Lady Rydale proffered. "Very well. What would you like to know?"

Lady Rydale set the scones down to clap her hands excitedly. "Oh, do tell us everything. Just start at the beginning, dear. How did you know you were about to be robbed?"

And so I did, sticking closely to Papa's edited account. That meant I had to leave out the part where the Black Unicorn shot and killed Buford, since Lord Beverley would naturally want to know why. All in all, even with Lady Rydale's frequent questions, my account took only a few minutes.

"It is very fortunate that no one was hurt," Lord Beverley said as I sipped my tea.

"Yes. Very fortunate," I agreed.

"Was he very handsome then?" Dorothea cut in.

"He was masked," Lady Rydale snapped. "Lady Delemere could not see his face. Er, isn't that correct, Lady Delemere?"

"Yes, he was masked." I set down my teacup and considered my scone. I was not fond of raisins, but Lady Rydale had provided a pot of clotted cream.

"And he did not say a single word?" Lord Beverley asked.

"No, not a word." I eyed the clotted cream.

Lady Rydale decided the issue for me by doling a healthy dollop of cream onto my plate. "He is probably mute. Or he stammers. Or perhaps he has a dreadful accent."

"Papa has another theory," I said, setting my teacup back down. "He thinks he is an aristocrat, and I agree."

Lady Rydale snorted.

"Really?" Lord Beverley fixed me with a skeptical look. "Like in a novel?"

"No," I said testily. "*Not* like in a novel." My mind called forth the memory of Sophie struggling on the ground beneath Buford's groping hands, the sound of her screams still vivid. "Not at all like a novel, Lord Beverley."

"Of course, Lady Delemere," he said. "My apologies. But why an aristocrat?"

❧

The evening after the robbery, I joined Papa in the coffee room of the Old Bull. He had just dutifully reported our encounter to the local magistrate.

"According to Sir Teegarden," Papa began as I sat down across from him, "the Northern Gang is originally out of Yorkshire, known in several northern counties for various criminal activities, but specializing in house breaking. Our attack in Lincolnshire was unusual on two counts: firstly, it is the furthest south of any of their known areas of operation, and secondly it is their first known instance of highway robbery."

"So what then was the Northern Gang doing so far south?" I asked. "And what was the Black Unicorn doing so far north? He only haunts the road to Bath—everyone knows that. And why did he intervene in a situation where he was so grossly outnumbered and then choose to let us go rather than robbing us?"

"These are all excellent questions, and I do have some theories." He paused, taking a sip of whisky. "To begin with the easiest answer: I believe that the Black Unicorn has changed his theater of operation. He has moved now to the Great North Road."

"But why?" I demanded. "That makes no sense. With the London Season over, everyone will be on the road to Bath."

Papa nodded. "But the key to successful highway robbery is isolation; one needs a lonely stretch of road with little likelihood that someone else will stumble upon the robbery while it is still in progress. The road to Bath is too crowded at present."

I considered this. "It seems an awful coincidence that both the Northern Gang and the Black Unicorn should choose to move into exactly the same territory at exactly the same time. Especially since the Northern Gang is not known for highway robberies."

"Too much of a coincidence," Papa agreed. "I do not believe that we are dealing with two separate parties here."

"You mean the Black Unicorn was working with the Northern Gang?" I demanded. "But why would he shoot one of his own men?"

Papa ran his finger thoughtfully around the rim of his glass. "I will tell you what I think is the only possible answer. The Black Unicorn has moved north. I believe that he has opted not to bring his previous group of accomplices with him, but has rather employed the Northern Gang, instead.

"Why this should be the case, I cannot imagine. It does not seem to make any more sense to bring the Northern Gang down from Yorkshire than to bring his Somerset accomplices north with him to the Great North Road. In both cases, he is introducing a large group of thugs into a new territory and that is likely to attract the notice of the local criminal element, as well as the local magistrates."

"So this attack was more violent because he is employing a new gang?"

"That is what I believe."

"Then why did he intervene? Why did he shoot that disgusting beast, Buford?"

Papa shrugged his narrow shoulders in a gesture I might have called nonchalant under better circumstances. "It seems counterintuitive, I agree. Unless what we witnessed was a power struggle over leadership."

I shook my head, not following.

"It seems to me that a critical danger in employing a pre-existing gang of criminals is that they will already have some sort of a leader," Papa explained. "In this instance, Red Jack. Red Jack would already have a certain way of doing things, and his followers would presumably follow his orders before those of the Black Unicorn. Especially given the fact that the Black Unicorn is clearly a man of education and breeding, possibly even an aristocrat. That, I believe, is why he remained silent throughout the encounter. He did not want us recognizing his likely origins through his speech. I also believe the Black Unicorn intervened and shot Buford to establish that he is the man in charge. Not Red Jack."

"Then he is no hero."

"No, my girl, the Black Unicorn is no hero," Papa said grimly. "Though I do owe the man a debt that I shall carry for the rest of my life. But if it were not for the Black Unicorn, we would never have been stopped in the first place. The Northern Gang were housebreakers until this day."

"And you truly think he is an aristocrat?"

"I think it very likely. That headpiece disguising the markings of his horse came from a very old set of equestrian parade armor. Probably of Spanish origin. It is not the sort of thing one can pick up in a shop. I would wager the rest of that armor is on display somewhere in a country house or converted castle."

"But why, Papa? Even the impoverished can live comfortably on the credit of their name alone. Why go to such dreadful measures for a few hundred pounds here and there?"

Papa sighed and turned his gaze meditatively to the flames in the hearth. "A man will resort to desperate measures to preserve his life, Elina, and even more desperate measures to preserve his honor. And can you think of any more obsessed with honor than those foolish young bucks from our own esteemed class?"

I returned my attention to Lord Beverley, and favored him with an appraising look. His interest seemed genuine, so I answered him. "An aristocrat would need to hide his accent and diction. If he identifies himself as a member of our class, it will narrow the field considerably in the authorities' quest for his identity."

"But if he is an aristocrat, why then would he take to the roads?" Lord Beverley argued. "Even if impoverished, he still has options. In these modern times, there are fewer and fewer restrictions on a gentleman's participation in trade."

I shrugged. "Perhaps you can ask him that when you catch

him. But it is not only his silence that suggests a distinguished pedigree to me. There is also the matter of his horse."

"But fine horseflesh is purely democratic," he argued. "Any man with the means can purchase as fine a horse as he wishes, and from what I have heard of this Black Unicorn, he certainly has the means."

I reached for my scone and began slathering it with cream. "His horse, from what I saw of it, was indeed very fine." I agreed. "But that is not to what I am referring. The beast wore an interesting headpiece. Papa said it looked like something taken from a suit of very old equestrian dress armor. Spanish, in point of fact. I cannot imagine that such a piece would be easy for one to simply purchase. It is rather the sort of thing handed down in a family from one generation to the next."

Lord Beverley frowned. "Perhaps he stole it. He is a thief, after all."

"A rather difficult thing to steal," I pointed out. "If he was that motivated to hide the markings on his horse, why not just use a different horse? Like you said, he has the means. It makes far more sense that he already owned the headpiece."

"Then why use it at all?"

"That, Lord Beverley, I do not know."

But Lord Beverley was shaking his head before I had even finished. "I just cannot accept that a man would risk not only his life, but the honor of his family name. It seems impossible to me."

My opinion of Lord Beverley plummeted. Nothing is so unattractive in a man as a lack of imagination. "But I was there, Lord Beverley," I reminded him. "And you were not. I have seen this man, and I am telling you that he is an aristocrat."

We settled into an awkward silence.

I drew a long breath, then set my scone back on my plate. "Very well. Then you and your like will continue to play the game according to *his* rules, and I shall have to wait a very long time before I have the satisfaction of watching the man who terrorized my family swing from the gallows."

"Well!" Lady Rydale exclaimed, her voice pitched a bit too high. "Thank you very much, Lady Delemere, for sharing your experience with us. It was most entertaining, wasn't it, Dorothea?" The good lady dug an elbow into her daughter's ribs, causing the girl to startle awake with an angry yowl. "Now!" she continued. "Cribbage anyone?"

CHAPTER 8

ON OUR FOURTH MORNING at Scarcliff Towers, I awoke to find myself in the mood for solitude. Thankfully, Lord Ashenhurst was away to York for business for a few days, though the rest of the guns were home from the moor for the day, so solitude might be in short order. Still, I had an idea where I might go.

I found the priest hole in the base of the southern tower, which made sense since the northern and southern towers were the two largest in the house and the windows on the ground floor had been bricked in for privacy.

Consequently, when I peered through the opening in the wall that until five years ago had been bricked in like the windows, I could not see anything at first.

But, as my eyes adjusted to the darkness, I noticed a clever little pistol tinder box sitting on a table just inside the doorway, with an attached candle-socket and a brass barrel full of matches. Checking the receptacle for tinder, I cocked the pistol, shut down the striker, and pulled the trigger. On my first attempt, I found the telltale little spot of glow in the tinder, and pulled a brimstone match from the barrel to transfer the flame to the candle. Moments later, my candle held high, I stepped over the threshold into the dark, cool hush of a little world kept secret for almost two-hundred years.

"Dear la!" I breathed.

The priest hole was set up as a chapel, just as Lord Rydale had said. But this was no rough approximation set up for expediency's sake during the days of the Reformation. The first thing I noticed was the wooden rood screen, elaborately carved by a Master, separating the room into a chancel, where the altar was set up, and a nave consisting of two wooden pews. Surmounting the rood screen was a large crucifix flanked by a statue of the Virgin on one side and a statue of some saint, possibly Saint John, on the other.

Passing through the rood screen's gate, I approached the altar. Set up on an elevated dais and covered in a moth-eaten black cloth, it stood complete with a golden chalice to the left, a stand holding a moldy Missal for the service of the Mass to the right, and a massive cross of what looked to be solid gold in the middle. Behind the altar an ornamental screen of wood similar to the rood screen covered the wall, and from the ceiling hung two sanctuary lamps flanking a large golden tabernacle for the Host.

Holding my candle close, I gingerly flipped through a few pages in the Missal, noting that it had been left open to Christmas Day. My Latin was good, but I still had trouble reading it due to the moldering corruption of the pages. Next I looked to the tabernacle, and the desire seized me to check and see if there was anything left inside it.

Something, however, held me back.

There was an undeniable sanctity to this place, and though not a Catholic myself, I still felt compelled to treat this sanctuary with respect.

I turned and passed back through the gate into the nave of the chapel. I noticed then the ancient rushes still strewn across the stone floor. I also saw the large wall painting on the southern wall, featuring a man with sorrowful eyes tied to a tree and bristling with arrows. There was another painting on the western wall, though I could not make out any of its details from where I stood.

Advancing to take a closer look, I slipped on something, yelping as I flung away the candle to catch myself on one of the pews.

After a few moments, satisfied that I was not going to fall, I carefully took a seat in the pew, then reached down to snatch the errant object up off the floor.

The light from the doorway did not penetrate to my position, and without the candle I could not see exactly what it was, though it felt like a string of beads. Unfortunately, the candle seemed lost to the darkness, so I brought the string of beads over to the doorway and discovered it was a rosary of jet with a crucifix of silver.

"What on earth are *you* doing here?" I wondered out loud.

Lord Rydale had said that he had left the chapel just as he'd found it, but I doubted that meant leaving rosaries on the floor where people could slip on them in the dark.

Besides, this rosary could not be two-hundred years old— the silver was still shiny, not covered in two centuries' worth of tarnish.

Suddenly I wanted to have another look at the room, but I needed that candle. I found it eventually in the far corner of the second pew. Lighting it once again, I returned to the altar.

Sure enough, I discovered that it had been recently cleaned of the thick layer of dust covering almost everything else.

Lord Rydale had not said anything about cleaning the chapel.

Passing back into the nave, I looked closer at the two pews and noticed immediately that the second one had been similarly cleaned of dust.

And on the floor, the rushes revealed something of a pathway between the doorway and that same second pew.

This chapel was still in use.

But, as Papa had said, the Bewforests were staunch Protestants.

Placing the rosary in my pocket, I walked back over to the western wall to take a closer look at the wall painting, which featured a strange flag of vertical red and gold stripes flanked on either side by two black unicorns rampant.

Bess had left money for Masses to be said for her lover, so it followed that the Black Unicorn was Catholic. This chapel must have been for him.

My candle began to smoke. Acrid enough to make my eyes water, I suddenly needed to be somewhere with sunlight and lots of modern windows. Only one place in this enormous pile could supply both those things.

The ground floor conservatory overlooking the gardens was clearly a recent addition to Scarcliff Towers. Built onto the western façade between the protruding northwestern and south-western towers, the long rectangular room boasted a wall of modern floor to ceiling French windows that flooded the con-servatory with light and opened directly onto the gardens. It seemed a good place to pass the time undisturbed.

However, as I entered the sunny room breathing with the vitality of lush green things, I found a tall man with luxuriously thick honey blond hair clubbed back in a queue seated on a wooden settle next to a potted orange tree. His back was to me, but I would know those massive shoulders anywhere.

I took a deep breath. "Sir Tristan?"

In an athletic surge of motion the man rose to his feet, turned, and bowed. When he righted himself, I found myself looking up into a brilliant pair of chiaroscuro eyes, opal green fired with darker bands of jade. But whereas my dear Charlotte's could at times be cold, with a touch of cynicism, her brother's held only warmth and gentleness.

"It is you!" I exclaimed, my enthusiasm a trifle forced. "How wonderful! Have you come to join the shooting party?" But then I caught sight of his troubled face. "Tristan, whatever is wrong?"

Tristan broke into a fatigued smile. "Zounds, Lady Delemere! You are more beautiful every time I see you!"

"*Elina*," I corrected gently. "Remember I have asked you to call me *Elina*."

We stood a moment in awkward silence. Things had been like this for years. Once upon a time, we had been children together, and he'd been my closest friend. Then, as adolescents, we became something a little more—happy in our private world of tentative touches and shy kisses. But in those days, Tristan had no prospects, and things had changed between us upon my sudden marriage to William.

Tristan had thrown himself into politics, becoming Papa's protégée. William had cut me off from family and friends, likely fearing the things I might say to them about his habits and strange appetites. But all of that now stood in the past. Tristan and I could start anew, though I was not sure I could tolerate that kind of close friendship with a man again. I felt that somehow it would not be fair to Tristan.

Finally, he motioned to the wooden bench behind him. "Come sit with me a moment? I am longing for some company."

"You were getting my company whether you liked it or not. I take it that you have not come to join the shooting party." The look on his face troubled me. If he came as the bearer of bad news, it could only pertain to Papa. Sir Tristan's association with Papa was closer than any he had with anyone else in the house. Except perhaps for me.

"I will be staying for a few days, so if Lord Rydale has an extra fowling piece, I am sure I will shoot a few moorcocks while I am here. But shooting is not the original purpose for my journey."

"Papa?" I asked tentatively.

Tristan's open, frank face had always been easy to read. The shadow that flickered across it now was answer enough. "I have some news I must deliver," he said. "Once I have discharged that duty, I can be more open with you."

I nodded, determined to keep my smile from faltering. "Did you arrive just this morning?"

"Last night."

"The journey from London must have been arduous."

He lifted a solid shoulder in a shrug. "I made good time. I sent my luggage ahead, but still have managed to beat its arrival."

Looking him over, I saw that he still wore his riding breeches, mud-spattered traveling frock, and linens yellowed from the dusty roads. With a shock, I realized he had *ridden* here.

Papa had come to Scarcliff Towers because the trip from London would be too onerous for one man to follow alone. It would be more convenient to write a letter, or so Sophie had said.

A letter that Papa could choose not to open.

And yet Tristan had made the journey, *on horseback*, knowing full well that Papa would not have ignored *his* letters. So Tristan's news must be the sort that could not be trusted to a letter.

"You must still be recovering from the journey." I stood and held out my hand. "How about we go find ourselves a cup of strong tea? And perhaps something to nibble on? You must not have eaten very well over the last two days."

"Tea? But you have only just come."

"We can continue our chat in the morning parlor."

He rose to his feet, towering over me, and begged my pardon as he arched his back in a quick stretch. He was a beautiful specimen of Saxon stock, his warrior's body too powerful for the modern men's fashions. In another time, he would have been standing with a battle axe in hand, holding the shield wall against the charge of the Norman invaders.

But today, he just took my hand. "I am a bit hungry," he said. "Has Lady Rydale employed a good cook?"

CHAPTER 9

Tristan's luggage arrived while we sat at tea, so I gave him leave to refresh himself.

Upon his return to the breakfast parlor, his spirits seemed improved, so I proposed a walk in the gardens.

We kept our chatter friendly and superficial, each of us careful to avoid any subject pertaining to Papa, though I knew his troubled specter haunted Tristan as much as it did me.

Later, as we sat in the window seat overlooking the fishpond in the garden banquet house, our laughter over recollections of shared childhood antics a bit forced, the first fat drops of rain fell upon the leaded glass.

"Rain?" I exclaimed. "But I did not notice any rain clouds when we were in the garden."

Tristan touched the window with his finger to follow a raindrop's progress down to the windowsill. "They say the weather in these parts is a fickle mistress, apt to change at any moment. The landlord at the inn I stayed at the night before last told me that this has been the wettest summer recorded in county history."

"That does not bode well for a shooting party." I traced my own drop of rain down its path through the tiny diamond panes.

"I think your shooting party is going to be spending a bit more time indoors than planned," he said. "That is probably where we should be headed ourselves, before this storm opens up in earnest."

It was not a very long walk back to the main house, though someone had locked the French windows of the conservatory, obliging us to wind our way around the northern tower to reach the front door on the eastern façade.

By then the rain was falling heavily enough to necessitate a change of clothes once we reached our chambers, though that was not too inconvenient since it was time to dress for dinner anyway.

Still, I planned to speak with the butler about the locked windows.

As we rounded the corner of the tower, I noticed a cloaked rider dismounting just in front of the porch. I remembered over-hearing Lord Rydale mentioning to Papa last night that he had some estate business to attend to today, and sure enough, as we approached I recognized our host. As we hurried into the hall together, the butler rushed forward, an urgent look on his face.

"Milord," he greeted Lord Rydale with a bow.

"Yes, Mr. Bartholomew, what is it?" The earl held out his arms for his servants to divest him of his drenched cloak and beaver hat. Tristan and I had no outerwear to surrender, but I lingered in order to speak with the butler once Lord Rydale finished with him.

"Lord Ashenhurst has returned, milord."

Lord Rydale's pale eyes widened in surprise. "But he is not due to return for another three days."

"Yes, milord. He has met with some misfortune on the road."

"Thieves?"

"It appears so, milord."

"Is he harmed?"

"A wound to the arm, milord. His valet has tended to it."

Lord Rydale sighed. "Lord Beverley is not going to like this—"

I did not stay to hear the end of the conversation, but took my leave of Tristan.

I needed to see Lord Ashenhurst immediately.

⤳

"Lord Ashenhurst!" I rapped on the door. "Lord Ashenhurst, open the door."

I waited. Nothing.

"Lord Ashenhurst!" I knocked again. "Either you open this door, or I will open it for you!"

This time I heard movements on the other side of the door. The handle turned and it opened a crack to reveal a very small man with white hair and a sour face.

"Lord Ashenhurst is indisposed at the moment," he said. "Perhaps madam can—"

"It is all right, Simon," came a faint voice from within. "Allow Lady Delemere to enter."

Simon glared at me, then nodded and stepped aside.

I hesitated, suddenly wary.

I could think of a hundred different reasons not to go forward. A man's bedchamber was a dangerous place, and probably none more so than Lord Ashenhurst's.

But he'd been attacked by thieves on the road.

I needed to know: had the Black Unicorn come to Yorkshire?

I took a deep breath and stepped into the darkness. To cover my nervousness, I snapped at the valet. "It is freezing in here! Why don't you—"

But the little devil slipped into the corridor, pulling the door closed behind him.

It took me a moment for my eyes to adjust. The heavy drapes were drawn closed, the only source of light flickering from the fire burning itself out in the hearth. In front of the fireplace stood Lady Rydale's full-sized copper bathtub, surrounded by empty water cans. Next to the bathtub stood a small table with a flannel washcloth, an amber bar of soap, and a crystal decanter of brandy with a matching tumbler next to it.

And in the bathtub sat the wretched figure of a man, head bent down, exhausted. A wet tangle of hair fell over his downturned face, the pale back of his neck looking vulnerable and exposed. Damp skin glowed in the firelight, shadows accentuating the sleekness of shoulders, arms, and the graceful curve of shoulder blades.

I closed my eyes, and focused on the sound of the rain lashing the windows. In the distance, thunder rumbled over the moors.

He was just a man, I reminded myself. But this great revelation seemed only to sharpen my senses. Yes, he was just a man, and I just a woman. And here we were, alone together. In the dark.

Nothing seemed more natural, nor more terrifying.

I inhaled deeply and opened my eyes. "Lord Ashenhurst—"

"Ashby," he mumbled.

His skin looked so smooth, so luminescent. I wanted to touch him, to feel the contours of bone and muscle, to flatten my palms and follow the graceful curve of his spine down, down, forever down into the water.

I clasped my hands behind my back and took a step backwards. All thoughts of the Black Unicorn vanished. "I beg your pardon?"

He sighed. "Lady Delemere, I am in the bathtub—"

I frowned, puzzling over the odd, dreamy quality of his voice.

"—titles seem rather ridiculous just now, yes?"

"I suppose they do." I bit my lip, hesitating. "Ashby?"

"Hmm?"

"Are you all right?"

He turned his head, looking at me through his hair. His eyes were dark, almost black, the firelight reflecting in them strangely. I glanced down to his left arm. It had been expertly dressed, but the bandages were soaked with blood.

"Are you all right," I repeated. "You have been shot?"

He shifted his position and leaned back, bringing his knees up as he slid lower into the water. Using his good arm to rake his hair back from his face, he fixed me with an expressionless look. His eyes still appeared black, lashes clumped together and heavy with bathwater. I noted the scar on his upper lip, and another just below his left nipple, a narrow length of shiny white tissue running about an inch long. A blade, perhaps? And on his right shoulder he had a large round knot of red scar tissue looking to be only a few months old.

"A superficial wound," he said. "Just a great deal of blood."

"And was it . . .? Was it the Black Unicorn?" I asked.

"It was."

Damnation. The possibility of the man coming to Yorkshire had crossed my mind. After all, we'd all been on the same North Road. But just now, with Lord Ashenhurst in the bathtub, I found myself oddly distracted from thoughts of the thief that had terrorized my family.

"You have been shot before," I said as I cast around for a place to sit. His clothing, crowned with his bloody shirt, covered the chair. I moved over to the bed and sat on the very edge.

"Winged in a duel last Christmas."

"Why do you do it?" I asked, setting my restless hands to stroking the smooth silk damask of the counterpane.

"Dueling?" He sounded surprised, "Believe me, it is never *my* idea."

"No. The women."

He turned to look at me, the firelight sliding around the angles of his face, emphasizing the sharpness of his cheekbones and casting his lower lip in shadow. He watched me for a long moment with those black eyes, then sighed and turned back towards the fire.

"I am a whore, milady."

"Have you ever loved any of them?" I asked.

"Any of *them*? No."

A strong gust of wind sloshed rain against the window. I shivered in my wet clothes, and scooted myself farther back on the bed, extending my arms behind me in a quest for the bed warmer's heat.

"But you have loved," I said.

"I apologize, Lady Delemere."

"Whatever for?"

"For not being there the night he died."

"Why do you call me Lady Delemere?" I continued to grope around on his bed, the ancient bed ropes creaking under my weight, but there appeared to be no bed warmer. "If I am to call you Ashby, then you must call me Elina. It is only proper."

"You told me you did not want me to call you Elina."

"Very well, Ashby. Call me what you like. You were about to tell me that you have been in love."

"*Am* in love," he corrected. "I still love her. And I suppose I always shall, which is as tragic as it is stupid."

"You cannot marry her?"

He closed his eyes. "I cannot marry her."

"May I ask why not?"

"Suffice it to say, I cannot."

"She does not love you?"

"Would you?"

I bit my lip, no longer able to ignore my conscience.

"Ashby?"

His eyelids fluttered open, and I could see by their gilded tips that his eyelashes had dried. "Hmm?"

"I must confess that I find your manner strange."

He tilted his head to the side, considering my words. "Laudanum has that effect. I believe I am also rather heavily in my cups," he added, gesturing to the decanter of brandy. "But if you are worried that I am baring my soul to you because my better judgment has been impaired, fear not."

"Then, why?"

"I do not know," he said. "Perhaps I should not. Too late now, I suppose."

"May I ask you another question?"

"You may ask, certainly."

"Isn't love supposed to inspire in one the desire to become a better man? Is not every shameful affair a discredit to the lady you love?"

"You sound like a bloody troubadour."

"Ashby."

He sighed. "Very well. I will answer, though I doubt you will be able to understand it."

"I am listening."

"I can never be with her, though I never wish to stop loving her. But I cannot live the life of a celibate. Nor do I wish the charms of a lesser woman to ever eclipse her."

I frowned. "So, what? You move from one dalliance to the next without ever allowing any one woman to linger long enough to challenge your lady's place in your affections?"

"I am a whore to honor my love. Not to discredit her."

"So you shall never marry then?"

"Marriage has nothing to do with love."

I snorted. "Indeed. But since you are being so candid, Ashby, may I ask you another question?"

"Must I answer it?"

"Yes, you must."

"Go on."

"Why do you torment me?"

His eyes snapped open. "I torment you?"

"We cannot carry on like this."

He remained quiet for a long while. If I had not been able to see the fire reflected in his eyes, I might have thought him fallen asleep.

"Ashby?" I prompted.

"I do not wish to torment you," he said, his voice hushed.

I stood up abruptly. "You mock me, sir."

"I wish you would not go. Not yet."

I glanced at the clock on the mantelpiece and started at the late hour. I hurried to the door. "I must go. It is almost time for dinner. I must dress."

"You will likely be partnered with Richmond tonight," he remarked. "I dare say you shall find him an improvement over my poor company."

Vaguely, I wondered how Ashby would know of Tristan. But since he spoke the truth, I chose not to answer and left without another word. Once in the corridor, I quickly closed the door behind me and blocked it with my body before Simon could slither back in. He glared at me while I lectured him, very quietly lest his master should hear me. The room was far too cold. He needed to build a bigger fire, change the dressing on his master's arm, and why in heaven's name was there no bed warmer in the bed?

The surly little man informed me that he did not own one, which I found appalling and so ordered him to borrow mine from Edith. I could sleep in damp bed linens for a night, since I feared Ashby's condition might make him more susceptible to catching a chill.

Finally, I ordered him to bring a full dinner up to his master immediately—no broth, since Ashby would need something substantial to dilute all the laudanum and brandy in his belly.

Then I let go of the incensed valet, and stepped into my own room to dress for dinner.

Later that evening, after the ladies retired to the saloon to await the gentlemen for coffee and tea, I found myself too restless for company. Making my excuses, I made my way down the corridor ostensibly in search of the water closet, lost in thought. But when I heard the low rumble of voices, I realized that I had come to a stop just outside the Great Chamber's withdrawing room. The doors to the Great Chamber stood open, and I could hear snippets of the gentlemen's discussion, a random word here, another few there. They sounded unhappy about something. Then I heard Tristan's voice, clear as a bell, say the only two words powerful enough to make me forget entirely my problems with Lord Ashenhurst . . .

"Black Unicorn."

I slipped quietly into the darkened withdrawing room, creeping silently in the shadows along the wall until I reached the large *secrétaire* cabinet next to the open doors which led to the Great Chamber. I quickly wedged myself into the small space between the side of the cabinet and the wall.

"So it is true then," Lord Beverley said.

"Aye, Charles," came Lord Rydale's resigned voice. "My neighbor, Julian Trevelver, sent word this afternoon, and I spoke to Ashenhurst just before dinner. He confirmed it."

"And where was he attacked?"

"On the same road as Trevelver, but further north, nearer to Thirsk."

"Both of them on their way to York," mused the Viscount.

"Apparently so," Lord Rydale confirmed. "He must have robbed Ashenhurst first, then Trevelver, who shot the Black Unicorn in the arm."

"That is very bold," said Tristan. "Two robberies in one day. How much did he take Ashenhurst for?"

"Not much," said Lord Rydale. "Fifty quid and a watch."

"And yet Ashenhurst struggled?" Tristan pressed.

"He must have," said Lord Rydale. "The Black Unicorn shot him. He did not shoot Trevelver, even though Julian was armed."

"A mistake the ruffian will likely not make again," said Tristan grimly.

"Well, he is injured now." The Viscount's odd falsetto was

toned down for the masculine company. "At the very least it will put him out of commission for a while. At the very best, it will scare him out of Yorkshire."

"Oh, he is not leaving anytime soon," said Lord Beverley unhappily. "I have known this was coming ever since Hertford told me he was using the Northern Gang. I figured the Black Unicorn ultimately planned to come poach in my territory. It was only a matter of time."

"But I thought Trevelver said Red Jack's gang was not among those assisting the Black Unicorn in the robbery?" Tristan queried.

"He did," said Lord Beverley. "In fact, the Northern Gang seems to have vanished completely. Nothing has been heard of them in over a week. Very strange."

"And what did Ashenhurst say?" Tristan asked. "Did he recognize anyone other than the Black Unicorn?"

"He claimed that the Black Unicorn was working alone," the Viscount said.

"*Claimed,* sir?" Tristan pressed. "You do not believe him?"

"It just seems very odd to me." The Viscount's words were accompanied by the clinking of crystal. "Why would the villain rob Ashenhurst alone, shoot him in the arm, then bring in the whole gang just a wee bit further down the road and allow himself to get shot? More brandy anyone?"

"Perhaps he had the gang already in place to ambush Trevelver, then happened upon Ashenhurst and decided on a whim to rob him as well." Tristan suggested.

"Then why did he shoot him? So far the Black Unicorn has not shot anyone else. Why Ashenhurst?" the Viscount pressed.

"Because he was alone, perhaps?" said Tristan. "Thus far, the Black Unicorn has never robbed anyone alone."

"And Ashenhurst struggled," Lord Rydale pointed out. "So the Black Unicorn, without the benefit of a gang for backup, was forced to subdue him by means of the way safest to himself, which was to shoot him."

"And Ashenhurst probably struggled," said Tristan, "*because* the Black Unicorn was alone."

"Which means," said Lord Beverley, "that he will likely never try to rob anyone alone again. I will take a spot more of your superb brandy, Eleezer. Who is your supplier?"

"I would prefer not to tell you, since I would like him to continue supplying me," came Lord Rydale's cheerful reply with more sounds of clinking crystal.

"Ah. I take it then that this brandy is not tariffed?"

"Of course not. Smuggling is so common in these parts, it is practically respectable. It is those dratted Runners and Excisemen you have to look out for—blood-thirsty devils, all of them. You should do something about *them*, Charles, and leave the free-traders alone. But that is a discussion best saved for another time."

"Indeed," Lord Beverley interjected. "What do you gentlemen think of Hertford's theory?"

"What theory?" Tristan asked.

"Hertford suggested the man might be an aristocrat," Lord Beverley said, "which is why he remains silent during his robberies. He does not want his speech giving away his membership to our privileged class. I did not credit it at first, but now I am not so sure. It has Lady Delemere convinced."

"It is certainly a valid hypothesis." Tristan sounded thoughtful. "The Black Unicorn would not be the first highwayman to claim elite status."

"*Claimed* is the operative term there," the Viscount replied. "Dick Turpin and his like were ruffians, all of them. Perhaps this Black Unicorn fellow simply does not speak. Perhaps he is a mute."

"It would certainly make matters easier if this Black Unicorn *was* of gentle birth," Lord Beverley mused. "Particularly if he were an aristocrat."

"We do not have enough evidence just yet to begin suspecting our friends and relatives," Lord Rydale declared. "What we do know is that the Black Unicorn is in Yorkshire. He is no longer working with the Northern Gang. He has targeted two gentlemen headed to York on the same road. And now he has shot a man. So, my question to you, Charles, is thus: as Lord Lieutenant of Yorkshire, what do you intend to do?"

"I have already sent word to the magistrates of York, informing them of the Black Unicorn's presence. Tomorrow I shall send word to Scarborough, Kingston upon Hull, and the largest of the market towns. I plan to offer a £25 reward for any information regarding the identity or whereabouts of the Black Unicorn, and a reward of £250 for his capture alive."

"That will certainly put the thief takers to work!" exclaimed Tristan.

"I dare say it will also sorely tempt the Black Unicorn's own band of thieves to turn against him," said Lord Rydale.

"That is precisely for what it is intended," agreed Lord Beverley.

I slipped back out to the corridor and wandered back towards the saloon, deep in thought.

Sir Trevelver had shot the Black Unicorn.

Ashby had been shot.

Could it be?

No. I shook my head resolutely. *Impossible.*

In any case, Lord Beverley certainly seemed to have matters well in hand.

We were safe while in Yorkshire. With any luck, we'd see the Black Unicorn captured before we headed back to Hertfordshire.

For Sophie's sake, I prayed it would be so.

CHAPTER 10

THE STORM HAD PASSED by the following morning, leaving behind it the bitter nor'easterly that had blown in from the coast.

I sat on a cold marble bench tucked into the corner of the flower garden nearest to the roses. A book lay open in my lap. I stared down, not really seeing the words. I was in the grips of a dilemma that had kept me from sleep for most of the night.

I knew information about the Black Unicorn that Sophie did not.

But the highwayman would be no threat to us until we left to go home to Hertfordshire. Any other planned outings would undoubtedly be in the company of all the gentlemen, and the Black Unicorn would be mad to attack a party that size.

Still, she should know. I longed to discuss the matter with Tristan, but then I would have to confess my act of subterfuge to him. I could always tell him that Lord Ashenhurst had told me, but then I would have to confess my presence in his bedchamber before dinner.

Lord Ashenhurst's bedchamber.

"Elina!"

I gasped, nearly falling backwards off the bench

"Blast you, Lord Ashenhurst!" I gasped as I righted myself. "Where the devil did you come from?"

"Language, language, Elina," he chided as he took an uninvited seat beside me. "And I told you to call me Ashby."

"Fine. Ashby," I said, swallowing my pulse. "I do not know why you insist upon sneaking up on me like that."

"I was not sneaking." He crossed his right hand solemnly over his breast, looking the very picture of innocence.

I frowned. "Where is your coat? You will catch a cold."

He waved his hand blithely, the scent of lavender water wafting from the billowy frills at his wrist. "My coat is inside; the sleeve would not fit over my bandages."

"Well then, you should not be outside."

"But *you* are outside."

I continued to watch him warily. There was something different about him this morning—something other than the lack of laudanum clouding his eyes, though I could not figure what it was.

Suddenly he broke into a smile. "Elina?"

"Yes, Ashby?" I shifted my position to face him, scooting as far away from him as I could without falling into the rose bushes.

"I wanted to thank you."

"For what?"

"Simon told me what you said to him in the corridor last night."

"Oh. Tricky devil. If I were you, I would find myself a valet who took better care of me. My maid Edith has brothers in service; I could give you a referral."

He glanced down, his thick fringe of lashes dark against the paleness of his cheek as he smoothed his hands over nonexistent wrinkles in his waistcoat. "It has been a very long time since anyone has taken care of me."

He glanced back up, and I abruptly realized what was so

different about him. It was the open, candid look in his eye, the shyness that hovered at the corners of his smile.

The mocking sarcasm and arrogant pretense of the fashionable libertine had been stripped away.

I felt myself relaxing. "How does your arm feel? Does it still pain you?"

The wind ruffled the lace at his throat, catching once more the scent of lavender. He lifted his good shoulder in a shrug. "It will pain me for a while yet. A pistol ball to the arm, even a graze, is not a pretty thing. Lady Rydale offered me some more laudanum for the pain, though I would prefer not to resort to it if I can help it."

"Ashby?" I asked suddenly. "May I ask you a question?"

He smiled that shy little smile again. "You and your questions. You may ask, though I still reserve the right not to answer."

"Are you here to court Dorothea?"

"Would it matter to you if I were?"

"I took tea with Lady Rydale in her dressing room a few days ago. Lord Beverley and Dorothea were in attendance . . . I think there's something you ought to know."

"Ah. If you are referring to Lord and Lady Rydale's hopes to wed their daughter to Lord Beverley, I already know. Lady Rydale made that perfectly clear to me my first night here."

"So you *are* here for Dorothea."

"Actually, I am here for my brother. Chrysander."

My eyes snapped back to his face. "Your brother?"

"Half-brother, actually. My father found himself an heiress from Oxfordshire shortly after my mother died. I also have three half-sisters."

"I do not think that match will work, Ashby," I said. "Not with the way Dorothea is pining after you."

Ashby looked horrified. "Good God, I am not here to marry Chrysander to Dorothea!"

I found myself smiling smugly, then immediately frowned as I realized how much his reaction pleased me.

"Then what is this about your brother?" I pressed.

"My brother is seventeen and will be entering Cambridge next year to prepare for a career in politics. The Harcourts and the Bewforests have been close allies since before the Civil War, though we have grown apart in recent years. I have come to rekindle that alliance. Rydale is the Duke of Newcastle's man, and I hope that Eleezer will sponsor my brother into an introduction. I would like to see Chrysander placed in the Commons in five or six years. And," he added irritably, "Dorothea is making things more difficult by alienating me from Lady Rydale."

"I see." I was still troubled over how much this news pleased me. What the devil did I care?

"Elina?"

I turned away from him, training my eyes on the rosebush next to me. "Yes, Ashby?"

"May I ask *you* a question?"

"I suppose."

"Last night you showed me kindness."

"That is not a question, Ashby."

"Do you . . . " His voice trailed off uncertainly.

"Yes?"

He drew a long breath. "Could it be possible . . . that is to say, do you perhaps see something . . . more in me? More than what my reputation advertises?"

I did not answer.

"Elina?"

He fascinated me, it was true. I had thought myself immune to such things; that I could be a fool for no one. And if I was not careful, I *would* become a fool for Ashby, right along with every other woman in the kingdom. He'd controlled every encounter from the very beginning, using the staggering power of his sexuality to keep me always off-balance.

He sighed, sounding almost sad. "You do not have to answer. But could you at least look at me?"

I did not move, but stared intently at that rosebush, its open blooms somehow seeming vulgar as they spread their petals for the watery sunlight.

"Please?" he begged.

The easiest course of action would be to get away from him. *Permanently* away from him.

It was the best solution.

"Elina, if you would just look at me once, I will leave you alone. I promise."

I should be cruel. I should make him hate me. He'd given me a glimpse of his soft underbelly; I should use it to my advantage.

Carefully arranging my features to mimic his own talent for inscrutability, I slowly turned towards him. I lifted my gaze to meet his, but when I looked into his eyes, so open and hopeful, I hesitated for just the flicker of a moment. Then I reached up and pulled him down to my kiss.

His mouth was as soft as it looked, and warm. He smelled clean, of soap and lavender. The area just above the dip on his upper lip was especially fragrant with his natural, musky scent.

His kiss was unexpectedly tender. He closed his eyes and leaned into me, tilting his head, molding his mouth to mine. I closed my own eyes, and he reached up to gently take hold of either side of my throat, his thumbs lightly stroking along my jawline until gooseflesh erupted in a surge of heat across my body.

I whimpered as he leaned further into me, suddenly full of intent as his tongue coaxed my mouth for entrance. I opened to him, and he plunged into me, the sudden penetration causing my stomach to drop abruptly while the secret and most sensitive parts in my body fired back to life. I barely registered the taste of chocolate and brandy before surrendering all thought as I sank into the glorious invitation of his body.

Ashby's hands slid down my back to my hips, pulling me almost into his lap. His mouth left mine to trace a line of fire along my jaw, his warm breath sending fresh shivers down my spine. He moved down my neck, teeth grazing my skin, then retraced his way back up with brushes of his soft, beautiful mouth. As he slowly found his way back to my kiss, I awaited him breathlessly, eyes closed, lips parted. But instead of returning to me, he pulled back, holding my face in his hands to keep me from following him. I opened my eyes to find him gazing down upon me, his hooded eyes dazzlingly seductive, his lips curved into a smile that fired a powerful jolt into the ache between my legs.

I knew this look for what it was.

Temptation.

Ruin.

"*Minha Amada*," he breathed.

He kissed me suddenly, bruisingly, releasing my face so he could twist one hand into my hair while he slowly moved the other down over the curve of my breast to take firm possession of my waist. He dragged me still closer, pulling me off the bench until I straddled his lap. I sank my teeth down hard into his luxurious lower lip, perhaps a bit harder than I'd intended. A curious noise escaped him, and I felt his mouth curve into a smile.

But even this was not enough, and I whimpered in my desperation for more of him. Releasing my hair, he dropped his shoulder and began scooping up under my skirts with his good arm, his hand moving possessively up the curve of my calf to the back of my knee. I gasped against his mouth as he moved with practiced ease past my garter, his touch searing into the naked flesh of my thigh.

Good God, I wanted his mouth all over me, kissing my throat, my breasts, my belly, my hips, and lower still. I wanted to feel his weight on top of me, pressing deep inside of me as I pulled my knees up over his hips. I needed him, and he needed me, too. I knew it. I could feel it.

But suddenly I felt his body go rigid. He broke away from me, letting his arms drop down to my sides. My body immediately protested this cold abandonment, and I opened my eyes to find that his were narrowed into a baleful glare directed over my shoulder at something behind me.

That something cleared his throat.

I twisted around and found Tristan standing there, outrage writ clearly upon his face.

"Really, Lady Delemere," Ashby said icily as he continued to stare Sir Tristan down, "how exceedingly careless of you. You arrange an assignation with one suitor, and then entertain another in his place. How dreadfully vulgar."

I blinked at him. "What? Ashby—?"

"Get off me, woman." Ashby seized me around the waist and dumped me roughly back onto the bench, his features twisted into an ugly sneer.

I stood, swaying a little on weak knees, then gathered as much dignity as I could. I smoothed down my hair, brushed out the wrinkles in my dress with deliberate care, then turned to look down on Ashby.

"Go to hell, Ashby Harcourt," I said.

Then I spun on my heel, and marched past Tristan out of the garden.

CHAPTER 11

THE CONSERVATORY WAS LOVELY.

The little orange tree had flowered overnight, perfuming the air and filling it with pollen dancing with the dust motes in the rays of the late-morning sun. Everywhere lush green things thrived, planted carefully in pots and climbing the trellises lining the walls, all of them perfectly pleased with their indoor existence free from insects and frost.

It was a room of comfortable ease, of harmony and contentment.

I wanted to tear it all down.

I think it was Congreve who determined 'Heaven has no rage like love to hatred turned / Nor hell a fury like a woman scorned.'

And I had allowed myself to be scorned by the most infamous rakehell of my generation.

Still, Ashby's reaction seemed bizarre for a rake. Obviously, some animosity existed between Ashby and Tristan. If I did not know any better, I would say he seemed almost jealous. But surely such creatures could feel no jealousy. And had he not just told me *yesterday* that his heart belonged irrevocably to another?

A gentle knock sounded from the doorway.

I did not bother to look up. "Hello, Tristan. Come sit down, if you like."

"I can leave you alone, Elina," he said. "I just needed to see that you were all right."

"I am not. I am very angry with myself. But your presence is soothing. I think I shall feel better with a little company."

Moving silently, as though the sound of his footsteps might send me into a fit, he crossed the room and took a seat on the bench opposite mine, worry etched in every line of his face.

"Elina—" he began tentatively.

I held my hand up without looking at him. "Don't. I could not bear it just now."

"There is something I feel I must tell you," he pressed. "About Lord Ashenhurst and myself. It might make this easier for you."

He looked miserable, his opal-green eyes dulled with melancholy. I said as much.

He nodded, and leaned forward to plant his elbows on his knees. "I feel it is my duty to inform you of our past, but I am worried it may kindle in your heart sympathy for a man who deserves nothing but your derision. When I came upon you in the garden, it was like coming upon a scene from a terrible nightmare. That a lady of your sensitivity and distinction—"

"Stop it, Tristan!" I snapped. "I already feel horrified enough at my own actions. And spare me any tales about your past with that vile creature. Nothing you say could possibly excuse him. I wish for you to tell me instead about Papa. He did not come to dinner last night, so I expect you've delivered your news, yes?"

Tristan shook his head, his eyes pleading. "Not now, Elina. Let us put off this discussion for another time. It would be better for both our nerves."

"I must know what has happened."

He sighed and looked down to his hands clasped loosely between his knees. "As usual, your wish is my command. But I must forewarn you that what I am about to tell you will most assuredly spoil your morning if it has not already been spoilt. I think that your little, ah, interlude with Ashenhurst must be affecting you more than you are letting on—"

"Enough, Tristan!" I cut him off sharply. I knew that later I would come to regret my treatment of my old friend, but just now I could not be bothered with anyone's feelings save my own. "I have waited long enough."

He nodded curtly. "Very well. I presume you know by now that your father has left the Whig party, yes? He and a number of his supporters, including myself, have gone over to Pitt's camp. The break was over France: the so-called "New Whigs," led by Fox, support the revolutionaries. They view the Revolution in France as a continuation of our own revolution in 1688. Your father, however, does not support the Revolutionaries and their wholesale murder of their aristocracy."

"Yes," I interrupted, "I do know most of this already. There were reprisals then? From the Party?"

"If it were not for the fact that we are about to declare war on France, your father would have never been singled out."

I took a deep breath and steeled myself for the worst. "Singled out how, Tristan?"

"First, I must go back a bit. After your father left, Fox continued to alienate members of the Party with his sympathy towards the French Revolution. Most notably, House leader the Duke of Portland, Lord Fitzwilliam, and a fellow named William Windham were becoming increasingly uncomfortable with Fox's radicalism. Rumor had it that they were preparing to defect over to Pitt's side, as well. And since Pitt is preparing for war with France very publicly, those in Fox's camp—the ones very strongly against war with France—panicked. They singled your father out as a scapegoat and effectively ruined him politically in an effort to scare his followers into rejoining the New Whigs, while discouraging Portland, Fitzwilliam, and Windham from defecting to Pitt."

"But how? *How* could Fox even touch Papa politically?"

"Well, His Royal Highness the Prince of Wales owed Fox a favor. A large favor, dating back to the king's madness. Fox helped secure limited monarchical powers for Prinny during that time. And it is rumored that should the king's madness return, Fox has promised that those limited powers shall be pushed into a regency with the full power of the monarchy behind it. So, when Fox called in his favor, the Prince answered. The Brinkleys no longer enjoy royal favor, Elina. Your father's enemies have presented some old essays of his, never published, which they are using to erroneously link him to Thomas Paine. The charge is ridiculous, especially since Lord Hertford has now crossed over to Pitt's camp in support of the war with France. But Paine will most likely be tried *in absentia* for seditious libel for his treatise *The Right of Man*, and there is a possibility that your father could be tried as well. I personally do not think it will come to that, but, then again, I never thought I would see the day when the Marquess of Hertford would be forced out of politics in disgrace."

"So the fact that Papa has served Britannia's interests for his entire life means nothing," I said bitterly.

"No, Elina. Not in this case."

"But what of the king?" I demanded. "Surely the king will not tolerate this mischief! He would not allow a loyal subject to be ruined upon a whim!"

Tristan stood abruptly, agitation radiating from his powerful body as he paced over to the French windows. "The relationship between the King and his son is a very troubled one. It always has been, though it has become worse since the Prince ruled in the King's stead as his regent. Old Prinny got a taste of power and was loathe to give it up once his father recovered. Consequently, the King avoids any direct conflicts with the Prince whenever he can. He will not counter the Prince's mischief in this case, because your father is not one of his ministers, which is exactly why your father was singled out by the New Whigs in the first place."

"And what will you do?" I asked, my voice sounding hollow in my ears. "Could you be in danger, as well?"

"I will stay with your father," he said. "But I do not think that I will be in danger. If it comes to pass that I am prosecuted, I will probably just take an extended holiday somewhere. I have always wanted to see America."

I watched him for a moment, noting his rigid posture and the defiant set of his shoulders. I wondered whether he spoke the truth, or was just attempting to assuage my worries. The selfish side of me realized that should Tristan be forced to flee, he would likely take Charlotte with him. And life would be terribly dreary without the two of them to share it with me.

And now what would Papa do? His whole life revolved around politics. I said as much to Tristan.

"I do not know, Elina." He drew a long breath, and I saw the tension ease out of him as he exhaled. His hands, clenched at his sides, relaxed, and he shoved them into his pockets as he turned back round to face me. "I just do not know. Hopefully, he will embrace the life of the country squire."

"You and I both know that that will not happen," I said sadly. "And now that we have been ruined, what will that mean for Sophie's marriage to Thaddeus? And Phosey? If we do not have the political card to play, we are nothing!"

"I think that Sophie's bond to Sir Thaddeus is strong enough to withstand this," he answered. "It is probably fortunate he has reached his majority and his father is no longer alive. As for Phosey? Hopefully by the time she is ready for marriage, the fortunes of your family will have reversed themselves. Right now, while Paine's trial is still pending, is the most dangerous time. I feel certain that once we officially declare war on France and once the Paine trial is over—hopefully without your father being brought up on charges—then things will die down. Your father will never be able to return to politics, but your family will almost certainly regain some of its lost position given time."

"I only pray that you are correct, Tristan," I said, closing my eyes wearily, "because I do not know what we shall do if you are not."

CHAPTER 12

I SPENT THE REST OF the day alone in my room.
I'd decided when I left Tristan in the conservatory that
I would not be coming up to dinner that evening.

But then I thought of Papa, and I realized that if he could be
brave enough to face company, so could I.

So when the clock chimed eight o'clock, I sailed into the
withdrawing room, shoulders squared, head held high, resplendent in a gown of green and ivory serpentine silk, my hair a
cloud of curls and ringlets dressed *à la Conseilleur* with my mother's diamonds.

Ashby did not yet count among the assembled company.
Though only a temporary reprieve, I still found it easier to
breathe. And there were two new faces joining our company
that evening: Sir Chauncey Dalingridge, a rather forgettable man
d'un certain âge with thinning brown hair and a weak chin; and
his new wife Lady Gabrielle Dalingridge, a young French actress
but recently come to England.

With her startlingly violet eyes, graceful figure, and forth-
right manner, she had already made a stir in fashionable society,
particularly when she'd chosen the homely Dalingridge for a

husband when she could have had virtually any gallant cavalier of her choice.

Some whispered she'd only chosen Dalingridge because of his tolerance for her many extra-marital affairs.

As I made my way across the room towards Sophie and Tristan, I found my progress halted abruptly by the person of Dr. Froggenhall. Swallowing down my irritation, I forced myself to smile and wish him a good evening.

"Thank you, Lady Delemere," he answered, his manner as somber as his plain black suit. "And may I wish you a good evening. You look lovely as ever."

"You are too kind," I responded. "But if you will just excuse me, I was—"

"I have just been informed by Lady Rydale," he interrupted, "that I have the very great honor of attending you this evening."

"Oh?" I replied, my elation at hearing that I was free from Ashby for the evening blending with dismay over the price I would have to pay for it. "How lovely. I look forward to your conversation at dinner, sir, but if you will just excuse—"

"I think that our pairing up, er, for dinner that is, is fortuitous for the both of us," he told me. "I think that you will find my conversation both stimulating and entertaining. I thought we could begin with a discussion over the difference between melancholy as a disposition, or melancholy as a habit. In the case of the former, as you will soon come to agree—"

"Excuse me, Phineas." Lady Rydale, Gabrielle Dalingridge following closely in her wake, muscled her nephew aside. "You will have plenty of time to regale Lady Delemere with your conversational talents during dinner. Right now, I need to make introductions."

Dr. Froggenhall flushed a mottled red as he was forced out of the way. He lingered awkwardly for a few moments, unsure as to what he should do, while Gabrielle Dalingridge and I bobbed curtsies and followed the protocol for meeting a new acquaintance. The poor little man then became the victim of a second act of rudeness when Lady Rydale firmly took hold of his arm and dragged him away with her so that Lady Dalingridge and I could continue undisturbed with the ritual of becoming better acquainted.

I watched his retreating form with satisfaction, then focused on the beautiful woman before me. She was taller than I had thought, besting me by about two inches. And I thought her to be about three to five years my junior, though her eyes bore the relaxed confidence of a woman of the world. The rest of her was flawless down to her elegant gown of the palest blush silk faille.

"Lady Delemere," Lady Dalingridge breathed in heavy French accents, "*Vraiment*, to meet you at last, this is such a great honor! So very many things have I heard about you!"

"You have?" I asked, taken aback. "I beg your pardon, Lady Dalingridge, but whatever for?"

"But you do not know? You are preceded by your reputation, Lady Delemere," she said, her gaze traveling over me from head to toe. "I have heard a great many things about you."

"Really?" I returned her smile guardedly. "It is funny that you should choose those words, Lady Dalingridge. It does not come across as a compliment."

She shrugged in typical Gallic fashion. Then she leaned forward, her quick movement making me jump, "You must call me Gabrielle," she whispered in a conspiratorial manner. "You say 'Lady Dalingridge,' and I do not know who it is you mean. May I call you Elina?"

"I suppose," I said, struggling against the desire to take a step backwards. Something about her made me increasingly uneasy, though I could not figure what. She in turn watched my face closely, sculpted eyebrows raised expectantly until I finished my sentence. "Gabrielle," I said belatedly, and her expression relaxed.

"*Bien*," she said, nodding to herself. "This is very good. *Voyons*," she continued, "there is another question I must ask you."

"Very well." There was something predatory about her. She was still standing too close, looking into my eyes so intently she seemed almost hungry. I blinked and refocused my eyes on some random object across the room.

"I was wondering, Elina," she said, her accent elongating and emphasizing the vowels, "if you could tell me please when Ashby will be coming back?"

"What?" Startled, my attention snapped back to her face. "What did you say?"

"*Ahhsch*-bi," she answered coolly, sinking her teeth into his name so luxuriously it brought to mind all manners of sin. She reached out and touched my upper arm, causing a wave of goose-flesh to rush across my body. "He and I are friends now a very long time, since he was just a young man at *l'Université de Paris. Naturellement*, he came often to see me at the Maison Moliere. I wish to know when he will return. He is the only reason I am here to join this party in your dull North Country, you see? So, you will tell me now, Elina, *oui?*"

"I was not aware that Ash— er, Lord Ashenhurst, had left," I told her. "I honestly do not know why you think *I* would know. Perhaps you should ask Lady Rydale. Surely Lord Ashenhurst would have communicated his plans to her."

"I see," she said. She'd been stroking my upper arm with her thumb, and now she released me, casually stroking the outer swell of my breast as her hand returned to her side. "I am glad you are here, Elina," she said. "I look forward to getting to know you better."

I stood utterly perplexed, and not a little flushed, when the butler and footman opened the double doors leading into the Great Chamber. As they took their posts on either side of the doorway, Dr. Froggenhall promptly materialized and presented his arm. Taking my place beside him, I nodded to her, then allowed him to pull me away towards the Great Chamber.

"Has milady made a new friend?" he asked caustically, clearly still smarting from Lady Rydale's rudeness.

"I do not know, Dr. Froggenhall," I answered, replaying the strange encounter in my mind, "I honestly do not know."

CHAPTER 13

G ABRIELLE PERFORMED ADMIRABLY DURING dinner, her wit and sparkling personality soon captivating everyone, ladies and gentlemen alike.

The only person impervious to her charms was Dr. Froggenhall, whose idea of good conversation turned out to be a lengthy lecture upon his chosen specialization: the study of melancholy. This suited me fine, since it only required me to agree with him every now and again, while I could devote the rest of my attention to my own thoughts.

Watching Papa as he sat in the place of honor next to Lady Rydale, I could not help but think he looked diminished. Old and somewhat frail to begin with, I noticed now that the fire in him seemed dampened. As he courteously paid court to Gabrielle, the twinkle in his eye had vanished and not even the French actress's sharpest witticisms inspired more than the shadow of a smile from him.

After dinner, the men did not dally long in the Great Chamber. Coming to join us in the saloon after only ten minutes, they continued to orbit Gabrielle like so many dark planets to her sun. Sir Chauncey looked on in quiet contentment from his seat in the corner.

Unfortunately for me, Dr. Froggenhall still seemed immune to her charms. And now that he'd spent all of dinner lecturing me about his study of melancholia amongst his patients at the York Asylum, he was asking me questions that required me to pay attention to him.

"Tell me, Lady Delemere," he said once he'd settled down into the seat next to me, "how do you like Yorkshire?"

"It is beautiful, Dr. Froggenhall," I answered, stirring two sugars into my tea, "though a little chilly for me. Hertfordshire is a bit milder of temperature."

"And are you very attached to Hertfordshire then?"

"Er, yes—" I responded. In the background the men were making a commotion.

Apparently, Ashby had not been the only one to see Gabrielle on the stage. Only natural, I supposed, given the amount of time she'd spent on the boards. She'd had a quite career in Paris. Glancing over Dr. Froggenhall's shoulder, I was surprised to see even Tristan bandying for Gabrielle's attention as he waxed poetic on her virtuosic portrayal of the virginal Junia in Racine's *Britannicus*.

Virginal indeed.

"Lady Delemere?" Dr. Froggenhall prompted, a touch of irritation in his voice.

I remembered then that I had been in the middle of saying something. "Ah, yes, Dr. Froggenhall. My apologies. Yes, I am very attached to Hertfordshire. I spent my girlhood there, after all."

"But your late husband's family is from Suffolk, unless I am much mistaken."

"No. You are not mistaken."

"And you moved to Suffolk then, after you married?" he asked, his tone a bit too casual as he sipped his coffee.

"Well, of course, I did—" I glanced once more over the little man's shoulder at Tristan. Gabrielle was favoring him with an engaging smile. He in turn seemed flushed as he chatted with her. Just at that moment, Gabrielle glanced towards me and caught my eye. She winked at me, slowly and deliberately, and her smile deepened into something impossibly seductive.

Very old friends, she had said.

I could see it perfectly: Ashby lounges in a large armchair in a fashionable apartment on the Rue de Richelieu with high ceilings and rococo plasterwork, wearing just his breeches and a snowy white shirt untucked and unlaced down the front to expose his bare chest. His sapphire eyes look dark in the candlelight, slightly unfocused in a drunken haze, and his loose, tangled curls tumble into his eyes as he leans forward to pour himself more wine.

Gabrielle materializes in the open bedroom doors behind him, clad only in a long silk dressing gown that clings to her body along with her long black tresses as she stalks towards him. The soft click of her Chinese slippers on the wooden floor stirs in him erotic memories from just a few hours earlier, and he smiles languorously as he pours the wine. But she stands behind him now, arresting his progress by playfully grabbing a handful of his hair. He settles back into the chair as she tilts his head back, exposing his long white throat and the strong line of his jaw as she kisses him deeply. Her gown slips off one shoulder, exposing a perfect white breast with its small pink nipple pebbling at the sudden exposure. He pulls her around and into his lap, his practiced hands once more making her body sing as the forgotten wine glass falls to the floor and shatters.

And now she has come to Yorkshire. For him.

But what the devil did I care?

"—But I am very glad to be back in Hertfordshire," I continued seamlessly, eradicating the unwelcome vision from my mind. "I do not mean to ever leave again."

"Hmmm." Dr. Froggenhall took another sip of coffee. "And your sister shall be moving to Kent upon her marriage?"

"Yes," I snapped. "She will." I glanced over to Sophie, seated across from me in the *fauteuile* next to Phosey's, and caught her eye. She sipped her tea, glanced pointedly towards Dr. Froggenhall, then smiled serenely.

"Do you know, Lady Delemere," the little man continued, "that I have never been to Hertfordshire?"

"Er, no Dr. Froggenhall," I answered, glaring at Sophie, "I did not know that."

"Perhaps—"

Suddenly Gabrielle released a loud peal of laughter, drawing everyone's attention. Everyone save Dr. Froggenhall.

"Perhaps," he pressed on, "I should make a trip—"

"*Sais vrais?*" the Frenchwoman exclaimed loudly, her face shining with delight as she turned from Tristan to Lord Beverley. "The Black Unicorn is indeed in Yorkshire as the newspapers say?"

"Why yes, Lady Dalingridge," Lord Beverley promptly replied. "That is correct."

"And still you do not know who he is?"

"Er, no, milady," he admitted, covering his sheepishness with a sip of coffee. "He has proven most elusive. But he will be caught, mark my word! I swear that he will not leave Yorkshire a free man. I have taken certain steps to ensure the rascal's downfall!"

"Well, if you cannot tell me who he is *monsieur*, then what good are you to me?" Gabrielle asked as she stepped closer to Lord Beverley and gazed up into his face. Lord and Lady Rydale glowered at the performance. Dorothea smirked.

"Well," the sportsman said once he'd recovered himself, "I cannot at present tell you his identity. But Lord Hertford and his lovely daughters were most fiendishly robbed by the very same miscreant while on their way to Yorkshire. What say you, sir?" He turned abruptly to Papa. "Would you be willing to entertain the ladies with your account of the dastardly fellow? I don't believe they will take 'no' for an answer!"

Papa favored Lord Beverley with a cold stare. It was bad form for Lord Beverley to single Papa out among mixed company without clearing it with him beforehand. But since Papa was keeping his promise to Sophie that he would not tell anyone of her near rape, Lord Beverley had no reason to believe that anything had occurred during the robbery other than inconvenience. Only we knew otherwise. I watched Sophie's face, looking for signs of distress. But her features remained schooled in a look of impassive calm, and her hands sat in her lap relaxed and still. Nevertheless, I thought she looked a little pale. Phosey, on the other hand, looked alarmed as she watched Papa's silent figure.

"I'm afraid there isn't much to tell, Lady Dalingridge," Papa said at length. "None of us got a very good look at the man. He was not present for most of the robbery and when he did appear, it was behind us and we couldn't see him."

Gabrielle looked in turn from Papa to Sophie to me. As she met my eyes I shook my head almost imperceptibly, willing her to let the matter go. Her eyes narrowed, and she looked about to say something more when she glanced to Phosey and caught the look on the girl's face.

"*Voyons*," she said with a shrug, "such a pity. But . . ." She paused significantly, a playful look warming her eyes as she turned her attention back to Lord Beverley. "When you do catch this *voleur romantique*, I will expect a full report from you, *oui*? You must promise me!"

Lord Beverley, belatedly realizing his colossal blunder with Papa, agreed to Gabrielle's request somewhat meekly.

"Excellent!" she declared. "And now for some music. Dorothea, *ma belle chèrie*, do come play and sing for us!"

CHAPTER 14

S UNDAY MORNING FOUND ME crammed into the close quarters of the Bewforest family box, squinting in the sunlight streaming down from lofty clerestory windows.

I sighed.

The morning service promised to be a long one.

The elderly vicar stood directly in front of us at the eastern end of the nave, droning on in his warbling voice from behind a small wooden lectern. He looked very insignificant in the great cavernous space all around him.

More cathedral than parish church, the minster of the local town had long since been stripped of its religious statuary and stained glass during the Reformation. All along the cool walls of each aisle behind the thick stone columns of the nave stood empty niches that once housed the Catholic pantheon of saints, conspicuous now in their absence.

"Lady Delemere," Lord Rydale's voice snapped me to attention. "I see you admiring our fine collection of county flags."

He hadn't bothered to lower his voice. But the vicar wasn't likely to shush the Earl of Rydale.

"The flags?" I replied, casting around for what he was talking about. I found them, a ratty assortment of faded colors upon the wall next to me. "Ah yes," I said, recognizing the stag on a yellow shield for Hertfordshire. But there were some flags that I did not recognize, and after a quick count, realized there were more flags than there were counties. I pointed this out to Lord Rydale.

"That is because some of them are for the old Anglo-Saxon kingdoms," he said with the pride of an antiquarian. "See that one of the gold saltire on the blue field?"

"Yes."

"That is for Mercia. And the white horse rampant on the red field is for Kent."

"And the three curved swords on the red field?"

"Those are Saxon seaxes, and that flag is for Essex," he replied. "And that one with the gold wyvern on a field of white is for Wessex."

"And what about the one with the staggered red and gold stripes?"

"That one is a bit controversial. It is supposed to be for the kingdom of Northumbria, though some, including myself, believe it to be a misrepresentation."

"How so?"

"Well, I believe that the proper flag of Northumbria is of plain red and gold stripes with no interruption in the pattern. I have asked them to replace that flag, but they are dragging their feet, as they seem to do with everything around here," he added testily. He seemed about to say something more when Lady Rydale elbowed him in the ribs, effectively bringing our conversation to a halt. Then the congregation rose to sing, and I realized I'd lost track of the service.

I stood with the others, mumbled obediently through the appropriate words, then sat down again as the vicar turned to the morning's lessons from the Scriptures. I pushed his dull drone to the back of my mind again, turning my attention back to Lord Rydale's description of the red and gold flag. I had seen a flag of red and gold stripes recently, but where? It had been just as Lord Rydale described, a row of uninterrupted red and gold vertical stripes.

Suddenly, it came to me. I had seen it in the Catholic chapel at Scarcliff Towers! It was in the wall painting, between the two black unicorns rampant.

Another clue!

I hadn't devoted much thought to the mystery in recent days, my mind having been absorbed by my games with Lord Ashenhurst. But now as I sat in this house of God, ignoring the vicar's readings, I turned my mind again to the old puzzle: for whom was the chapel built? And who still used it today?

The answer to the first question was Bess Bewforest's lover, a man whose surname presumably began with the letter "H" and whose device adorning the chapel's eastern wall held the old flag of Northumbria flanked by two black unicorns rampant.

And as for the second question, I thought I might have a more concrete answer to that. I figured that, judging from the quality of the rosary I had found—fine jet beads and heavy silver—the individual must be a person of some wealth and therefore could not be one of the servants.

That left the Bewforests and their guests, all but two in attendance this morning.

Gabrielle had journeyed with us into town, but she managed to disappear when we'd entered the minster. This was not surprising since France had been Catholic until the recent troubles, and now those French men and women interested in maintaining a healthy distance between themselves and Mam'zelle Guillotine proclaimed themselves atheists devoted only to the religion of the Republic.

But the rosary could not belong to Gabrielle since she had only just arrived a few days earlier.

That left Ashby Harcourt, the very same man whose mother had come from a Catholic country.

Could Ashby's father have also been Catholic?

Could Ashby himself be a secret Catholic?

This made perfect sense, since Lord Ashenhurst needed Lord Rydale's assistance to launch his brother Chrysander into politics. Papa had explained to me once that because Catholics could not attend Cambridge or Oxford, they could not tap into the political networks formed by their Protestant brethren at these universities. Nor could Catholics develop their own political networks outside of these schools, since it was impossible for Catholics to hold political office in England.

So, Lord Ashenhurst must be Catholic.

The only problem with this reasoning was that he intended Chrysander for a political career, but wouldn't Chrysander also be Catholic? Even if Chrysander's mother was Protestant—and as an Englishwoman from the landed gentry, she most likely was—Ashby's father would presumably have remained Catholic.

The congregation stood again, and this time we sang the Jubilate. Then we sat back down, the vicar continued with the service, and I continued with my own thoughts.

Ashby's father was a spendthrift who financially ruined the family. And since his second wife was an heiress, it likely meant that Ashby's father married her for her money.

And if Ashby's father needed his bride's money to keep himself financially solvent, that would give the young woman's guardians some leverage—perhaps enough leverage to insist upon a conversion to Protestantism and a Protestant upbringing for any children that might come of the marriage.

And this conversion might not have been too onerous for the senior Lord Ashenhurst since his eldest son and heir to the family title and estates, Ashby, would remain Catholic. Therefore, the titled branch of the family would continue the Catholic line so long as Ashby produced a male heir.

And fortunately for Ashby Harcourt, they were an ancient

family with strong ties to other ancient families that could be exploited when he needed to further the chances of his Protestant siblings.

And then . . .

My God.

It was true.

Like quicksilver, my mind raced from the robbery in Lincolnshire to Bess's lover, the B intertwined with an H crowning the parapets of each tower at Scarcliff Towers, the device on the Catholic chapel's wall . . .

And Ashby's wounded arm.

Suddenly, I struggled to breathe.

The Bewforests and the Harcourts: two ancient families whom Ashby claimed had been closely allied since before the Civil War. He'd said that they were very close in those days, though they had drifted apart in recent years.

And the red and gold striped flag suggested that the device in the wall painting in the Catholic chapel belonged to someone with ties to the ancient region of Northumbria, the territory of which largely coincides with the modern county of Northumberland.

Bess Bewforest's lover was a Harcourt.

And flanking each side of that ancient flag were two black unicorns rampant.

No.

I rose automatically with the rest of the congregation for the State Prayers, the Prayer of St. Chrysostom, and the Grace, though the words were little more than a dry rasp forced between my lips. Then we sang another hymn, but I felt too dazed to bother following the words in the book. I sat down once more with everyone else, and the vicar left his lectern to climb his pulpit and begin the morning's sermon. Dimly I became aware that his words urged us to reconcile ourselves to God through the act of forgiveness.

Surely other families must employ black unicorns in their

heraldry. And maybe the highwayman's sobriquet had nothing to do with heraldry in the first place.

And there was the question of motivation. If Lord Ashenhurst was so financially desperate, why did he not marry an heiress? With his looks and pedigree, he could probably have the pick of England's rich beauties. And if his faith stood in his way, he could marry an heiress from a Catholic country.

But . . . the Black Unicorn had attacked us on our way north while Lord Ashenhurst was presumably making his own journey north on the same roads.

And the Black Unicorn and Lord Ashenhurst had taken up residence in Yorkshire simultaneously.

And the first robbery had occurred while Lord Ashenhurst was away from Scarcliff Towers.

And during that robbery, Sir Julian Trevelver shot the Black Unicorn in the arm on the same day, and on the same road that Lord Ashenhurst himself was shot.

Lord Ashenhurst's claim had been that the Black Unicorn shot him. But the highwayman had never shot anyone during a robbery before.

Except for Buford.

Then I remembered the gentlemen's conversation I'd over-heard the evening that he returned wounded. Their words came back to me, fraught with new shades of meaning:

"He claimed that the Black Unicorn was working alone," the Viscount had said.

"Claimed, *sir*?" I could hear the speculation in Tristan's voice. *"You don't believe him?"*

"It just seems very odd to me. Why would the villain rob Ashenhurst alone, shoot him in the arm, then bring in the whole gang just a wee bit further down the road and allow himself to get shot?"

I felt very cold.

How could I have been so stupid?

And how could he *be so* reckless?

The sermon ended, though I'd barely registered a word. As the congregation stood for more prayers, and the final hymn, I squeezed out of the box, ignoring the looks of concern from Sophie and Lady Rydale, and hurried down the aisle to the massive arched doorway leading to the market square.

The day outside was perfect. The sun shone brightly in a sky the color of the Mediterranean in June, while a light breeze carried the fresh scent of growing things from the surrounding countryside. But I hardly noticed it at all, rubbing my hands briskly up and down my arms to chase away a chill that defied nature's best efforts.

Knowing that Lord and Lady Rydale would be a while exchanging pleasantries with their tenants and neighbors, I struck out across the marketplace towards the white gazebo in its center, hoping to hide unobserved in its shelter until the time came to depart. I needed time to think, to get myself back together.

So intent was I upon making my escape unnoticed, I did not realize that the gazebo was already occupied until it was too late. And to my dismay, one of the occupants proved to be one of the very people I was hoping most to avoid. The other was a small, wizened old woman with darkly tanned olive skin, obsidian eyes, and layers of tattered rags.

The two were bent together in close conversation over Gabrielle's opened hand, the old woman jabbing a long, crooked finger into the French woman's palm as she muttered in some language full of too many hard consonants for English. At first the two did not seem to notice my presence. I paused at the foot of the gazebo's steps, thinking for a moment I might yet make good my escape. Then Gabrielle spoke.

"*Bonjour,* Elina," she called without looking up. "Please come to join us, *oui?* This is Daciana. She tells fortunes," she added. The old woman continued with her muttering without looking up for the introduction.

I sat down, barely registering surprise when Gabrielle answered the woman in the same foreign tongue. "I did not know you spoke Romanian."

"There are a great many things that you do not know about me, Elina," she replied.

The market square was now filling up with people leaving the minster. Gabrielle seemed to be finishing up with the fortune-teller. The Frenchwoman said a few more words to her companion in Romanian, then pulled something from her pocket and placed it in the old woman's hand, folding her fingers over it so I could not see what it was. Payment of some sort, I assumed. Then she turned to me.

"Elina, give your hand to me now," she commanded.

"Why?" I asked, though I still gave her my hand.

Gabrielle grasped me around the wrist, pulled me closer, then shoved my hand at the fortuneteller as she said a few more words in Romanian.

"No!" I exclaimed, snatching my hand back as though burned. "I do not want my fortune told." I scooted away from them, clutching my hands to my chest in case Gabrielle might try to grab me again. But she just fixed me with an appraising look. Daciana also stared at me and said a few words in Romanian to Gabrielle. Gabrielle nodded without taking her eyes off me, then replied in the same language.

"What are you saying?" I demanded.

Gabrielle did not answer, but continued to watch me. Daciana also stared at me, the expression in her black eyes as opaque as her language. She said something more to Gabrielle, and the latter nodded.

"Daciana tells me that there is a very great secret you are guarding—" Gabrielle answered.

I felt the color drain from my face.

"—But if your secret is what I think it is," Gabrielle continued, "then I will tell you that I know it now for a very long time. And there are many more secrets I know, Elina. Many, many more."

I knew in that moment that it was the truth: Lord Ashenhurst was the Black Unicorn. Gabrielle knew it. And now I knew it, too.

"How?" I demanded.

Gabrielle's lips curled up into a smile as she held my gaze. "*Voyons! Comment je le dis en anglais?*" She frowned a moment in thought, scraping together an English translation.

My French was actually quite good. Better than Gabrielle's English, in any case. But I saw no reason for making matters any easier for her.

"Men are very vulnerable after they make love, *oui?*" she said. "*Tristement*, I do not think that you have been with enough lovers to know very much of that. But why that should be, *je suis stupéfaite.*"

She paused then, allowing me the opportunity to counter her. Though what she expected me to say, I could not imagine.

"You say nothing, so now I will instruct you," Gabrielle continued mercilessly. "After a man makes his love and you hold him in your arms while he sleeps, he will say many things to you he should not say. It is because in those moments, a man truly loves a woman and he will trust you very much with his life. He will tell you his secrets and have trust for you to keep them. *Mais naturellement*, some women do keep them very well, and some women do not. It is why the very best *espionnes* are the mistresses, *oui?*"

"*Espionnes?*" I asked weakly.

"Spies."

Footsteps on the gazebo's stairs behind me saved me from answering.

"There you are, ladies!" Tristan announced. "We have been looking all over for you two! Did you not hear us calling?"

"Er, no, Tristan." I turned around to face him. "We did not hear a thing. Is it time to go already?"

"Indeed, milady," he answered as he gallantly offered me his arm. Then he turned to hand Gabrielle up, "Are you ready, Madame?"

Gabrielle gazed up at him coyly as she accepted his other arm. I noticed then that Daciana had made her escape.

"Tell me now," Tristan continued as he escorted us back towards the carriage, "what in blazes were you two just talking about that left you so insensible to our cries?"

"*Les questions du coeur, mon bel ami*," Gabrielle answered with a mischievous smile.

"Really?" Tristan turned to look at me in astonishment. "Matters of the heart, Elina?"

"Indeed, Tristan," I replied evenly. "Matters of the heart."

CHAPTER 15

ON THE WAY BACK to Scarcliff Towers, Lady Rydale told us what she'd learned of two more robberies that had taken place in Yorkshire, both of them since Lord Ashenhurst's departure from the house.

I spent the remainder of the day alone in my room, sitting at the little writing desk in front of the window, wondering what I would do.

ᔓ

The coffee room was crowded when I left Sophie and Phosey tucked in bed and came down to join Papa at his little table by the fire. I appropriated the seat across from him, still warmed from the Newark magistrate's person.

Some residual instincts of self-preservation impelled us to lean in close to each other as we spoke, keeping our voices low despite the din of noise. We needn't have worried; the patrons of the Old Bull Inn were giving us our space. Our clothing and speech formed an impenetrable barrier that set us apart from the quaint company of Nottinghamshire farmers and craftsmen. But we were still in shock, and hypersensitive to the fact that we were surrounded by strangers.

"So how did it go?" I asked.

"As well as could be expected," Papa answered. "'Tis not a pleasant thing to be informed that a notorious band of outlaws has moved into one's territory. But Sir Teegarden accepted my account and promised to send word to the magistrates in Lincoln upon the morrow."

The door swung open, causing us both to jump, but it only admitted a large, red-faced farmer accompanied by a chilly gust of rain-scented wind.

"Did you tell him about Sophie?" I asked.

Papa sighed, and ran his hand over his face. "No. I swore to her that I wouldn't, and I cannot go back on that. Keeping my word to the child is the very least I can do for her. But Sir Teegarden knew I was neglecting to tell him something. He did ask me rather pointed questions concerning you ladies. Apparently, the Northern Gang is well known for their appalling treatment of women." He glanced up at me briefly, then looked away. "But I told him nothing. He was too refined a gentleman to question me further."

For a little while, we said nothing. Papa stared off at some point over my shoulder, and I watched the fire sizzle and spit in the hearth as heavy rain drops began falling down the chimney chute.

Beyond our quiet table, the rest of the inn's patrons appeared in fine form this blustery evening, talking stridently in animated voices, guffawing loudly, and hallooing for pretty Mary and buxom Eliza to refill their pewter tankards with the Bull's rich, honey-colored ale.

"How is Sophie?" Papa finally asked. "Did she take any supper? Has she said anything since—?"

I returned my attention to his face, so deeply lined now with fatigue and worry. "No. I just checked on her upstairs. She's in bed with Phosey, pretending to sleep. Phosey ate her supper, but Sophie hadn't touched her tray."

Papa placed his head into his hands, the picture of defeat. I knew how he felt. Sitting back in my rough wooden seat, I commandeered his untouched glass of brandy and took a sip, thinking back over the last few hours.

The trip to Newark—our final planned stop for the day—had taken us only two hours, but it was a dreadful two hours, each of us too entangled in the grips of our own personal turmoil to speak.

Only Sophie herself had spoken just after the terrible incident as we remained fixed in place, staring stupidly after the Northern Gang as they abandoned us for the woods.

Then Sophie made us each promise to never speak of her assault to anyone, particularly Thaddeus.

"Promise me!" she had raged. "Swear to me on your lives! Never speak of this again; Thad shall never know! If he learns of this, I shall know that one of you betrayed me, and I will count you all dead to me!"

She had seemed so wild, so crazed, we all agreed.

Though the rape had not technically occurred, and Sophie's "honor" remained intact, what had happened seemed too terrible a secret to keep from one's intended. But we were too shaken for rational deliberation.

We stood rooted in place like statues, looking around at each other, at the woods, at the body of Buford, at the place where the Black Unicorn had stood just moments before.

When we'd gathered enough wits about ourselves for communication, we decided to press on with our journey rather than travel back to Lincoln to report the crime. Though it would have been better to alert the magistrates of Lincolnshire of the Northern Gang's activities within their county, we were loathe to pass through that isolated stretch of road again.

Papa's voice abruptly snapped my attention back to the present. "You know I never wanted sons," he said, bowed head still resting in his hands. "I always wanted daughters."

I frowned. "I beg your pardon?"

Papa straightened up and fixed me with his red-rimmed blue eyes—ice blue, just like mine. "Even after I inherited the family patrimony from my brother, knowing full well that the Hertford estates could only descend to my heirs through a son, I still only wanted daughters."

I took another sip of brandy and nodded. The Hertford estates were held in entail and therefore could only be inherited along with Papa's title by a male heir. My uncle Robert, Papa's younger brother, would inherit Brinkley Abbey and all the Hertford lands while Sophie and I would split the remainder of mama's portion and Phosey would inherit the portion of our step-mother, Agnes.

"I thought that sons would always be waiting for my death, since only then could they assume the mantle of manhood, while daughters would cherish me for the doting Papa I knew I would become. Only daughters would mourn me once I was gone. I was a selfish fool," *he added bitterly.*

"A fool, Papa? You do not think that we cherish you?"

"No, my dear girl," he said, his voice impossibly sad. "I know you love me more than any man deserves to be loved. I'm a fool because I did not understand then the great responsibilities that come with raising girls. I did not comprehend just how much more protection daughters need from this horrible world of men. I failed you, Elina, on your wedding day. And today I failed Sophie. In both cases I was too weak and too old, and today it took the intervention of another man to keep you all safe. God only knows in what ways I shall fail poor Phosey"

I reached across the table and grasped his hand. "Papa, you have not failed us in any way. You are a good man. My marriage was no one's fault but my own. I was young and headstrong and refused to see in William what was plain to the rest of the world—"

"You were seeking to escape the influence of Agnes, the shrew I introduced into our harmonious house."

"Phosey's mother was a shrew," I agreed. "But without her, we would have no Phosey." I hesitated, not sure of what to say next. I decided to lie to him. "I cannot blame you. Your initial inability to see the baser aspects of Agnes's nature was no different from

my inability to see those baser aspects of William. I cannot blame you for crimes for which I too am guilty. Hypocrisy is not one of my shortcomings."

But I was a hypocrite.

I did blame him.

He was a man—far wiser about the ways of this world than I could ever have been at nineteen. Agnes had sold me into marriage, seduced by the wealth of the Throckmortons. She'd convinced me that William was just a little wild, in need of a wife to settle him down, and Papa had been content to go along with it.

But this was not a conversation I cared to have with him in the crowded common room of an inn.

"Now, you said that Sir Teegarden had mentioned some previous knowledge of the Northern Gang. Did he say anything else?" I continued.

"I am sorry, Elina."

Not wishing to exacerbate his misery, I forced myself to nod, then finished the remnants of his drink.

The sun set and Edith brought my dinner down to my room.

In truth, though I'd married a psychotic man with the blessing of a complacent father, I'd never been alone in that house. Lord Ashenhurst had been William's constant companion these past seven years, and as such he'd been there during the worst of William's moods, always seeming to distract him when things threatened to turn violent. It was in no small part thanks to Ashby that in the final, terrible months of my marriage, I'd seen less and less of William—until the night he died, when Ashby had been away from the house. Though I abhorred the dissolute, womanizing life he led, I couldn't dismiss the feeling that I may have owed Ashby quite a lot.

Still, Sophie deserved vengeance. And it was the Black

Unicorn's fault that we'd been stopped in Lincolnshire. Buford had been his man.

But blindly turning Ashby over to the authorities wasn't so simple.

A while later Edith woke me from where I had fallen asleep at the window to help me out of my clothes and prepare for bed. I was exhausted and went through my ablutions in a daze before climbing into bed and immediately falling back to sleep.

My dreams were strange. I stood in a vast crowd of people, dressed in black mourning clothes with a heavy black crepe veil that reached down to my toes. The people around me jostled me, and I wrapped my arms protectively around the sleeping infant I held in my arms. Next to me I heard a familiar voice laughing, and I turned to find Gabrielle standing there, similarly dressed, with an infant in her own arms. With one hand, she pointed in front of her, and I turned to see that we stood just in front of the gallows at an execution. Daciana, the fortune-teller, was leading the hooded prisoner out in front of the howling crowd. I did not need to see the prisoner's face to know that it was Ashby.

"He'll die a good death," Gabrielle cooed to the babe in her arms. "Don't you worry, *mon petite,* Papa will make you proud!"

Then she began to laugh again, louder and wilder with each passing moment until her cackles began to sound more like sobs. I felt the babe stir in my arms, and I looked down and recognized Tristan's blunt features and Saxon coloring in the infant's face. He began to wail, mixing his voice with Gabrielle's. Then ashes began to fall all around me, thick and heavy like snow. At this one familiar detail, I realized I was dreaming. I abruptly woke up.

Immediately I knew that someone stood just outside my door. Throwing off the covers, I swung my legs over the side of the bed and silently made my way over to the door.

It was him.

He was there.

My attention fixed on the handle, I watched it slowly depress and heard the soft metallic click as the mechanism disengaged from its seat. I waited, barely daring to breathe as the seconds ticked by. Then the mechanism re-engaged as the handle returned abruptly to its original position. Across the corridor, Lord Ashenhurst's door opened and closed.

CHAPTER 16

I QUIT MY CHAMBER EARLY the following morning, and made my way first to the library.

In the section Lord Rydale had designated for antiquarian studies, I found what I was looking for in a thick volume, handsomely bound in red leather with gilt-edged pages. With a little effort, I pulled the book down off the shelf, then brought it over to a table and cracked it open to the title page: *Créatures Effrayantes de Savoir et de Légende: Un Bestiarum Vocabulum pour l'Âge de la Raison* by Christophe Charbonneau, Bordeaux 1757.

Flipping through the pages, I saw that it was indeed what the title advertised: a bestiary, or compendium of magical beasts, without the appending moral lesson usually to be found in the earlier medieval versions. Once I came to the page entitled *La Licorne*, I gently smoothed down the stiff pages and began to translate.

The unicorn, according to Monsieur Charbonneau, was a proud and untamable beast of legend commonly depicted as a white horse with a goat's beard and a large, pointed, spiraling horn called an alicorn projecting from its forehead. Mentioned first by the Ancients of Greece as a monstrous animal, with a closer resemblance to a rhinoceros than to our modern understanding of it as a horned white horse, it later became the most important magical animal of the Dark Ages and then the Renaissance.

During these centuries, the unicorn became characterized as an animal of impossible beauty, a symbol for purity and grace, which could only be captured by a virgin. Because of its wild and untamable nature, it became a popular heraldic symbol during the chivalrous age, where it was commonly portrayed rampant with a collar attached to a broken chain, indicating that it had broken free from its bondage and never to be taken into captivity again.

Beneath this excerpt were two fine drawings of unicorns rampant, one with the cloven hooves of a goat and the tail of a lion like the unicorns from the chapel, the other just a horse with a spiraling horn and a broken chain around its neck. Both were white.

Nothing at all was mentioned of a black unicorn, which could suggest its use as a heraldic device might be rare. And what did a black unicorn signify? If a white unicorn stood for purity and grace, could a black unicorn be taken as its opposite? Black commonly stood for the color of sin and death. But it seemed odd that a family would adopt such symbolism for its device.

Once again, the words of my father came back to me. *Four types of men run this world, my dear.*

Which type of man was the Black Unicorn? A good man who did bad things? Or a bad man who did good things?

I needed to know before I decided on what to do. And likely only the man behind the unicorn knew.

I needed to find Lord Ashenhurst, and I knew just where to look.

The chapel appeared just how I'd left it.

And it was deserted. The candle and tinder box remained

where I had left them, but this time I preferred to remain in the dark. Slowly following the faint pathway in the ancient rushes from the doorway to the second pew, I took a seat and waited for my eyes to adjust.

Gradually the shadows began to take shape: the intricately carved rood screen, the altar with its giant gold crucifix, the outlines of St Sebastian's martyrdom painted on the southern wall.

I do not know how long I waited for him in the dark, but I knew at once when Ashby arrived. I felt him pause a moment in the doorway, then the air stirred next to me, and he was seating himself, his boots silent upon the floor, his breath still as a ghost's.

But I knew, even in the charged atmosphere of the chapel, that he could be no ghost. I could feel the vitality radiating from him, the heat of his body warming me from its close proximity. And I could smell him: soap, leather, lavender, and that muskiness peculiar only to him. Breathing him in, his scent hurtled me back to the garden with the feel of his body pressed against mine, the taste of chocolate and brandy in his kiss.

My body wanted him; I'd been forced to admit that. And honestly, I'd wanted him for a long time.

And because of this, I'd inadvertently handed over control to him.

And this was something I could not allow.

"Ashby—?" I ventured.

"Estephânia," he responded quietly.

I frowned. "I beg your pardon?"

"Estephânia Alfaiataria-Delgadinho was my mother's name," he continued. "She was but a child of sixteen when she married my father. He was a man of forty-five in need of an heir. I cannot imagine there to have ever been much affection between them. I remember her exuberant love of life and the vitality of her youth seemed always an affront to him. She took to Northumberland better than one might have expected a young girl from Iberia's

Douro Valley, but she always told me that her love had more to do with the fact that half of me was of Northumberland and she could never grow to hate anything that was part of me."

"You were very close then," I murmured. "You and your mother."

"We were," he affirmed. "Which my father interpreted as just another affront to him. He sent me away from her on my seventh birthday, to a small boarding school in Shropshire famous for the rigorous nature of its discipline.

"But without me to keep her occupied in Northumberland, the dreariness of my father and Castle Ashenhurst became intolerable. Her letters became more infrequent as she grew restless. She told me once it was because she could not bring herself to write to me of anything unhappy, knowing as she did how I suffered at the hands of my jailors. Then one day shortly after my tenth birthday, she arrived unexpectedly at my school. The headmaster could not very well turn away the Countess of Ashenhurst, and so she took me on a short holiday in Cheshire to visit some friends. When she returned me a week later, she told me that she was living in London, and, since she was happier, she would write to me more frequently. She also told me she had made some influential friends, and she planned to have me removed from the boarding school and brought to London to live with her. That was the last time I saw her, alive or dead."

"Ashby . . ." I reached out to touch his arm, but something in his posture warned against it. "What happened?"

"My father arrived one day to take me from the boarding school down to Eton. I wanted more than anything to ask him what had become of her. I felt certain that he must have murdered her, for I knew she would never willingly leave me alone like this. But I could not, though to this day I cannot say exactly why. I never feared my father, but I felt almost as though if I asked him about my mother, he would give me a reason to fear him. I suppose I also felt that if my mother had managed to escape him, it was only because he had forgotten her existence. I did not want to be the one to remind him of it.

"Eton was a vast improvement over the boarding school in Shropshire, and I settled in easily. There was a tall boy that I particularly liked, a year older than I, named Tristan Richmond. He was a natural leader, even in those days, and he took me under his wing. I grew to worship him with the devotion a boy might usually reserve for his father or an older brother—even came to wish that I'd inherited my father's lighter coloring rather than my mother's darkness so that I might look more like my golden idol.

"Then the scandal broke."

"A scandal?" I repeated, unable to mask the incredulity in my voice. "Involving Tristan?"

"Involving Sir Tristan's father, Sir Richard Richmond, and his Portuguese lover Estephânia Harcourt. Despite Sir Richard's marriage to Tristan's still-living mother, and despite my own mother's legal attachment to my father, the two had taken up open residence together in Sir Richard's London townhouse, and were hosting dinner parties together and making the rounds of the London Season's soirees and balls. Once word of this reached Eton, the boys whom I had thought my friends became cruel. They called my love for Tristan unnatural. But none were so harsh as Tristan himself, who defended his downtrodden mother and vented his outrage against the Portuguese whore who'd usurped his father's affections by inflicting every conceivable misery upon me."

"*Tristan* did this to you?" I demanded. I could hardly believe it. I had known Tristan for my entire life, and I'd never known him to ever be anything but the kindest, gentlest man.

"He was just a boy, Lady Delemere. A boy, taking upon himself the role of champion for his mother because no one else would do it for him. It crushed me, but even then, I could have forgiven him if not for what happened next. You see, while my mother cohabitating openly and socializing with his father was certainly scandalous, it was nothing compared to the scandal that rocked Society when he set aside my mother for an opera singer. My mother found herself left with nothing, and when she tried to return to my father, the doors barred to her and all her belongings burned on the rubbish heap. She had no other recourse than to leave England and return to her family in Portugal in disgrace. I heard sometime later that she had tried to see me before she left, but my father had written the headmaster with strict instructions that she was under no circumstances to be allowed to do so. I do not know how she managed to scrape together the money for her voyage, but I figure she must have had some small jewels to sell. She died less than a year later. My father would not even grant me permission to see her buried."

"And what of Tristan?" I demanded. "Did he continue to persecute you?"

"No, he did not. Once his father had destroyed my mother, his anger seemed to fizzle. But the damage was done. The boys called me the Portuguese whoreson, as well as many other things too dirty to repeat. Tristan's belated kindness counted for too little, too late. When I learned of my mother's death, I blamed him for it just as he had blamed me for his father's infidelity. He got to keep his mother, while I'd lost mine. I hated him for it."

Slowly I began to piece together what had happened after Ashby kissed me. "So when we were in the garden, and he came upon us . . . "

"I thought, irrationally I admit, that Tristan . . . " His voice trailed off.

"Would take another woman away from you."

"I know what kind of a man Sir Tristan Richmond is. I also know that he is your father's heir apparent in the world of politics. He will likely fill the vacuum created by your father's forced retirement. No woman of any sense could possibly choose my suit over his."

"Choose . . . your suit?"

"I leave Scarcliff Towers tonight, milady. I will trouble you no further."

"Ashby," I said, "it was a stupid misunderstanding, that is all. Tristan came to the garden to tell me about my father, not to make love to me. Let us move past it now."

I reached out to touch his face. His body suddenly went rigid, but then he relaxed as he leaned into my hand while I traced along his cheekbone and then stroked along the line of his jaw. When my fingers reached the point of his chin, he captured them with both hands and brought them to his lips.

"I leave tonight," he said.

This wasn't going well. An apology I expected, but Ashby banishing himself from my company did not factor well into my plans for him. Before I confronted him, I needed him to trust me. As Gabrielle had said, *after a man makes his love and you hold him in your arms while he sleeps, he will say many things to you that he should not say . . . He will trust you very much with his life. He will tell you his secrets and have trust for you to keep them.*

"Oh, sod it!" I stood, grabbed up handfuls of my skirts, then threw one leg over him so that I straddled his lap. I heard his sharp intake of breath as I sank back down and ground my hips into him. I kissed him, suddenly, my heart thundering in my chest.

At first he was too surprised to do much of anything. Then he took me firmly by the shoulders and began to push me away. "No, Elina. I cannot. Not like this. Not with you."

I sat back. This was not what I wanted from him.

"But the garden," I said.

I felt him look away. "That was a mistake."

"A mistake?" I did not understand. He'd been chasing me for years. What was this nonsense? I thought back to the kiss in the garden—the softness of his mouth, the luxurious fullness of his lower lip. Not knowing what else to do, I leaned forward and I bit him—tentatively at first—then sank my teeth into him, hard.

A deep, guttural sound escaped him. He pushed me back again, then touched his fingers to his lip. In the dim light from the doorway, I saw them come away with blood. He looked at them a moment, meditatively rubbing his fingers and thumb together.

"You like to bite," he said.

"I do."

Then he chuckled, a deep, rich sound; the naturalness of it surprised me, something I would like to hear him do more.

"Very well, milady," he said. "How shall we proceed?"

"Kiss me."

He kissed me hard, his baser instincts winning supremacy, and repaid my attentions in kind by biting down hard on my lower lip.

"If this is how you want it," he murmured against my mouth, "then this is how you shall have it. But tell me," he continued, moving his lips close to my ear, "what exactly is the nature of my penance."

I pulled back, not sure how to respond.

"Making love to you can hardly be called punishment."

"Punishment?"

"For tormenting you. You told me that I torment you. Perhaps you should just use me for your pleasure."

This only confused me more. I was not at all sure how using him for my pleasure could be accomplished without lovemaking. I shook my head.

"As you wish."

But the balance of power had shifted between us, and for all my brave overtures at seduction, Ashby was back in control. And as his hands slid up under my skirts to stroke my bare thighs, I knew at once that I was in very capable hands. This knowledge both thrilled me and frightened me. Trembling slightly, I reached back to pull the ends of my white fichu out from where my sash kept them secured at the small of my back. I unwound it from across my breast, and pulled it out from behind my neck, the friction of the soft lawn sliding against my skin sending a shiver through me as I dropped it to the floor.

Ashby leaned forward and brushed his lips over mine, and I tasted the copper of his blood. He slid his hands up to my naked hips and began lightly stroking the hollows under my hip bones with his thumbs. Brushing my lips again, he tantalized me with just the barest hint of a feather touch, then pulled away until I found myself leaning into him, impatient for something more substantial. I growled in frustration, and he suddenly pressed his mouth more firmly to mine. His tongue pressed for entry, and I granted it. Whereas he had kissed me so sweetly and passionately in the garden, this kissing seemed more calculated and skillful. More purposeful.

Leaving off my mouth, his lips burned a trail down my throat, pausing a moment to bite me gently at my pulse point, and then his lips traced lightly along my collar bone.

His touch was the sweetest agony, building up my desire as he carefully avoided the places I wanted so very badly for him to touch. I opened my thighs wider, as I used every ounce of my self-control to keep from shoving his face into my breasts. My shyness forgotten, I arched into him, pressing myself ever closer into his body. And then, just as I reached the point where I couldn't take it any longer, he dropped his head and kissed the top of my breast.

Moaning softly, I pulled down my chemise to the edge of my bodice, and rolled my head back as he captured a nipple and I felt the gentle pull of his mouth followed by a sharp nip of his teeth. His hands at my hips began slowly to stroke their way inward, settling into the hot crease of my inner thigh, so excruciatingly close to the throbbing, aching place in between.

God how I wanted him to touch me there, and I moaned again in frustration as he continued to stroke just along the periphery.

"Shhh," I could hear the smile in his voice as he murmured into my breast, "we must be very quiet. There could be others close at hand."

Though I had been so convinced that I did not want to be just another conquest, I realized now that I had been lying to myself. I was so tired of being the strong one, the dependable one; the prospect of giving myself to a beautiful rake who'd mastered the art of love on the bodies of countless women before me proved intoxicating.

But what of his talk about choosing Tristan's suit over his? For a fraction of a moment, I wondered guiltily if this seduction might mean something more to him. Surely he didn't tell his heartbreaking story of his mother to all his lovers. But then Ashby moved his hands around to my bottom, and I forgot everything save the sweet agony of his touches that teased me while I squeaked and squirmed, finally forcing me to the expedient of biting his shoulder to keep from crying out.

Chuckling softly, he pulled one hand out from under my skirts and brought it up to my nape, guiding me back into his kiss. As his tongue pressed once more for entry, his other hand found the wetness between my legs. I opened my mouth to gasp, and he invaded with his tongue at the same moment he pushed one long finger up inside of me. I broke away from him, crying out. His rough kiss silenced me as he began to pulse inside of me with his finger while using his clever thumb to stroke my throbbing pleasure point. My hips began to move with him, and soon, far sooner than seemed possible, he'd brought me nearly to the peak of my climax. Suddenly I realized what he'd meant about using him just for my own pleasure.

And at that very moment, using him sounded like an excellent idea.

But even as my hips continued to move with his virtuosic touch, I knew that this sort of climax would do nothing to fill my aching void. Only one thing could satisfy my body's hunger, and that thing was still locked up in Ashby's breeches.

"Stop," I gasped, using all the willpower I possessed to pull away from him. He complied immediately, surprising me with his ability to take orders during the heat of passion. It hinted towards powers of self-control that I found deeply erotic.

Leaning back, I began to fumble with the buttons of his waistcoat, seized by a sudden need to explore his body with my hands. My progress was slow in the dark, but eventually I succeeded. He shrugged out of the garment as I pulled his shirt out of his breeches. Next I set to work on his cravat, and soon the entire lot, shirt and neckstock, was coming off and over his head. I ran my hands over the warmth of his smooth skin, up over the ridges of his abdomen and then the flat planes of his chest. I traced the curve of his collar bones with light fingers, swept over his broad, muscular shoulders with my palms until I felt the sharp angles of his shoulder blades. Then I brought my hands back to his chest and brushed his erect nipples lightly with my thumbs. I dropped my hands down to his breeches, seeking the buttons of his falls, aware all the time of the great pressure in his lap stretching the fabric of his smallclothes taut. I knew that once I freed him from his inadequate prison, there would be no turning back for either of us, which was exactly what I wanted.

As the last button popped open, I pulled down the flap of fabric and took him into my hands. His breath caught at my sudden touch, the muscles of his flat belly contracting as he swallowed a strangled, guttural moan. His reaction pleased me, seeming altogether too natural and too intimate for a man of such sexual infamy.

The size of him was alarming, but his skin felt so smooth and soft and warm. I gripped him, gently moving my hand back and forth along his shaft. Ashby tilted his head back, his breath shuddering out of him, and I wished I could see his face in the darkness. Scooting myself forward, I prepared to guide him into my body, when suddenly I stopped short.

"What is it, my little seductress?" he asked, and I could hear the amusement in his voice.

"This isn't going to work," I said, crestfallen. "My knees have nowhere to go." I knocked my knees up against the back of the pew for emphasis.

"No, it isn't," he answered, his voice still warm with humor. "I take it you've never made love in a church pew?"

"Perhaps if you just slide your hips down a bit?"

"I have a better idea." Without another word, he stood, scooping me up with his hands under my bottom, and carried me over to the wall where St. Stephen mournfully endured his martyrdom. Pinning me against the wall with his hips, he winced slightly as he allowed me to put my right foot down, and I remembered his pistol-shot wound. But before I could comment, he pulled my left knee high up over his hip and pressed the blunt tip of his cock against my opening. A flash of panic coursed through me; my back hard against the unyielding wall, I had nowhere to go.

I was really going to do this.

Ashby paused, for just a heartbeat, then pushed.

I gasped, and he abruptly stopped.

"How long has it been?" he murmured in my ear.

"Long," I panted.

"Months?" he asked. "Years?"

"Years." Four long years since I became brave enough to bar my door against William.

Ashby pushed a little further, pausing to allow me a moment to become accustomed to him, then pushed a little further still.

He stopped again when I made a frustrated noise in my throat. "Am I hurting you?"

"No," I gasped. "But the angle. I want all of you."

"Give me your other leg."

Using his grip on my left leg and the wall behind me for leverage, I obediently gave a little hop and hitched my other knee up over his hip as his hand caught me beneath my bottom. He readjusted his stance while settling me against him more securely, and shifted his hips to ease the strain on his wounded arm as much as possible. My stays dug into my abdomen, but the pain barely registered.

His balance was extraordinary, as was his strength; the muscles of his arms, chest, and abdomen taut as he supported my weight. I nodded my readiness, and he pushed all the way inside of me, his size continuing to shock me as he filled me up until he pressed against my barrier. We stayed like that a few moments, our bodies fitted together perfectly.

Ashby bent his head down to kiss me slowly, tenderly. He began to move his hips, pulsing into me so gently at first, but picking up momentum, his control slipping with every stroke, until soon he was pounding me against the wall.

I cried out first, agony and ecstasy taking me together in a massive wave that started in my core and radiated outwards to my fingers and toes, my vision becoming corrupted by little flashes of light. Then he crushed me to him, shuddering, shuddering, shuddering again as he continued to plow through my exquisitely sensitive tissues until he cried out softly at the blinding rush of release.

"I am your slave, milady," he gasped. Then, so softly I almost couldn't hear him, he murmured, "Always."

I felt the urge to laugh, but was far too spent. "You're talking silly nonsense in the dark, milord," I gasped. "Not very much like a libertine, you know."

Ashby sighed, resting his forehead against mine. "No, not so very much."

CHAPTER 17

EVERYTHING WAS QUIET, SAVE for the hammering of Ashby's heart against my breasts.

"I think we may have committed an act of sacrilege," he said as he slowly eased out of me and set me back on my feet. "Though I do not think this chapel was ever properly consecrated."

"God will forgive us," I told him, wobbling on shaky legs, "It's not like we were on the altar."

"God might forgive *me. You*, on the other hand, took His name in vain repeatedly."

"That was entirely your fault."

He captured my hand and brought it to his lips. "How are your legs? Can you walk?"

I snatched my hand away from him, "They are perfectly fine, sir!" I took a step and did an undignified dip towards the floor, catching myself on his arm before I fell to my knees. "Er, perhaps I should sit down a moment".

"I thought that might be the case," he said, his voice rich with masculine smugness. "But tell me, *Minha Amada*, is there anything I can do to make it up to you?"

"Make what up to me?" I demanded.

"For temporarily crippling you, my love."

"Well, yes, Ashby," I said, my tone suddenly serious, "there is something important I need to talk to you about."

"Very well." He quickly righted his clothing with a practiced expertise I tried not to dwell upon. "But I've had enough of this darkness and I would like to freshen up and change my linens. Will you allow me to postpone our chat for half an hour? Then I will be happy to meet you anywhere you like."

"Let us make it an hour," I said, rewrapping my fichu with considerably more effort than it had taken his fingers to fly down the buttons of his waistcoat."

"And where shall we meet, milady?"

"The park. I think that is sufficiently secluded."

"The park it is," he pronounced with a kiss.

One hour later I made my way down the main path cutting through the Scarcliff Towers park, wondering where on earth in this vast acreage I was supposed to find my new lover. But just about the point when I'd given the search up for futile, I turned a bend and found Ashby seated in the yellow pimpernels at the base of a large oak, a book in his hand and an ancient hound snoozing with his great head in his lap. Ashby looked up at me then, his eyes soft, candid. I dropped my gaze down to the ground, suddenly flustered.

"Who is your friend?" I asked by way of diversion.

"Ah." He closed his book and placed it on the folded blanket next to him. "This is Brutus. He's blind and long since retired from the hunt, so he does not get out much anymore, though his heart and spirit are still willing. I bring him with me whenever I come out here. He's a decent chap and good company."

"Well, hello, Brutus," I addressed the dog, still reluctant to meet Ashby's eyes. "How do you do?"

Brutus graced me with a single thump of his tail. Ashby stroked him affectionately on the head.

"Well," he said, "now that the proper introductions have been made, Brutus and I were wondering if you would like us to show you one of our favorite spots here in this wood?"

Mentally I cursed myself for not switching my slippers out for boots.

"I'm afraid I am not dressed for lengthy walking," I admitted.

Ashby eyed my morning dress with a new look of appraisal, and a little smile pulled up the corners of his mouth.

"Perhaps we should have this talk another time," I said hastily, turning to walk back down the path. "I am not suitably attired."

Suddenly he was on his feet, catching me by the arm.

"Then it will only become harder for us to be around each other. Now that we are lovers, we need to relearn how to be friends. Please trust me when I say that it will soon get better."

I did not budge. Though I'd reveled in his experienced notoriety in the chapel, I found that now I did not like to be reminded of his expertise in such things. This was going to be more complicated than I'd anticipated.

"I am not properly dressed," I repeated.

"Elina?"

"Yes?"

"Will you not look at me?"

"No."

"Please? If you will just look at me, it will be better. I promise."

I turned to look at him, and my breath caught in my throat; with his expression so open, he looked just a boy. I found myself reminded with all the force of a great revelation that there was a man behind that face, with a heart that could be broken. And he guarded his heart as carefully as I did mine. He was, in that respect, no different from me. And now he seemed willing to let me in.

"The place I have in mind is not far," he said, releasing my arm and holding out his hand.

I nodded. "All right."

He bent down to kiss me lightly on the lips. I stood perfectly still, not daring even to breathe as he pressed his mouth against mine. Our lovemaking from just an hour earlier flooded back from memory, but he was correct: now it no longer embarrassed me as we stood in the dappled sunlight beneath the canopy of trees.

Ashby pulled away and smiled down at me, pulling me off the path.

"Come," he said, "there's a deer path to follow. It'll only take ten minutes to get there."

And true to his word, we walked easily through the wood on a narrow path, led unerringly by the blind Brutus, who snuffled along with his nose bent close to the earthen floor. Our ease of movement was partly due to the deer path, and partly because the wood was not a natural forest: the trees were still relatively young, and there was little in the way of undergrowth to catch and twist my ankles or snag my clothing.

At just about the time the light began to get a little brighter, Brutus released a great bellowing woof as he joyfully bounded forward. Ashby and I abruptly left the shelter of the trees and came upon a large field ablaze with hundreds of thousand, perhaps even millions, of bright red poppies.

"Dear la!" I breathed as we paused to take in the great sea of fiery color. "I have never seen anything like it!"

"It's a sight," he agreed. "Brutus brought me here one morning last week. It's full of butterflies and small animals for him to track, so we shall not be seeing him again until it's time to head back."

We stood a moment longer admiring the view, then Ashby began to wade through the flowers to the center of the field where he laid out his blanket. I followed close on his heels, and once he'd arranged the blanket to his satisfaction, I knelt down rather awkwardly with his assistance. He joined me much more gracefully with his usual boneless flexibility, convincing me more than ever that someone among his ancestors had coupled with a cat. He took off his coat, wadded it up into a tight bundle, and placed it under his head as he stretched out languidly on the blanket. I watched him, acutely aware that my current position had my corset digging into my belly, then shrugged and stretched myself out next to him. Ashby gave me his coat to use as a pillow and then propped himself up on one elbow so that he was looking down on me.

We lay quietly for a while, soaking up the warm sunshine. I cracked my eyes open once to look at him through my lashes and saw he had his closed eyes, his mouth curved into a little smile.

"Ashby?" I began tentatively.

He opened one sleepy eye, "Yes, *Minha Amada*?"

"There is something I must talk to you about."

He straightened up a little more as a light breeze ruffled through his hair. "I gather from your tone this is not a good something."

"No," I said, sitting back up. "It is serious."

"I'm listening."

"You owe me an explanation, Ashby."

Slowly I reached into my pocket and drew out the rosary I'd found in the chapel. I handed it to him.

"It's a rosary," he said, looking it over.

"It's *your* rosary."

"Very well," he said after a moment. "It is my rosary. Where did you find it?"

"On the chapel floor, when I went exploring last week."

"And is this what our little talk is going to be about?" he demanded, a slight edge to his voice. "The fact that you know I'm Catholic?"

"No!" I exclaimed. "It is much bigger than that. I couldn't care less that you're Catholic!"

"Truly?"

"Yes!"

"Very well." He exhaled a long breath, and his shoulders seemed to relax. "Then what is this about?"

And so I told him: I told him that I knew Bess Bewforest's lover was a Harcourt. I told him I knew from the chapel that the black unicorn rampant was the Harcourt device. And finally, I told him I knew he was the highwayman known as the Black Unicorn.

He stared at me a long while in silence. So long, in fact, I'd thought we'd reached some sort of tacit understanding. His next words, therefore, were unexpected.

"I do not know what you are talking about," he said.

"*Ashby!*" I cried in exasperation, "Haven't you been listening? I *know*."

"Elina, this is nonsense."

"No, it isn't." I said, suddenly angry "And I am not the only one who knows. Gabrielle Dalingridge knows, as well!"

"*Gabrielle?* Gabrielle *Dalingridge?* She is here? At the Towers? But when did she arrive?" he demanded, a huge smile on his face. "I am amazed she has not come to find me!"

I struggled to my feet. "She probably has not been able to find you, sir, since you have been entertaining *me* this morning. I have no doubt she is looking for you even now."

"But, Elina," he shaded his eyes as he squinted up into the sun at me, "what on earth is the matter with you? Gabrielle and I are old friends; I've known her since—"

"Gabrielle has already told me the nature of your relationship," I cut in.

"Very well, then I fail to see what is the matter."

"Is she the one?"

"The one what?"

"Never mind," I snarled. "If we could just leave off for the moment our discussion of Gabrielle, I was in the process of trying to warn you that you're in danger!"

"But I cannot be in danger, Elina, since I am *not* the Black Unicorn!"

"I do not understand," I said. "How is it that you trust her and yet you do not trust *me*? Especially after this morning?"

But then I remembered with whom it was I was dealing. His soubriquets came rushing back to me: libertine, scoundrel, rake.

I was a fool.

I had thought myself so morally superior, and yet I had played the tart—a role with which he was thoroughly familiar.

"I am sorry she said that to you," he said, his voice neutral. "But she and I are the oldest of friends—"

"So you admit it then," I said softly. "You admit that you confided in her; that you told *her* that you are the Black Unicorn!"

"I admit nothing, Elina."

"You owe me the truth, Ashby. And you owe us all, especially Sophie, an explanation."

"I do not owe anything to anyone."

"What?" I choked back a sob. "Then I suppose it won't matter to you that you are likely already suspected by Lord Beverley and that your movements in and out of Scarcliff Towers are being tracked."

I caught then a glimmer of surprise flash in Ashby's eyes. It was enough to confirm what I knew to be true.

"Very well," I said, voice shaking, "I do not care what Gabrielle is to you, nor do I care how long you have known her. The fact that you privilege *her* in your confidence over *me*, especially after I have just made the egregious mistake of making love to you, is *unforgivable*. I know that you do these sorts of things all the time, but I do not. Do not come near me again."

"Elina!" he called after me as I marched through the flowers back towards the wood. "Elina, wait!"

I could hear his progress through the field as he followed after me. When I reached the line of trees, I sensed he was close. I whirled around to face him just as he was lunging forward to catch my hand.

"Stop!" I cried, yanking my hand back out of his reach, "Enough!"

"But—"

"No, Ashby," I told him. "Stay away from me!" But I knew even then that false lover or not, I was not strong enough to cast him away forever with no chance for reconciliation. So I amended my earlier declaration. "Stay away from me, Ashby Harcourt," I pronounced, "until you are ready to tell me the truth. And yes, you *do* owe me the truth."

I looked into his stricken face for just a moment, then whirled around to find my way back through the trees. I hoped that he would follow me, that he would close the growing distance between us, pull me back into his arms and hold me tightly as he told me that this morning had meant something to him. But just like every man who has ever disappointed a woman, Ashby followed me no further.

CHAPTER 18

IGNORING ASHBY SHOULD HAVE proven easy.
Lady Rydale ceased to partner me with him at dinner,
selecting Gabrielle to partner him instead while I now had
Sir Tristan to attend me.

But I could not get the man out of my head. My whole body
ached for him, and I remained acutely aware of him at every
moment. When he moved, I knew it; when he breathed, I sensed
it; when he looked at me, I felt it. In a crowded room, I seemed
able to hear only his voice, and at night as I lay alone in my bed,
my mind burned with thoughts of him sleeping in the room just
across the corridor from mine.

Meanwhile Tristan, and sometimes even the loathsome Dr.
Froggenhall, made nuisances of themselves. While my heart
broke over Ashby, they were relentless in their attention. And
since a rainstorm had relegated the party indoors for the past
several days, I was at my wits' end in my attempts to get rid
of them.

Then, after a week of poor weather, we woke Saturday morning
to sunshine and clear blue skies. The good weather arrived just in
time for Lady Trevelver's ball that very same evening, honoring
the birthday of His Royal Highness, The Prince of Wales. The

only good news was that we were far too north, and the Trevelvers—despite their massive wealth—far too socially insignificant to warrant a royal visit, so Prinny himself would not be gracing us with his presence at his birthday celebration. The bad news was that the roads would be impossible, though with the rain now dried up, not impossible enough for us to send our regrets.

And so, at noon we set out on the road to York along with our attendants in four carriages and a wagon carrying our luggage. The roads were far too mucky to travel at night, so we—along with most of Lady Trevelver's other guests—would spend the night at the great baroque house.

The journey promised to be long and tedious. While the others slept, I passed the hours in a dream of rolling fields of velvety-textured greens and meadows of gold, dotted with rustic old stone barns and fine farmhouses partially hidden by thickets of broadleaf trees, all crisscrossed by an intricate latticework of dry-stone walls.

Four hours passed before we finally turned off the main road to York and onto the little road leading to Sir Julian Trevelver's vast acreage. In the far distance, we caught our first glimpses of the magnificent house, easily the size of a royal palace.

"There are 145 rooms," Lady Rydale informed us through a yawn.

"Does Sir Julian ever get lost?" Phosey asked.

"Perhaps when he was a child," Lady Rydale replied. "And maybe he still does, though I doubt you'll ever get him to admit it."

When the coach finally came to a stop, liveried footmen materialized to assist our descent, while several grooms rushed from the stables to collect the gentlemen's horses. I could not help but admire Ashby's gorgeous thoroughbred stallion, black on black except for the white star between his eyes. Immediately the beast began to dance nervously about with flattened ears once his reins had been transferred from master to groom.

"He's gorgeous, Lord Ashenhurst," Dorothea gushed as she strode towards him, earning herself a sneer from Gabrielle.

"Don't come too close," he warned. "Diabo bites."

Diabo obligingly bared his teeth, bringing Dorothea to a sudden stop.

"I think it's those long plumes in your hair," Ashby said. "Perhaps you should take a step back."

Diabo bared his teeth again and pawed at the ground. His brave groom wrapped the reins around his meaty forearm several more times for good measure and attempted to haul the horse towards the stables.

Diabo didn't budge.

Ashby bared his teeth in a fair imitation of his charger. "Now you've upset him," he said testily to Dorothea. Then to the groom, "Give him to me. He won't move now until he's killed those ridiculous plumes."

Dorothea's cheeks turned pink as she spun on her heel and stomped off towards her mama. A safe distance away, I remained rooted in place, fascinated by the transformation in the animal once his master took hold of his reins. Ashby stroked the horse's neck, murmuring to him soothingly in a language I gathered to be Portuguese.

Diabo stopped pawing at the ground, perked up his ears in amiable curiosity, and suddenly adopted a whole new attitude about his immediate surroundings.

"What does his name mean?" I asked, careful to keep my voice low and soothing.

"Devil," Ashby replied in the same soothing tones.

"Is that Portuguese you were speaking to him just now?"

He nodded, reaching his hand up to tenderly stroke down

the stallion's satin-smooth nose, causing Diabo to whuffle softly and lean his great head into Ashby's touch.

≼

We'd arrived at four, just in time to join Sir Julian and his family for a light repast. Then we retired to our rooms for a rest until eight, when our maids arrived to dress us for the ball. This proved an exercise in patience for Sophie, Phosey, and myself, since the three of us shared a single room. Our maids, Edith and Harriet, didn't seem too pleased with the arrangements, either. At ten Sophie and I went down to the ballroom, leaving a frustrated Phosey behind with a hot iron in her hair.

Lady Trevelver's modern ballroom—the very latest addition to Trevelver Court, with a white marble floor and gilt-edged mirrors lining the walls—was a vision to behold. Richly bedecked in floral arrangements and garlands taken from milady's gardens and hothouses, and lit with hundreds of beeswax candles in massive candelabras and the four glittering French crystal chandeliers, the ballroom was a triumph of tasteful extravagance.

Still, despite the grand trappings, Lady Trevelver's ball seemed like something closer to an assembly. A country dance was currently underway. Instead of an orchestra, I could see just a small grouping of violins and violas, with two cellos and a tambour. The only peers in attendance looked to be those from our own party, and even they would likely not have been present if not for the fact that Lord Rydale was Sir Julian's patron. The rest of the gentlemen appeared to be country squires and some members from the more respectable professions.

Lady Trevelver must have been waiting for us, for the moment we arrived she descended upon us at once and drew us over to a large group of people clustered together in the far corner. As we crossed the room in the worthy lady's wake, I glanced discreetly around the room for Ashby and found him soon enough opposite a gaggle of simpering young ladies doing their very best to attract his attention. But he had eyes only for Gabrielle who, unlike Sophie and myself in our old ball gowns a few seasons past the height of fashion, apparently saw no need to tone things down for this company. She looked a veritable goddess in a shimmering cream silk *cannalé* gown of the very latest Grecian fashion, diamonds glittering in her shining black hair dressed *à la Venus*. But she paled in comparison to Ashby, himself resplendent in velvet of the deepest blue, tailored perfectly to emphasize the graceful lines of his body, his tailcoat laced in gold and his waistcoat richly embroidered to match.

Just then the dancing master called for the minuet, and I saw Ashby offer his hand to Gabrielle, who smiled radiantly up at him. As they made their way onto the floor with the other couples, I found myself almost tempted to watch. But instead I turned my back on the pair, and focused with a show of interest on a certain Mr. Sykes, who was describing in detail the bloodlines of a mare he'd just purchased. Sadly, this topic failed to hold my attention for long, and soon my mind drifted back to the couple on the dance floor, picturing them perfectly in my mind's eye.

Some find the minuet a tedious dance, but I am not amongst them. It is so much like a courtship—teasing and tantalizing, bit by bit, coming together then breaking apart, causing that feeling of erotic frustration to grow until the couple loses themselves in the madness of their sexual desires. A madness from which they can only be released thought the physical act of consummation. I think it no coincidence that the minuet is the traditional celebratory dance of man and wife after the completion of their nuptials.

I listened to the delicate strains of the harpsichord, imagining in my wretched mind each step of Ashby's courtship answered by each step of Gabrielle's coy encouragement. Together they built their tension, so perfectly, so inexorably, that I could imagine him sinking into her thighs, her head thrown back in ecstasy as she brought her knees up around his naked hips.

The heat of the ballroom suddenly became oppressive, and I realized that my head was swimming. I took a faltering step backwards. Sophie touched my arm, refocusing my attention. Mercifully, I heard the final chords of the music ring throughout the room. Relieved, I exhaled the breath I had not known I was holding.

"Are you feeling poorly, my love?" Sophie murmured behind her fan.

I snapped open my own fan, and attempted to smile. Meanwhile, Mr. Sykes pedantic lecture on horse breeding continued, though now he seemed to be talking about a stallion named Red Bishop. Whether Red Bishop belonged to Mr. Sykes or not, I could not say, which was unfortunate since at precisely that moment the gentleman decided to address me with a question.

"Lady Delemere," he said, focusing his small, piggy eyes onto my bewildered face, "I would be interested to hear your thoughts on the matter. Lord Delemere, God rest him, was quite knowledgeable on the subject of horseflesh, was he not?"

But at that very same moment someone softly cleared his throat behind me. My thoughts immediately flew back to Ashby. I smiled at Mr. Sykes and begged his pardon, then turned.

"Tristan!" I exclaimed.

"Elina," he said, smiling down on me. "Would you do me the great honor—"

"No!" I gasped, then quickly amended when he looked taken aback, "I mean, yes! But could we perhaps find a secluded corner for a bit of refreshment instead of a dance?"

"Certainly," he said, offering his arm. "But if you are unwell, Elina, perhaps we should ask Sophie to take you back to your room."

"Oh, no," I replied, "tempting as that sounds, I am not

unwell. I just need a quiet place to rest for a few minutes and have a glass of punch."

"Very well." His boyish smile returned. "Your wish, as ever, is my command. I know just the place."

Tristan took me to a sheltered boudoir some distance from the ballroom where we could enjoy a few moments undisturbed. I took a seat at the window and began to fan myself in earnest as Tristan left in search of some punch. He returned shortly, two crystal cups in hand.

"Milady," he said, handing me one of the cups.

He took a seat across from me and I thanked him, then proceeded to gulp down the precious liquid in a manner not at all complimentary to my governesses. Tristan pretended not to notice as he stared pensively out the window into the darkness. I set my empty cup down on the windowsill and hiccupped loudly. The corners of Tristan's mouth twitched. Leaning back in my seat, I continued to fan myself as I looked at him appraisingly.

Sir Tristan Richmond cut a dashing figure this evening. Dressed in rich silk satin of the darkest green, richly laced and embroidered in silver, the excellent cut of his tailcoat showed off to perfection his massive shoulders, and his pale silver waistcoat and snug breeches emphasized the rest of his well-proportioned figure. Even Tristan's calves, so often a source of embarrassment for gentlemen of otherwise fine physique, were strong and shapely beneath his silk stockings. Ashby, without a doubt, was the gentleman breaking the most hearts tonight, though Tristan could not have been very far behind him.

"Tristan," I said suddenly, "may I ask you an impertinent question?"

He turned away from the window to gaze at me with his opalescent eyes, now softened with amusement. "How could I ever deny such a request as that?"

"Well, it is just that we have known each other for so long,"

I explained, flushing slightly. "I regard you as more of a brother or a cousin than just a friend. And a certain amount of impertinence is allowed between family members, yes?"

"Yes," he agreed. "I suppose it is. Only I would prefer to be your cousin rather than your brother, if you do not mind."

"Why are you not married, Tristan?" I asked. "You are so handsome, so kind, and surely you'll be prime minister someday. You could have any lady you wanted! Are you so afraid of the bonds of matrimony?"

"That is a fine question coming from you, Elina! Are you not the same lady who has sworn never to be enslaved by the bonds of matrimony again?"

"Marriage is different for a man than it is for a woman," I pointed out. "The same rules do not apply to both the husband and the wife. A man is not enslaved by his vows the same way a woman is."

"There is truth in that, I suppose," he agreed. "But must we discuss this now? We are in the middle of a ball, and I'm afraid my answer will make me rather wretched company."

"Oh, yes!" I urged. "I have been meaning to ask you this for ages. And now you have me intrigued!"

He sighed. "To answer your question, it is not because I fear the bonds of holy matrimony that I remain unmarried. In fact, I believe marriage between a man and woman who love each other could be sublime."

"Then why are you not married?" I pressed as I reached out to take his hand. "You must tell me, Tristan, because I think you would make some woman a very good husband."

"I will not marry someone I do not love."

I nodded sagely. "So you have not yet found someone to love."

"That is not it at all," he said, gently freeing his hand. "I love someone very much. But she married another."

"Well then, she's a bloody idiot!" I pronounced. He looked at me, clearly startled, and I thought it necessary to add, "I'm sorry, Tristan, I'm afraid the punch has gone to my head. But surely you could find another to love, couldn't you?"

"She is no longer married. Her husband died seven months ago. In a fire."

"Oh!" I exclaimed. Then, touching my hand to my lips, "*Oh*."

"She has told me that she shall never marry again," he continued, "even though I would spend the rest of my life finding some way of becoming worthy enough to stand beside her. If she wanted children, I would gladly give her children; but if she wanted instead only to write novels, I could content myself with just being her husband and growing old with her at Richmond House. Because, Elina, without her, nothing matters. I could never love another; I can only love her. And if I cannot marry her, I shall marry no one."

I had been sixteen the last time Tristan had looked at me in this way. He had been a young man of twenty, though still a boy in so many ways. There had been a time when I'd thought I would marry Tristan, but fate had led me down a different path.

When William asked Papa for my hand, Tristan was in London working on his political career. I wrote to him, expecting him to ride up to Hertfordshire immediately to press his suit. But he did not even reply to my letter. I had thought then what I'd interpreted as devotion from Tristan had been only an idle flirtation. I'd convinced myself that the hurt was nothing more than my wounded pride. It was not until several years into my marriage that I realized my letter had likely been construed as an announcement of my intent to marry another man, rather than the entreaty for Tristan's interference I actually intended.

"Oh, Tristan," I whispered. "I—I do not know what to say."

"Do not worry, my love," he said, an infinite sadness in his voice. "This is not a proposal. I already know what your answer would be. But if I could . . . just one more time . . ."

And with a speed remarkable for someone his size, he closed the distance between us and kissed me. Only his lips touched mine, though I sensed in him the need for something more. Before I knew what I was doing, I found myself responding to the warm, firm pressure of his mouth. My body slowly awakened, and I leaned in closer to him, raising my hand to softly touch his cheek. But then he abruptly broke away.

"I can't—" he began to apologize, but then his body tensed as he glared at something just over my shoulder. "Can I help you, sir?" he demanded, his voice low and threatening.

Struck with a terrible mixture of *déjà-vu* and foreboding, I turned to see whom it was Tristan challenged. The object of his ire stood in the doorway, one shoulder leaning gracefully against the door jamb, the very picture of elegant repose except for his dark eyes scorching me where I sat.

"Ashby!" I cried without thinking. "How long have you been standing there?" Then I cursed myself for my guilty words.

"Long enough, madam," he said. "Long enough."

CHAPTER 19

Lady Trevelver's ball did not last long past midnight, when the musicians packed up their instruments and left. There was still some activity in the card rooms, and a few lovers lingered in the more secluded boudoirs, but for the most part everyone had sought out their beds long before the *bon ton* would even have arrived at a London soiree.

I sat in the window seat of the room I shared with Phosey and Sophie, listening to their gentle snores coming from the dark recesses of the bed. Eyes closed, the night air damp and cool on my face from the open casement, I sat and I mourned what could have been.

Poor, dear Tristan. How different my life could have been had he only made that journey to Hertfordshire. We were so young, so stupid—neither of us able to tell the other what we truly wanted.

And now? Could I start over?

No. I could not. Things had happened in William Throckmorton's house. I was no longer the same girl Tristan had loved. I'd become something darker, more savage, and I could not bring that into Tristan's life. He was the best of men; he deserved better.

And what of Ashby? What could he possibly be thinking of me now?

I opened my eyes and gazed out upon the vista outside my window. Our room was located above the conservatory, overlooking the garden. The silvery crescent moon glowed faintly behind a smattering of clouds. At the edges of the garden below, the night mists were gaining ground, steadily working their way across the lawns to press thickly against the stones of the house.

Just as I was thinking it a night for the spooks and specters to be out, a soft click below caught my attention as someone exited the conservatory through the French doors. Moments later I saw her, unmistakable in her gold faille dress, no cover for her bare shoulders on this chilly night, as she glided out towards the garden maze.

She was alone, and my decision was instantaneous.

Edith had already prepared me for bed, but surely she'd packed me a pelisse. A quick search of the armoire proved that she had, and grabbing this, I left to find Gabrielle in the gardens.

The mists swirled around my feet as I stepped out through the conservatory's doors. The garden was dark, and there was no telling how far she'd gone, but I figured she'd likely not strayed too far from the house. Not on a night like this. And sure enough, as I turned the first corner around the hedge, I found her seated on a stone bench, looking almost as though she'd been waiting for me.

"Good evening, Elina," she said.

"Gabrielle."

She looked a goddess of the night in her Grecian gown, diamonds just a faint sparkle in her hair and at her throat.

"I need to talk to you," I said.

"I know. I knew you would come to find me."

I took a seat on the bench next to her, and gathered my pelisse closer around me. Gabrielle seemed unconcerned by the cold; the soft, bare flesh of her breast and arms glowed slightly in the wan light of the moon. My eyes lingered a moment on the edges of her low-cut gown, I suddenly wondered what she looked like beneath the clinging material—was she truly as perfect as I imagined?

She sniffled, and I looked up sharply. "Have you been crying, Gabrielle?"

"Ashby is very angry with me." She sniffled again. "He's never been this angry with me before."

She looked so young, so forlorn. I could detect no trace of the brazen Parisian actress in her now. Despite myself, I felt my heart go out to her.

"What happened, Gabrielle?"

She shook her head, and glanced away.

"Gabrielle?" I prompted after a few moments.

"I tell you a story now," she said. "Then you will understand."

"Very well."

"I met Ashby when I was fifteen. I was all alone, and Paris is a very dangerous place for a girl, all alone.

"But I was lucky—until one night I wasn't. I had a job at a little theatre as a cleaner, and one night I was alone in the green room, when a man came in and locked the door behind him. I screamed, but no one came. When he was finished, and I was broken and bleeding on the floor, he spat upon me and told me to be ready for him the next night. I knew then that my life was over.

"I do not know how long I lay upon the floor, when someone came in and lifted me up into his arms. He carried me to a coach, and from there he took me to his apartment. I thought he meant to do me more harm, but I was too weak to resist. At his apartment, I caught my first glimpse of his face and I recognized him from the theatre—he was the lover of one of the actresses. He told me his name was Ashby, and that he was going to take care of me. He told me the name of the devil who raped me was Delemere, and that I was never to return to the theatre. He would get me work elsewhere.

"And the rest is history, as you English say. He had connections at the Maison Moliere, where I started as a cleaner, then became lady's maid to one of the actresses, and then finally an actress myself in a little *comédie*. I lived with Ashby, he was my everything, and I his. We were happy . . . but one thing we were not, was lovers."

Gabrielle glanced up at me, as though to make sure these words resonated.

"We were not lovers," she repeated. "I could not be with a man after what Delemere did. Ashby and I love each other as brother and sister. *Naturallement*, everyone in Paris thought us lovers, but it wasn't true.

"Then one day, Ashby came to me and told me he had to leave. Someone needed him in England, and he knew that I would be all right on my own. I was famous by then, the darling of the Revolutionaries, no one would dare lay a hand on me. My heart broke, and I resolved to hate whomever was stealing him away from me."

I nodded. "So you are the *one*."

"What do you mean, the *one*?"

"Ashby told me he was in love with a woman he could not marry."

"And you think that woman is me?"

I nodded again.

"*Merde*. You really do not know anything, do you?"

"You are not the woman Ashby loves?"

She flashed me a smile. "Oh he loves me, make no mistake about that, *ma chérie*. There is simply . . . another."

I frowned. "But Ashby only mentioned the one."

"Ashby is *tres stupide* in matters of the heart. As are all men, *oui*? He does not understand that he can love more than one. He loves me, but he also loves another . . . another for whom he left me in Paris seven years ago."

"Seven years ago?" I whispered.

"He always hated William Delemere. Did you know that? Even before he raped me and ruined me, he hated Delemere."

"But he never left William's side!"

"He never left *your* side, you stupid cow. Always close," she pressed on, "because he knew what Delemere was. He'd seen— we'd all seen in Paris—what he was capable of. After me, there were others. Many others. But he was an *aristo*. He was untouchable. The girls at the theaters knew to stay away from him. He had a reputation for entertaining certain appetites. And then Delemere married you, and poof! Ashby left me in Paris, because he could not leave you alone with that monster."

I shook my head. "Impossible! I did not even know Ashby before my marriage!"

She shrugged in typical Gallic fashion. "This is perhaps a conversation you'd best have with him, *oui?*"

"That will not be happening anytime soon," I said bitterly. "Not after what has happened between us, and not after this evening."

Gabrielle's lip curled. "You tried to force the truth out of him through a crude manipulation. That never works. Ashby cannot be forced, and he cannot be manipulated."

"But he told *you* the truth!"

"He did, *oui*. But that is because I am a part of it."

"You are a highway robber, too?"

"Ah, Elina. You do not even begin to know what this . . . this *thing* is, that we do. But please, *mon petite*, do us all a kindness. Leave Sir Tristan alone. He has no place in this. He is a complication we do not need."

"We?"

"Understand this. Though you may hold primacy over Ashby's

heart, my place is with him. I will always be by his side. Always. I will kill, if I must, to keep him safe. Someday, perhaps, I will extend that to you, too," she added softly. "I know now that I cannot hate you. I did, for many years . . . but now that I know you . . . now that I see the way he loves you, and you love him . . ."

I glanced up at her, and saw her watching me with a curious look in her eyes that I couldn't quite identify. It seemed almost . . . wistful. Then she shivered, and I noticed gooseflesh erupting across her bare skin.

"You *are* cold." I scooted close to her and wrapped my arm around her shoulders, sharing the warmth of my pelisse with her. I felt her sharp intake of breath, and then she snuggled close into the warmth of my body.

"We should not be enemies, Elina," she said. "I am sorry I lied to you. I am sorry I made you think Ashby was my lover."

I nodded. "I do not want to be your enemy, Gabrielle. I do not know what to make of this story you've told me, or even if I believe it, but I know that I do not want to be your enemy. And I'm sorry."

"For what?"

"For what William did to you. My God, you were Phosey's age."

Gabrielle rested her head on my shoulder. "He was the Devil," she murmured.

"Indeed, he was."

CHAPTER 20

TIME MOVED SWIFTLY AFTER the night of Lady Trevelver's ball.

With the fine weather holding for nearly a week, the Guns, along with Gabrielle, returned with their fowling pieces to the moors while we ladies settled into a dreary routine of letter writing, card playing, and squabbling. On the fifth day of this tedium, a nasty row erupted between Lady Mildred and Dorothea, where the younger called the elder a tiresome old maid with the face of a horse and the voice of a donkey. This convinced Lady Rydale of the need for another group outing.

So, come Saturday morning, I found myself stuffed into the corner of a smart yellow-bodied conveyance, dressed sensibly according to careful instructions. The gentlemen accompanied us on horseback, in addition to Gabrielle for whom no room could be found in the carriage. If I had not already experienced first-hand the bitter chill of the north Yorkshire wind as it howled down relentlessly from the scoured plateau of the moors, I might have envied Gabrielle her comfort and freedom.

Our destination was to be a surprise, though I guessed from the two large baskets strapped to the back of the carriage that our host and hostess had planned a picnic for us. Lord Rydale rode alongside us, pointing out landmarks and curiosities as we passed them while regaling us with his impressive knowledge of the local folklore.

"This is superstitious country," he informed us, "full of barghests, fairies, hobgoblins, ghosts, and witches."

"And what is a barghest?" I asked, adjusting my hat to a better angle against the wind. "I've never heard that term before."

"Tis a great black devil dog," he answered, rolling his eyes in pretended trepidation towards Phosey. "York is supposedly rife with them, haunting the snickleways and gobbling up those who have lost their way. But some have claimed to see them out here as well, stalking the misty moors and lurking in the shadows of the dales. Should you see one, and you've no doubt in your mind if you do—their great, burning red eyes immediately give them away as something evil and otherworldly—then it is a very bad omen, and your death is said to follow very shortly."

"And witches?" Sophie prompted. "You still have witches?"

"Aye, indeed we do," replied Lord Rydale. "North Yorkshire has a long history of witches. But the most famous witch from these parts was old Mother Shipton, who lived some two hundred years ago. Some say her true name was Ursula Soothtell, and she was a famous soothsayer supposedly born to a witch in a cave."

"And what did she foretell?" I asked. "Anything that has come to pass?"

Lord Rydale frowned. "She foretold some very strange things. There is a rhyme about some of her predictions, though I confess I do not know it."

"She did predict the Great Fire of London," Ashby interposed.

I turned to look at him for the first time since we'd left Scarcliff Towers. He'd been silently riding next to me, his proximity constantly threatening my determination to ignore him as completely as he had ignored me since the night of the ball.

"I do not believe in witches anyway," Phosey declared. "I

think it is all just make-believe told to frighten children into behaving. I should like to hear another story, a *true* one."

Lord Rydale smiled with approval. "Clever girl! Which would you like to hear? The exploits of Robin Hood? The fairies of Fairy Cross Plain? Or the secret chamber beneath Freeborough Hill where Arthur and his knights slumber? Or perhaps the legend of Wade the giant, who built the great road across Wheeldale Moor for his wife to walk from Mulgrave Castle to tend her flocks in Pickering?"

"Have you any stories about love?" Sophie asked.

"But, of course!" Lord Rydale exclaimed. "There is the story of Beggar's Bridge, spanning the Esk at Glaisdale. It begins with a young man of humble origin named Tom Ferris. He loved Agnes Richardson . . . "

And so we continued on our journey, listening to Lord Rydale's endless store of entertaining stories while enjoying our beautiful surroundings and the fine weather.

Presently we came to a handsome little village with houses made of mismatched grey stone, and here we made our stop in front of a whitewashed inn with planters of brightly-colored gillyflowers blooming beneath each of the casements. Boys from the stables rushed out to take the horses, and as they led them away, the gentlemen came to help us climb down from the carriage. When my turn came to disembark, I found myself suddenly face to face with Ashby, waiting to assist me with his outstretched hand. I hesitated, momentarily taken aback by the flinty look in his eyes, then took his hand. Ashby's cold expression remained unchanged as he helped me down the steep steps, then tucked my hand snugly into the crook of his arm as we fell into step behind the others and followed them behind the inn to a broad grassy terrace.

The view was extraordinary, overlooking a peaceful valley protected by lofty, wooded hills and the undulating country of purple moorlands beyond. Beneath the wooded precipice just below our feet, a broad river flowed past bright green meadows, thickly wooded glens, and the solemn, roofless ruins of the most spectacular Cistercian abbey I had ever seen. Those ruins spoke to me, promising me hours of good fun, and I immediately began tugging my companion towards the steep path that led down through the wooded escarpment to the valley below.

Once we reached the bottom, Lord Rydale suggested we take a stroll through the ruins while the footmen prepared our picnic. Most of our party headed for the remains of the great Gothic church, while Phosey and I struck out towards the buildings down by the river. Phosey and I had always been the explorers of the family, seeking out the darkest corners of every old house or estate we found ourselves in since she was a very small child.

Naturally, we headed for the largest building first, a two-storied rectangular structure with an underground *cellarium* and a perfectly-intact winding staircase in the southeastern corner. I began to climb the steep steps, Phosey following close behind me.

"Elina!" she exclaimed once we emerged on the first floor.

"Indeed." I turned slowly, taking in the panoramic view. "You can see everything from up here! The river, the woods, and all the rest of the abbey!"

"What do you suppose this place was?" She moved over to a massive pointed-arched window frame in an intact segment of wall.

I came to look out a similar window frame overlooking the river. "Whatever it was, it's very large. The chapter house? And this would have been a dormitory on the first floor?"

"Maybe," she said, frowning slightly. "But these large windows would have made it very cold for sleeping. I think it might have been the scriptorium, with the library on the ground floor."

"Of course!" I exclaimed. "They would need all this light to see the texts they were copying. You are devilishly clever, Phosey!"

She shrugged her shoulders in a charming, childlike gesture. "I know."

Closing my eyes, I listened to the slow-moving waters of the river. "The Cistercians knew how to select a spot. Though," I added, opening my eyes, "I think it helps that everyone is still in the church. I don't think I would find this place nearly as peaceful if Dorothea were within earshot."

Phosey came to stand beside me. "I don't think so, either," she said solemnly. "I do not like her very much."

I nodded. "We shall have to explore the church after our repast. Once everyone else has moved on."

"Um . . . Elina?"

I turned to look at her, something in her tone arresting my full attention. "What is it, Phosey?"

"May I ask your advice about something?"

"Of course," I said, studying her troubled face. She was losing some of the childlike roundness in her features, and it occurred to me that Phosey wouldn't be a child for much longer.

She took a deep breath. "What do you do if a gentleman is paying you special attention and you do not like it?"

"That's a very good question. I confess it is not something I excel at myself. Why, Phosey?" I smiled gently. "Has someone been paying you special attention?"

She nodded. "Yes."

Immediately I thought of Ashby and the regard he'd been showing the girl. "He is probably only doing that to be kind," I said. "And because he doesn't want you to be lonely."

She looked uncertain. "Oh."

"Has he touched you?" I asked sharply.

"No."

"Has he said anything untoward?"

"No, nothing like that. He just . . . he just always seems to be where I want to be. I'm never alone."

"Would you like to tell me who it is?"

"You won't be angry?"

"Of course, not!" I exclaimed. "Well? Out with it, little love! Saying his name won't—oh damnation!"

Startled, Phosey turned to follow my line of sight over her shoulder. In the distance Dr. Froggenhall had broken away from the group and was heading in our direction.

"I thought I'd shaken the little worm," I muttered.

"Oh! And here comes Sir Tristan, too!" Phosey exclaimed.

I swore again. I had not spoken to Tristan since the night of the ball. But unlike Ashby's silence, *I* had been the one determined to remain *sine communicatione*, mainly by making damn sure I could never be caught anywhere alone when I knew Tristan might be around. In fact, between Ashby's determination to avoid me and my determination to avoid Tristan, I'd only had to put up with Dr. Froggenhall's nauseating attentions for the past week.

"Phosey? Would you be a dear and head them off while I go hide in the *cellarium*?"

"What?" Phosey looked alarmed.

"I'll explain to you later! And thank you!" I kissed her quickly on the cheek, then hurried down stone stairs into the darkness below.

CHAPTER 21

THE *CELLARIUM* WAS COOL and quiet.
As my eyes adjusted, I found myself in a long, tunnel-like room with a packed earth floor and a low ceiling of rib vaults whose rows upon rows of pillars supported the heavy foundation above. The walls, ribs, and pillars were made of the same solid gray stone as the superstructure, but for the ceiling panels the medieval builders had opted to utilize cheaper bricks, porous and crumbling now from extreme old age. At the far end of the room, dust motes and pollen floated lazily in the sunlight that streamed through the partially collapsed ceiling.

As I stood wondering whether or not death would be instantaneous should the entire structure suddenly come crashing down upon my head, I heard the sound of footsteps coming down the stairs behind me. Quick and light, they bespoke both the grace and agility of their bearer, as well as the excellence of his Bond Street boot maker. Such a tread could only belong to a man who'd devoted decades to studying the arts of dancing and fencing. I groaned inwardly without bothering to turn around.

"Hello, Tristan," I greeted him quietly.

"I am sorry to disappoint," came the cool response, "but I am not Tristan."

I sucked in my breath, my pulse leaping at the sound of Ashby's voice. I remained perfectly still. Nothing could induce me to turn and face him now. This bloody ceiling could come down on my head, and I would let it crush me where I stood so long as I would not have to see again that same look of scorching contempt I had seen the night of Lady Trevelver's ball.

"I beg your pardon, sir," I replied evenly. "Hello, Ashby."

"Will you not turn around?"

"I think it better, sir, if I do not." I could feel him standing directly behind me now, so close I could feel his breath stir the air. I sought to suppress the unwanted reminders of what had happened the last time I found myself alone with him in a cool, dark place.

"Very well," he replied, the cold tone of his urbane voice nearly breaking the spell. "If you are going to force me to address the back of your head," he continued, "I shall get to the point. I have come here to offer you the truth."

"The truth?" I kept my tone nonchalant.

"But only if you promise to meet my terms. Then I will tell you everything you want to know."

"Your terms, sir?" I narrowed my eyes as my pride gained the upper hand. "And what terms might those be?"

"Promise me that I shall never have to see that brute's hands upon you again."

Anger flared within me. "Tristan is not a brute! And I can promise you nothing of the sort. *He* kissed *me*! Not the other way around!"

"From what I witnessed, you appeared lax in your efforts to resist him."

"He took me by surprise!" I exclaimed, though a part of me acknowledged the truth of his words. "And I fail to see why I need to defend myself to you."

"I am not asking you to defend yourself," he pointed out. "I am asking you not to kiss him. And in return I shall give you full disclosure of my recent, ah, *unorthodox* activities."

A triumphant thrill coursed through me: I had been *right!* But then I paused a moment to think. It wasn't that I balked at any restrictions on my future kissing activities with Tristan, since I never intended to kiss him again.

But the idea of any conditions at all irked me, especially since Gabrielle had not needed to enter into any contract before Ashby allowed her into his confidence.

"Is it such a terrible thing I ask?" he asked, his voice suddenly gentle. "Have I misinterpreted your intentions towards Sir Tristan Richmond?"

I closed my eyes, focusing on his voice as I forced Gabrielle out of my mind. I thought of him as he stood behind me, dressed for riding in his buckskin breeches, striped silk waistcoat, and double-breasted tailcoat of deep blue superfine with fashionably-wide lapels. His cravat was perfect, of course, and the priceless ruffles at his wrists still impossibly white despite the day's out-of-doors activities. A velvet ribbon tied his softly curling hair back to the nape of his neck, and his jet-black lashes like smudges of perennial shadow in the hollows beneath his eyes. And what about those eyes? What look did they hold?

Slowly, I turned to face him. He stood leaning against the stone wall, arms folded across his chest, one foot crossed casually over the other. He was backlit, the sun shining down upon him through the stairwell and casting his face in shadow. I took a step towards him. He immediately pushed off the wall and followed suit, so I took another and so did he. When I could finally see his face, I froze. In his eyes I saw a naked longing so powerful, the packed earthen floor seemed to drop out from under me.

The next moment, I was in his arms.

"*Minha Amada,*" he murmured into my hair.

At first, all I could do was listen to the sound of his beating heart. But then I drew a long, shaky breath. "Can you forgive me?" I asked, my voice small and hesitant.

"Forgive what?" He brushed his lips tenderly against my temple. "I am the one who has behaved like a fool."

"If you can forgive me, then I can forgive you."

His chest rose and fell in a heavy sigh, a curiously sad sound when I was feeling so happy. And then he pulled away from me so he could look into my eyes. "No, *Minha Amada*. You cannot forgive me yet. There are some things I must tell you first."

I frowned, confused. "But I already know you are a highwayman, Ashby, and I do not care! I do not understand why you do it, but whatever your reasons, I do not care!"

"But you *should* care, Elina!" He released me and turned away to pace a few steps. "What happened to your sister was my fault! What could have happened to *you* had I not intervened in time, would have been my fault! Even if you do not care that I am a common thief, you should care about that!"

"But you saved Sophie, and she has recovered. And I know you killed those horrible men. I heard Lord Beverley say that the Northern Gang has disappeared, and I know it is because you killed them."

Ashby turned around to face me, his expression pained as he searched my face. "You seem terribly unmoved over the death of your fellow man, Elina. You accuse me of murdering five men and two boys, and unless I am much mistaken, you seem pleased that I did so."

"They were monsters," I said, lifting my chin. "I am glad they are dead."

"You should not be so quick to judge those less fortunate," he said. "Poverty is nearly impossible to overcome by honest means, and hunger can transform the most admirable and praiseworthy of men into savages in a very short time. But I did not kill all of the Northern Gang," he continued. "I rid this world of Buford and Red Jack only. The rest, except for two of the boys, were caught by thief-takers and now await trial in Cambridgeshire."

His words, though truthful, still rankled. I did not appreciate being lectured, even by Ashby, on matters for which he only understood half—the male half—of the story. "It is an easy thing for you to disapprove of my lack of compassion," I told him. "Perhaps you are even a little shocked at my bloodthirstiness. But you are a man who knows no master save God, King, and Country. You know nothing of the terrors women are subjected to when we, through no fault of our own, find ourselves in the power of men like Red Jack and his wretched accomplice, Buford. They were rapists, Ashby, and I am glad you rid the world of them. But I bear no ill will towards the boys," I added. "What has become of them?"

"They are with me still," he said as he leaned a shoulder against the nearest pillar and assumed his favored attitude of repose, "though I no longer employ them on the highways."

"Surely you have not sent them up to Castle Ashenhurst!" I exclaimed. "They may be young, but they are still criminals, Ashby."

His expression darkened. "I assure you they are nowhere near Castle Ashenhurst," he said. "Those two ruffians do not even know my name, let alone where my estate lies. Should they ever venture that far north, it will be their last mistake."

"Then how are they in your employ?" I asked, moving into the sunlight and rubbing my hands up and down my arms against the chill. "I do not understand. Have you gone into trade?"

He glanced at me briefly, then pushed himself off the column and set to pacing. I watched him prowl back and forth like a restless tiger in a cage, and began to feel uneasy. "We have reached the point in our conversation that I have been dreading," he explained grimly.

My stomach clenched with a brief premonition of hurt. This was not going to be the simple confession I had been expecting.

"It is all right, Ashby," I assured him, though I could feel my confidence rapidly eroding from beneath me. "Whatever it is, it is all right. Please tell me."

"As you wish." He ceased his pacing and looked up at me, holding me with his eyes. "You have been asking me for the truth, Elina," he said. "So I shall tell you the truth now and submit myself to your judgment, whatever that might be. But I warn you, it will change things."

I nodded for him to continue.

"You asked me just now if I was in trade. The answer is 'yes,' I am in trade—*free* trade. And other things."

"Other things?"

"I'm a smuggler, Elina. I also have several counterfeiting operations. And . . ." His voice trailed off.

"And?"

"And I own brothels. Now do you see why I wished to keep my secrets from you?"

"But you are a highwayman!" I argued. "You are the Black Unicorn!"

"The Black Unicorn is nothing but a phantom, a diversionary tactic designed to keep the authorities' attention focused on the *interior* of the island so they do not notice the very, *very* large smuggling operation I am running along the eastern coast right under their noses."

I frowned, taking a few moments to absorb this. "But, *why?*" I finally asked. "I do not understand why you should risk yourself this way! Why can't you marry an heiress like everyone else? If you're caught, either as a smuggler or a highwayman, you'll be hanged! My God! If you're caught as a counterfeiter, you could be burned!"

"And here we've come to it," he pronounced, his eyes full of bitterness. "The price of the truth."

I knew I did not want to hear what was coming. I had no idea what he was going to say, but I knew instinctively that this would be the source of the hurt I had been afraid of. He watched me, waiting for my cue before he went any further. I stood on the edge of a precipice, and I could still turn back. I could still remain comfortably ignorant of whatever it was he didn't want to tell me.

But no, that was not true. Ignorance as a conscious choice is never comfortable. I had William Throckmorton to thank for teaching me that lesson.

"Tell me," I said.

"I am betrothed to the Barrington heiress," he said, his eyes still intent upon my face. "I am sure you know the family, out of Kent?"

I nodded. "Little Violet Barrington. Family fortune made two generations ago through shipping. No brothers, no sisters. Only eight years old. The greatest matrimonial prize in Great Britain. Who doesn't know little Violet Barrington?"

"Her guardians wish to keep the betrothal secret until her twelfth birthday. The wedding will take place soon after she turns eighteen."

I looked away and studied the smooth grey stones in the wall next to me. "In just ten years, you shall be one of the richest men in England."

"Yes."

I felt numb. The pain had not hit me yet, though I knew it would. I glanced back to his face. "Then why are you doing this?"

He sighed and ran a hand over his face. "My father left me with a mortgaged estate, three sisters who will wish to wed soon, and a brother I must launch into a political career. These things cost money—a great deal of money. My sisters are nearly of marriageable age, and, as I told you, Chrysander is about to start at Cambridge. I cannot wait ten years. So, in the meantime, the

Black Unicorn must haunt the turnpikes and—" Ashby stopped abruptly, his expression intent as he cocked his head to the side, listening.

"What is it?" I whispered, a cold knot suddenly forming in the pit of my stomach.

Ashby raised his hand to silence me. In the tomb-like stillness of the subterranean chamber, we both heard the sound of a single pebble rolling unhurriedly down the staircase. In a flash, Ashby shot up the stairs, looking for eavesdroppers while I stayed frozen where I stood. He seemed gone a very long time, the moments ticking slowly by as I imagined all sorts of dreadful scenarios, most of them involving Lord Beverley. But then I heard his footsteps tripping lightly back down the stairs.

"I did not see anyone," Ashby reported when he came back in view, "but I think we should be heading back. I am sure everyone is wondering where we are."

I nodded silently, unsure of what to say.

"I am sorry, Elina. I did not want this."

"I know," I said, smiling at him bravely. "I forced the truth out of you. I am upset, but I have only myself to blame."

"I hate to leave things like this. Will you meet me in the park? Tomorrow morning?"

I hesitated for just a moment, then nodded again.

"Thank you, *Minha Amada.*"

He offered me a smile, but made no move to touch me again. As we made our way out of the *cellarium* and walked back in silence through the ruins, I couldn't make up my mind whether or not I regretted his distance.

CHAPTER 22

THE WEATHER MATCHED MY mood the following day as I tromped through the wooded park.

The night before, the massive darkness of the lonely moorland had pressed threateningly upon the house. A bitter wind howling down from the north sounded like the cries of lost souls left to haunt the chilly heath. It was a wind that brought with it evil tidings as it railed against my windows.

And now the sky, an ominous greenish grey, appeared to be pressing the bloated clouds too close to the earth. A chill north wind picked up by the second; it threatened to tear my bonnet from my head, whipping me in the face with the strings tying my pelisse. It was weather for staying indoors, to be sure. But I was on a mission. I was headed towards the patch of yellow pimpernels, where part of me hoped to find Ashby.

The other part hoped not to find him at all.

A light rain began to fall, slanting through the trees. I clutched my pelisse closer around me as the rain hammered down harder. If I did not find Ashby in the flowers, I would return immediately to the house. I would not wait for him. We'd had our tryst, and it was time to end it. Ashby could have all the young heiresses he liked.

The rain came down harder still, and I realized tetchily that whether I found Ashby or not, I would soon be soaked through. There would also be some explaining to do back at the house, since I'd pled a headache earlier so I could meet Ashby instead of attending Sunday service. If I believed in such things, I might have thought this was God's way of punishing me for my lie and truancy from church. As it stood, I would have to come up with another lie—and an inventive one at that—to explain why I'd decided to go out for a walk in the rain with a headache.

A shiver ran through me, and I pulled my head down between my shoulders. The rain seemed to grow steadily colder. But if memory served, the bend just up ahead was where I'd found Ashby before. I could smell the inviting scent of a wood fire burning in someone's fireplace close at hand. Probably the game-keeper's cottage, and no doubt that worthy soul sat enjoying a hot cup of tea next to the blaze at this very moment. I would join him in spirit, I decided, as soon as I returned to the Towers.

The wind continued to pick up, and I felt mildly uneasy. The world around me grew darker by the moment, and besides the sound of rainfall, everything fell eerily silent. No birds chir-ruped from the trees, and the woodland critters were nowhere to be seen. Following the path around the bend, I found Ashby's clump of pimpernels vacant with the little star-shaped flowers closed tightly against the dark skies. I sighed and felt a pang in my heart, a phantom twinge of loss for something I never really had in the first place. My mind tried to bully my heart into com-pliance with its resolution. This was not a romantic assignation.

Suddenly, a flash of lightning illuminated my dreary sur-roundings, followed closely by an ear-splitting explosion of thunder directly overhead. I shrieked, instinctively covering my head with my hands as the sky opened up and unleashed a torrent of freezing rain. I was instantly soaked, the rain so intense I could barely see my hand in front of my face. Then it began to bounce off the packed earth of the path in large pieces of hail. Over the roar of the rain and the hail, the trees creaked and groaned around me. I stood frozen in place, unsure of what to do. The house was some distance away, and this was the North Country; people died regularly of exposure in storms such as this.

Instinct propelled me blindly towards the foot of the large elm tree where Ashby had been seated the last time I'd come here, seeking shelter from the hail. Suddenly a blinding light seared my eyes, and I was blasted back against the tree as the world exploded around me. My head cracked against the trunk, and I fell heavily to the ground, stunned. Everything smelled burnt, and I had just enough time to wonder vaguely if I might be on fire when two hands grabbed me roughly by the arms and jerked me to my feet. My shriek of surprise was swallowed by the rage of the storm as my assailant yanked me back onto the path, and I noticed stupidly that my bonnet had been dislodged.

Ashby bellowed something into my ringing ears, but I could not make out the words. He took off running, dragging me along behind him. Fortunately I'd worn my boots, so I could run, though my wool pelisse was so heavy with water it was tangling around my legs and tripping me up. Realizing this, Ashby stopped and tore the thing from around my shoulders, then flung it to the ground. Another flash of lightning streaked overhead, followed by more thunder. Ashby took off again deeper into the wood. I had no idea of our destination, but since my spotty vision couldn't penetrate three feet in front of me, it did not really matter.

Ashby's grip hurt my arm; I yanked free from his grasp, but still kept up with him as we ran. The hail, now the size of robin's eggs, pelted me relentlessly, and I knew I would be bruised on the morrow. I tried to press my chin down into my chest to save my face from the worst of it. Then, all at once, a large stone structure loomed up ahead of us. Ashby sprinted up its steps three at a time without breaking stride and yanked the large oak door open for me. He shoved me inside, then followed, pulling the door closed behind us.

I slid down to the floor, back against the door, holding my head in my hands. Ashby squatted in front of me and roughly pulled away my hands. He studied me intently, then grasped my jaw and turned my head this way, then that.

He took a deep breath, and let it out slowly. "I think you are undamaged."

I pulled his hands away from my face. "What happened?"

"A lightning strike. Hit the tree across the path," he said. "You could have been killed."

I nodded. I'd thought as much. "Where are we?" I gasped, rubbing my hands up and down my arms, shivering. Now that we were not running any more, I realized I was chilled to the bone. And this strange place, whatever it was, was absolutely freezing.

"This is Lord Rydale's hunting lodge." Ashby stood and offered me a hand. "If you can move, we should go upstairs. I have a fire burning up there, so it should be warmer by now."

That was all the encouragement I needed. Allowing him to hand me up, I followed him across the large room, which appeared from its rustic decoration and furnishings to be yet another banqueting room.

"Bess certainly liked to entertain," I observed through chattering teeth. "This is the third banqueting room I've seen on this estate."

"Yes," he agreed, leading the way up the oak staircase, "though this place is a little different than the others. You'll see once you get to the top of the stairs."

But that was where he was wrong. All I felt was the warmth, and as soon as I'd climbed the final stair, I pushed rudely past Ashby and hurried over to the fireplace. Holding my hands out to the cheerful blaze, I rubbed them together and then fell to my knees so the fire's warmth could envelop me. But the fire seemed to be making matters worse. The more the heat washed over me, the harder I shivered until my teeth were chattering so loudly I knew Ashby could hear them.

"Elina," he said, his voice strangely neutral, "you need to get out of those clothes. You are sure to catch a chill otherwise, and they will dry faster without you wearing them."

I nodded. I was shaking so badly now, my body ached. I felt his hands upon me, pulling me to my feet and turning me to face him.

Without another word, he began unpinning my dress, then pushed it back off my shoulders and peeled the sleeves off my arms. Then he leaned in close, sliding his arms through mine to reach the silken cord knotted in the small of my back. I felt the cord give, and my overskirt and hip pads slid down to the floor with a sodden thump.

Ashby took a step back, allowing me to breathe a little easier as he deftly unfastened the tapes around my waist and unpinned the stomacher from my stays, and then he was yanking at the cords of my petticoat until they too fell to my feet. Ashby grasped me by the shoulders, turned me to face the fire, and continued with a rapid economy of movement to unlace my corset. Soon it joined the hip pads and petticoats on the floor, and he was gathering up my soggy chemise. I raised my arms up over my head and off it came.

In an impossibly short period of time, I found myself standing naked in front of the fire, clad only in my stockings and boots. Ashby turned me around to face him again, studiously keeping his attention bent on my feet as he knelt to undo my boots and slip them off my feet.

Finally, he untied my garters and then quickly rolled my stockings down my legs. Ashby stood, his eyes carefully focused on my face, and turned me around once more to face the fire.

I was now more naked than I had ever been in front of anyone before, and I did not care. The warmth of the fire's heat on my bare skin was sublime. Moments later, a heavy blanket draped around my shoulders. I pulled it tightly around me, then allowed Ashby to draw me towards a large, winged armchair just to the side of the fireplace.

"Is this all right, *Minha Amada*?" he asked. "Or would you like to be closer to the fire?"

"Just a bit closer." I stretched my bare feet towards the blaze. He pushed me closer. I began to relax as he came around my chair to add another log to the fire. He had been correct. The moment my clothes were off, I stopped shivering and my teeth no longer chattered.

Outside the storm raged, punctuated continually by punches of light and great booms of thunder. I could hear the torrents of rain coming down overhead. I expected Ashby to take a seat in the matching chair opposite mine, but he disappeared behind me instead. I sat for a few moments, listening for his movements, but I couldn't hear him over the noise of the storm and figured he must have left the room.

Without thinking, I turned to look for him and found him standing with his back to me, next to a giant four-poster bed, stripping his waterlogged cambric shirt off over his head. I sat transfixed, watching the way the sleek muscles of his back shifted beneath his skin, and the way that skin glowed in the firelight just as it had that night I'd interrupted his bath. Then I quickly turned back around as he began to unbutton the falls of his breeches.

"So this is a bedroom, then," I said.

"It is," Ashby affirmed. "I think, from the excessive number of black unicorns all over the place, this may have been Bess's and Alastair's favorite trysting spot. They could entertain downstairs as they liked, and then quietly retire up here whenever they chose."

"Bess's secret lover's name was Alastair?" I asked.

"Yes."

"Alastair Harcourt?"

"Yes." He came to take the seat across from me with another blanket from the bed wrapped tightly around his waist. "My great great grandfather."

I frowned as I watched him. "Why did you decide to use your family device as your sobriquet? It is very reckless, you know. This estate is crawling with black unicorns, and once anyone realizes that Bess's secret lover was a Harcourt, it follows that the Black Unicorn might also be a Harcourt."

"Yes, well, we Harcourts are known for our recklessness," he admitted, his tone suddenly pensive. "Some more than others. My father was reckless with money; I am reckless in other ways. Besides, Rydale already knows."

"He does?"

"Yes."

"And he'll keep your secret?"

"He will."

Neither of us spoke for a while, each of us lost in our own thoughts. My gaze moved from the flames to the tattered tapestry mounted above the fireplace. It had been beautiful once, though now it was little more than a moth-eaten rag.

"Can't you stop?" I asked.

He did not answer me at first. As the minutes slowly ticked by, I thought he wouldn't answer me at all. In the tapestry, a black unicorn lay sleeping with its head in a yellow-haired maiden's lap. I glanced back to Ashby's face, watching the way the firelight danced around the contours of his face as he studied the flames.

When he spoke, his voice was very soft, but it still startled me enough to make my heart jump. "I will stop, *Minha Amada*. Soon."

I looked back to the tapestry. Around its edges, hunters

moved in for the kill. They had the maiden and the unicorn surrounded, intent upon destroying it with their clubs and axes. I wondered if the maiden worked in concert with the hunters, or if she too would be their victim. Would her heart break to watch something so rare and beautiful being destroyed in front of her? Because of her? I glanced at the wound on Ashby's arm, still angry and red. Nowhere close to being healed.

"Not soon enough," I said quietly.

"How about this," he said, leaning forward in his chair and causing his blanket to slip a little down his hips. "I promise I shall not rob anyone else while I am in Yorkshire."

An inch of black hair trailed enticingly from beneath his navel down the flat plane of his abdomen. I gathered my own blanket closer around me and transferred my gaze to the fire. "I think it only wise. Lord Beverley is not an idiot. If I can figure out your identity, so can he."

He snorted. "I doubt that. You are a woman of singular intelligence and intuition. If you were a man, you would have caught me and hanged me months ago."

I shivered. "Do not joke of such things."

He held me a moment with his gaze, his expression enigmatic as ever. But then his eyes softened, and when he spoke, his voice was gentle. "My life is in the palm of your hand, *Minha Amada*. You hold the power of life and death over my head."

His attraction was as overwhelming as the storm outside. I struggled against him, willing myself not to drown in him as he drew me inexorably into his vortex. Anger at my own weakness flared within me, and I desperately latched onto it and sought to turn it against him. "And so what?" I demanded. "You seduce me then to keep me from dropping the axe? To keep me quiet and warm your bed while little Violet Barrington grows into your beautiful bride?"

"No." He lurched forward with the abruptness of a cobra

strike, and in a flash he knelt at my feet, his blanket puddled loosely around his hips. "I seduce you, *Minha Amada*, because I love you. Because I have always loved you."

And with a resounding crack, I slapped him across the face.

CHAPTER 23

"O UCH." Ashby sat back on his heels as he rubbed his cheek.

"I am not sorry," I said, clutching my blanket closer around me. "It serves you right."

"I do not understand."

"Do not seduce me with the same words you've used on others. Now, please return to your seat. Your closeness is making me uncomfortable."

And indeed it was, his blanket having now slipped down to a good inch below his hips, leaving the long line of his torso naked all the way down to his pubic bone. It was enough to befuddle the senses of any hot-blooded woman.

His eyes suddenly blazed with anger. He planted one hand on each arm of my chair and leaned in closer. "I see. You think I have told others that I love them? That I am as free with my heart as I am with my body?"

"Ashby," I begged, "please sit in the other chair. I do not wish to slap you again."

"Or perhaps you think my love is so common a thing, it is worthless? Is that it?"

"Ashby . . . " I repeated, but the look in his eyes froze the words on my lips.

"Answer my question."

Ashby's face was so close to mine, he took up my entire field of vision. But as he'd risen off the floor to box me in with his arms, I knew that the blanket had not come with him. Ashby was now totally naked, his blanket protecting only the modesty of his knees. At first I felt a glimmer of relief that he was too close for me to steal a peek at things I should not, but then I felt a surge of shame wash over me. His heart was breaking before me, and all I could do was think of his body.

Damn. Damn. *Damn*. How had he turned this all against me?

"Answer my question."

"I do not think your love worthless," I whispered.

The moments ticked by as I burned under his scrutiny. But gradually I sensed his body relax, and his eyes softened a little.

"You think I am not sincere, because I have told others that I love them? That the words have no meaning, because I have used them so many times before?" he asked, his voice barely audible.

I nodded. "Yes."

His eyes softened further, and I knew he was beginning to understand. He leaned into me a little closer, and I struggled to keep my attention on him and not solely on his body. "And what if I were to tell you," he murmured, his mouth now so close to mine that I could feel the warmth of his breath on my lips, "that the only other woman I have ever loved, or even professed to love, was my mother? Would you slap me again if I told you once more that I love you?"

"Yes," I whispered. "I mean no. I do not know."

"I love you, *Minha Amada*." He brushed his mouth over mine, just the barest hint of a touch. I leaned into him, wanting more of him, and felt my entire orientation of mind, body, and spirit center on him with a permanence that I found terrifying.

"I love you," I whispered.

I had never spoken the words before to any man except Papa. Not even to my husband, even during the early days when he was still hiding his dark nature from me. I had been saving the words, protecting them by burying them so deeply within my heart. And now I realized it was for the power of this moment.

Ashby closed his eyes, and his brow puckered as if my words had brought him pain. But when his lashes fluttered and lifted, I could see only the reverent glow of a peace so profound it confused me.

But then I realized *this* was Ashby—the man behind the libertine.

The man who until this moment had only allowed me to see him in glimpses.

And he was looking at me with love in his eyes.

Ashby closed his eyes again, the fan of his lashes so dark against the translucent skin, and leaned in to press his soft mouth to mine. I closed my eyes, and everything in the world seemed to melt away.

I am not sure at what point my knees parted, but suddenly he was between them, pressing his body still closer to mine as he broke away from my mouth. I whimpered, mourning the loss, but then he began delicately tracing along the line of my jaw with his lips.

"I could drown in your skin," he murmured as he continued down my throat, then dropped down to my collar bone with feather-light lips and followed it to my bare shoulder. He returned to my mouth, his kiss firmer, more insistent, as he pulled open my blanket and slid it off my shoulders and down to my waist.

Breaking the kiss, he leaned so close that the peaks of my hardened nipples brushed lightly against his chest. His breath tickled my ear as he whispered, "You come to me often in my dreams, *Minha Amada*."

I gasped, arching into him as I parted my knees wider.

"No, no." He pulled away, a flash of humor in his dark eyes. "The chapel was yours. Now it is my turn."

With a frustrated groan, I leaned back into the chair and scowled at him.

"You must learn to trust me, *Minha Amada*," he murmured. "I do not wish to sound arrogant, but I believe that I am very good at this."

I was attempting to think of a suitable retort when he stood in a smooth, graceful movement that treated me to my first glimpse of his nakedness. The sudden sight of the thick thatch of dark curls between his legs and the long length of his erection shocked me into silence.

He paused a moment, submitting to my hungry inspection. I had never thought the male figure particularly attractive in the nude, and had always wondered why Classical and Renaissance sculptors had been so enamored of it.

But looking at Ashby's nakedness, I understood. I was out of my chair before I knew it, my blanket forgotten. I explored him the way I had wanted to that night I'd caught him in his bath. I dragged my fingertips along his collarbones to the points of his shoulders, then flattened my hands over the flat muscles of his chest, down over the ridges of his upper abdomen, then traced lightly the groove over his lean hip bones that led down to the dark, dangerous area between his legs. I marveled at the beauty of his skin, so perfectly smooth in places, and then rough when marred with scar tissue.

I leaned forward to kiss his shoulder, tasting him with my tongue.

Salty.

Then I dropped down to lick the tight little nub of one of his nipples as I cupped his testicles with one hand, causing him to suck in a breath as I ran my fingers lightly up the length of his shaft with the other.

He closed his eyes and tilted his head back, his expression almost pained as a deep, primal groan tore loose from deep within him. I continued to stroke him, and then, on a strange impulse, bent down to take the blunt tip of him into my mouth. He gasped, the muscles of his abdomen contracting, and I felt him tremble as his hand came down to cup the back of my head. Encouraged, I brought him as far into my mouth as I could, running my tongue over his soft, smooth skin, then pulling back to suck again on his tip.

Saltier than his shoulder.

Curious to see what else I could discover about him, I breathed him in, and discovered that his skin's unique musky scent seemed strongest here. He pushed gently on the back of my head and I drew him back down into my mouth as he uttered another strangulated moan, but then jerked himself away from me and pulled out of my reach.

I stood before him, at a loss. "What . . . "

Ashby chuckled. "That, *Minha Amada*, was sublime." In a sudden burst of speed, he closed the space between us, swept me into his arms and turned to stride towards the bed. "*Too* sublime. If I allowed you to continue any further, I would not be able to stop. You would have me unmanned within a few short moments, and that doesn't factor well into my plans."

He lowered me onto the bed, then sat next to me, the stuffed mattress dipping under his weight. He looked me over from head to toe, his dark eyes devouring every detail of my body. I wondered what he saw, how I measured up to all the other women he'd been with. I became embarrassed again as every one of my flaws seemed to become larger than life under his scrutiny, and I flushed deeply.

"You are blushing," he murmured, tracing his finger lightly down my arm. "All over your body. I had always wondered . . ."

"Always wondered what?" I demanded, cursing Fate for making me a redhead.

"Nothing." He brushed his finger in a whisper-light touch from the point between my breasts down to my navel. "Open your legs for me."

"*What?*"

His eyes, half closed so that his lashes tangled appealingly in their corners, looked like nebulous pools of seduction in the dim firelight, and he curved his beautiful mouth into that devastating smile responsible for so many broken wedding vows. When he spoke, his voice resembled a roughened purr. "Open your legs for me, *Minha Amada.*"

I tried to be angry with him for using his tricks on me, but it was no use. The only thing I could do while he looked at me that way was to slowly move my hand across the bed for the sheet. His smile grew to something close to a grin as he bent to kiss me, his hand arresting mine in its quest and bringing it up over my head. His kiss became hot and languid, his tongue plunging through my parted lips as he brought my other hand up and pinned my wrists together. Then, transferring his hold on me to just one hand, he dropped the other between my knees.

He tore his lips from mine, and nuzzled the tender spot just where neck meets shoulder. "Open your legs."

I parted my knees, and he smiled in approval as he began slowly tracing his fingers up and down my inner thigh, teasing me by coming ever closer to the place my body yearned for him to touch. Meanwhile, his lips had moved down to my breast, and as he gently pulled one nipple into his mouth, I arched against him and struggled against his hand restraining my wrists. He chuckled again, holding me easily as he brought his lips back up to brush over my mouth, then traced their way leisurely to my ear.

"Open your legs wider *Minha Amada*," he whispered as he slid his hand up to the hot crease of my inner thigh. I complied immediately, and he plunged his tongue into my mouth as he slid two fingers through the folds of my tender flesh. But the moment he touched me, another groan tore loose from him. In a swift movement, he was suddenly on top of me, his body forcing my knees wider apart. I spread my legs to accommodate his hips, knowing I had him in my power.

But he jerked away, just as he had earlier. He shook his head as a corner of his mouth kicked up, his smile wicked and boyish at the same time. "Not yet, *Minha Amada*."

I sighed, then tested his grip on my wrists again. "What does that mean?"

"What?" His voice had turned meditative as he released my wrists and lowered his head to move his lips down the channel between my breasts.

"*Minha Amada?*"

"Hmmm." He continued down the length of my body to lightly burn a trail across the smooth plain of my belly with his tongue. Then he shifted his body down to my hips, kissing each protruding angle while his hands stroked my thighs. He lifted one leg and kissed the inside of my knee, sending another hot flush across my body as his mouth moved down my inner thigh.

"Well?" I panted, desperately fighting the obscene compulsion to thrust my pelvis into his face. "What does it mean?"

He paused to glance up at me, a thick lock of hair tumbled over his brow. I hadn't noticed when he'd pulled his hair loose. His soft black tresses, shining with unexpected sparks of copper in the dim firelight, tumbled down into my tight cinnamon curls as he rested his cheek against my inner thigh. "My Beloved," he said.

"In Portueg—"

But my question was cut-off with a gasp. With no warning, Ashby dropped his head and pressed his mouth down between my legs, where he delivered a long, paralyzing stroke with his tongue along my opening.

At first I did nothing, stunned into obedience by the wickedly soft and wet sensation of his tongue. But when he moved his head down to do it again, I snapped out of my stupor.

"No!" I squeaked as my thighs convulsed. "Ashby, what are you doing?"

But he'd been expecting this reaction, and he pinned my hips easily to the bed. I moaned as I covered my face in mortification. But he was devilishly clever with his tongue, and I was soon forced to admit that the sensation of him tonguing me so leisurely, so comprehensively, was the most intense pleasure I had ever experienced.

My legs relaxed, and I felt myself opening to him, blooming under his mouth like the soft petals of a very wanton flower. I lowered my arms, forgetting everything but the feel of Ashby's mouth. I looked down at him, at the sight of his dark head pressed between my thighs, and found him watching me with those sultry eyes.

He dragged his tongue up to my pleasure point and sucked it into his mouth, kneading me with his tongue in a slow, pulsing rhythm that I soon matched with my hips. A low, shuddering moan escaped my lips and I ran a hand through his hair, grabbing a handful of it as my hips moved from gentle pulses to something harder and more demanding. I began thrashing around on the bed, whimpering and begging as his strokes became firmer and faster.

At the median where the spectrums of pleasure and pain overlap, an exquisite tension began to build and radiate from that epicenter under Ashby's tongue. My legs began to tremble and I cried out as I bucked against him, burning in a bliss unlike anything I had ever felt before. I lay there panting on the bed, a fine mist of sweat covering my skin, my body suddenly loose and pliant.

Ashby rested his chin on my hip, his sinful mouth curved into a smug smile. I had once thought that mouth a gateway to ruin, and I laughed now in my panting delirium as I realized just how close to the truth I had been.

"What's so amusing?" he demanded, calling my attention back to him with a gentle nip on my inner thigh.

I shook my head. "Nothing. But what was *that?*"

"*That*, milady, was your clit," he answered, his tone matter-of-fact. "I thought it time the two of you became better acquainted."

"My clit?"

"Mmmm-Hmmm."

"Oh . . ."

He closed his eyes and rubbed his cheek against my inner thigh in a leonine gesture. "You sound uncertain."

"I just thought it was called something else."

"Hmmm, I think I know the source of the confusion," he replied. Then he dropped his head down for another quick lick along my opening, "*That* is your quim. *This*," my hips bucked involuntarily as he flicked his tongue lightly over my pleasure point, "is your clitoris, or 'clit' for short. It's a tragedy you had to wait for me to introduce you, since you really ought to be intimately acquainted by now."

"Oh, we've met before," I assured him. "I just didn't know it had a name. You've been very educational."

"Mmmm. I aim to please." He closed his eyes and returned to nuzzling his cheek against my inner thigh.

I watched him, wondering just how many others had seen him like this. But immediately I chased those thoughts out of my head. For now, at this very moment, he was mine and mine alone.

When he opened his eyes again, I saw the warmth of his amusement had given way to something darker and more sensual. He prowled back up my body on his hands and knees, hooking one arm under my knee and drawing it up towards my shoulder until we were once again face to face.

He kissed me, plunging his tongue deep into my mouth as he slid his cock smoothly into my feverish body. I cried out against him, his sudden penetration sending sharp echoes of my climax throughout my body. Then he stilled, eyes shut tightly and frowning in concentration as he kept his passion in check. He seemed much larger than I remembered, pushing up firmly against my barrier, this position with my knee pulled up leaving me feeling vulnerable and exposed as he held me pinned to the bed.

But I kept very still, sensing instinctively that this was a critical moment for him. And it was a moment of revelation for me, since I now suspected that my body moved his just as profoundly as his moved mine.

Soon his shoulders relaxed and his lips curved once more into a little smile as he opened his eyes. My body relaxed into him, and he kissed me again as he began moving his hips back and forth in a slow, steady rhythm.

He pulled his lips away from mine and drew back a little so he could watch me, and I no longer felt so vulnerable. I liked having him on top of me. It felt very natural, as though my body had been designed to wrap around his.

I reached up to brush the scar on his upper lip with my thumb, and he closed his eyes and leaned into my touch. His rhythm began to gain momentum, his pulses becoming a bit longer and stronger. He bent his head down to kiss me again, then pulled me to his chest and rolled us both over until I found myself suddenly on top.

We paused a moment as I caught my bearings. I had known

that women could make love on top, and I'd even been a bit curious about it, but now that I found myself in the position to explore its possibilities, I did not like it at all. This couldn't possibly work, the angle of his penetration was too deep, and I struggled to pull away from him.

"Relax, *Minha Amada*," he murmured, his hooded gaze reassuring as his hands held firmly to my hips. "Relax and let your body take me."

He released my hips and began stroking my body from the indent of my waist down to the tops of my thighs. I closed my eyes and released the breath I had not realized I'd been holding. My body began to feel more pliant and I unclenched the muscles of my abdomen, settling down onto his hips as the last of my tension eased out of me. The fullness inside of me that had felt so much like an unwanted invasion just moments before, now felt wholly sublime. Tentatively, I began moving my hips back and forth and was instantly rewarded by a low groan of pleasure from him. I looked down at him beneath me, his body stretched out with his muscular arms thrown up over his head, his hair strewn wildly across the pillow.

"My God, you are beautiful, Ashby," I whispered.

This made him smile. "As are you, *Minha Amada*. Take down your hair."

Reaching up, I began to pull out the pins. Slowly my curls unraveled, still damp from the rain, tumbling over my shoulders and breasts to hang in wild curlicues down to my waist. Ashby caught a lock in his fingers, pulled it down gently to straighten it, then released it to bounce back up into a curl. I gathered it all in my hands and piled it up on top of my head as I closed my eyes and leaned my head back.

I smiled when I heard him catch his breath.

His hands cupped my breasts, then slid down to my waist before finally coming to a rest back on my hips as I continued to rock back and forth. Gradually my hips increased their tempo, the pulses becoming stronger and faster. I leaned forward, planting my hands on his shoulders for leverage as I felt the crescendo beginning to build.

Suddenly he pulled me roughly down to his chest and rolled us over again and with a few quick thrusts brought me to the agonizing moment just before another climax. Once more my pleasure exploded inside of me, shattering my senses as waves of heat scorched out to my fingers and toes like ripples of fire.

My muscles contracted around him as he cried out, shuddering within me, against me, again, and again. His arms gave out and he collapsed on top of me, his heart hammering against mine.

"*Amo-te*," he said, burying his face into my neck. "*Sempre, amo-te, minha amada.*"

I did not understand the words, but the reverence in his voice was clear enough. I closed my eyes and brought my hand up to stroke the back of his neck.

"I know, Ashby."

CHAPTER 24

I AWOKE SOME TIME LATER to find myself alone on the bed, wrapped tightly in the blanket I had been wearing earlier. With a gasp, I sat upright and scanned the room for Ashby, then breathed easier when I saw him pacing in front of the fire with his own blanket wrapped around his hips. He glanced up, hearing my audible sigh of relief, and the deep frown etched into his features melted into a smile.

"I thought you'd left me," I admitted a little sheepishly.

"*Left* you?" He sauntered over to the bed, the flow of his movements reminding me more than ever of a tom cat. "Are you in the habit of being abandoned by your suitors?"

"I am not in the habit of having suitors," I said. "Nor am I in the habit of trysting. I confess I am ignorant of the proper etiquette."

One corner of his mouth twitched as he offered me his hand. "You would have found yourself in a predicament had I left you here."

I took a seat in my abandoned chair in front of the fireplace. Outside I could hear that the violence of the storm had ebbed to just a light patter of rain on the windows.

"Papa is restless," I said. "I think we will be leaving here soon."

"I must soon leave here myself," he replied. "I have business I must attend to, and I have been away from Northumberland for too long."

We sat for a while in silence. There were so many things I wanted to say, so many things I wanted to ask him, but I was afraid I already knew the answers. I glanced at him out of the corner of my eye and saw that his scowl had returned as he gazed into the fire.

"Ashby?"

"Yes, *Minha Amada*?"

I hesitated a moment, then looked down. Through my lashes, I could see him waiting patiently while I struggled with my courage. He loved me, and I loved him. But still, nothing had changed in our situation. I had to ask him; I'd spent much of the night before trying to figure out just how to do it. Finally, I took a deep breath and squared my shoulders.

"If your criminal operations eventually negate your need to marry an heiress, will you still marry Lady Violet in ten years?"

Ashby swore under his breath. He rose from his seat suddenly, and set to pacing in front of the fire. I could tell he was angry.

I watched him, the cold knot of despair I'd been battling since his confession in the *cellarium* settling into my stomach. "Ashby," I finally said, "forget it. I am sorry I asked you."

He stopped abruptly, his hands on his hips, his head tilted back as though he were staring at the ceiling. "I must provide an heir, Elina. I cannot allow my burden to fall to Chrysander. My lands are not held in entail, so it matters not whether the child is a boy or a girl. But it must be legitimate, so I must marry."

I clasped my hands tightly in my lap, focusing on their discomfort as I crushed my fingers till my knuckles turned white.

"I must marry, Elina," he repeated. "And you will not marry again. And you cannot even be my mistress, because you live now in your father's house, under his protection. Perhaps if you'd stayed at Lord Delemere's house, the situation might have been different—"

"But what if things were different," I interrupted. "What if I changed my position?"

He looked at me sharply, his expression guarded. "What do you mean?"

"What if I changed my mind?" The words came slowly and deliberately, as though some part of me hesitated, waiting for my rationality to catch up and halt my progress before my irrational heart took matters beyond the point of no return.

"About what?" His eyes narrowed, his focus intent upon my face.

"Marriage," I said.

"Marriage?" he repeated slowly, a strange look flickering through his eyes. "Marriage to *me*?"

I nodded. My rationality still hadn't caught up with me.

"You mean you would consider remarrying?"

"Only if I married you." I watched his face, but he gave nothing away, keeping his features carefully controlled. I felt a pang in my heart as I reminded myself that this was a man whose relationships with women were characterized generally by artifice and betrayal.

Wordlessly, Ashby moved over to where our clothes lay out to dry on a nearby table. He reached for his breeches, and for a horrifying moment I thought he was going to dress and abandon me without an answer. But instead he pulled something out of his pocket, too small for me to see what it was. He returned then, and knelt before me with the dignity of generations of Harcourts resting easily on his shoulders, though he wore only an old blanket knotted loosely around his hips.

"We were only children when first we met," he said, his eyes suddenly clouded with memory. "Though I know you do not remember it. I wouldn't either, except that when I saw you again at your presentation at Court the Season of your eighteenth birthday, I saw in you so much of the girl who had been my first love ten summers before. Right then, I fell in love with you all over again. But my father was systematically destroying my inheritance, and although the title I would soon inherit was an ancient one, it was disgraced. I was just another boorish brute from the north, with no wealth, no political connections, no favor at Court, and no chance of ever aspiring to the station of a daughter of the great Percival Brinkley. But I was young, and I still believed in the miraculous power of love, so I began carrying this around with me, just in case. Later, when I grew into manhood and came to a greater understanding of the jaded ways of the world, I carried it to remind me always of you, and of my own innocence, once upon a time."

He paused then to show me what he held concealed in his hand: a ring, very old but still beautiful with two polished sapphires set vertically in a rectangular setting of gold. He handed it to me, and I ran my finger over the smooth stones, then noticed tiny hinges connecting the setting to the gold band. Rolling it over, I saw that the other side featured a raised enamel black unicorn rampant with the words *Amour et Honneur Éternels* lettered around it in gold.

"Love and Honor Everlasting," I murmured.

He nodded. "This ring has been in my family for generations. It is the only piece of jewelry my father did not sell. When my mother died, her family sent this to me and I hid it from him, treasuring it as my only remembrance of her. I always knew that one day I would give it to the woman I would marry, just as generations of Harcourts had done before me, and when I saw the red-haired daughter of Lord Hertford, I began to carry it with me. It was a fool's wish."

I rotated the ring to show the sapphires again, and once more ran my finger over the smooth stones, polishing them absently with my finger just as so many Harcourt ladies must have done before me.

"What are you thinking?" he asked softly.

I kept my eyes focused on the ring, not daring to look up just yet. "I am thinking that I remember you. It was at the Groffhurst estate in Cheshire—Plumley Green was it?"

"In the spring."

"We were visiting my mother's family," I continued. "You were there with your mother."

"It was the holiday I told you about—when she took me out of the boarding school."

"We used to play in the orchard, and you kissed me under the big cherry tree in the center." I touched my fingers lightly to my lips. "It was my very first kiss, with all the pink blossoms falling down around us."

"It was my first kiss, too," he said, reaching up to brush a wayward curl away from my face. "It was your hair that first ensnared me, such a vibrant color of red I had never seen before. And you had freckles then, though now they are all but disappeared."

I sighed. "And then I married a lunatic."

"You did," he said. "Though his lunacy was not widely known in those days. But I knew."

"Gabrielle said you hated William."

He nodded, turning his face away. "He was known amongst our circle for his violent ways with women. When you married him . . . it was the darkest day of my life."

"Ashby," I said, "please do get up—your poor knees must be aching terribly by now."

He shook his head. "No. Though this is not at all the way I imagined I would do this, I must do it correctly." He captured my hand and raised it to his lips, then shifted his position as he brought one knee up before him while straightening his back and squaring shoulders. When he spoke, his voice was solemn. "Elinamifia Brinkley, will you honor me by becoming my wife?"

The enormity of the situation bore down upon me, and I felt a wave of panic.

Could I really do this again? Could I place my faith in another man? And this time, I could not blame my naiveté if things should go wrong. I *knew* the man kneeling before me now; I *knew* his reputation and the failings of his family. I could very easily find myself forsaken up in the wilds of Northumberland with only my bitterness for company. Or, worse yet, I could find myself witnessing his execution, listening to his final words on the scaffold as a crowd of thousands howled for his aristocratic blood.

"It won't happen," he promised softly. "Whatever it is you are thinking, it will not happen. I swear to you, on my life, that I love you and will continue to worship you for the rest of my life. I will make my vows to you, and I will never break them. You will have me," he grinned suddenly, "all of me, for better and for worse, forever."

"But what if you die?" I pressed. "What if you are caught? I could not bear to have you taken from me in that way, Ashby. I could not bear to watch, nor could I bear for you to meet with that cruel fate alone. I am not strong enough."

"You are strong enough," he said, "But please believe me when I tell you that you do not have to worry about me on that account. I will not be caught."

I opened my mouth to protest, but he held his hand up for silence.

"I am reckless, I know," he said. "But I am not without my resources. I think it best that you do not know too much about my various activities, but if anything should happen that might compromise me, I would simply abscond to my family estate in Portugal while I put certain plans into motion that I have ready should I need them. It would be your choice, of course, whether you chose to come with me or not."

"What are your plans?" I asked, frowning. "I thought you said you don't have any political connections?"

He shook his head, a little smile playing at the corners of his mouth. "I will tell you, but only after we are married. For now, suffice it to say that I have certain skills and connections that our government shall find far too useful, especially now that we are about to embark on another war with France, for them to do away with me at the end of a hang-man's noose."

"But you won't tell me—"

"—until after we are married," he finished firmly. "For now, you just need to know that I will not make you a widow again. I swear it."

"And what if you are thrown from your horse? Or you are shot again on the road? Or if you contract the plague? Or the sweating sickness?"

"I never fall from my horse," he replied. "And we Northumbrians have far too vigorous constitutions for us to be susceptible to sickness. What you should be worried about is how on earth I'm going to keep you warm up there! It's unbelievably cold in the winter!"

"But too cold for the plague."

"Far too cold for the plague."

"And what about the Black Unicorn?"

His smile faltered. He looked at me a moment, his eyes serious. "I will retire the Black Unicorn, if you will become my wife."

"You swear it?"

"I swear it."

"Then I guess you leave me no choice. But you must ask me again," I added.

Ashby's mouth curved slowly into a smile that suddenly

reminded me of the boy I had almost forgotten, standing under the cherry tree.

"Elina," he said. "Marry me."

"Yes, Ashby. I will."

CHAPTER 25

THE TWO OF US arrived back at the main house just as everyone was dressing for dinner, and in time for Ashby to begin preparations for his immediate departure.

He had a shipment of Portuguese rum arriving, and he needed to be present for its unloading and transfer. Tonight, he explained, would be ideal for such activities since the heavy cloud cover would eclipse the moon and stars, thus ensuring total darkness, and the rain would keep most of the Excise men indoors next to their fires.

"But what about . . . " I demanded as we stood in the corridor outside our rooms.

Ashby shook his head firmly. "Retired. Just as I promised. Besides," he continued with a sly smile, "who on earth would I rob? No one in their right mind will be on the roads tonight unless they, like me, are up to no good. And those sorts are usually best left alone."

Dinner proved to be a dull affair. The Harcourt heirloom I now wore on my right ring finger—Ashby had requested we keep our engagement secret until he could seek an audience with Papa—absorbed most of my attention. The rest of the party had spent a long day in the private parlor of the tavern, where they took refuge after the morning service until the worst of the storm had passed. Then they'd spent a harrowing four hours on the muddy road back to the house, arriving wet, bedraggled, and exhausted only moments before we had. It was a wonder any of them showed up for dinner.

Things proved a little livelier after dinner. Sophie and I sat in our customary places on the giltwood couch in front of the fire, fixing the coffee and tea. Phosey sat in her favorite chair across from us, swinging her feet back and forth as she stared into the fire.

Sophie finished with the coffee and poured me a cup. Then, setting it down in front of me, she took hold of my right hand. She ran her finger over the Harcourt sapphires, favoring me with a pointed look. I read the question in her eyes, and I nodded with a shy smile. Sophie beamed at me as she squeezed my hand.

"*Lord Ashenhurst?*" she mouthed.

I nodded.

"*Tell me everything!*"

I nodded, feeling the color creep into my cheeks.

Sophie's smile grew wider. She abruptly leaned forward so that our foreheads were almost touching as we huddled close. "*Everything!*" she whispered, mouthing the word slowly, emphasizing each syllable.

"Er, I am sorry to interrupt, ladies," interjected a jovial voice, "but I don't suppose I could trouble one of you for a spot of that coffee?" Looking up, we found Lord Beverley taking a seat across from us in the chair next to Phosey's, watching us with a look of masculine condescension.

"Of course, Lord Beverley," I said, giving Sophie's hand a final squeeze. "And you still take it black, sir?"

He broke into a cheerful smile. "Indeed I do, milady. You have an excellent memory. Now," he continued, taking the cup and saucer from me, "I don't suppose you ladies would like to tell me what you were just giggling over?"

"Certainly not, sir!" Sophie exclaimed in mock consternation. "You must leave us ladies with our secrets!"

"And our gossip!" I added gravely.

Lord Beverley chuckled, the few lines on his tanned face crinkling charmingly. "Ladies and their secrets and gossip. I dare say, most of it must be about how you members of the fairer sex can ensnare our hearts and so bend us to your gentle will." He glanced over my shoulder as he said this, and from the look of tenderness I saw in his eyes, I knew he looked to Dorothea. Poor fool.

"Though I do wonder," he said softly, almost to himself, "why it is you ladies do not share your secrets and gossip more with Lady Dorothea. I notice that the young lady seems to spend a great deal of her time isolated from other members of your gentle sex."

Sophie cleared her throat, flashing me a stricken look as she quickly guided the conversation away from Lord Beverley's unpleasant intended. "Do tell us, Lord Beverley, have you heard any more news of the Black Unicorn? Are you any closer to figuring out the elusive figure's true identity?"

Unfortunately, the effect of Sophie's words on me was immediate. I nearly spit out the mouthful of coffee I had been about to swallow, and in my efforts to thwart this natural response, I managed instead to swallow it down the wrong passage.

"Yes," Lord Beverley replied as he frowned at me, "we have several leads. But my dear Lady Delemere, are you all right?"

"Yes, Lord Beverley," I assured him between choking spasms. "Just inhaled a little coffee." I dabbed my tearing eyes with a handkerchief as he continued to watch me doubtfully. "I do assure you, I am fine. But really you must tell us, what of these new leads?"

"Well," he said, watching me as though I might suddenly keel over, "as I said, we have several leads. Though in my mind, there is only one man who fits the bill."

"Indeed?" Sophie topped off his coffee. "And can you tell us his name?"

"Alas, no," he replied, "not yet. Though I can tell you," he lowered his voice as he leaned forward, "that your insight, Lady Delemere, into that tricky devil's origins—namely that he might in fact be a member of our own privileged class—has proven invaluable! In fact, dear lady, I confess that I owe you something of an apology. I am rather ashamed to admit that I initially dismissed your theory as romantic fancy. But if it were not for you, we might never have considered our prime suspect in the first place! It seems you will have the satisfaction of seeing the man who terrorized you and your family brought to justice very soon!"

"Is that so?" I smiled weakly at him, reaching for my coffee.

"And what of this justice?" Sophie asked. "Surely the man's aristocratic birth shall afford him some clemency, will it not? A royal pardon, perhaps? If the man agrees to make financial restitution to his victims?"

"Oh, no," Lord Beverley assured us. "There shall be no clemency in this case. Perhaps there would be if the man had only committed robberies, but unfortunately he is also a murderer. And not even the Prince of Wales could get away with murder. There will be no royal pardon."

"M-murder?" I stammered. "But whom is it he is supposed to have murdered?"

"Two, perhaps three, of his former accomplices. Members of the so-called Northern Gang. We have the rest of the gang in custody, and they have given testimony. Seems that one of the murdered men was their leader."

Sophie's mouth tightened at the mention of Red Jack and his gang.

"But those men were the very worst sort of brutes imaginable. Surely the Black Unicorn has done a public service ridding the world of them!" I said.

Lord Beverley shrugged. "Perhaps. But murder is murder,

and King George does not pardon murderers. The Black Unicorn will hang for his crimes. You have my word."

"Then you must know his true identity for certain," Sophie pressed, "if you've got his accomplices to testify against him."

"*I* am certain, yes." Lord Beverley paused to take a sip of his coffee, "But unfortunately the members of the Northern Gang are not. You see, the fellow was clever and never divulged his true identity to them—they do not even know what he looks like, and he never spoke to them directly. All communication was either written, since apparently the gang's leader—"

"Red Jack," Sophie supplied quietly.

"Er, yes. Red Jack," Lord Beverley agreed, "I keep forgetting that you ladies have met these repulsive individuals. Red Jack, apparently, could read. The Black Unicorn also communicated through middle men, though we have not been able to find any of them."

I felt a tiny glimmer of hope. "So you do not know then. Not for certain."

"Oh, I am certain," Lord Beverley assured me. "I have the fellow under constant surveillance. He will slip up sooner or later, and my men will be there to catch him in the act!"

"So he must still be in Yorkshire then," Sophie said.

"Oh, yes," Lord Beverley declared, "he is still in Yorkshire. And he is closer than you might think!"

I returned my coffee cup to its saucer on the table. "You are very clever, Lord Beverley," I said, forcing out the words. "I have no doubt that you shall catch your man."

"You are too kind, Lady Delemere," the gentleman answered. "And correct. Now," he continued, "if you ladies will excuse me, Lady Dorothea has consented to play and sing for us this evening, and I think she is about to begin."

CHAPTER 26

"A PLAGUE ON LORD BEVERLEY!" I seethed as I marched up and down my bedroom *en chemisier*. "Devil hang that confounded man! May the earth open up and swallow him whole!"

"Elina." Sophie's calm voice held the note of long-suffering patience one would expect of a sane person trying to converse with a lunatic. From her perch on the edge of my bed, she'd been watching me rant now for ten minutes. "Are you going to tell me what is wrong, or are you just going to curse poor Lord Beverley into oblivion?"

"*Poor* Lord Beverley?" I halted my progress to turn on her. "You are *defending* that wretched man? How can you *defend* him, Sophie? Tell me *that*!"

"I can defend him," she said, "because I do not yet know what he has done. Are you going to tell me? Or shall I leave you to your ranting?"

I resumed my marching, ignoring the coolness of the floor-boards on my bare feet. Sophie waited patiently while I made up my mind. Finally, I spun on my heel and stalked over to where she sat.

"You must swear that you will tell *no one* what I am about to tell you!" I said, pointing my finger into her face. "*No one!* Not even Thad! *Do you swear!*"

Her eyes narrowed, and when she spoke, it was through gritted teeth. "I will swear, but only after you've taken your bloody finger out of my face!"

I stood there a moment, shocked. Sophie never cursed. I dropped my hand limply to my side.

"I am sorry," I said.

"I accept your apology," she replied. "And I swear. Now tell me."

I took a seat next to her, and scooted back until my feet dangled in front of me. "It is about Ashby," I said carefully. "About . . ." I paused, suddenly at a loss for words. I thought back to my conversation with him in the abbey's *cellarium*. "About his 'recent unorthodox activities,'" I finished, quoting his words.

She nodded curtly. "I see. Then I must first make a confession. If you are about to tell me that Lord Ashenhurst is the Black Unicorn, I already know."

"*What!*" I surged back to my feet. "*How?* Does *everyone* know?"

"If you do not keep your voice down," Sophie snapped, "then everyone soon shall know. Please calm down and have a seat." She patted the bed where I'd just been sitting.

"Very well," I grumbled as I climbed back onto the bed. "How long have you known?"

"Since our second night here."

"*What!?!*"

"Elina," she said warningly.

"Right. Sorry." I stood, padded over to the vanity and took a seat so that I faced her. "How is it you learned of this on the second day?" I asked in as reasonable a tone as I could manage. "Did *he* tell you?"

"Yes and no—"

"And what the bloody hell is that supposed to mean?" I demanded.

"If you will let me finish, Elina, I will tell you!" she replied, her porcelain complexion flushing angrily.

I knew better than to push Sophie too far, so I did my best to sound contrite. "Sorry. Please continue."

She nodded. "As you wish. I'd slept only very little that night. When you'd come to check on me after dinner, I did my best to put on a brave face and convince you that I'd recovered from my ordeal in Lincolnshire. I did not want you to worry. I also felt that if you all thought me recovered, you would stop hovering around me, trying to get me to speak of things you could never understand. Every time I saw the worry in your eyes, it reminded me of things I was trying my best to forget.

"Once you'd left me, Elina, I retired to bed. But every time I closed my eyes, I could see that beast's leering face in front of me, and feel his rough hands all over me as he pinned me to the ground. Just before dawn, I found myself wide awake and so decided to come down for an early breakfast in solitude. Unfortunately, I found that the Guns were all in the breakfast parlor when I arrived, preparing for their day's activities. The last thing in the world I wanted was to be alone in a room full of men, so I stole out to the gardens to watch the sunrise and wait for the gentlemen to vacate the house.

"It was dark outside, but peaceful and quiet. A light mist still covered the ground, muffling my steps as I made my way to the pleasure garden, thinking it the most likely place to find a secluded bench tucked away in a corner. But when I turned the corner around the boxwood hedge, I found to my great dismay that I was not alone. The gentleman did not see me at first, lost in his own meditations.

"I discerned from his dress that he was one of the Guns, and I wondered irritably what he was doing away from all his jovial companions. Still, good manners prevailed, and I cleared my throat quietly to alert him to my presence. When he saw me, I thought he did a double take, though I couldn't see his features clearly.

"He quickly rose to his feet as I reluctantly approached him, and he introduced himself at once as Ashby Harcourt, Lord Ashenhurst. Then he offered me his seat and begged me for a moment or two of private conversation.

"I remembered him from the Foreign Secretary's Ball, and was well aware of his reputation with women. So naturally, I found myself in a hurry to remove myself from his presence at once. But he repeated his request, pleading with me to stay. I found something so compelling about the look in his eyes, I couldn't find it in my heart to turn away from him."

"You've always been too good, Sophie," I murmured.

"Indeed. But he seemed so strangely pathetic. He looked, in point of fact, exactly how I felt. Haunted. And it was clear from the shadowy circles beneath his eyes, he had not slept any more than I had.

"Lord Ashenhurst, with a gentleness I found rather at odds with his rakish reputation, asked me about the robbery. And, much to my surprise, I found myself obliging him with my tale. I began to weep, the first tears I'd shed since the robbery. I also found myself detailing for this man everything down to the most intimate indignities. I relived every terrible moment, from the rough feel of Buford's hands upon my breasts, to the way he drove my legs painfully apart with his knees and the foul stench of his breath as he muttered filthy things into my face. But as I recounted every horrible detail to this stranger pacing agitatedly before me, I realized that I was cleansing my soul of the whole ordeal.

"After I'd finished, Lord Ashenhurst stood by quietly as I cried. The birds began to twitter as dawn broke, and slowly my sobs subsided into sniffles and hiccups. Lord Ashenhurst, always maintaining a respectful distance, handed me his hand-kerchief, which I accepted gratefully and blew my nose. Then he said the strangest thing to me, his expression deadly earnest. 'Lady Sophronia, I am sorry for everything you were forced to endure—sorrier, in fact, than you can ever understand. But please know that none of those brutes shall ever harm you, or any other woman, ever again. I swear it to you upon everything I hold dear. You have my word of honor.'

"It was such a bizarre thing for a stranger to say to me, and even more bizarre was the fact that I instinctively knew it to be true. I suddenly knew, as positively as I knew my own name, that this liber-tine had been the man who killed Buford before he could complete his rape. This man, Ashby Harcourt, was the Black Unicorn."

When Sophie finished her tale, neither of us spoke for a little while. As the minutes ticked by in silence, I sat torn between my powerful feelings of pride and love for Ashby, and the hurt I felt towards Sophie for keeping this from me. She could see that I had been falling in love with him, and still she'd said nothing.

"Why?" I finally asked. "Why didn't you tell me?"

She sighed and spread her hands out before her. "Lord Ash-enhurst's secret wasn't mine to tell. At first I was afraid of what you might do with such information, for I knew you had ven-geance in your heart. But then when I saw the strength of his love for you, I knew that he would tell you in his own time. And if he didn't, I knew that my clever sister would figure it out on her own anyway."

She smiled at me tentatively when she said this last bit. I couldn't help but smile back at her.

"Do you love him?" she asked.

"I will marry him," I said. "But first I must save him. I'll be damned if I'm going to allow Lord Beverley to send Ashby to the gallows."

Sophie frowned. "Do you really think he is in danger? We're not even sure it was Lord Ashenhurst that Lord Beverley was speaking of this evening. It seems rather odd to me that he would be so candid about a man with whom we have been living and socializing for the past several weeks. And even if he were, surely Lord Ashenhurst is clever enough to know he's suspected and therefore take counter-measures."

I shook my head. "I cannot risk it. I must assume that Lord Beverley does suspect Ashby; to do otherwise would be folly. And while Ashby certainly is clever, he is also reckless. *And* he does not know that the Black Unicorn will be tried for murder. He thinks he will receive clemency if he is caught, and that belief might make him less careful than he would be otherwise. I must find a way to warn him."

"But how on earth do you propose to do that?" Sophie exclaimed. "We do not even know where he is, do we?"

"He's somewhere near the coast," I said. "That is all I know. He's also a smuggler," I added in response to her quizzical look.

"Well, that could be just about anywhere, Elina," she pointed out. "Do we even know if he's still in Yorkshire?"

"I do not know. But I think I know someone who will. Ashby did not take his valet with him, and I'll wager that evil little man knows exactly where to find him."

Sophie looked dubious.

"He's a terrible valet," I explained. "Totally inept at even the most basic requirements of a manservant. I figure Ashby keeps him in his employ for other reasons, such as skillfully removing pistol balls from his employer's arm."

Sophie nodded, immediately catching on. "And perhaps serving as the middleman Lord Beverley was talking about."

I nodded, pleased to see her thoughts ran alongside mine on the matter. "But I cannot speak to Simon tonight without raising suspicion. As much as I hate to do it, I will have to wait until morning. Then I can have Edith summon him on some pretext."

"You should take a bath," Sophie suggested. "Edith will need help carrying the water cans up the stairs."

"Perfect!" I exclaimed. "Tomorrow I shall have a bath first thing. I'll write the letter out tonight, give it to Simon in the morning, then send him on his way while Lord Beverley and the rest of the guns are out on the moors!"

"Perfect only if this rain stops," Sophie pointed out. "Otherwise we'll have the guns at home with us, and Simon might have some difficulty in getting away unobserved."

"Hmmm." I watched the rain slide down my darkened window. "But this is August, and though it may be the county's wettest August within living memory, the damned rain has to stop sometime. God willing it will be tomorrow."

"Yes," Sophie agreed. "God willing."

CHAPTER 27

GOD WILLED MORE RAIN the following day. But Simon was crafty, and the little fellow made good his escape from the house without anyone save the stable boys the wiser.

Meanwhile, I bathed in Lady Rydale's hip-bath, soaping myself mechanically through my sodden flannel chemise as I did my best to calm my frayed nerves. I had not slept much the previous night, writing draft after draft of the missive I would send with Simon. I found it a tricky line to walk, trying to be cryptic enough in case my letter disastrously fell into the wrong hands, while simultaneously impressing upon Ashby the gravity of the situation.

After I'd bathed and dressed, I dismissed Edith to find some footmen to help her dispose of the bathwater. Once she'd closed the door behind her, I sighed in relief as I stared out the window into the blustery cold. The rest of the party would undoubtedly be in the library today, reading and playing cards. But I had no taste for company. At first I thought of taking refuge in the quiet hush of the chapel, but soon realized that wouldn't do at all. Sitting all day, alone and in the dark where things with Ashby had changed forever, was not a good idea. No, I needed a neutral place, and that narrowed my options.

≈

The gallery was deserted. I moved over to a window seat near the fire crackling in the hearth, and arranged myself comfortably on the cushions. I could feel the cold radiating off the window's thick glass, and congratulated myself on my decision to stay away from the conservatory. As I sat a moment, watching the rain pouring steadily outside, I wondered where Ashby was just then, and hoped that whatever he was doing, he was safe and indoors. I heaved a heavy sigh, and turned my attention to the book lying closed on my lap.

"You sound as though you carry the weight of the world on your shoulders, Elina," came a soft voice very close behind me. With a yelp, I leapt up and whirled around to face the intruder.

"Tristan!" I gasped when I caught sight of his somber face.

"I apologize for startling you, but I did announce myself. Twice."

"I am not in the mood for company, Tristan."

"So I perceive," he replied dryly. "But I have a matter of very great importance that I must discuss with you."

"Now?"

"I cannot in good conscience allow this to wait."

"Very well. Pray come take a seat with me." I kept my tone casual, but as he settled down on the cushions opposite mine, my nerves got the better of me.

"Well, come on, man," I said, "out with it then!"

"I am trying to find the gentlest way to break this to you," he said, frowning as he gazed out the window into the rain. "But I think it best if I just tell you."

Tristan turned to look at me then, his opalescent eyes softened with compassion.

"What is it?" I whispered, a stab of fear knifing through my heart. "Papa?"

He shook his head. "I am afraid this news has only to do with you."

My shoulders relaxed. Not Papa.

"I have just this morning received a letter from a client of mine in the Doctor's Commons in London," he continued. "It seems that your former step-son, the new Earl of Delemere, is challenging your jointure in the ecclesiastical courts. He is expected to win, Elina."

I stared at him, not comprehending.

"It's true," Tristan said grimly. "I've sent word back by courier for verification, but my man is extremely reliable."

"But . . . but that is not possible," I said. "My jointure was part of my marriage contract."

"He is seeking to dissolve your marriage. If he succeeds, everything pertaining to your contract will be null and void."

"But he cannot do that!" I said stupidly. "How can he do that, Tristan? I was married to his father for seven years!"

In a flash, the compassion in Tristan's eyes burned away to reveal something darker. His massive hands balled up into fists, the skin straining over his white knuckles.

"What is it?" I whispered. "What has Sebastian done?"

Tristan tore his eyes away from mine, transferring his baleful glare to the miserable elements outside. "That *bastard*," he growled, "has claimed to have had an adulterous affair with you that commenced on the night of his fourteenth birthday. And he has claimed that before that, you had liaisons with several of the household servants—both male and female—that began immediately after your wedding to his father."

I felt the blood drain from my face. Everything suddenly seemed very loud—Tristan's raspy breathing, the pounding of the rain.

"Elina!" Tristan was leaning forward now, clasping my freezing hands in his. "*Elina*! Are you all right?"

"There must be some mistake," I said, my voice trembling. "Your contact has made a terrible mistake."

"There is no mistake, Elina."

Suddenly agitated, I tried to stand. I needed movement. But Tristan took me gently by the shoulders and pressed me back down onto the cushions.

"No one will believe him, Tristan," I said. "This will ruin him. He is only seventeen. He can't possibly realize the consequences."

Tristan's face looked pained. He leaned forward and recaptured my hands. "There will be a trial, Elina. Sebastian has witnesses, members of the household whose false testimony he has secured through money and fear. The only witness you could bring on your own behalf would be Edith, and he is claiming that she was one of your lovers."

"But how can you believe that!" I cried, snatching my hands back. "How can you believe such filthy things, when you have known me all my life!"

Tristan surged to his feet. "I do not believe it! How can you think that I would? But there *will* be a trial, Elina. Your father's enemies will make sure of it. First him, and now you. You will be publically humiliated and personally ruined! Without your jointure, you will have no way to support yourself! You will have to marry again!"

Suddenly I saw the implications of my ruin clearly. "But with my family ruined and my reputation destroyed, no one will have me," I said hollowly. "It would be social and political suicide." I rubbed my thumb over the Harcourt sapphires and thought about Ashby's family: Chrysander's hopes for a career in politics, his sisters' hopes for kind husbands of noble birth and good fortune. Then I thought of my own sisters. Would Sophie's impending nuptials with Thad be threatened by this?

And what of Phosey? What chances could Phosey have of finding a husband with a politically obsolete father and a ruined sister?

Tristan sank back down into his seat. He leaned forward and planted his elbows upon his knees, leaving his hands to dangle in between them. "Not for everyone, it wouldn't," he said quietly. "Not for me."

I glanced up at him. "What do you mean?"

"I love you, Elina," he said. "And I swear to you that I will do everything in my power to block this trial, do you understand? But if you are my wife, it will be much easier for me. I can then place your family under my protection, and I doubt that young Delemere would be stupid enough to tangle with me directly."

I tried to pull away again, but he held me tightly. "I know what this is," he said, his voice gentle as he held my knuckles up, causing the light to refract off Ashby's ring. "He wore it on a chain around his neck after his mother died. The boys at school used to tease him about it, but after a scuffle or two, they soon learned to leave it alone."

I wrested my hand out of his grasp and covered the ring protectively with my other hand. "And did you ever scuffle with him?" I demanded. "Were you one of the boys who learned to leave it alone?"

"I have never started a fight. But I have never walked away from one, either. However, I plan to change that policy with Delemere. I have already invited him to join me in a little trip over to the Continent at his earliest convenience."

"A *duel*?" I exclaimed. "But Tristan, you cannot endanger yourself for me!"

He looked at me incredulously. "Of course I can! I love you. Whether you will become my wife or not, it is my prerogative— my duty even—to fight for your honor. And I will not lose. If I kill him, there will be no trial."

"I do not want you to kill him . . ." I began.

He nodded and transferred his gaze once more to the window. "For that reason, I shall try not to. But I hope you will excuse me for hoping that I succeed anyway."

"Tristan, I cannot marry you."

"You have known me all your life, and I have loved you for most of it. Please . . . " He turned the full weight of his gaze upon me in earnest entreaty. " . . . *please* just promise me, you will think about it! Though Ashenhurst is a peer of the realm, I am not sure his family's reputation would be able to withstand Delemere's treachery in the same way that I could."

I looked down to the Harcourt sapphires on my right hand. "I am not sure it could either," I admitted quietly. "I am not even sure how you could."

"I can," he said firmly. "That is all you need to know."

I took a long, shaky breath. "I cannot give you an answer right now, Tristan. I need some time alone."

"I know, Elina. But you will promise to think on my offer?'

I wanted to refuse, but I couldn't.

Tristan was the very best of men, the most perfect of gentlemen, and I knew that he spoke only the truth about everything. Including Ashby.

"I will think on your offer," I promised.

Tristan smiled shyly, his eyes suddenly full of a hope that tore at my heart. "Thank you, Elina. That is all I ask."

CHAPTER 28

I GHOSTED THROUGH THE REST of the day in a daze.
Thankfully, Lord and Lady Rydale retired early for the
night, freeing up the rest of the household to do the same.
I kissed Sophie and Phosey good night at their door, then continued slowly down the corridor towards my own room.

At my door, I glanced towards Ashby's chamber. A powerful need to step inside—just for a moment, just long enough
to catch the scent of him off a pillow—suddenly eclipsed my
better judgment.

Before fully realizing my intention, I found myself inside the
dark hush of his chamber, closing the door softly behind me. I
closed my eyes and drank in the faint scent of lavender and soap.
I glanced towards the door to Simon's closet. Edith had informed
me of his return just before dinner, which told me that wher-
ever Ashby was, it was not too far away. But I could see no light
glowing underneath Simon's door, and so relaxed a bit. I held
my candle up high, chasing the shadows into the corners of the
room, and looked around. On the bed lay the object of my quest.
I grabbed the two pillows, intending to replace them with my
own, then backed hastily into the corridor and closed the door.

I turned then, and very nearly collided into my father.

I froze, horrified.

"You know," he said, stooping to retrieve the chamberstick I hadn't realized I'd dropped, "I always thought your mother's pillows smelled like jasmine." Handing me the guttered candle, he then pulled his snuff box from his pocket and flipped open the lid. "I never cared much for the smell of Constance's pillows," he continued as he took a pinch. "They always smelled slightly of vinegar to me. I suppose that should have been a warning; but then again, by the time I discovered it, we were already married."

I had no idea what to say. I stood silently, clutching Ashby's pillows.

"I am afraid I must speak to you urgently," he said, regarding me coolly. "And privately. I would suggest we retire to the library or some such, but it is late and I am too weary to climb up and down any more stairs. So as outrageous as it sounds, I beg you to humor an old man and invite me into your chamber for our chat. I would suggest mine, except that it is next to Dr. Froggenhall's, and I think it likely he would be listening at the wall."

"Certainly, Papa," I replied, my voice remarkably even. "Please do come in."

I eased past him, not wanting Ashby's pillows to touch him, and opened my door. Edith had already lit a candle, and sat snoozing on the bench at the foot of the bed as she waited to assist me out of my clothes. But when she caught sight of Papa behind me, she rose quickly and bobbed at the knees before removing silently to her closet.

"Please have a seat, Papa," I said as I laid Ashby's pillows on my bed. He pulled out the chair to the dressing table and sat down while I took Edith's spot on the bench.

"I am sorry for my distance these past weeks," he began. "Tristan has told me that he informed you of my forced retirement from politics."

I nodded.

"I knew it was coming," he said, his tone pensive as he cast his gaze out the window into the misty darkness. "The signs were all there, and a few good friends warned me. But it was still a shock when it actually came to pass."

He looked so old and frail in the dim light. In truth, *I* had been the one neglecting him in his time of need. So taken was I with Ashby, I had little room for thought about anything or anyone else. Suddenly I felt in my heart what I had known since Tristan told me of Papa's disgrace: he would not last without politics. We did not have him for much longer, perhaps only months. All at once, I couldn't breathe as the danger of my predicament became clear to me. I was about to lose everything. My father, my home, my jointure, my name, my character.

And my Ashby.

With a lump in my throat, I realized that Tristan was not just an option—he was my only means of survival.

"Tristan has asked me for your hand," he said.

I nodded. "I figured that he probably spoke to you. He has already proposed."

Papa looked up sharply. "And what did you say?"

So Papa was here to champion Tristan's suit. Not that I was at all surprised; Tristan had been a family friend my entire life, and Papa was, or I should say used to be, Tristan's patron. It was only natural Papa would welcome Tristan as a son-in-law.

"I told him I would consider it."

"So you have not said 'yes,'" he pressed, his eyes strangely intent.

I shook my head slowly. "No. But I have not dismissed it. I told him I would consider it, and I meant it."

Papa's shoulders relaxed a little. "Good. I gave him my blessing. Tristan is like a son to me, you know."

I did my best to sound cheerful. "I know, Papa. And if it makes you happy to know, I will probably marry him."

At this, Papa sat bolt upright. "No! You cannot! Elina, you must not marry Tristan! You must not!"

I stared at him, shocked. "But why not? You just said yourself that you gave him your blessing!"

Papa bowed his head, and suddenly he sounded terribly weary. "He loves you. So naturally I gave him my blessing. I do not think you could do better for yourself than Tristan. He is the very best of everything a man dreams of for his daughters. But I do not give *you* my blessing, Elina."

I sat back, stunned. "You feel that I am not good enough for Tristan? Is that it?"

Papa looked up at me, his gaze solemn. "In a manner of speaking, yes. But not the way you are thinking. You have in you the best of both your mother and me. Sophie is too much like your dear mother, and Phosey, thank heavens, is too much like me. But you, my girl, are everything that I could have hoped for—dreamed of—in a child."

"Well, if Tristan is the best of everything you could have hoped for in a son-in-law, then why in Hades can't we be married?"

"Because I love Tristan more than just a son-in-law. I love him as a son. And I cannot abide his marriage to a woman who does not love him, even if that woman is my own lovely daughter."

I considered his words. The candle Edith had left on the dressing table flickered, casting strange shadows across Papa's face. He sat leaning forward, shoulders stooped, elbows resting on his thighs with his hands clasped between his knees. It was a classic pose of his, at once casual as well as energetic. Tristan, I had noticed, had adopted it of late, though I wasn't sure he was conscious of it.

I had made a critical error—the decline of Papa's body had nothing to do with his mind. He was still as sharp as ever. And though I feared that mind might become enervated in the coming months as he tried to acclimate to the life of a country gentleman, it had not yet come to pass.

"I see a lot of things, dear girl," he continued gently. "Even in my preoccupied state, I can see that my eldest daughter is in love. And," he continued, "I know from the wisdom of my years and from the heartache I felt when I lost your mother, that your love will endure undiminished for the rest of your life. This is the very best trait—and also the trait hardest to live with—that I had to give you. If you marry Tristan, there will always be three people in your marriage. And even if you learn to love him over time, you will never love him like you love Ashby Harcourt. Tristan, my dear, does not deserve to live out his life with Ashenhurst's specter haunting him in his marriage bed."

Papa was correct, of course. Suddenly I felt disgusted with myself for even entertaining the notion of using Tristan that way. I had only been concerned with self-preservation, blinding myself in the process to the fact that I would effectively be ruining three lives—four, in fact, if I counted whomever Tristan was truly meant to marry. What a wretched and selfish creature I was. I bowed my head, a single tear sliding down my cheek and landing with a fat plop onto my folded hands.

Papa moved to sit next to me. "Do not cry, my dear. The answer here is very simple: you must kindly decline Tristan's offer and accept Ashenhurst's. I presume," he added, his voice suddenly sharp, " Ashenhurst has made you an offer?"

I nodded with a sniffle.

"Then why these tears, my girl? This is a cause for celebration, not for sorrow! You love Ashenhurst, and you will marry him. It is very simple."

"But it's not simple, Papa!" I cried. "It is anything but simple! I cannot marry Ashby; I cannot bear to tarnish the Harcourts with my ruined name and character. Ashby has wonderful plans for his siblings, and for raising the Harcourts back to greatness. I cannot destroy that for him. But I must marry, and my only other option is Tristan! But now I see that I cannot marry him, either!"

Papa took my hand and clasped it firmly in his own. "I will not lie to you, my girl," he said. "The Harcourts will be affected by Delemere's treachery. But the damage will not be so great as you fear. Ashby, as you call him, is a peer of the realm, an earl from an ancient and honorable lineage. His father's profligate lifestyle humbled the Harcourts a little, but not nearly so much as young Ashenhurst fears. Has he voiced any concerns over your name and character?"

"He does not yet know."

"Do you think he will once he finds out about Delemere?"

I shook my head. "No. But he is very reckless, Papa; he does not often take the time to consider the consequences of his actions."

Papa chuckled. "I know very little about your Ashby, my dear, but I do at least know that."

"Yes." I smiled briefly. "I suppose you would. Rakehells do not often seem to nurture a healthy concern for consequences."

"Indeed, they do not," he agreed. "So you feel it is up to you to look out for him if he is not going to look out for himself?"

"Yes."

Papa reached over and gently took my hand. "But the decision is not yours, Elina. He is a grown man, and he can look out for himself. If he does not deem you a risk to his family obligations, then you must accept that and honor that. Do not let your pride ruin your chances for happiness, my girl."

I frowned and glanced up into his wizened face. "Pride?"

"Yes," he replied. "Pride. *You* would like to be the one to save the Harcourts, and yet *they* will be the ones to save you. I know you well enough, daughter, to know how much that must rankle."

HEATHER E. F. CARTER

I dropped my gaze back down to my lap. "But I can bring them nothing except ignominy."

"Wrong," he said. "You will bring yourself and your love, and despite what others may tell you, that is worth so much more than a prestigious name or connections at Court. And you will also bring a respectable portion, so do not worry on that account."

"No, Papa!" I exclaimed in dismay. "I cannot ask you to do that. You were more than generous with the portion I brought to William! I cannot ask you to do that again."

"I should have never allowed you to marry that brute," he said softly. "And the very least thing I have lost in the matter is the portion I settled on you. Besides," he added, "you are the daughter of a marquess. Our name might not mean much at Court just now, but our honor is still intact. No daughter of a Marquess of Hertford will ever go to a marriage empty-handed."

"But Papa . . ."

"If you are worried about where the money will come from," he said, "Don't. I inherited a few small estates from a cousin some ten years ago. They are not entailed with the rest of the Hertford lands, and I had been planning to leave them to you and your sisters. I can sell one of those now—perhaps the one in Somerset, I think. Since we lost our connections at Court, I'd been thinking of selling off some land anyway to augment Sophie and Phosey's portions. I also have a small estate in Scotland that I can rid myself of if I need to."

"Very well, Papa," I said, letting the matter drop for the moment. "But there is something else . . ."

"Yes?"

"I am scared, Papa." I bowed my head, unable to meet his penetrating gaze.

"I know, Elina," he said. "But that is normal, my dear. Doubly so for someone who has survived a bad marriage. But you must have faith—faith in yourself to know the difference between love and a momentary infatuation, and faith in your Ashby to know the same."

I sighed. "I know, Papa."

"Forget this nonsense with Delemere," he said. "We do not even know for certain that your character will, in fact, be ruined. That will not be determined until the trial, and a lot of things can happen between now and then."

I nodded absently, trying to absorb everything that Papa had said. It seemed too good to be true, too cruel to hope, but Papa was making a great deal of sense. However, I stumbled over this last bit. "What do you mean?" I asked. "*What* things can happen?"

"These are dangerous times we live in," he replied blithely. "People get run down in the street all the time. Or shot by thieves, or killed in duels."

"Tristan has challenged Sebastian to a duel."

"Indeed, he has," Papa answered. "And I know no one better with a pistol or a blade than Tristan. Except perhaps your Ashby, but that is only because I have heard he has had a great deal of practice with pistols and blades."

"Meeting at sunrise," I said.

"Precisely."

I frowned, still unable to accept this turn of events. "So let me get this correct, Papa. You are in fact encouraging me to marry a notorious libertine?"

He chuckled softly. "Ah, Elina. I am old enough to know that I really do not have any say in the matter, now do I? You are an independent woman now, free to make your own choices and your own mistakes. But!" He held up his finger to emphasize the point. "If your Ashby does go back to his wicked ways after you've married him—"

"You'll send Tristan up to shoot him in a duel?" I asked with a wry smile.

"Good heavens, no!" he exclaimed. "Tristan might get shot. If it becomes clear after marriage that certain of his old habits should resurface, I am confident, my dear, that you will shoot him yourself. In fact, I think I will make you a wedding present of my old dueling pistols, since I won't have any use for them now that Tristan is going after Delemere."

A shudder ran through me as I imagined Papa meeting Sebastian at dawn, and suddenly found myself intensely grateful to Tristan for taking that possibility out of play. "Very well, Papa," I said, "I shall accept your dueling pistols. But you will need to show me how to shoot them first."

"Indeed, I will, my girl," he said, stifling a yawn. "Indeed, I will. But now I think I shall bid you good night. It is time these old bones found their bed."

I rose and followed him over to the door. "Papa?" I said as he stepped out into the corridor.

He turned back, his eyebrows lifted in a question.

"Thank you."

He leaned forward to kiss my forehead. "You are very welcome, Elina. Now goodnight. I shall see you in the morning. But," he added, a mischievous twinkle in his eyes, "do remember to replace Ashenhurst's pillows with your own. Otherwise the housemaids will gossip."

"Yes, Papa," I murmured, dropping my gaze down to my toes as I blushed furiously. "Good night, Papa."

Chuckling softly, he closed the door behind him.

CHAPTER 29

I AWOKE THE FOLLOWING MORNING feeling peculiar. Sunlight sparkled in the window, flashing off the diagonal lead muntins and streaming through the diamond panes. I smiled, and it struck me: I felt *happy*. My smile graduated into a grin as I stretched my arms up over my head, and when I caught sight of the Harcourt sapphires on my right hand, I remembered:

Ashby.

I would marry him.

And he loved me.

It should be enough, for a while at least.

But no doubts could put a damper on my mood. This told me my euphoria must not be solely attributable to Ashby. Eventually my mind turned to Papa, and I realized what it was.

This feeling was forgiveness.

The sense of having been betrayed by the one man I had loved and trusted beyond all others was now absent

Humming a little tune under my breath, I sat up and pulled Ashby's ring off my right hand and replaced it on my left. It felt good: weighty and substantial.

I chuckled as I reached for the bell pull. My life wasn't the only one about to change drastically. Edith would move to Northumberland with me, no question about that. And possibly to Portugal, as well, though I didn't know how often Ashby visited his Iberian estate. I wondered how she would take the news: it was going to be bitterly cold that far north, and unlike me she wouldn't have a man to keep her bed warm for her at night.

An hour later, I was still smiling as I sat alone in the flower garden. I had chosen the same bench where I had first kissed Ashby, and the memory of that moment warmed me in the chilly sunlight. I'd slept much later than I was accustomed to, and when I finally made it down to breakfast, I discovered that I was alone in the house. The gentlemen were back on the moor today, and the housemaid who'd given me my morning chocolate told me that the ladies had all gone to town. Ironic, considering it was the first time since our arrival that I desired company.

Footsteps crunching on the gravel on the other side of the thick boxwood hedge alerted me to someone's approach. I frowned, tracking his movement along the outer periphery of the garden. Since I was the only one left at the house, perhaps a servant had been sent to check up on me.

Unless . . .

Ashby! Could Ashby have returned so soon?

But by the time the footsteps had made their way down to the opening in the hedge, I knew it couldn't be him. They were far too graceless, plodding along slowly with no hint of energy. Still, when Dr. Froggenhall turned the corner, I was taken by surprise.

"Good afternoon, Doctor!" I called out with an expansive smile. "Well met, sir!"

This cheerful address caused the little man to freeze a moment in place, startled.

"Please do join me, sir," I said. "It is such a beautiful day, is it not?"

"Er, yes, Lady Delemere," he ventured once he'd recovered enough to continue his progress towards me. "A bit chilly, perhaps."

"Bah!" I waved my hand at him good naturedly. "I find the cold greatly invigorating."

He frowned at me as he took the proffered seat. "An odd sentiment, coming from one so enamored of Hertfordshire. Perhaps it is indicative that you are ready for a colder climate?"

I looked at him, slightly taken aback. "Why, Dr. Froggenhall! I do believe you must have a knack for clairvoyance!"

The little man looked at me appraisingly. "You are in a rather frivolous mood, madam, and I confess I am a little relieved. I had noticed that you've been rather distracted of late, and I worried that you'd fallen victim to melancholia. And melancholia is but a small step away from more serious ailments."

"Er, yes, Dr. Froggenhall," I replied, suddenly reminded of my reasons for not liking him. "We've had this conversation before. You've already explained to me the bit about widows being susceptible. Possibly more than once, in fact."

He leaned forward. "It's the sudden cut-off from sexual intercourse, you know. Male semen corrects the intrinsic imbalances of the female body by keeping the levels of heat and moisture even. That is why I, and other gentlemen of my profession, council widows to remarry as soon as they are able."

"I beg your pardon, sir!" I exclaimed, shocked at the strange fellow's sudden temerity.

"Still," he continued as though I hadn't spoken, "I believe I would approve of a little more sobriety from you just now, since I have something very important to discuss with you."

I nodded curtly. "What is it?"

"A proposal," he replied, "of marriage."

I frowned. "A proposal of marriage? To whom?"

"To me."

"A proposal of marriage to *you*?"

"Yes, madam," he replied. "I am asking you to marry me."

This was not the first unwanted proposal to ever come my way, though in truth it was certainly the most bizarre.

Still, there was a script to follow.

I began the speech solemnly. "Why Dr. Froggenhall, you pay me a very great compliment, and I am truly flattered by such a great honor—"

"Tell me, Lady Delemere," he interrupted, "have you ever witnessed an execution?"

"I beg your pardon?"

"An execution madam. Have you ever witnessed one?"

"What in Hades are you talking about, sir?"

"I attend them regularly at York," he replied.

"I cannot marry you, Dr. Froggenhall," I said, no longer caring for proper etiquette.

"They do not all die right away, you know. Some of them do; their neck snaps when they fall. But most of the time they strangle to death. It can take a long time. I imagine it is a horrible way to die, kicking desperately while being throttled to death. I've heard that sometimes their eyeballs burst—"

I stood up abruptly. "That is enough, Dr. Froggenhall. Good afternoon." I started to walk down the path, eager to put as much distance between us as I could.

"They're not recognizable afterwards, you know," he called after me. "Their faces are distorted beyond anything human. They shit and piss all over themselves. It would be a terrible pity to see a man like Ashby Harcourt come to that end, don't you agree?"

"What did you say?" Slowly, I turned to face him.

He was still sitting on the bench, watching me impassively.

"If you refuse," he said. "I will deliver this letter" —he pulled a letter from his breast pocket for me to see— "to Lord Beverley, denouncing your lover Ashenhurst as the Black Unicorn, and guilty of a host of additional crimes including murder."

I walked back down the path towards him. "I presume you can prove these accusations."

"You presume correctly, Elina. And *do* call me Phineas."

I came to a stop a few meters away. William had taught me to stay out of the reach of men I did not trust. "And the nature of this proof?"

He raised his eyebrows expectantly.

"*Phineas.*"

"Does it matter, Elina?" He patted the place where I'd been sitting next to him. "It is solid and irrefutable."

"If I am to take your threat seriously, I must know the nature of your proof."

"Come have a seat, Elina. I shall tell you everything you want to know."

I paused a moment, deliberating, then came back to join him on the bench.

"That's my girl." As he turned to face me, he crowded his knees into my skirts. It took all my self-control not to shove him backwards off the bench. To my utter disbelief, he began inching closer still, leaning into me almost as if he would kiss me. I quickly brought up my hand to block his face. "I am waiting."

His little smile grew wolfish. "Secrets are best not shared in public places, Elina. Not even in dark little corners beneath the ruins of a Cistercian abbey."

Ashby's confession.

"You heard us then." I had terribly underestimated the mad-doctor.

"I did. And your lover nearly caught me. But he was far too preoccupied with his thoughts for you to give the area a very thorough search. I probably have your considerable charms to thank for saving my life. Though," he added with an unpleasant leer, "once you are *my* wife, you will tone down those charms when we are in public."

My mind struggled to make sense of this baffling mixture of the menacing with the farcical. Meanwhile, he was continuing to gain ground on the bench, but if I leaned back any further, I would fall backwards into the rose bushes. "Your word against that of a peer will be meaningless. I assume you have stronger proof than that?"

He nodded. "I have had my valet tailing Ashenhurst since that afternoon. He is with him even now."

Good God. First-hand testimony of witnessed crimes. And Froggenhall's testimony identifying Ashby as the Black Unicorn coupled with Lord Beverley's evidence from the living members of the Northern Gang could be enough to secure a death sentence.

"Then I wonder why it is you would choose me for a matrimonial partner," I replied, shifting my approach. "Who is to say I would give up my lover once married to you?"

He made a move as if to touch me, but then seemed to think better of it. "Any contact you have with Ashenhurst from this moment on, even if it is just a shared glance, will destroy him. Am I making myself clear?"

"Perfectly." I narrowed my eyes. "I am unclear as to why you would go to such lengths for an aristocratic bride. From our first conversation, *Phineas*, I recall that you do not hold a very high opinion of aristocratic women in general."

"In my circle, marriage to the daughter of a marquess will be a triumph. With a peer of the realm for a father-in-law, my bid for municipal office in the next elections will be assured."

"Municipal office?" I snorted. "You have connections through your uncle. And Lord Rydale would have far more influence in York than would a marquess from Hertfordshire."

He shrugged. "My uncle has disowned me."

"Whatever for?" I asked dryly.

"That is no concern of yours," he said, oblivious to my tone. "With your father's support, I'll most certainly become Lord High Mayor in York within the next ten years."

I shuddered at the thought of ten years married to this worm. Froggenhall noted it, and his smile grew more pronounced. He reached out to touch my shoulder, his thumb stroking as I summoned every ounce of my-self-control to keep from smacking his hand away. Emboldened by my apparent acquiescence, he continued the unwelcome touch down the length of my upper arm, his thumb tracing casually around the swell of my breast. Then he gripped me by the elbow as he leaned in close, and I knew he meant to kiss me. At the very last moment, I turned my face to the side so that his lips found my cheek. I felt him smile against me as he gripped my elbow harder and pulled me towards him until his lips hovered over my ear.

"I require your answer. Now."

My mind worked rapidly. I had no intention of marrying Froggehnall. Ashby had landed himself in a mess, and I was not about to martyr myself to save him. At least not when I knew Ashby to be clever enough to have some sort of contingency plan in place. The best thing I could do for him now would be to play for time, and the easiest means of doing that would be to accept Froggenhall's offer. But if I did that, the mad-doctor might very well demand proof of my sincerity, and with the house deserted of everyone save the servants, I had a fairly good idea as to what that proof would entail. That left me with only one other option that I could think of.

"*Phineas*," I breathed into his ear as I pressed my body in closer to his. "I must be allowed time to think it over." I leaned back so I could look him in the eye and dazzle him with what I prayed to be a smile saturated with feminine charm.

Unfortunately, I could see from the contempt in his eyes that my efforts were not well received. He gripped my arm harder still and yanked me back towards him, his mouth slamming painfully into mine.

Memories of William flooded my mind as every instinct in my body screamed for me to fight. Instead, I opened my mouth to Froggenhall's filthy kiss and forced myself to relax against him. If I couldn't convince him with my smiles, I must do so by other means. The hand he'd been using to hold my arm now moved up to grip the back of my neck, allowing me no room for retreat as he nearly gagged me.

But then something in his attitude shifted, and I realized that despite his small size, he could still easily overpower me. I acted instinctively, shoving at him with all my strength. Fortunately, I startled him enough to release me, and I leaped off the bench and staggered backwards before my mind had fully registered that something was wrong. And I knew from the look in his eyes as he got to his feet that I had underestimated him yet again.

I couldn't hope to outrun him, so I sucked air into my lungs in a huge gulp and prepared to scream for assistance. Then I heard the crunch of footsteps from the gravel path on the other side of the hedge. I froze, as did Froggenhall, and together we silently tracked their progress down the length of the path to the edge of the hedge. The footman who turned the corner into the garden showed no sign of surprise at our strange attitude, but bowed to Froggenhall and handed him a note.

As the mad-doctor read the missive, I hurried out of the garden and back towards the house. I had no idea whether I'd managed to buy Ashby any time, though my instincts warned that I hadn't: Froggenhall wasn't stupid enough to think that I would ever accept his suit. But then again, he did not know women well, a fact made only too clear by the look I had seen in his eyes as he'd come off the bench after me.

I had seen that look in my late husband's eyes, and I knew what it meant: Froggenhall thought he had me in his power. He thought that his letter to Lord Beverley had me neatly caged. It therefore followed that, so long as he wanted to keep me, he couldn't give Lord Beverley that letter. At least not until he realized that his blackmail was not so effective as he'd supposed.

In the meantime, I knew what I needed to do.

CHAPTER 30

THE CASTLE, LONG SINCE reduced by the ravages of time and war to piles of weathered grey stone, loomed up ahead of us. Its medieval builders had known what they were doing, situating it on a promontory of calcareous rock overlooking the North Sea.

My guide silently urged his gelding up to the foot of the steep slope leading to the remnants of the gatehouse, and dismounted. I urged Rupert up next to him, then followed suit, anxious to stretch my legs after the three hours it took us to reach this desolate stretch of coast somewhere between Whitby and Scarborough.

The wind howled around us like restless ghosts in the fading light, angry at our trespass into their haunted domain. Catching my hat as those unhappy spirits sought to tear it off, I squinted into the stinging wind, looking for signs of life. From our current vantage point, it was impossible to tell. It certainly didn't look like any sort of headquarters.

Simon called out a signal, and two shadows detached themselves from the base of each projecting tower on either side of the gatehouse. Another materialized in a crenel of the battlements at the top of the gatehouse itself.

I checked my time piece and saw that it was only six o'clock, two hours yet to go until sunset. God willing, it wouldn't be for another couple of hours that anyone noticed my absence from Scarcliff Towers. Not that there was anything they could do about it. In the letter I'd left for Papa, I'd only explained that I'd left to join Ashby. I did not say where I planned to join him.

The conference between Simon and the two guards concluded. The little valet began to make his way back down the hill, followed by one of the men.

Both looked very grim, and it suddenly struck me that Simon might have played me false. I could see no sign of Ashby anywhere; the only structure still intact beyond the gatehouse was the crumbling remnants of the keep some distance away.

They were almost upon me, and the guard behind Simon wouldn't look me in the eye. I had Papa's Turkish pistol in my saddle bag. I didn't know how to use it, but I wouldn't go down without a fight. Stepping back towards Rupert, I turned and casually moved over to the saddlebag. Groping through its contents in a manner I hoped communicated nonchalance, I finally felt the butt of the pistol and yanked it out just as Simon reached me.

"Come on then," he growled, gesturing over his shoulder towards the ruins. "You'll not be needing that." The guard moved past me and caught up Rupert's reins, then moved over to gather those of Simon's gelding.

Still too shaken to feel foolish, I indicated with a shake of the head that I would be keeping the pistol. Simon looked from my ashen face, to the beautifully ornate weapon, and shrugged.

"Suit yourself," he said, "but I'm not holding it for you when you climb down the ladder."

Without another word, he turned and set a challenging pace back up the slope and through the gatehouse. I hurried after and followed him across a courtyard paved in large flat stones, broken apart and reclaimed by the grass and dandelions. Once at the dilapidated keep, Simon moved to a grassy patch in the center of the floor, and with two cleverly concealed rope handles, moved aside what turned out to be a flat wooden cover disguised with a thick layer of turf over the top. Joining him, I found myself looking down into a small, pitch black hole just large enough for a person to fit through. The small size was further compounded by the fact that about half of it seemed taken up by a rickety-looking ladder.

"I'll go first," Simon said, "so I can light the torch at the bottom." Then with the nimbleness of a chimney sweep's climbing boy, he disappeared down into the hole and the awaiting darkness below.

"Well?" came the caustic demand a few moments later. "Are you coming down or not?"

"I thought you were lighting a torch."

"I can't do that until we're through the door. Now get down here, you bloody woman."

Looking down at the pistol in my hand, I realized what he'd meant about not holding it while I climbed down the ladder. With no pockets, my choices were either to stay up here and hold onto the gun, or leave it up here for one of the guards to pilfer while I descended into their lair. With a silent apology to Papa, I quickly laid the pistol down behind a large pile of crumbling stones, and then followed Simon's lead down into the dark.

Once at the bottom, I found myself in a damp chamber not large enough for two people to stand in comfortably. Simon didn't seem like our close quarters any more than did I, so I'd barely time to set both feet on the ground before he pushed open a heavy wooden door with a terrific grunt of effort.

I hurried through the doorway close on his heels and was immediately glad I did when the door's deafening slam reverberated up and down the darkened tunnel. On a hook near the door hung a lantern, its candle burned down to just a bit of wick floating in a liquid pool of wax, with only the tiniest spark of a bluish flame. Using a paper spill from a pile on the table beneath it, Simon lit the torch in the wall sconce next to the lantern and proceeded silently down the tunnel.

I had only the impression of smooth rock walls and a rounded ceiling as I trotted after my guide. The ground had a slightly gravelly texture, like sand scattered over stone. And the temperature was cool, the air surprisingly fresh and briny, which led me to believe that there might be additional access points to the surface other than the one we had just used.

I followed Simon through several twists and turns, and after what seemed an eternity, his pace slowed a bit. I could see from the light of his torch that this tunnel terminated in a heavy door of oak planks. And I could hear voices on the other side of it.

Despite the coolness of the tunnel, sweat beaded on my upper lip, and I hastily wiped my damp palms on my skirts. I'd had three hours on the journey to the coast to prepare what I planned to say to Ashby, but now I considered the questions I had not allowed myself to ponder. What would he think of my intrusion? Would he be angry? Would he think my warnings about Froggenhall sufficiently important to warrant this invasion into a part of his life he'd been so determined to hide from me?

Should I just have sent Simon alone with another letter explaining everything?

The answer to *that* question was most certainly *yes*. But then Ashby would just put his contingency plan into effect, and I might never see him again.

And that would do nothing for my own contingency plan.

As Simon pounded heavily on the door three times, paused two beats, then pounded twice more, I squared my shoulders, and lifted my chin.

At first, nothing happened. I couldn't even detect any pause in the voices on the other side of the door. Then the door wrenched open just wide enough for a nasty-looking countenance to glare through over the barrel of a pistol. Simon, unperturbed, leaned in close to mutter a few words I couldn't make out. After a moment, the man nodded, then the door creaked open a little further so he could get a better look at me as he leveled the pistol at my chest. Simon muttered a few more words, then shrugged in a manner that plainly cleared himself of any further responsibility for me.

The ugly man looked me over thoroughly, almost leisurely, in a manner so devoid of any sexual interest that I thought myself doomed for sure. But then he nodded curtly and opened the door with something like a welcoming flourish from the hand holding the pistol. Simon stepped aside so that I might precede him into the den of smugglers. I rallied my courage and prepared to make as dignified an entrance as I could, but when the door slammed shut immediately behind me I spun around and yelped in alarm.

And this, unfortunately, did bring all conversation in the room to a halt.

"Elina?"

Slowly I turned to face the silent room. It was long and narrow, dimly lit by lanterns set upon the upended crates the men were using as tables. I counted six of them in the room: Ashby, standing in the center next to the largest crate/table with a large map strewn across the top of it like a tablecloth, and five others seated on short casks of liquor gathered around a smaller crate/table bearing the paraphernalia of a card game in progress. Lining the walls were many larger casks and stacks of crates reaching almost to the ceiling, with still more stacked at the end of the room behind Ashby.

"Elina?" he repeated, his tone sharper this time. "What are you doing here?"

He looked tired and slightly disheveled in just his shirtsleeves and riding breeches. He watched me, his expression guarded, though the same couldn't be said of the rest of his company. Even in the muted light, I could read clearly the suspicion and hostility on their grim faces.

I cleared my throat. "I need to speak with you. Alone."

Ashby glanced towards his men and caught the eye of the largest fellow with a nasty scar running from his eyebrow, through a milky-white blind eye, down to his heavy lantern jaw. The latter gave a brief nod, then rose along with the others.

As the heavy door slammed shut behind the last man, I turned my attention back to Ashby. His expression was still guarded as he indicated a seat for me to take opposite his, though I thought his eyes and the line of his mouth seemed a bit softer. I sank down on the proffered cask, and he disappeared into the gloom behind a stack of crates at the end of the room, reemerging a few moments later with a bottle and two wine glasses. Wordlessly, he uncorked the bottle and generously poured the golden amber liquid into both, then handed me one as he took his own seat. I took a tentative sip, my eyebrows climbing in surprise before I took a larger gulp.

"What are you doing here?" he repeated. "I got your letter yesterday. You didn't need to come here yourself."

"Froggenhall knows. He overheard us in the *cellarium*, and he's had his valet following you ever since. He claims that the man is watching you even now. He told me that if I do not marry him, he will expose you and your operations to Lord Beverley. I half expect that he'd do it anyway, just out of spite."

"Christ." Ashby shook his head. "This couldn't have come at a worse time."

"*And*," I continued, "as you'll know from my letter, I think Lord Beverley may already know."

"Lord Beverley suspects that Sir Julian is the Black Unicorn."

"*What?*"

"Yes." He flashed an almost apologetic smile. "As you'll recall,

I had to claim that I too was attacked by the Black Unicorn on the same day that Sir Julian was. Lord Beverley had it correct in suspecting that one of us was lying, but fortunately for me, Lord Beverley found my story to be the more trustworthy of the two."

"But—but that makes no sense, Ashby!" I said. "Sir Julian is fabulously wealthy. Why on earth would he be going around robbing people on the highway?"

Ashby shrugged. "He and Lord Beverley have been bitter rivals in county politics for some time. Sometimes a man simply sees what he wants to see."

"But how do you know this?" I demanded. "And what about poor Sir Julian? Is he in any danger?"

Ashby paused a moment to refill both glasses. "I know this, because I am not completely inept. This business with Froggen-hall is unfortunate—"

"I know," I interrupted miserably. "If I hadn't forced you to confess to me, none of this would have ever happened."

"That, possibly, could be true," he allowed. "But then again, it might have happened anyway. I said I wasn't *completely* inept. That does not mean that I am claiming supreme competence. My eventual exposure was inevitable, though I was hoping it wouldn't be for a while yet.

"And do not worry about Sir Julian. He is in some ways the most ideal diversion. Other than a gambling habit, he is the most upstanding citizen. No jury will ever convict a man of Sir Julian's wealth and influence on theory alone, even if it is the Lord Lieu-tenant of Yorkshire's theory. Evidence is needed, *Minha Amada*, and there is none, since Sir Julian is not his man."

"But if that is true, Ashby," I countered, "then how can you know that Lord Beverley still suspects Sir Julian?"

"Lord Beverley has his spies, and I have mine."

I shook my head. "I suppose it doesn't matter anyway. Froggen-hall will be informing Lord Beverley of his error any moment now."

"You mean you do not plan to throw yourself away on the diabolical mad-doctor to save my life?" he teased.

"How can you even joke about such things?" I demanded. "The mad-doctor is mad himself. He wishes to marry me so that Papa can use his influence to further his political career!"

Ashby's playful expression vanished. "His desire to wed you has nothing to do with politics, *Minha Amada*, and everything to do with money."

I frowned. "I don't understand."

"Froggenhall formally asked for Dorothea's hand a few days before you and your family arrived at Scarcliff Towers. Naturally, Lord Rydale refused him—the match was almost too ridiculous to countenance, which made him suspicious of Froggenhall's motives. So, he asked me to look into Froggenhall's affairs discreetly and to report back to him. I didn't like what I discovered, and neither did Lord Rydale."

"Which was?"

"Froggenhall is in very serious trouble with the Royal College of Physicians. He's been accepting patients into his asylum without orders from doctors, which is highly illegal, and there are allegations of sexual misconduct with some of his female patients. In particular, there is the case of a Miss Mona Sinclair, whose family is claiming he has kept in a state of virtual imprisonment for the last four years. The unfortunate young woman is due to give birth to his bastard any day now. He needs a substantial amount of money for a few well-placed bribes to make all of this go away. Otherwise, the York Asylum could be closed, and he'll be ruined and probably tried and incarcerated. An aristocratic marriage will bring with it aristocratic connections and an aristocratic portion, and *this* is his proper motive, not a career in municipal politics."

"Good heavens!" I shivered with disgust. "I am shocked that Lord Rydale hasn't sent the man away!"

"He's keeping all this from Lady Rydale, which is why he asked me to look into the matter rather than making enquiries of his own. He doesn't want to trouble her with such a sordid business until it's certain that all of this will be made public."

I bit my lip, thinking for a moment. "But even so, I'm not so sure Froggenhall is entirely motivated by money. Papa has agreed to settle a second portion on me, but Froggenhall cannot know that."

"He is either gambling on your father's love, to settle you with a second portion, or he plans to turn me in to Lord Beverley after your wedding to collect on the reward."

"Yes, you are probably right," I said, tracing my finger around the rim of my wine glass. "But still, knowing Froggenhall's motives doesn't help our case, Ashby. You will be tried for murder. Not just highway robbery. There can be no pardon. There are no mitigating circumstances that will save you from the noose."

"There are *always* mitigating circumstances, *Minha Amada*," he said, his voice suddenly gentle. "I will still need to leave the country for a short while, which is damned inconvenient with all this," he motioned to the casks and crates stacked all around the room, "still to be moved. I shall have to delegate authority to Simon, and I really hate to do that."

"I am coming with you. If you'll have me, that is."

"If I'll have you?" Through my lashes, I saw a corner of his mouth kicking up into his familiar half-smile. "What a curious question coming from a lady already wearing my ring."

"Ashby, there's something I have to tell you."

CHAPTER 31

"FIRST SOME FOOD," HE said.
    "Ashby, this cannot wait."
    "You haven't eaten since this morning, have you?"
"No," I admitted. "But, Ashby . . . "
"This won't take long."

True to his word, he left me alone only for about ten minutes. But ten minutes can seem like an eternity to a troubled mind.

When he reappeared, he held a sturdy tray overladen with dishes. One of his men accompanied him to hold open the door, though the lackey made no other move to help his leader. I raised my eyebrows at this as the door slammed shut behind Ashby.

"We don't pay much heed to rank in this organization," he explained when he saw the look of surprise on my face. "Things run more smoothly without all of the bowing and scraping, and it's good for morale. Any resentment they harbor tends to be aimed at each other rather than me, which I can use to my advantage if I need to."

"Do they know who you are?"

"My lieutenants do," he said as he set the tray down on the crate. I could see a small crock of stew, a loaf of coarse brown bread, and an elegant crystal carafe of water that looked a bit out of place amongst the earthenware crockery. "The rest obviously know I am a gentleman of some sort," he continued as he began dishing out the stew into two bowls, "possibly even an aristocrat, though they do not know my name. My lieutenants guard that secret very carefully."

"You trust them?" I asked as he handed me a bowl.

"I trust their greed. And so long as I am making them money, they'll continue to do things as I see fit. Besides," he added, "in an organization that does not recognize rank, my lieutenants are jealous of anything that separates them from the rest of the rabble. And knowledge of my name is one of those few things."

"How many lieutenants do you have?"

He shrugged. "One for each county, from County Durham down the eastern seaboard to Kent. But I'd rather steer our conversation in another direction, if you don't mind. Why do you wish to come with me? Are you afraid I won't come back for you?"

Reluctantly, I set down my spoon. "I do not think you are taking this threat to your life seriously, Ashby. I think the danger is far greater than you are appreciating. I think you will leave me, and I will never see you again."

He leaned forward, planting his elbows on the crate. The light from the lantern flickered in his eyes. "You are wrong about that," he said gently. "But let us set that aside for a moment. If you come with me, *Minha Amada*, your reputation will be ruined—"

"But I thought reputation meant nothing to you."

"*My* reputation means nothing to me," he corrected. "And only because I have ruined it beyond any possibility for recovery. If I had a choice in the matter, I would prefer to enter a room and not cause all conversation to suddenly halt. But *your* reputation means a great deal to me; so much so, in fact, that I lay awake at night troubling over what *my* name will do to you once we are married."

I dropped my gaze down to my hands clasped tightly in my lap. "Then we cannot be married."

I pulled the Ashenhurst heirloom off my finger, tearing my skin as I dragged it over my knuckle, then slid it towards him across the paper of the map. I could not bring myself to look into his face, though I felt the intensity of his gaze.

"What has happened, Elina?" His voice was deceptively soft.

I swallowed down the lump in my throat, then told him of Sebastian and his treacherous accusations against me. It did not take long.

"There will be a trial," I finished. "He has witnesses. *My* reputation will soon be ruined beyond any possibility for recovery. It would not be *your* name that would pollute my reputation, but *my* name that will pollute yours."

In a sudden movement, he snatched one of the crystal tumblers and hurled it against the wall, shattering it. Then he was out of his seat, ranging back and forth like a caged animal.

"Ashby, don't," I pleaded when he paused to seize the other tumbler off the table. "Tristan has already challenged him, and if he fails, I'm afraid Papa will stand up next."

Ashby froze. "Then Richmond will kill him. He's the best shot I know other than myself. If he *doesn't* kill him, then I will kill him myself, and I will not wait to meet him on the Continent to do it!"

"That would be murder," I said. "Do not speak of such things."

Ashby flung the second tumbler against the wall, then set to pacing once more. "I am already a murderer!" he declared savagely. "My soul will be no more damned if I add Delemere to the list. In fact, God would probably count it as a penance since I'd be doing the world a favor."

"*God* might call it a penance," I pointed out, "but England won't. Ashby, you would hang for killing Sebastian. He's a peer of the realm now, like you."

"*Not* like me," he said, his voice suddenly quiet. "*Nothing* like me. I am his darkest nightmare, and I swear to God I will see him destroyed."

I sat back and watched him helplessly as first one tear, then another, slid down my cheeks. After a moment, I was forced to sniffle, which brought Ashby's agitated pacing to an abrupt halt.

"You are crying?" he demanded, his expression incredulous. "Are you crying for *Delemere*?"

"No." I sniffled again. Ashby hadn't brought any table linens with the food, so I was forced to wipe my nose on my sleeve. "Sebastian has made his bed, let him lie in it."

"Then why?"

"I do not know," I admitted in a small voice. "I suppose I had just become used to the idea of marrying you."

He frowned. "I do not understand, Elina. Why can't you marry me?"

His use of my given name told me everything I needed to know. He was a gentleman, and so would not abandon me. But the tenderness encapsulated in '*Minha Amada*' was gone. I shook my head as he came to take his seat across from me. He picked up his ring and studied it for a moment.

"Why can't you marry me?" he repeated.

I shook my head again. "I know what you are doing. And I won't let you do it. I won't let you throw yourself away on me."

"*Throw* myself away on you? What the devil are you talking about?"

A surge of anger briefly eclipsed my despair. I slammed my fist down on the crate, causing the crockery and silverware to jump. "My reputation! It is ruined! You cannot marry me. You must go find another woman with a *good* reputation to marry in order to save your family! I cannot do it!"

"You think I am marrying you to save my family?"

"No. But I know what your plans are for your family, and I do not want to stand in your way."

"You are already standing in the way, Elina," he said. "To carry out my plans, I need to marry an heiress. But I cannot because I love you, and have always loved you. I cannot marry another woman."

"But my reputation! You said my reputation was important to you!"

He heaved a heavy sigh and shook his head. "You little nitwit. I don't care a damn about your reputation. I only meant that I did not want you to suffer from Society's harsh judgment the way that I do. I *earned* my bad reputation, and I did not want my sordid past to be the cause of your ruin!"

I sat quietly for a moment, thinking. Papa had told me not to let my pride ruin my chances for happiness. And he had been correct: *I* wanted to be the one to save the Harcourts, not the other way around. To tarnish their name—Ashby's name—was almost too great a strain for my pride to bear. Papa had also told me that my love was enough, but was Ashby's?

"You still want to marry me?" I asked tentatively.

He snorted. "Of course I want to marry you! I still don't understand how you could have thought I wouldn't!"

"My ruined reputation means nothing to you?" I pressed.

"Nothing."

My smile was a slow thing, tentative at first, then passing through the stages of tenderness and love before blooming gloriously into triumph. "It is settled then: I will be accompanying you to Portugal."

For a moment, he looked thunderstruck, and I congratulated myself on eliciting yet another honest expression from my closely guarded libertine. A low, smooth chuckle acknowledged his defeat.

"If you will permit me," he said, holding up his ring.

"I will." Slowly he slid the ring onto the ring finger of my left hand, then brought my knuckles up to his lips for a kiss.

"I still do not think it a good idea," he said at length. "Your father will never forgive me, and I'd hoped to have been on better terms with Lord Hertford."

"I left him a note. I told him we were eloping."

"Ah. I do hope he's not the bellicose sort—he isn't going to demand a reckoning, is he?"

I couldn't help but laugh. "I do hope not! He is as likely to shoot himself in the foot, or perhaps his second—which will probably be Tristan—as he is likely to shoot you. But," I continued quickly, "he has already given his—"

My words were cut off by a loud pounding on the door. Startled, we both looked up to see the heavy door swing open to admit a flunky with a scarf tied over his head and a rather piratical-looking eyepatch.

Swearing under his breath, Ashby begged my pardon and rose to go find out what the fellow wanted. I tracked his lithe movements for a moment—struck, as always, by his perfect blend of grace and swagger—before I busied myself once more with my cooling stew, listening as best I could to their agitated conference. Finally, I heard Ashby sigh irritably, then say, "Fine, bring her here."

Startled, I looked up to see him returning to our table as the door slammed behind the exiting flunky.

He looked profoundly unhappy as he took his seat opposite me.

"A woman has arrived?" I asked.

He favored me with a long, measured look. "Yes."

"Gabrielle?"

"How did you know?"

"She told me she was involved with this."

Another great pounding on the door signaled the return of

the piratical flunky. Shoving the door open, he stood aside for Gabrielle, though I would have been hard pressed to identify the cloaked figure if I hadn't already known it was her. She glided silently into the room, and didn't startle when the door slammed shut behind her—apparently she was used to the heavy doors of this place.

Ashby was on his feet immediately, striding over to where she awaited him. "What is it?" he demanded. "What has happened?"

Two ghostly pale hands emerged from the folds of the cloak, and slowly drew the hood back from their owner's face. The muted lighting was not kind to Gabrielle, making her look old and drawn. Her eyes looked tired as they glanced at Ashby, then came to settle on me.

"I have a message for Elina," she said, her already strong French accent made stronger by her fatigue. She must have set a challenging pace on the roads to have caught up with me so soon.

I eyed her warily. "For me?"

"What is it?" Ashby demanded.

Gabrielle shot Ashby a cryptic look. "The message is for Elina. But it is not for me to tell. To hear it, she must come with me."

"Gabrielle," Ashby said, a dangerous edge to his voice, "who have you brought here?"

Gabrielle did not flinch. "I had no choice. You will see, once you have heard the message."

"*Who* have you brought?" he repeated.

"Sir Tristan," she replied. "He is waiting outside *le château.*"

CHAPTER 32

W E LEFT THE UNDERGROUND labyrinth the same way
I came, though it was evident from the size of the
crates and casks in Ashby's storage room that there
must have been a far more convenient point of entry for the
movement of large, bulky items.

Gabrielle led the way through the chalky tunnel, with me in
the middle and Ashby bringing up the rear.

None of us spoke a word.

When we finally emerged from the hidden trapdoor, the
cool dampness of the sea air hit me in a rush. It was dark now,
with only a faint glow of pink tingeing the heavy clouds to the
west. It would be another hour or so till moonrise, but I could
still see Tristan clearly through the ruined curtain wall as he
patiently walked his stallion Bellerophon back and forth to cool
him down after the strenuous journey. Behind him, Gabrielle's
sorrel gelding received similar treatment from one of the guards.

Tristan, I knew from long experience, had ears like a bat,
and so had heard our approach long before he chose to acknowl-
edge our arrival. As we stood somewhat awkwardly, watching
him continue with Bellerophon, I wondered at Ashby's strange
silence. It was not at all what I would have expected from a man

whose enemy has appeared upon his doorstep. But Tristan finally chose to speak before I could pursue that thread any further.

"Lady Delemere," he said, his manner cold as he brought Bellerophon to a halt in front of me.

I greeted him with a nod. "Good evening. What has happened?"

"It's Phosey," he said, without preamble. He kept his eyes trained so carefully on my face, effectively banishing the others from our conversation. "She is gone."

"What do you mean she's *gone*?"

"She was not in the house when the ladies returned from town."

"But that's impossible," I argued. "She went to town *with* the ladies!"

"She was suffering from one of her headaches this morning and could not go to town. The last Sophie saw of her, she was in bed with the drapes drawn and a cold piece of flannel over her eyes."

"But when she's having one of her migraines, sometimes she becomes delirious. She must be somewhere in the house, lost or unconscious."

"The house has been searched," Tristan said. "Several times, by all of us and all of the servants. The grounds have also been searched, just in case she wandered outside. She is not on the property. And there is something else . . ."

"What?" I demanded.

"Froggenhall is gone, too." he said, his expression grim.

"Oh, my God," I whispered.

"What?" Tristan demanded sharply. "What is it? What do you know?"

"Oh, my God," I repeated. My hands shook as I pressed my fingers to my temples. "I left her alone with him."

"Elina," Ashby cut in. "You did not know she was in the house. This is not your fault."

"But I *should* have known!" I cried. "She's my sister! And she is just a child! And I left her alone with him!"

"*What?*" Tristan roared. "What is it?"

My blood was rushing in my ears. The world around me pitched and swayed.

"Harcourt?" I heard Tristan demand as I stumbled over to the side to wretch. Sinking to my knees, I heard Ashby's voice as he told Tristan about Froggenhall's proposal this afternoon in the garden, careful to leave out the part about the blackmail.

I was sweating, despite the cool night air. As I struggled to stand, I discovered that two slim arms were wrapped around me, one around my waist, the other around my shoulders, supporting me with surprising strength.

"I did not tell Ashby everything," I said. "They must know."

"Then they will come over here to you," Gabrielle said. And then she called out, demanding Ashby's and Tristan's presence. Moments later Ashby's arms encircled me.

"Are you well enough to stand?" he asked.

I nodded and he lifted me back up to my feet.

"There's something else," I said. "Something I did not feel worth mentioning earlier, but now I think it important you should know. I saw it in his eyes. He meant to attack me, but was interrupted by a footman." I sucked in a shaky breath. "Phosey is only fifteen—we cannot leave her alone with a man like that."

"Froggenhall needs money," Ashby said. "So his intentions will be marriage. That will buy us some time."

"We came to the same conclusion," Tristan said. "Rydale told us what you learned about his legal troubles with the Royal College of Physicians and that poor girl's family. Lord Hertford and Lord Beverley are already on their way north to overtake Froggenhall and Phosey before they reach Scotland."

"But Froggenhall won't be heading for Gretna Green," Ashby said.

"Of course, he will!" Tristan argued. "Where else could they be headed? No one in England will marry a fifteen-year-old child without the consent of her father!"

"They can go to the Continent," Ashby pointed out.

"Why on earth would the fool do that?" Tristan exclaimed. "That will take days, and we are already in Yorkshire! He could be in Gretna Green by tomorrow if he rides hard enough!"

"He could." Ashby agreed. "If he were traveling alone. But he's got Phosey with him, and she is ill."

"He will have had to hire a coach," I said. "Phosey cannot ride with a migraine."

"And a coach would be easily overtaken by two gentlemen riding two of Rydale's champion thoroughbreds," Ashby said. "But if he's headed for the Continent, all he needs is a port. And there are many ports to choose from."

"Oh, God," I said, nausea overwhelming me again. "We'll never find them. It's hopeless."

"No," Ashby said softly. "I think there can only be two places he's likely to be heading. Either York or Kingston upon Hull."

Tristan snorted. "Really. And what fortuneteller, pray, has told you that? Why Hull? Why not Whitby or Scarborough? And why York? York is not a port!"

"He will have to choose a very large port," Ashby explained. "Otherwise, he'll be too easy to track. Hull is the closest large port. York, though landlocked, is linked directly to London—the largest port in the country—by way of the Great North Road. He needs only to catch a stagecoach to London, and he can be safely out of English jurisdiction in two days. The mad-doctor also happens to maintain his residence in York, and so it will have the added benefit of being familiar territory to him. Rydale and Hertford," he concluded, "are headed in the wrong direction."

"Then we must go ourselves!" I cried. "Right now! We must delay no further!"

"Two of us will have to go to York," Ashby agreed. "The other two will go to Hull."

"No." Tristan's firm negation startled us into silence.

"Why ever not?" I demanded.

"Your father has sent me here to bring you back to Scarcliff Towers," he said. "*That* is my duty."

"You cannot mean that!" I exclaimed. "You would really allow Phosey to be abducted and brutalized just because you lack the ability to be your own man and think for yourself?"

"Elina," Ashby said warningly.

"Papa would surely not want you blindly following his orders," I continued, "if he knew the information that you now know!"

Tristan spared me a long, measured look. I could tell by the anger in his eyes and his clenched jaw that I had truly struck a nerve. *Good*, I thought mercilessly. *I don't care whose feelings I hurt, so long as Phosey will be safe.*

"It is not I who would allow Phosey to be abducted and misused, but *you*, madam," Tristan said. "If you had not chosen to elope with your lover, to abandon your family, then I would never have been sent on this fool's errand to rescue a daughter from her own poor choices. A daughter," he added, "that clearly does not deserve the family she is rejecting, nor my foolish efforts to save her from herself."

"*C'est ridicule,*" Gabrielle muttered next to me. "*Hommes stupides, avec fierté stupide.*"

"Tristan," I said. "I am sorry. But Ashby and I will go to York. You and Gabrielle will go to Hull. It is the right thing to do," I added. "You know it is. It is what Papa would want you to do."

"Fine," he said stiffly. "But it will be you and I who go to York, and Harcourt and Gabrielle to Hull."

"It's *Ashenhurst* now," Ashby pointed out quietly. "Our school days were a long time ago. *I* will be going to Hull, and Elina will be coming with me. You and Gabrielle will go to York."

"No," Tristan and I declared in unison. For a moment, Tristan looked supremely pleased, but then I continued firmly, "Ashby and I will go to York. Tristan and Gabrielle will go to Hull."

"What does it matter who goes to where?" Gabrielle demanded. "We are wasting time with this bickering, *non*?"

Ashby turned to look at me. Taking me by the shoulders, he explained, "I know Hull well, Elina. I do business there and I am well-known on the docks, so the people there will talk to me. Otherwise, trying to track Phosey down will be like finding a needle in a haystack. York, on the other hand," he continued, "will be relatively easy to check. All Tristan will need to do is search Froggenhall's residence—he may have stopped there to pack, and his servants might talk—and to check the stagecoaches to see if anyone matching their descriptions has booked passage. It will probably be a matter of checking only a handful of coaching inns."

"Very well," Tristan said. "Then Elina and I will go to York."

Ashby shook his head, and looked prepared to argue the point. Catching his eye, I held up my hand, pleading for silence. He glanced from me, to Tristan, then nodded and took a step back.

"Tristan." I reached out to gently touch his arm. "I am going with Ashby. There is nothing you can do or say to alter my decision."

Tristan did not argue. He regarded me steadily for a long moment, and I saw the hurt in his eyes before he could master it. I knew at once that he understood I was not just talking about accompanying Ashby to Hull.

A chilly breeze smelling of the sea ruffled the stray golden tendrils curling at his temples and the lace at his throat. Then he blinked, his lashes resting on his smooth cheek just a moment too long before they lifted again. He turned his head to watch the horses, dismissing me from his line of sight so that I was left studying his strong profile.

I sighed inwardly and let my hand drop down to my side.

"Elina?" Ashby's voice came from beside me, soft and tentative.

Turning to look at him, I told him flatly. "We shall be going to York."

York, I was convinced, was where I would find my sister. And I was determined that I would be the one to save Phosey from her captor. It was the very least I could do after failing her so terribly. What matter if Ashby knew Hull like the back of his hand if Froggenhall had not taken her there in the first place?

"Elina," Ashby's voice was still soft, but a commanding strength had replaced the tentativeness of just moments before. "You must trust me in this. We shall go to Hull."

I shook my head emphatically, prepared to argue with him.

"Do you trust me?" he asked.

"Yes."

"Good." He nodded curtly, then turned back to Tristan. "Richmond, you and Gabrielle will go to York. If you do not find Froggenhall, I want you to meet us at the port. It will be a long ride, but you will find fresh mounts at the Black Swan Inn on Goodramgate. The proprietor is named Alice. She should remember Gabrielle, but in case she does not, show her this." Ashby reached into his sleeve and pulled out what appeared to be a playing card, which he handed to Tristan.

Tristan stared at the card a moment, squinting slightly to make out the image in the darkness, then replied "This is a tarot card. The Sun."

At this, Gabrielle's eyes widened briefly in surprise.

"Turn the card over," Ashby said.

This Tristan did, and suddenly he looked startled.

"What?" I demanded. "What is it?"

Tristan glanced up at Ashby. "It's true, then?"

"It is," Ashby replied.

Tristan continued to watch Ashby, his eyes narrowed in

speculation. Seeing that he wasn't going to answer me, Gabrielle moved forward to pluck the card out of Tristan's hands and held it up for me to see. Like Tristan, I had to squint to make out the figure painted on the back, but since it was painted in black, I couldn't see what it was supposed to be.

"A black unicorn," Gabrielle volunteered helpfully. And all at once, the outline of the figure resolved itself into a unicorn rampant, just like the two painted on the wall of the chapel at Scarcliff Towers.

"You are the Black Unicorn," Tristan said.

"I am," Ashby confirmed. "But you knew that . . . didn't you?"

"It had occurred to me, yes. I didn't know for certain until I saw this." Tristan gestured towards the dilapidated castle and the guards. "Still, highway robbery? Why?"

"That, my dear fellow, is a story better told over a bottle of wine," Ashby replied dryly. "And unfortunately we have no time for such things. We must leave at once."

"I will hold you to that, Ashenhurst."

And without any further ado, we made ready to rescue my sister.

CHAPTER 33

WE MADE GOOD TIME in our rush south.

After thundering down the coast for two hours, we turned inland at Bridlington, to head due west into the low hills of the East Riding Wolds. We reached the market town of Kilham in under an hour, then turned south again to make the run over the hilly terrain to the minster town of Beverley. As I caught my first glimpse of the great medieval church's towers breaking through the town's lesser buildings, I felt a glimmer of hope. Beverley was close to Kingston upon Hull—its smaller dot less than an inch from Hull's larger dot on the map of Britain Papa kept framed in his library.

If Phosey was truly in Hull, it wouldn't be long before I held her safe in my arms.

As we slowed to pass through the sleeping town, the staccato beat of our horses' hooves on the cobblestones and Diabo's labored breathing were the only sounds reverberating through the close streets. Ashby twisted in his saddle to speak to me for the first time since our departure.

"This is the last town before Hull," he said, confirming my surmise. "From here we will head southeast for about sixteen kilometers. I expect we shall reach the port in just under two hours."

"So long?" I said, suddenly deflated. "Surely we can close that distance in under an hour."

"Beleza certainly could," he agreed, indicating the Arabian mare he'd provided me for the journey. "But Diabo is spent. We must slow our pace until he recovers."

I didn't say anything, but sat in silent dissatisfaction. He was correct, of course. It was evident from the silvery sheen of sweat on Diabo's flanks and the animal's heavy breathing and snorting that the horse had reached the limit of his endurance.

Fortunately for Diabo, the journey from Beverley to Hull proved an easy one. The hilly landscape of the Wolds melted into a broad, pastoral plain of fields and meadows. Gradually, the countryside began to shift into a more urban ordering of things. The scent of the cool night air took on that ripe quality that heralded one's approach to a large settlement of people living together in dirt and squalor, spiced with the acrid stench of heavy industry.

As we entered the town from the east, rows of houses on the north side of the street suddenly gave way to timber yards, and up ahead, over the shallow roofs and plain chimneys, I could see the tops of a forest of ship masts from the river.

Ashby conversed with the night in a language I did not understand. Things caught his attention that missed mine, while he ignored other noises that sounded threatening and alien to my ears. He urged Diabo closer to me, and I saw that he had let the horse's reins drop, each hand now occupied with a pistol resting casually on each thigh.

The ship masts from the haven steadily grew larger until the houses suddenly gave way, and I saw the ships—small galleys, brigantines, dories, and great three-masted barks—all of them with their sails reefed and tied. Many lay quietly midstream in the sluggish waters of the river Hull, while others pressed almost haphazardly two or three ships deep against the staithes of the west bank. All along the east bank, as far as my eyes could see, lay more timber yards, while the west side looked to be a solid wall of warehouses.

The road narrowed to a bridge that crossed the river, post lanterns fueled with whale oil hanging at intervals, lighting our passage, but casting the world beyond into deeper darkness.

I glanced down the haven to where the Hull eventually emptied into the great River Humber some thirty kilometers from the open sea, and I saw a small spot of smoldering fire burn near the mast of one of the ships. As I watched, it slowly grew more intense for the space of a few seconds, then suddenly winked out. Then it reappeared, only now on another ship further down the river. Then another appeared on another ship, and another, until the entire harbor looked to be populated by very large, very sluggish glow worms, slowly throbbing in and out of existence.

"Guards," Ashby murmured before I could pose the question.

"Sorry?"

"Guards," he repeated. "On the ships. They're smoking tobacco to pass the time."

"Oh." I preferred the glow worms. "But why are they in the dark?"

"They can see better in the dark. And people cannot see them."

"Can they see us?"

"Oh, yes. They're watching us."

"Oh," I said, glad of the pistols on Ashby's lap.

Once across the bridge, the road widened once more. We passed a series of businesses and facilities that looked related to the quay and the harbor, and a number of public houses, taverns, and inns. We passed more timber yards and inns until the road swept up in a broad curve and then resolved itself back into a long straight avenue, and we found ourselves transitioned abruptly into a clean, smart suburb with newly-paved streets and more light.

A neat row of brick shops with large bow windows ran along the northern side of the street, and the southern side was almost wholly taken up by a long row of fashionable bourgeois terrace houses, four stories high with matching white doors and white-painted ironwork gates protecting their narrow, uniform frontage. All the windows of these homes were dark, though each was brightly lit by a lantern hanging over each door and more post lanterns hung in intervals along the street and at each intersection.

This, I knew immediately, was not the neighborhood where we would find my sister.

"Ashby . . . " I began, but the mournful hour-song of the night-watch interrupted me before I could continue. It was three o'clock in the morning.

"Ashby," I repeated, "what are we doing here?"

"I must go back to the quayside," he replied, "but I cannot do it with you accompanying me. Too dangerous."

"But shouldn't we be checking the inns?"

"No," he said flatly. "It is too late. If any of them opened their doors to us at this hour, it would likely be to sailors waiting to rob us and slit our throats. Besides," he continued, "servants talk. I don't want to alert Froggenhall to our presence here before I first know where he is."

"Ashby," I said quietly. "I cannot allow her to spend the night with him. We don't know . . . "

"I know," he said gently. And to his credit, he did not point out that whatever Froggenhall planned to do with Phosey, he'd likely done it hours ago. "Let's get inside before we discuss this any further. Ah," he said, bringing Diabo to a halt. "here we are."

Beleza pulled up next to Diabo with no urging from me, and I looked up to see the house that held Ashby's interest. It was new, its bricks not yet faded by the sun, and roughly twice the size of the other houses on the street. It stood on a corner, detached from the terraced row with about twenty feet in between. And a good thing, too, since the level of noise coming from the place would have driven anyone to distraction who had to share a wall with it.

The prominent windows on the *piano noble* were all lit, as were many of the sash windows in the bedrooms above. From where we stood on the street, we could hear the din of voices punctuated frequently by women's laughter and underscored by the faint strains of music. There were probably more people awake in this one house than sleeping in all the other houses on the street.

Ashby dismounted, then helped me from my saddle as two grooms materialized to take the horses. We passed through the gate and moved up the shallow flagstone stairs just as the front door opened silently upon well-oiled hinges. Ashby exchanged a few murmured words with the officious-looking butler, asking to see the lady of the house while doing his best to block me from view as much as possible. It was then I remembered I was dressed in buckskin breeches on loan from Gabrielle so that I could ride astride to Hull. With a dawning sense of horror I realized I was about to disrupt some fashionable lady's soiree dressed like a man, with no corset to blunt the curves of my figure.

I must have gasped, because at exactly that moment the butler peered at me over Ashby's shoulders, and then did a double-take once he saw me. I began to back down the stairs, mortified and furious at Ashby for placing me in such a humiliating predicament. I didn't get far, however, before he caught me by the arm and hauled me into place beside him.

"I will see your mistress," he growled at the butler, his expression brooking no argument.

The butler, who had a rather Teutonic look about him, furthered the impression by clicking his heels together with a sharp snap of his head. He stood to the side to allow us entry. Much to my anxiety, the sound of voices and laughter increased markedly. Fortunately, the door we were shown through opened only onto a deserted drawing room. My relief was so profound, I did not hear what Ashby murmured to the butler before the latter turned to leave, though I did catch the brief, almost speculative look he threw my way before closing the door silently behind him.

I had not any time to question Ashby, however, before a soft knock roused my anxiety once more. This turned out to be the housekeeper, who after gracing me with a quick assessment, asked me to follow her. Thinking I was on my way either to the kitchens or to a chamber where I might don something more appropriate, I followed without hesitation. The housekeeper deposited me upstairs in a bedchamber, her only words before she left were that my gentleman would be joining me shortly.

I frowned at the door as she closed it behind her. Something seemed distinctly off about this place. The women's laughter filtering up through the floorboards held a bizarre quality, almost bordering on the hysterical. It seemed calculated, as though the soiree's female guests were all pretending to be tipsy. It was indeed an affectation that some women adopted, to be sure, but an entire party filled with such women seemed strange. And I could not detect the mellow timbre of any masculine chortles, though I could occasionally hear the low thrum of a few words spoken here and there.

Eventually I wrenched my attention away from the noises below and turned to find myself a chair, but this bedchamber did not have any, not even a bench at the foot of the bed. So I sat down gingerly on the mattress edge, careful not to disturb the fine counterpane of red cotton chintz. I attempted to keep my posture as rigid as it would have been had I been wearing a corset. It was not long, however, before my shoulders bowed inward, my head drooping as I crossed my arms over my belly and folded in on myself.

HEATHER E. F. CARTER

I was exhausted.

I lay back and closed my eyes. My body ached from the long hours in the saddle. I wondered if Tristan and Gabrielle had reached York yet.

And then I thought of nothing.

CHAPTER 34

I KNEW I WAS DREAMING right away.
    I stood at my chamber door in Delemere House, staring
down at my miniature greyhound laid out upon the threshold. Fredericka had been a wedding gift from Sophie, a little
companion to keep me company in my new home with William.

I squatted down easily, not yet laced into my stays for the
day, and ran a hand down the sleek little body. So cold. I moved
my hand up to pet her narrow head, then stroked behind one
velvety ear the way she liked, careful to avoid the gaping wound
in her neck that had caused her to bleed out all over the carpet.

I awoke abruptly.

A man was leaning over me, his breath disturbing the little
hairs curling around my face.

He was not Ashby.

My eyes flew open, then struggled to adjust their focus. He
was a blond man in his thirties, with a narrow face, and deeply-
set hazel eyes spaced too closely together. He was smiling with a
small, cruel mouth. And he was well-dressed, judging from his
cravat of expensive lace.

"Not a boy," he pronounced, his cultured accents slurred by

the wine I smelled upon his breath. "But not Amelia, either," he added softly.

Then he reached out to touch my hair, the scented frills at his wrists spilling across my face as my instincts began to scream *Danger*.

"Mmmm," he murmured, "lovely, in fact. Yes, you'll do nicely, my dear. To hell with that pock-marked whore."

With a shriek, I shoved at him with all my strength, but since I was already flat on my back, he had me at a disadvantage. Finding that he was intractable, I changed tactics and went for his face with my nails.

"Now, now," he chided, dodging my hands with practiced ease. Quick as a viper, he caught one wrist and pinned it roughly over my head. I made a grab for his hair with my free hand, but he was ready for that as well. Then he had both my wrists pinned to the bed.

"You are going to have to be nice," he said.

I suddenly remembered I wore breeches. I hauled my knees up as sharply as I could, aiming for his groin. He evaded the blow, then released my hands to grip my knees and shove them apart. I screamed again, and he struck me hard across the face with his closed fist.

The blow staggered me. I blinked rapidly, trying to clear from my vision flashing spots of light. The next thing I knew, he was stroking my swelling cheekbone almost tenderly as he spoke. " . . . not a whore. Your skin is too fine, I think. I've only ever encountered this degree of fight in a little fresh girl. But surely you couldn't still be a virgin?"

It took a moment for me to get my mouth working. "I am not a whore. Get off me."

"Oh, I don't think so," he crooned. "I haven't had a fuck this good in a very long time." And to further telegraph his intentions, he suddenly rammed his groin into mine. Through my breeches, I felt his erection slam into my pubic bone.

I began to scream.

"Shut up, you bitch!" he snarled, clapping his hand roughly over my nose and mouth.

He cut off my ability to breathe. I tried to pry his hand away from my face, but the brute was too strong. I began feeling dizzy from the lack of air. My struggles became more desperate, while my pulse thundered in my temples.

Then time seemed to leap forward again, and he was slapping me lightly on the cheeks. So relieved was I to suck some air back into my lungs, I didn't fight him when he grabbed me and rolled me over onto my stomach and pinned my hands behind me.

"Tell me," he said meditatively, "since you dress like a boy, does that mean you take it like a boy?"

"Get *off* me!" I had meant to scream the words, but since he was crushing my lungs with the weight of his body, it came out as more of a hiss.

"Wha' th' 'ell?" came a coarse female voice from somewhere near the door. "Sir Bertram, it's me yer supposed t' be wi' tonight, not some *boy*."

"Please!" I cried as loudly as I could. "Help me!"

"Go away, Amelia, you filthy slut," Sir Bertram said mildly, shoving my face into the mattress. "You were late. I found this little piece in your bed, and I mean to have her."

"Bu', Sir Bertram," the girl pleaded, " 'e don't work 'ere."

"*She*, you blathering bitch, seems to work just fine."

"Wait!" the girl suddenly yelped. "Sir Bertram, look out!"

With a startled shriek, Sir Bertram was wrenched off me. Quickly, I rolled over just in time to see Ashby smash Bertram face first into the wall, crushing the plaster and leaving a bloody smear where his nose had been crushed.

"I am going to kill you," Ashby murmured into the man's ear. "But I think I will castrate you first."

I looked down, and saw the reason for Sir Bertram's strange stillness. Ashby had a large knife nestled close beneath the man's testicles. The pervert's breeches were now around his ankles, though I did not remember him removing them. I looked down at my own breeches and saw to my horror that they had been pulled down to my knees, and my drawers were bunched around the tops of my thighs.

I screamed. Ashby turned to look at me, eyes ablaze. He stared at me a moment in dumb confusion, his mind clearly fighting the picture I presented before him. Then the fire in him seemed to fizzle out, and his features went slack.

"Elina" he said, his flat voice foreign to my ears, "get out of the room. Now."

"No!" Bertram shrieked, breaking the spell. "I didn't touch her, I swear it!"

"Liar!" I screamed. "You bloody filthy liar!"

"I only had a little fun, but I didn't poke her! Dear God, I swear to you it's true! Please, I swear!" He sagged against the wall, sobbing.

Bertram's admission did not seem to have the desired effect on his executioner. Dragging the man back a few steps, Ashby suddenly flung him hard against the wall and pivoted to aim a pistol into the man's face.

"I am going to kill him," he told me quietly. "If you do not want to see it, leave the room now."

"I want to see it."

Sir Bertram squawked and cast about wildly for a savior. Then they settled on a figure in the doorway.

"Madam," he cried, "you will allow this murder in your house? I am a Justice of the Peace, for God's sake!"

"Milord," came a smooth voice, "please do not shoot Sir

Bertram. I fear that should he die on my premises, I would find myself ruined."

Ashby nodded and allowed his arm to drop. Then he pivoted again and brought the knife's blade down across Sir Bertram's face in a diagonal slash. The movement was so sudden, the slash so brutal as it tore through eye and nose, that we all stood frozen in place. No one uttered a sound except for Sir Bertram, who had doubled over onto the floor, screaming wildly.

The madam, a tall, almost mannish-looking woman with black hair and a severely-cut black gown, looked no more shocked than Ashby, who was now carefully pulling up my drawers and breeches. She nodded to me soberly, glanced down at Ashby's bloody knife ruining the carpet next to his feet, then quietly left the room.

"I am sorry." Ashby sat on the edge of the narrow bed, elbows on knees, head in hands.

We were up in the attic where the servants slept. A housemaid scheduled to work through the night had 'volunteered' her bed for me to sleep in until she came up to rest after breakfast. The room left much to be desired, but I did not complain or object. The door leading to the attic stairs boasted a solid lock, and each of the tiny attic rooms locked from both the inside and the outside.

"For what?" I asked dully.

"For not seeing that you were safely settled before I went to speak with Elizabeth."

The housekeeper, apparently, had made a gross mistake by leaving me in one of the 'working' bedchambers. I was never to have set foot on that floor. The housekeeper had been let go. Judging from Ashby's wrath, she had been lucky.

"You are not sorry for bringing me to a brothel?" I asked, mildly curious.

He straightened up just enough to turn and look at me, his face haggard. "I had very good reasons for bringing you here. But I am sorry for what happened—I will never forgive myself." He reached out to touch my swollen cheek, but let his hand drop. "I will kill him."

"Madame Elizabeth said that killing him will ruin her, and I take it you have some sort of *relationship* with the lady."

Ashby scowled and turned his face away from me. "She said that killing him *on her premises* would ruin her."

"Why did you mutilate him?"

The ghost of a smile flit across his features, though it held no hint of humor. "Because I wanted to. Because I cannot kill him right away, and I want him to suffer as much as possible until I can kill him. And because it felt good."

"I bet it did," I said, not bothering to disguise the wistfulness in my voice. "I wish I could have done it. Someday, though, I think I should like to know what it feels like to fight my own battles."

He turned to look thoughtfully at me. "Then there are a few things I will have to teach you."

We said nothing for a while. I strained my ears to listen for any traces of the business being conducted two floors down. But all I could hear was the faint whistle of the early-morning breeze passing through a missing pane in the broken window. The air seemed to hold that special chill that signaled the hours just before the break of dawn, and I wondered how much time had passed since we'd arrived at this dreadful place.

Where could Phosey be at this moment? Sleeping peacefully, I prayed, and oblivious to discomfort and danger, if only for a short while.

"Elina?"

"Hmmm?"

"That relationship you spoke of . . . the relationship with Elizabeth?"

"Yes?"

"It is only business."

I had to smile at that. "Isn't that always the way with whores?"

He snorted. "I suppose it is. Though my business has nothing to do with sex. I buy other things from her. And she buys some things from me."

I raised my eyebrows.

"I buy information from her," he clarified.

"Information?"

"I brought you here tonight, because I needed a safe place to leave you—" His face twisted at the painful irony of this statement. "—while I went down to the quayside. And I needed to ask Elizabeth if she's heard anything of Phosey."

"Why would the madam of a brothel know anything of my sister?" I asked sharply.

"Because that madam trades in flesh," he explained. "Phosey is exactly the sort of commodity that Elizabeth keeps a look out for. Even if there is never a question of Phosey becoming one of Elizabeth's whores, she is still likely to know of the girl's arrival in her town. Especially if that arrival is under questionable circumstances."

"And has she heard anything?"

"No."

"Ashby . . . " I began warningly.

"That does not mean she isn't here," he cut in quickly. "She did just arrive this evening, which is really too soon for it to reach Elizabeth's ears, but I had to try. Elizabeth will likely find out where she is sometime tomorrow, but I plan to have found her myself by then."

"And Froggenhall?"

"I will kill Froggenhall."

I nodded. "You should go. I will be fine."

"I don't like leaving you."

"I am not coming with you down to the quayside at this time of night. Madam Elizabeth has posted a footman by the door at the foot of the stairs, and this door has a lock."

"I know," he said. "Elina . . . "

"We are wasting time. It will be dawn soon, and then Froggen-hall will be able to move her. You must find them before that."

He continued to watch me with haunted eyes, but I turned away towards the dirty window and gazed out into the darkness. The squashed filling of the mattress barely shifted when he rose to his feet. A moment later, the door opened and then quietly closed behind him.

I had not even begged him to be careful, though I knew he risked his life by going to the quayside at this hour.

With a heavy sigh, I scooted down into the bed and pulled the threadbare quilt up around my shoulders. Slowly the heaviness of sleep began to take me, and my last thoughts before abandoning myself to oblivion were of Tristan. He would have reached York by now, and would have begun his search with Gabrielle.

Tristan, I knew, would never have brought me to a brothel.

CHAPTER 35

I WAS AWAKENED EARLY THE following morning by the sound of thunder.

It filtered through the layers of sleep, incorporating itself into my dreams. At just about the moment I realized something was wrong with it, I woke up.

I sat up in bed, wondering how on earth anyone in this wretched town could sleep with such a racket going on.

"It's the dock," Ashby said. "They're unloading cargos, only a few streets over."

He sat next to me in a chair tilted back precariously onto its two back legs with his shoulders resting against the wall and one booted foot propped up on the rickety washstand, with the other crossed over. His eyes were closed, and in the clear morning light he looked very young. His lashes resting on the bruised-looking hollows beneath his eyes fluttered and lifted, and he turned to focus his eyes sleepily on me.

Then I remembered: Phosey!

Ashby had gone to the quayside last night to look for her.

My posture went rigid, as though an electric current had shot up my spine. "Did you learn anything about my sister? Do you know where she is?"

He let his chair drop back down to its four legs and shook his head. "No. But, I know where she will be. I found the ship on which they have booked passage. They leave tonight."

Relief washed over me. "My God. She really is here?"

A corner of his mouth twitched, and he inclined his head. "She really is here."

"Then we must find her!" I declared, throwing the quilt off my legs. "We must find her now! I cannot allow her to remain with Froggenhall until tonight! He may change his mind and take her to another ship!"

"Or, if he is very clever, he will book passage on several ships to throw us off his trail," he said. "But, we do know she is here. That is a start—a very good start. And there is one more thing . . ."

"What?"

"He is traveling with her as his sister."

I frowned, not comprehending.

"They are not traveling as man and wife. Yet."

"So . . . they will have separate rooms," I said slowly.

He nodded. "And if that is the case, there is a chance . . . " He let his voice trail off, not wanting to voice the delicate assumption.

"There is a chance she is still a virgin," I said quietly. I glanced up at him, my eyes suddenly shining with tears. "Thank you," I whispered, though I knew not whether I spoke to Ashby or to God.

Ashby's plan, he told me, was to head down into the old medieval portion of Hull, located south of the great Queen's dock, the source of all the thundering noise that had disturbed my sleep.

It was by far the most populous part of town, with the most inns, and he thought that its crush of people would be the ideal place for Froggenhall to conceal himself and his charge while he waited for his ship's departure come evening. Due to the press of humanity, as well as the nature of the narrow medieval streets, we would travel by foot.

So we set out from Madam Elizabeth's establishment—now silent as a tomb—at about half-past eight. One of Madam Elizabeth's girls had been kind enough to lend me clothing more suitable for a lady than breeches. The dress proved simple and rather conservatively cut, with just a hint of lace at the elbows to embellish the dark green wool. The borrowed corset was a bit long at the hip, but other than that I had no complaints.

As we headed out of the suburbs down towards the haven, the noise became almost overwhelming. Lining the south side of Dock Street were timber yards, adding their cacophony to the noise, and through the gaps between them I could see some of the frenetic activity of the Queen's Dock. Sailors, watermen, dockworkers, and men whom Ashby identified as stevedores and longshoremen swarmed over the decks of the ships and the quay, their activities looking no more sensible or coordinated than dozens of chickens running about with their heads cut off.

Great cargo nets swung down from booms mounted on the ships' decks, or from one of the several massive cranes mounted on the quay, accompanied by a terrific amount of shouting from all directions. Everywhere there were casks, barrels, hogsheads, bolts of cloth, stacks of timber, pigs of iron, piles of exotic-looking fruit, and even crates of books being unloaded from ships, then reloaded onto carts.

And I had never in my life seen so much rope—coils of rope, tangles of rope, lines of rope pulling against each other at seemingly cross purposes. And yet no one ever tripped, though everyone's eyes always seemed tilted up towards the great, heavy loads of valuables descending from above.

I, however, had no such instincts for avoiding danger. Dock Street was almost as busy as the quay itself, as the carters moved the cargos from the quays to their various warehouses lining the haven, with no regard for the life and limb of any unlucky pedestrian in their way. There were no walkways of flagstones, nor even safety posts lining the street to separate street traffic from foot traffic, and so it was entirely up to Ashby to keep me from being flattened while I ogled the activity of the dock.

After a particularly close call involving myself and an irate carter, hauling an incongruous load of pig iron and oranges, we turned off Dock Street to follow the dock's curve down through the comparatively quieter Dock Office Row. We crossed the bridge, and from its high point I admired the striking skyline of the old medieval town. Twin forests of masts rose to the east and west respectively from the haven and the dock. To the south jagged rows of sharp-pitched gables radiated from the somber, age-blackened towers of St Mary's like the concentric rows of a sea monster's serrated teeth. Those towers, which dominated her prosaic surroundings with all the dignity of a great French cathedral, would serve as our compass as we moved through the tangle of streets.

Once we reached Lowgate, the main artery that would lead us straight to the central Market Place, the town took on an entirely different character from the smart suburb north of Queen's Dock. I realized at once what Ashby had meant when he'd spoken of the crowds.

The number of people was staggering, and the further south we moved, the more crowded it became. The streets, as Ashby had indicated, were far too narrow to support the amount of vehicle and pedestrian traffic attempting to squeeze through. On several occasions where the traffic clogged itself into an intractable mass of cursing humanity, we were obliged to leave the main thoroughfare and continue along the dark, twisty side streets until we cleared the blockage.

Though our progress was slowed by several diversions down

side streets, it probably took us no longer than twenty minutes to reach the market place. Here, the freshly-paved cobblestone street widened substantially, causing the throng of traffic to clear, and the surrounding buildings bore the stamp of recent construction. It was market day, which explained some of the vehicle traffic, and everywhere there were temporary stalls set up to sell everything from farm produce of every imaginable variety to linens, knives, hardware, candles, woodwork, leather, and earthenware.

Ashby strode purposely towards a large coaching inn called the Cross Keys Hotel, and I hurried to catch him up. Posing as my employer, he could not walk me through the streets on his arm, but he still could not bring himself to allow me to open the door for myself. Remembering that I, too, owed my "betters" deference, I acknowledged Ashby's courtesy with a quick bob at the knees before I hurried through the door.

But Phosey was not at the Cross Keys. Nor was she at the Dean's, the Fleece, the Queen's, the Black Swan, or the Bull and Sun. Having exhausted the possibilities within the immediate environs of the Market Place, we continued further south, past the large Guildhall and the four-story draper's emporium, through the narrow shambles of the Butchery to the Golden Lion public house on the corner of Blanket Row and Queen's Street. The sun had risen now to its zenith, its rays beating down upon me through the handkerchief I had tied over my hair as my dark woolen dress absorbed its heat. My growing sense of desperation urged me to press on, but I was forced to admit I needed some refreshment first.

The Golden Lion was an establishment that had seen better days, though it was still busy with custom. Ashby led me to a small table in the back corner somewhat separated from the rest of the patrons. Offering me the seat facing away from the door, he took his across from me and then raised his hand for the barmaid. Once she had been dispatched with our order, he quickly scanned the room before settling his gaze back onto me. I sensed he had something to say to me, and so held off for the moment on my questions about how and where we should next proceed.

"He hurt you," he said after a few moments.

Startled, I moved to touch my swollen face, then thought better of it since I didn't want to disturb the thick powdery paste Madam Elizabeth had used to conceal the bruise. I lowered my hand back down to the table. "Yes, I know."

He shook his head. "I'm talking about Delemere. William. He hurt you. He . . . struck you?"

The barmaid arrived and set down two tall pewter tankards, then left as silently as she had come.

I watched the foam sliding down the side of my tankard. "Sometimes," I said. "Sometimes he did . . . other things."

"He forced himself on you?"

"Never when you were there," I said, my voice flat. "But, yes. Eventually he grew bored of his sport, and found other ways to torture me. He killed my miniature greyhound Fredericka."

"Elina," he said softly. "What happened the night he died?"

"The night of the fire?"

"Yes."

I looked away. "I cannot speak of it. Not yet."

"When he died, you thought you were free."

"I did."

"You thought you would never allow anyone to treat you that way again."

"Yes."

"But last night . . . "

I glanced up at him. "Last night it happened again."

"Because of me."

I couldn't read his expression; he was leaning back, keeping his face in the shadows. I heard the resonance of deep regret.

I sighed and cast my eyes back down to the foamy tankard in front of me. "I know you stayed close to William to protect me. And you succeeded. When you were around, William found his amusement elsewhere. But Ashby, there's something you should know about me . . . before we are married."

"Yes?"

"I am not ready to give details yet. But you should know . . . I am not his victim," I glanced up into his face, then back down at my tankard. "William's death was no accident."

"I know," he said quietly.

I glanced up sharply. "That's impossible. The only other person who knows . . ."

"Is Hugh. The footman who assisted you."

Slowly, realization dawned on me. "He was your man."

"I placed him in your house. To watch over things when I was gone."

"Then you already know."

"I do."

I laughed, a bitter, mirthless laugh. "And still you would marry me."

"He was a monster. What he planned to do to you . . ."

I held up my hand. "Enough, Ashby. I am not ready."

"I would someday like to hear the story," he said quietly. "From you."

I shrugged. "Perhaps someday you will. But Ashby?"

"Hmmm?"

"Does Hugh still work for you?"

"He does. He's here, actually. In Hull. He works now on my yacht, *The Estephania.*"

"I will see him again?"

"Is that a problem?"

"No. I should like to thank him."

"Drink your ale, Elina," Ashby said. "We must continue on, and you'll need your strength. I am not sure when we shall be able to stop again."

Ten minutes later, we left the Golden Lion to continue our journey south on Queen's Street. I paused a moment just outside the pub while Ashby held the door open for a trio of giggling shop girls, and turned to find a small, wizened woman standing under the jetty. She watched me intently. Despite the heat of the day, she wore a heavy cloak, its hood drawn well over her head.

When she caught my eye, the intensity of her gaze sharpened and she looked about to say something to me. But Ashby joined me at that moment, and the strange woman suddenly shied away.

He offered me his arm, and I took it. We'd abandoned our original stratagem of him being my employer. This far down in the old town, amongst these people, it no longer seemed to matter.

The woman puzzled me, and I wondered what she could have wanted.

But by the time we approached a large establishment called the London Hotel, I let the matter of the strange woman drop.

I needed to dedicate all my thoughts and feelings to one goal: finding Phosey.

Nothing else mattered.

CHAPTER 36

"This is starting to feel futile," I said. We stood together under the London Inn's pronounced jetty shading the door. The proprietor, a Mr. Fitzeherbert, knew nothing of Phosey.

"I agree," Ashby replied. "I'm beginning to wonder whether she's in an inn at all."

"But where else could she be?"

"She could be in someone's private house," he replied. "The fact that these people are so reluctant to speak with us is making me suspicious."

"Suspicious of what?"

"I think it possible that Froggenhall may have a protector in this town. Someone well-known and feared."

"Have you any idea who he could be?" I asked, a note of hysteria creeping into my voice. It was now almost tea time, and we'd made no progress.

Ashby shook his head. "Not yet. But now that I am convinced of his existence, I think I know what to look for. Let's move on to the King William. I doubt anything will come of it, but since it's only a short way up the street, we may as well."

The King William was indeed just up the road, across from

the large Custom House of faded red bricks. As we walked, we could see the great expanse of water where the filthy Hull River emptied into the broad, fresh-smelling waters of the Great Humber. Just across from us was the southern tip of the sixteenth-century citadel, revived with a fresh garrison of soldiers to prepare for what seemed an inevitable war with France. Across the water came the sounds of building activity as army engineers diligently updated the old fortress to withstand any barrage from modern French weaponry.

The King William proved to be of much the same character as the London, though a bit smaller. Like Fitzherbert, the cross-eyed innkeeper Humphries did not want to speak to us, nor did he want us speaking with his staff.

Finally, when this line of questioning seemed to be getting us nowhere, and Humphries refused to be tempted by anything shiny in Ashby's pockets, Ashby pulled me aside and politely asked me to take a seat at one of the tables across the room.

It was then I caught sight of a familiar face in the opening of the William's door. She still wore her heavy cloak, just as she had outside the Golden Lion. She watched me intently, her black eyes glittering from within the dark recess of her hood.

I knew she wanted to speak with me, and it must have something to do with Phosey. This was our first solid clue, and I would not let it slip through my fingers. Ashby, busy threatening Humphries, did not notice me slip out the front door.

Back outside in the fading heat of the late afternoon, I felt unaccountably exhilarated. I took a moment to calm myself; I didn't want to appear too eager for the woman's information, especially since I had no money on me. I needed her to think that my allowing her to unburden her soul was an act of charity on my part, not a negotiation for a valuable commodity.

She'd motioned me to follow her down a short alley, and

when I turned the corner, my breathing had calmed, and I'd almost managed to coax my pulse back down to normal.

Still, I hesitated a moment on the street, peering down the snickleway. Ashby had told me repeatedly not to stray out of his line of vision, but that was surely just due to his lingering anxiety over last night's unfortunate events at the brothel.

At first I could not make out the strange woman, but as I stepped further into the alley, my eyes adjusted to the darkness. I saw her standing alone about halfway down to the other side. Behind her I could see the Hull River, and the citadel. I took another step into the alley, wondering irritably why she had to make me walk so far down, then chided myself for my cowardliness. She was alone; there was clearly no one else in the alley, and just as clearly no places for anyone to hide. I could see the smooth lines of solid wall all the way down to the river, so there were no little niches between buildings for a robber or thug to hide. Squaring my shoulders, I marched my way resolutely towards her, reminding myself not to appear too eager.

As I came closer, I saw that she was younger than I'd thought. Wisps of light brown hair escaped the matronly bun beneath her hood, and her lined face still possessed the firmness of middle age. In her late forties, I thought, but certainly no older than fifty. Her cloak was still shut tightly over her clothes, and in a moment of silliness I wondered if she had anything on beneath. I smiled at the thought, and she, seeing it, looked suddenly miserable. For a horrible moment, I thought she might be about to cry.

I rushed forward. "What is it? What is wrong? Has something happened? Is Phosey all right?"

"I am sorry, milady," she whispered. "You must believe me, I had no choice."

"No choice to what?" I cried. "Have you done something to my sister? Where is she?"

"I am sorry."

As her gaze shifted to something behind me, I knew we were not alone. I whirled around to face my attacker, but he caught me with a rough hand over my mouth before I could catch sight of him. Another hand wrapped around my waist, pulling me into his body and holding me immobile as I tried to squirm and kick. I couldn't scream with his hand over my mouth, so I bit down instead. The man howled, and I tasted the coppery saltiness of his blood in my mouth.

"Roger!" he snarled into my hair. "Get over here and help me. The bitch is biting me."

"Then bite her back," came a surprisingly urbane voice from behind us.

He transferred one hand to my hair, and yanked back savagely, exposing the line of my throat. At this angle, I lost much of my teeth's crushing power, and he slipped his hand back out to safety. Then he yanked harder on my hair, forcing me to bend backwards until the boning in my corset began to snap. He gripped my throat, and slowly began to squeeze.

"You had better behave yourself," he growled. "You are about to have a nice long stay somewhere very cold and dark, and you don't want me in there with you, waiting for you to wake up, do you?"

"Please," pleaded the woman from somewhere in front of me. "You promised you wouldn't hurt her!"

"Shut up, woman. Else I might have a mind to hurt *you* and then dump you into the river."

"Gerald, are you going to hit her or not?" Roger queried behind us. "Her bloke's going to come 'round looking for her any minute, and then things will get very messy."

"Let him," Gerald replied, "I'll blow a hole through him the size of my bloody fist."

"Fun as that sounds," Roger mused, "I think it you'd better just hit her."

"Please," I gasped, "I don't have any money. I have nothing of value. My companion will give you anything you want, I swear it."

Of course, Ashby would do nothing of the kind, but I needed to stall the brutes long enough to give him time to find me and kill them. He was probably already looking for me.

"Nothing of value, lovely lady?" Gerald crooned into my ear. "I'm afraid you are undervaluing the worth of your goods. You could be the highest-paid whore in Hull, do you know that? Or we could take you to London, if you like. I hear that the whores down there live like aristocrats, dining on venison and truffles every night."

"She *is* an aristocrat, you bloody idiot," Roger snapped. "Now get on with it!"

"Why, that's even better!" Gerald crowed. "Maybe I *will* have to come visit you in the dark!"

He released me so suddenly, I bowled forward into the cloaked woman, who caught me in her arms.

As I looked up into her sad face, something struck the back of my head with brutal force, gnashing my teeth painfully against each other. I dropped to the ground, the rough pavement cutting into my knees through my skirts. A wave of nausea rolled over me, and I felt a strange moment of confusion as I stared beyond the cloaked woman towards the smooth green waters beyond.

Then a second blow sent me tumbling down into the darkness.

CHAPTER 37

I FIRST BECAME AWARE OF a throbbing pain in my head. I lingered in limbo for a while, dancing through that strange liminal space that separates the waking from the dead.

When I did open my eyes, I met with a darkness so complete, I blinked several times to assure myself my eyes were indeed open.

I seemed to be on the floor.

And *why* did my head hurt so damn much!

I sat up, and suddenly everything came back to me in a rush.

Hull; the alley next to the King William; the strange woman.

Panicked, I surged to my feet, then staggered as pain lanced through my head. I closed my eyes, forcing myself to calm down.

My God, he had me. *They* had me, if Ashby was correct that Froggenhall had a protector.

But I knew from long experience with my late husband that fear, when allowed to run wild, was a useless emotion. Right now I needed my wits about me.

When I opened them again, my eyes had adjusted somewhat to the darkness.

Right. First order of business: take stock of my surroundings.

I was in some sort of storage room. Piles of crates were stacked in haphazard fashion all around.

And there was a door.

I stumbled towards it, propelled by the instinctive need to try it though I knew it must be locked. But then I tripped over something and nearly fell. The bottle rolled off to the side, its progress trackable by the sound of its glass grating against the uneven stone floor. I continued over to the door and grabbed the handle.

Locked.

Panic rose again like bile in my throat. Taking a few fortifying breaths, I turned back to face the room and tried to figure out the next best course of action. There were no windows. There was a place up close to the low ceiling that looked like it had once held a window, but it was now almost seamlessly bricked over. However, the placement of the window, and the height of the ceiling, told me I was most likely in a basement.

I closed my eyes again and tried to focus on what my other senses could tell me.

It was cool. Not very cool, but cooler than it had been outside the King William Inn. Perhaps it was later in the day, but not yet nightfall. I hoped so. I had no idea how long a good smack on the head could incapacitate someone, but twelve to twenty-four hours seemed a bit excessive without causing permanent damage. There was a possibility I was still in Hull.

Right, what next?

I tried a few of the crates, but they were sealed. I had no blankets, no bed, and no food. But there was the object I'd tripped on. I wandered over to the corner where I'd heard it clink against the wall. It was a bottle of wine, the wax broken, the cork jammed in just far enough to keep it from spilling.

I snorted. Did they think me a fool?

I eased myself down onto the floor, thankful for the snapped boning of my ill-fitting corset, and prepared to wait for either my captors, or my rescue, whichever came first.

◆

Several hours later, I still waited.

And I was terribly cold.

Night must have fallen, judging by the drop in temperature.

I'd been careful to keep quiet, not wanting to alert Froggen-hall and his protector to the fact that I was conscious.

But perhaps my captors were waiting for me to wake up before they provided me with a blanket for the night. Since keeping quiet had gotten me nowhere, I decided it was time to yell. It took some warming up, but after a while I got into the swing of things, and began yelling in earnest. When my voice began to give out, I switched to screaming. But I couldn't keep that up for long either. I was just too thirsty, and my strained voice was exacerbating the problem.

Time passed. I lay quietly, thinking about Ashby. Would he come? How could he know where I was? What did Froggenhall have planned? Was Phosey in this house, too?

Poor Phosey. I'd failed her. She'd been with Froggenhall far too long.

At some point I fell asleep. When I woke, my throat felt like fire. I tried to swallow, but my tongue seemed too large for my mouth. It was time to start screaming again, but my current state made that impossible.

What had they done to the wine? Was it meant to kill me? Likely a sip or two wouldn't do the job. I just needed the tiniest bit of liquid. I needed to let Phosey know I was here, in case she was being held nearby.

Desperate, I reached for the wine. But before I knew it, I'd drained half the bottle. My lips and tongue tingled oddly, but I was already feeling warmer as the wine sat in my belly and spread through my extremities.

Gradually, an odd sense of well-being came over me. I felt peaceful. My arms and legs grew pleasantly heavy, and my headache evaporated. Vaguely, I wondered if this was what death felt like.

Sleep would be the best thing. It would pass the time faster, and when I woke Ashby would be there with Phosey and we could all go home together. With that pleasant image in my mind, of Ashby, Phosey, and me walking together hand in hand, I drifted off to sleep.

I woke sometime later, confused and with a bad taste in my mouth.

It was still dark, though the room seemed a bit warmer. I staggered to my feet, and went to attend to nature in a corner behind some crates. My headache was gone, though my thoughts seemed sluggish and dull.

I was terribly thirsty.

I looked down at the wine bottle, and saw that the cork was back in. Frowning, I reached down to pick it up, and found that it was full.

Ah-ha! I thought triumphantly. Someone *was* here! I was not alone after all!

And good God was I thirsty!

I walked over to the door and tried the handle. Still locked. I began pounding on the heavy oak planks, shouting for someone to hear me. It wasn't long before I'd bruised my knuckles from the effort, and my voice was hoarse from the thirst.

Defeated, I turned back towards the bottle of wine and eased myself back down on the floor. I would only drink a little; this might be my only sustenance for the rest of the day. But when I set the bottle back down, it was already half empty. I stared at it, frowning. It *had* been a new bottle, hadn't it? Could I have somehow mistaken it for the same bottle as the night before? Was I that confused?

Maybe I'd been knocked out longer than I'd thought! Maybe I was no longer in Hull!

Maybe I was alone.

I'd been buried alive.

I braced myself for the familiar surge of panic, but instead I felt a growing sense of peace spreading through my body. My lips and tongue tingled, but it no longer seemed odd, and my limbs grew heavy as a pleasant drowsiness covered me. I reached again for the bottle, and drained it.

Ashby would be here soon.

I awoke again with a strange taste in my mouth, and the same raging thirst. I felt uneasy, the unrelieved darkness pressing down on me. I'd lost all track of time; I couldn't quite remember how long I'd been down here. And the bottle was not where I'd left it, but when I picked it up, I felt a tremendous sense of relief: it was a new bottle. Sitting up, I uncorked it with my teeth, and drank deeply. The temperature seemed chillier, and I was a little hungry, so I decided to drink the whole thing as there was still nothing to eat. Soon, I began to feel better, and I lay back down. My hands trembled. It wouldn't be long now before Ashby came.

I slept in fits and starts, always waking to the same oppressive darkness.

At some point, I began to hallucinate.

I woke to find the strange woman from the alley in the room with me. She stood over me, dressed as a housemaid, and she looked very sad.

The next time I woke, my mother was in the room.

"Mama?" I said, rubbing my eyes in confusion. "Where is my wine?"

"It is over there," she said in French, gesturing to where the strange woman stood in the corner holding it.

"Give it to me," I said. "I need it."

"Just a moment, *ma belle fille*," she continued in French. "First you must take this."

There was a candle on the floor next to her, and its light hurt my eyes. I had to squint to focus on the object she held in her hand, but realized I didn't care what it was.

"Then I can have my wine?" I asked.

"*Oui*," she said. She was dressed like a boy in breeches and boots, and her eyes were a striking shade of the deepest violet. This seemed odd, since my mother's eyes had been gray like Sophie's.

"Fine," I said. "Give it to me now."

My mother measured some liquid from a dark brown bottle into a large spoon, then held it steady for me to take into my mouth. I did so without hesitation, not even flinching at the very bad taste, and swallowed all of it. Then I reached for the wine.

"Just a moment, *ma belle fille*," said my mother.

I opened my mouth to argue, but then was suddenly, very messily sick all over the floor. My vomit was a dull red color, like blood. But it wasn't blood, it was the wine. I was vomiting up all my precious wine.

"Why?" I wailed, once my retches had died down. "Why would you do that to me?"

"The wine is poisoned, *chèrie*," she said. "I have brought you better wine." She nodded to the strange woman in the corner.

"Give it to me!" With a final look to my mother, the woman handed it down to me, shying away when I snatched it out of her hands. It was already uncorked, and I drank it greedily. Then I lay back down, waiting for the pleasant warmth of oblivion to wash over me.

I woke a short time later with a terrible headache. I felt sick, and my hands shook. When I opened my eyes, everything seemed to have a red haze around it. I closed them again as someone pressed something against my lips. I opened them just as the smell of the bread hit me. Shoving it away, I rolled over and vomited.

"You must eat," my mother said. "You will feel better."

"The wine," I muttered, keeping my eyes firmly shut. "Is there more wine?"

"You must eat," she repeated. But then I fell back to sleep.

Every time I woke up, the strange woman or my mother was there, pressing me to eat bread or drink water, and when I refused to do either, feeding me that noxious poison from the brown bottle and only then giving me the wine after I'd been sick.

But the wine, I noticed, was not the same. It tasted different, and it wasn't having the same effect. And when I woke, it was with a headache and a very poor stomach. My chamber was starting to smell terribly, and I was becoming more and more anxious.

My hands shook all the time now.

At one point, my mother held out an object for me to see, and asked me if I knew what it was. I took it into my hand, and studied it: a ring with two sapphires. I struggled to focus; the ring seemed familiar. She took the ring back from me, and rotated its face, then held it up for me to see. I looked at the enamel figure of the black unicorn, and suddenly felt very sad. I began to cry, and she repeated "Do you know what this is?"

"It's Ashby's ring," I said.

"Do you know who Ashby is?" she asked.

I thought hard a moment, but concentrating made my head hurt more. No face was coming to mind. "No," I said.

One time, when I woke, I found myself alone. I got up to go relieve myself, and as I shuffled back behind the crates, I noticed a lump on the floor on the other side of the room, concealed behind another stack of crates. Shuffling over to the lump, I looked down and discovered it was a body. A woman, in fact, stretched out on the floor.

This seemed odd. I kicked at her leg, to see if she were alive or dead. She didn't move, so I kicked her harder, this time in the stomach. I didn't want a dead body in here with me.

"*Merde!*" she hissed. "Stop kicking me, you fucking bitch!"

I frowned. "Gabrielle?"

"Yes, of course it is me!" she snarled. "Who else would it be?"

I squatted down and poked her just to be sure.

"Do that again, and I will kick *you* in the stomach," she said.

"It *is* you," I said. "What are you doing here? Where *is* here?" I added, looking around.

"You do not remember?" she asked, sitting up.

"No," I said, shifting my position. "Should I?"

"You have been here a week," she informed me. "What is the last thing you remember?"

I shifted my position again, and sat down next to her. "I do not know," I said. "I don't think I remember anything."

"Do you know your name?"

I thought about it a minute. "Is it Elina?" I asked.

She nodded. "Yes."

"I think I thought you were my mother," I said.

Before she could answer, the sound of a key moving the reluctant mechanism of a heavy lock signaled someone's arrival.

"Get away from here!" she hissed. "Go over to where you were lying, and lie still like you are sleeping."

Confused at the sense of urgency in her voice, I complied and lay my head down just as the door swung open. I kept my eyes tightly closed, though I very badly wanted to see who it could be. I heard someone walk over to where I lay, and sensed them leaning over me, but still pretended sleep. Then I heard Gabrielle's voice.

"Oh, good," the Frenchwoman said in English. "It is only you. I feared the worst."

"The little chick still sleeps?" A familiar voice asked. "Poor dear. I would have thought her better by now."

"Oh, she's better," Gabrielle said, and I heard her stand and come to join the other woman. "She kicks like a fucking mule." I opened my eyes then, and looked up at them both. The other woman, I saw, was the strange woman from the alley.

CHAPTER 38

I'D BEEN THERE FOR a week, alone for the first three days.
That was how long it took Ashby to break the brothel-
keeper Elizabeth, the only person in Hull who knew of
our presence.

That was four days ago.

We were, it turned out, in a house at the bottom of High
Street.

Once Ashby knew where I was, it took him, Gabrielle, and
Tristan another day to turn Mrs. Armstrong, the strange woman
from the alley and also a housemaid belonging to this house.

And she certainly had a strange tale to tell.

Her master was away on business, she explained, but, two
weeks ago, a man fitting Froggenhall's description visited the
house in the company of another man, whom she knew to be
one of her master's business associates. Froggenhall was clearly an
outsider, but the other man was very well known and respected
in the town, and so the household did not hesitate to open their
doors for him.

A few days later, Froggenhall visited again, this time with
a letter from the Master, and gave instructions that he would
be journeying to Hull shortly with a young lady—a very rich

daughter of an ancient aristocratic line, and therefore at great risk for kidnapping. This was his excuse for demanding chambers for his lady guest that, in effect, would prove to be a prison.

The serving staff followed Froggenhall's instructions to the letter. Then, eight days ago—the day before I woke to find myself in the basement—he arrived in the middle of the night with a young girl who was obviously ill and insensible to her surroundings. This could only have been Phosey, still suffering from her migraine.

But this strange arrival, Mrs. Armstrong told us, was only the beginning. Several hours later, during the dark hours of the morning, there came a great banging on the door. The above stairs servants, suspecting that Phosey was more a prisoner of Froggenhall's than a guest, thought the authorities had arrived, perhaps with Phosey's enraged father and some headstrong brothers. Not sure what they should do, they bickered amongst themselves until the racket brought down Froggenhall himself.

Froggenhall, armed with a pistol, shouted through the door for the men to cease their noise and leave the property if they valued their lives. The men announced that they were in the employ of Froggenhall's associate, and that he was outside in his coach in very bad need of a doctor.

More conversation passed between Froggenhall and the men on the porch until finally Froggenhall had enough confidence in the veracity of their claims to go out and check the coach himself. When he came back, his face was ashen, and he ordered all of the serving staff to retire immediately.

No one saw what it was that had Froggenhall so shaken.

The following morning, Mrs. Armstrong was awakened early and summoned to the master's library where Froggenhall awaited her. He told her he knew of Michael, her sister's youngest son, who was ailing from a terrible affliction of the lungs. Should she follow his instructions implicitly, Froggenhall would pay for

Michael to see the finest doctor in Hull. But should she refuse, or should she not follow his every order to the letter, he would make sure that Michael disappeared, never to be seen again.

Mrs. Armstrong hesitated only a moment, then agreed. She was told of me, the role she was to play in bringing me to this house, and the means by which she was to keep me here. She mixed the poisonous concoction into the wine. By the time Gabrielle approached her, she felt her soul in terrible danger of damnation and thought the French woman sent from heaven. She still feared for Michael, of course, but she found Ashby's promises more heartening than Froggenhall's threats.

So, Mrs. Armstrong smuggled Gabrielle into the house to care for me and wean me off the drugged wine. It had taken her almost four days of round-the-clock care before I finally had enough of the poison out of my body to recognize her.

Also, one of Ashby's crew from the *Estephania* had been smuggled into the house, to attempt to find Phosey.

"And so Ashby and Tristan now watch the house," Gabrielle said. "They cannot remove you until they can discover where Phosey is being held. We cannot risk losing her while you escape."

Unfortunately, Mrs. Armstrong had not seen Phosey since that first night she arrived, nor had she seen any of the other servants whom she knew to be caring for the girl. The house did have a very large warehouse attached to the back of it, so it was possible the girl could be in there somewhere.

"But surely Phosey and Froggenhall must be long gone by now," I said, despair sitting in my guts like a lead weight. "They'd booked passage for the night I was brought here."

Mrs. Armstrong shook her head. "I do not think so, milady. Deliveries have been made here throughout the week of ready-made dresses and other articles of clothing specific to the wardrobe of a young lady, and the master has no daughters."

I squeezed shut my eyes, offering a prayer of the most fervent gratitude to any power that might be listening. Then I opened them, and glanced to Gabrielle with a frown. "But I don't understand why I've been kept here so long. Clearly they mean me harm, but poisoning me slowly seems a very odd, not to mention unsatisfying, way of going about it."

Gabrielle shrugged. "I do not know," she said. "But whatever they mean to do with you, I wish they would hurry it up."

I snorted. "You are too kind, Gabrielle."

"You do not understand me," she said, waving my sarcasm away. "They wish to harm you, that we know. Why they wait so long to do it, I do not know. But when they do decide to do it, I think they will bring your sister into the room to . . . How do you say?"

"Afflict with mental anguish?" Mrs. Armstrong suggested helpfully.

"*Oui*, to afflict with mental anguish."

"Okay," I said. "So we are assuming my captors will eventually wish to see me, and that when they do, they will bring Phosey in to afflict me with mental anguish. Then, what?"

"Then I will give the signal, and Ashby and Tristan will come in and save the day," the Frenchwoman declared. "Now, time for more wine I think."

"No," I said flatly. "I don't want it." Especially since every fiber of my being yearned for it desperately. "No," I said again, crossing my arms.

"But your hands, dear," Mrs. Armstrong said. "Look at how they tremble."

"I don't have to look!" I snarled. "I can *feel* them. And that is exactly why I won't take any more!"

"Elina," Gabrielle began in the tones of the long suffering, "we have already explained this to you. You must drink it, or you will begin to shake all over and they will know you haven't been taking the drug."

"And poor Michael," Mrs. Armstrong said, her voice trembling slightly. "I fear what they will do to him. Your Lord Ashenhurst assures me he will be safe, but he cannot take Michael out of harm's way before you and your sister are free, for fear of alerting Dr. Froggenhall. And with both his lordship and the other gentleman spending all their time watching *this* house, there is no one to watch over Michael!"

These arguments had, of course, already been presented to me. But still, it helped hearing them again as I prepared to face my demon.

"Besides," Gabrielle said as she thrust the wine into my hands, "there is not so much poison in here as before. You will not even feel it, I think."

I sighed. "Very well."

And then I drank.

∽

They came for me the following day.

Gabrielle and I sat alone in the room, Mrs. Armstrong attending to her daily duties upstairs. We heard their heavy footsteps trudging down the stairs, and so were prepared with Gabrielle safely concealed when they finally opened the door.

The first one spat as he came in the room. "Shite! It stinks in 'ere."

"Aye," his fellow wheezed as he set something heavy down with a thunk and some sloshing. "Think it's 'er?"

The third man, a great hulk of a brute whom I would soon dub 'the quiet one,' came to stand behind me and gently grasped me under the arms and hauled me to my feet. I let my head roll back theatrically, as though incapacitated with drugged wine.

"Aye, it's her all right," he said softly, his familiar voice shaped by a Welsh lilt. "But I hear she's been down here over a week, so can't be her fault."

"But she's supposed to be Quality, right? I thought them don't stink like other women," said the second man.

"Only your women stink, Georgie," said the first. "And this one. Now slide a barrel over here and put the bucket down on top of it."

Georgie dutifully complied, his tremendous grunt accompanied by the sound of wood being dragged heavily across stone and more sloshing. A premonition struck me that I was not going to like what was coming next.

"All right," said the leader, "get her into position. Georgie, take her by the hair."

Both men followed their orders, and I began to get an idea of what they were up to. It was very difficult to keep myself from tensing.

Suddenly Georgie plunged me under water, all the air in my lungs forcefully expelled in a startled whoosh as he abruptly bent me in half. My natural instincts took over and I began to struggle, despite the fact I was supposed to be unconscious. This, however, did not seem to engender any suspicions in my tormentors, who decided to keep me submerged despite the clear evidence that I was awake. Once I realized they were not going to let me back up, my instincts of self-preservation propelled me into a full-fledged panic. I thrashed so hard, it took all three of them to hold me down as I screamed underwater.

Then, just as suddenly, they hauled me out of the water. I sagged in the quiet one's brawny arms, choking out water, desperately trying to suck in air. But they only allowed me to carry on for a short while, before it was back down into the water. I don't know how long they tortured me this way, or how I got through it. By the time they finished, I was bruised and shivering, and more afraid than I'd ever been.

In the end, I was probably in worse shape than I would have been had I been under the influence of the drugged wine.

I sagged in the quiet one's brawny arms, my knees buckled, my legs no longer able to hold my weight. I'd tried talking to them at one point, but the leader hauled back and punched me in the mouth. I was too far gone to see the blow coming, but the brute holding me must have sensed it because he jerked me back suddenly, causing the leader's fist to leave me only with a split lip instead of missing teeth.

But now I couldn't have uttered a word if my life depended on it. For the last two rounds, I'd sucked both water and air alike into my lungs. My eyes felt like they were about to burst, my ears ringing so loudly I couldn't hear what they were saying.

I was going to die.

Even my thoughts of Phosey faded beneath the veil of my torment, and I hoped that Ashby and Tristan would not risk their lives trying to save me.

Very quietly, I began to cry.

"All right, lads, ready for another go?" the leader asked.

"No," said the one holding me. "She's had enough. We're done here."

"Awe, Hugh," sneered the leader. "Have you gone soft on this aristocratic cunt? That's too bad, considering the gaffer's plans for her."

"Enough," Hugh repeated, his voice a low and menacing. "Georgie, get your hands out of her hair if you value them. Eddie, check her now."

The alacrity of Georgie's compliance left me wondering in a sort of detached way which one of these brutes was really the one in charge. Eddie, the one I had thought to be the leader, stepped in close and snapped my head back into Hugh's chest, peeling back an eyelid as he held a lantern up close to my face.

"Aye, she's awake," he pronounced. "Hugh, since you like her so much, you can carry the stinking bitch up the stairs. Georgie,

HEATHER E. F. CARTER

you dump out the water and see if you can't wash away some of this filth."

Hugh adjusted his hold on me, then swept me up into his arms almost gallantly. As we followed Eddie out of the room that had been my home for over a week, I heard Georgie grunt as he tipped over the bucket behind us, and I spared a thought for Gabrielle's safety.

Then I turned my thoughts to the ordeal ahead. What was it the 'gaffer' had planned for me?

CHAPTER 39

I FOUND HUGH TO BE a strong and reassuring presence.
I was positive now that he was indeed my Hugh; the same footman who'd helped me the night William had died. He was the member from Ashby's crew who'd been placed in this house.

Thank God.

Hugh didn't seem to mind when I nestled against his chest, conserving what little strength I had. He took me up two flights of stairs, down a long, carpeted hallway, then through an open door.

At this point I raised my head to have a look around, and immediately choked on the thick cloud of noxious smoke hanging in the air. Through the haze, I could see a large desk with two pistols and a knife laid out like a surgeon's tools, a long couch pushed up against the wall in the far corner, and a table and chairs in front of the fireplace. Most of the walls were lined with bookshelves full of books with mismatched bindings.

Hugh gently deposited me on the oriental carpet in front of the empty desk, then left me with a nod, taking up a position next to the closed door.

"So, as I suspected, not a whore," a dreamy, disembodied

voice said, "but a lady. The daughter of the Marquess of Hertford, no less."

Glancing wildly around the room, I finally discerned in the corner where the smoke was thickest, the dim outline of a figure sitting at ease on the couch, one long leg crossed casually over the other.

"You have me at a disadvantage, sir," I said.

These words elicited a soft chuckle. "But not at as much of a disadvantage as I would like. Your lover saw to that."

"Won't you come into the light so I might see your face?"

"Ah, my face." He blew out another plume of smoke. "Indeed, I think you would most certainly know my face. But I've been told that the light will pain me for some time still, even with the opium; lovely stuff, don't you think?"

"You put opium in my wine," I said.

"Oh, not opium, Lady Delemere. Though my elixir shares with opium a common genealogy from the poppy plant, to be sure. But it is far, far more potent. Opium is but a gentle lamb compared to the tiger's ferocity of what I've given you. By now you should be ready to make a pact with the devil himself to keep your wine in supply, hmmm?'

He rose, and made his way over to the desk. His movements were slow and surprisingly graceful as he stepped into the light. Though Mrs. Armstrong had told me his identity, it was still a shock to see his face; or as much of his face as remained visible beneath the half-mask he wore to hide Ashby's handiwork. Still, I could see the ends of the deep gash at his temple and down by his jaw, an angry, puckered black line of dry blood crisscrossed heavily with stitches. And beneath his mask, over his left eye, a thick pad of cotton covered the orbit where his eye had been.

"Sir Bertram," I said coldly.

"The one and only, my dear lady."

"Why am I here? And where is my sister?"

Bertram snapped to attention, his reptilian gaze like a viper ready to strike. "Your sister? What makes you think I have your sister?"

Immediately, I knew I had blundered. I was not supposed to know that he and Froggenhall were working together.

I stood frozen in place, thinking rapidly. The drugged wine was still affecting me, slowing my reactions and making me stupid.

"Well?" he prompted.

The most convincing lies are always those spun from truth. "I thought it was Froggenhall who took me," I said. "I was looking for my sister when I was attacked."

"No," he said finally. "Froggenhall was not the one who took you. Your presence here has nothing to do with your sister. But it has everything to do with me. And I am sorry for detaining you for so long. You see, I was in no condition to receive any guests."

I felt a spark of panic. I needed him to bring Phosey into the room before Tristan and Ashby made their move. If things had gone according to plan, Gabrielle had already slipped out of the basement, and joined the men. They were supposed to wait for ten minutes, to give Bertram enough time to bring Phosey into the room, but I knew my rescuers would be chomping at the bit after their week of inactivity. Timing was critical.

But we had not planned for the possibility that Bertram might decide to enact his revenge upon me without Phosey and Froggenhall present. Tristan and Ashby would still make their move, which would allow Froggenhall the perfect opportunity to escape with my sister under the cover of their commotion.

All hope of rescuing Phosey would be lost.

Then something occurred to me.

"If Froggenhall has nothing to do with my presence here," I said, "where did you learn my name?"

Bertram chuckled darkly. "So, I was correct: the drugs have

not turned you into a complete imbecile. I was afraid that the good doctor was giving you too much, but I am thrilled to have been mistaken."

"The 'good doctor' must be Froggenhall. And he told you who I was."

"Hmmm, yes," Bertram said. "You are correct. That whore Elizabeth could only give me Ashenhurst's name, but not yours. Still, Froggenhall is not responsible for your presence here. He was prepared to slink away like a dog once he learned you and the infamous *Black Unicorn* were here in Hull looking for him, especially when he learned you had found his ship. But I convinced him to stay. I needed his services anyway." He indicated the diagonal slash across his face.

I needed to speed things along. "I do not care about that filthy little worm," I said. "I just want Phosey returned safely."

"Phosey, is it? How charming. Froggenhall refers to her only as Lady Tryphosia. I admit, I do like Phosey better." He picked up a silver bell and rang it.

The door to my right opened and a boy was shoved through. He shrieked, stumbled over his own feet, and landed in an ungainly heap on the floor.

For just a moment, my instincts took over and I forgot where I was. I took a step towards the child, my hands outstretched to help him. He bent his head down to the soft carpet and began to cry.

"Phosey?" I froze, staring down at the waif in disbelief. "Is that you?"

"Elina?" She lifted her head until she met my gaze with her red-rimmed blue eyes.

"Dear God!" I exclaimed, rushing over to the huddled figure. "It is you! Oh, thank God, Phosey! Thank God!"

"You found me, Elina," she murmured into my shoulder as I wrapped my arms around her. "I knew you would."

Sir Bertram cleared his throat.

Jerking my head up, I glared at him. "What are you doing with my sister?" She was dressed in the boy's clothes I had borrowed from Gabrielle. Bertram must have retrieved them when he returned to the brothel to speak to Madam Elizabeth. "Where is Froggenhall?

"Ah, I see that the joyful reunion has cleared your head somewhat," Bertram crooned. "But to answer your question, Dr. Froggenhall is behind you."

I turned just as Froggenhall landed a vicious kick. I grunted from the impact and went sprawling. Phosey screamed and rushed to help me up, but Froggenhall backhanded her, knocking her flat on her bottom. I struggled to sit up, as Froggenhall loomed over me, his back to Bertram's desk as he prepared to kick me again. But Bertram's voice stilled him momentarily.

"That's enough, Phineas. Remember what we talked about."

"I don't give a damn what we talked about!" Froggenhall snarled over his shoulder.

"How unfortunate." Bertram fired the pistol he had trained on Froggenhall's back.

Phosey screamed again, and kept on screaming as I instinctively curled into a ball and braced for Froggenhall's dead weight. But Froggenhall, with a startled look on his face, staggered forward a few paces. Blood poured through the hole in his chest where the pistol ball had exited, drenching his white linens. He veered off to the side before collapsing onto the floor in a heap.

"We had a little difference of opinion, I'm afraid," Bertram explained.

"A difference of opinion?" A dreadful chill crept over me. I got back to my feet, then dragged Phosey up in front of me, pulling her shaking form close. "Over what exactly?"

"Well, my dear. Once I learned that dear Lady Tryphosia was your sister, I realized I just couldn't allow the child to waste herself on Dr. Froggenhall. I have much grander plans for her, which Phineas did not find appropriate for his soon-to-be child bride. He did not mind me having a little fun, of course; he only wanted to marry the chit for her money. But I wanted more than a *little* fun, and he was concerned— rightly, I might add—that the dear child might never recover."

Bertram looked to Froggenhall, moaning pitifully on the floor. "Don't worry, dear fellow. I missed your heart, but that hole will still finish you off quickly."

He turned back to me, "While the good doctor and I may have parted ways, he still had his uses. Until now, that is. You should know that, at first . . ."

Bertram was rambling, and I thought the best way to keep his hands off Phosey until Tristan and Ashby arrived was to keep him talking.

"Yes?" I prompted, stroking Phosey's hair to quiet her.

" . . . I thought only to ruin her face, as your lover has ruined mine," he said. "Naturally, Froggenhall had a few things to say about that. Didn't you, you cheeky bugger?" He addressed the bleeding lump on the floor. "Are you still alive down there?"

Froggenhall moaned weakly.

"But then," Bertram said, picking up the thread of his narrative, "I thought to myself, 'Bertie—there are so many more *enjoyable* ways to ruin a girl.' In fact, I confess the possibilities suddenly seemed endless. Wouldn't you agree, Lady Delemere? It seems to me I remember hearing somewhere that the dearly departed Lord Delemere entertained some rather *unusual* appetites, did he not? It's a shame I never knew the man, for I think I may have found in him a kindred spirit."

"Take me," I said desperately. "I am the one you want. I will go to you willingly. Just leave my sister alone." *And keep talking!*

"*Willingly?*" Bertram scoffed. "And where is the fun in that?"

Just then, I heard a commotion coming from downstairs. *Oh dear God. Please let them get here in time!*

"Well," Bertram said, at the first of the shouts, "I think I've chatted with you ladies long enough. Phosey, come here, my dear."

"No!" the girl cried, burrowing into my chest. I wrapped my arms around her and dragged her a few steps back.

"Phosey," he said, his tone gentle enough to coax a frightened kitten. "We do not have much time. If you do not come here, I will shoot your sister in the face."

Phosey looked up at me. I shook my head as I tightened my arms around her.

"Phosey," he tried again. "Would you like to be a mother someday? Would you like to have babies of your own, to love and cuddle and play with as they grow up? Hmmm?"

"Enough!" I cried, dragging Phosey further back. The shouts sounded closer, but still too far away.

Bertram had captured her attention. Reluctantly she turned just far enough to peek at him with one eye.

"Yes, that's right, my child," he said soothingly. "I can see that you do. But if you do not come to me right now, I will make sure that you can never have babies. I will—"

"No!" I shrieked, clapping my hands over Phosey's ears. "Enough, you filthy pervert!"

"Then make her come to me," he said. "Or I will do exactly what I just said. It doesn't take very long, you know," he added. "I can do it, and still have time to blow a hole through Ashenhurst the moment he steps through that door. That is, if he somehow miraculously survives the fifteen armed men between him and this room."

As if to underscore his point, a pistol fired somewhere on the floor below us, followed immediately by two more.

"Dr. Froggenhall told me about it once," Bertram continued,

picking up the knife to catch the candlelight with its edge. He held it steadily over the flame, heating it. "The procedure, that is. They employ it over at the madhouse to keep the female patients from getting with child. Doesn't always work, the good doctor learned to his chagrin, but I think that's only because they are so concerned to keep the young ladies alive. I personally do not care whether Phosey survives. I am sure though, she'll wish she doesn't."

Slowly, I let my hands fall away from Phosey's ears. I was out of time. "What are you going to do? If she comes to you?"

"That's a surprise."

Another shot rang out, and I heard more shouting. They sounded much closer, and I began praying, pleading, *begging* God, Jupiter, Heaven, the Mysteries of the Universe, *anyone* or *anything* to allow Ashby and Tristan to reach us in time.

"If I come to you, Sir Bertram, will you promise not to hurt Elina?" Phosey asked.

"But of course, child!" he exclaimed. "That is the whole point of this. You shall suffer so she doesn't have to."

Phosey sniffled, then nodded. "Very well."

Phosey began pulling away from me, struggling out from under my arms. But I tightened my grip, hauling her back into safety of my embrace. Bertram was out of his chair like a shot, startling me with the suddenness of his movement and destroying the last hope I had that maybe all the opium he'd been smoking might have made him somehow less . . . vigorous.

"Mr. Llewellyn," he said as he strode around the desk to where Phosey and I still struggled with each other. "Hold Lady Delemere, if you please." He grabbed Phosey by the arm, and dragged her away from me.

I lunged after them, but stopped short when he grabbed the second pistol and aimed it into my face. "Now, Mr. Llewellyn. Or you will have the pleasure of watching me blow a hole through her gut." He lowered his aim to my midsection. "It is, I am told, the most miserable way to die."

Hugh came up behind me, his movements stealthy on the plush carpet. He grasped me firmly by the arms and pulled me backwards away from the desk. "Can't you *do* something?" I hissed as I struggled against his hold. "Are you just going to watch this happen?"

"There is nothing he can do," Bertram said as he bent Phosey roughly over the desk. She cried loudly, but did not otherwise resist. "He is armed only with a knife, and he knows I will kill you before he manages to get close enough to me to use it." He turned his attention back to Phosey and ordered her to cross her hands behind her back. As she complied, he grabbed her wrists, tugging them viciously up her back at an angle fit to break them. She cried out.

"Remember this, Lady Delemere?" Bertram asked. "I do hope that your sister is as charmingly-made as you are."

I struggled harder, but Hugh held fast. "They are close," he murmured into my ear. And indeed they were, the shouting coming from just outside the door. A pistol suddenly fired very close at hand; I flinched, then turned with Hugh towards the closed door as Bertram let loose an enraged scream of pain.

Confused, we turned again to see Bertram aiming his second pistol at Froggenhall, who clutched a smoking pistol in his feeble, outstretched hand. I had just enough time to register the blood streaming down Bertram's white stocking when the door behind us burst open in an explosion of splintering wood. Bertram pivoted on his good leg, took aim at whomever was coming through the door and fired.

Time began to slow. I heard a grunt as the pistol ball found its target, the sound of a body being thrown back into the wall from the force of impact, then the heavy sound of it crumpling to the ground. Hugh's grip on me weakened as he became distracted by the activity near the door.

As Bertram raised the spent pistol over Phosey's head, I lunged at him, just as he struck savagely. I slammed into his shoulder, and what might have been a killing blow glanced off Phosey's ear instead.

Still, from the way her body suddenly slumped forward, I knew that he'd knocked her unconscious.

I shoved Bertram away from her with a strength I did not know I possessed, dislodging his mask in the process. He stumbled backwards, his remaining eye wide with shock. I snatched the knife up off the desk and plunged it into his throat, using all my strength to rip it upwards along his windpipe into the soft tissue beneath his chin.

I knew what I was doing; I'd done it once before.

Over the rushing of the blood in my ears, I heard men's voices shouting everywhere, and a woman was screaming like Boudicca from just outside the door.

Bertram staggered to the side, clutching at his throat. Blood spurted out of the wound, pulsing between his fingers. He fell to his knees, his movements awkward and abrupt like a newborn foal. He retched and choked, vomiting blood. Behind him the door that Phosey had been shoved through earlier burst open. Tristan charged through, saw Bertram on his knees, and strode over to him almost casually, placing the end of his pistol against Bertram's skull.

But I heard, rather than saw the shot. Tristan's appearance had filled me with dread. Who had been shot coming through the door? I turned, and saw him.

Ashby.

His broken body was crumpled on the floor, a thick bloody trail smeared down the wall behind him.

My blood froze in my veins.

I struggled to my feet, tripping on my skirts and lurched over to where Ashby lay.

I threw myself down next to him, frantic at the sight of so much blood. I tugged at his body, pulling his head into my lap. The source of the blood was gaping wound in Ashby's chest, just beneath his collar bone. I pressed my hands over it, as though I could catch his blood and press it back into him. Two small hands suddenly grabbed at my wrists, and yanking me away from my task. I screamed, my teeth bared in a feral snarl.

Gabrielle struck me hard across the face. "I must have a look at him," she said, the calmness of her voice at odds with the power behind her hand. "He is not dead. But he will be soon if I do not get him back to his yacht."

I bent my ear over his mouth to listen for his breath.

It was there; very faint, but there.

My God, how could he still be alive?

Gabrielle focused on his wound, still bleeding freely, but she did not seem overly anxious about it. I realized, with a bit of a start, that I trusted her with his life.

She loved him; she would not let him die.

"I have what I need at the yacht," she said, sparing me a distracted glance. "But I must staunch his bleeding. Tear off a piece of your petticoat. Now."

I hauled up my overskirt and began to tear large strips off my flannel petticoat. The room was now full of men, everyone running every which way in confusion like an ant nest under attack. Some men had clustered around us to look down upon Ashby with worried faces. A few averted their eyes, while others watched me with open curiosity. I took them for household servants. All the fight had fizzled now that Bertram and Froggenhall were dead.

Gabrielle wadded up one of the flannel strips, then used two of the others to fasten the pad into place against Ashby's chest.

He was unconscious, and pliant as a sleeping baby. I watched him as he lay in my lap, so helpless, so vulnerable, so utterly beyond my reach.

"Find Hugh," Gabrielle ordered without looking up as she made some final adjustments to the bandage. "We must leave. Now."

CHAPTER 40

ASHBY'S YACHT WAS MOORED nearby at the bottom of the haven.

From the merchant's house on High Street, it took us ten minutes to reach it, and only that long because Hugh was burdened with Ashby's dead weight, while Tristan carried Phosey. The hour was very late, the streets dark since the street-light ordinances apparently weren't enforced in this part of town.

Once on the uneven boards of the quayside, Gabrielle found the *Estefània* quickly. The Captain, a short, swarthy man, stood by as Hugh carried Ashby across the gangplank first, followed closely by Gabrielle.

As I stepped onto the narrow causeway after her, Tristan called after me. "No. Elina, you cannot."

I froze, then turned impatiently. "Tristan, we do not have time for this."

Light from the lamp swinging from the *Estefània*'s mast flickered across his blunt features. I could see his brows gathered into a frown, the stubborn set of his jaw. "Your place is with your sister and your family," he said. "And with me."

I felt a twinge of guilt as I looked upon Phosey's unconscious form still cradled in Tristan's arms. He was correct, on all counts, and I knew it. Eloping with Ashby in this manner, as he fled for his life from the jurisdiction of Britain's courts, was folly. I would bring ignominy to myself, as well as to my family, at a time when the Brinkley name could withstand no further assaults.

And Tristan. Leaving him after he'd risked his life to save me was a terrible thing to do.

But Ashby had also risked his life. And in that moment, when I saw Tristan charge through the doors to the merchant's study, and I knew that Ashby had been the one to take Bertram's pistol ball behind me, I had made my decision. Papa was correct: Tristan deserved a better wife—a better woman—than me.

"I cannot, Tristan." I wanted to say more. I loved him, and I wanted to tell him so. But then I would have to tell him that my love for him just wasn't enough, and that seemed cruel.

"I can save him, Elina." His voice was soft, but I could hear it clearly.

At that moment, the moon slipped her cover, casting a pale, silvery light along the quayside. Tristan's face, earnest, pleading, stood out in sudden stark relief.

"Save him?"

He nodded. "There will be a trial, Elina, before a jury of his peers."

I hesitated, frowning. "I do not follow, Tristan. How can that be saving him?"

"Before his *peers,* Elina. He is a Peer of the Realm; he will be tried before the House of Lords."

I shook my head. I stood with one foot still on the causeway. "I don't follow, Tristan."

"I can supply him with whatever alibis he needs," he said. "Do you think there is any man in the Peerage who would not take me at my word?"

"You would do that?" I said, the uncertainty in my voice clear. "You would perjure yourself for the sake of a man you hate?"

"Perjure myself, yes," he said. "And most likely ruin my chances for Prime Minister. But not for a man I hate. I would do it for you, Elina. Because I love you. Because I need you."

"Oh, Tristan." All of my strength suddenly left me. I exhaled heavily, bowing my shoulders. "For that very reason, I cannot marry you. I do not deserve you. You shall never know just how true that is until you find the woman who *does* deserve you."

"Never!" he cried, the vehemence in his voice startling me. "You do not know what you say! You've been through a terrible ordeal, Elina! It can all end now. Come home with me, I beg you! Come home and let me love you!"

I began to pull away. Slowly, I took another step backwards onto the causeway. "Tristan. I cannot."

"If not for me, then do it for Ashenhurst. Do it so that he may remain in England with his family. They need him."

Tristan was correct; if I stayed, then Ashby could stay, too. But we could never be together. I tried for a moment to be angry with Tristan for thrusting this choice upon me. But then I realized he was being more kind than cruel by not stating the obvious: Ashby might very well die before the night was through. And then I would be truly lost—cast away at sea in a ship with no anchor; homeless, friendless, with no family, and a reputation so ruined that I could never set foot in England again. Not even Tristan, with all his wealth and strong political connections, could marry a woman of such low character.

But if I did step off this gangplank, back onto the quayside with Tristan, I knew that Ashby would die. What little chance he did have rested upon my presence at his side. It was egotism of the highest order to assume I might have such powers of life or death over a man like Ashby, but I knew in my heart that it was the truth.

And that was ultimately the deciding factor: Tristan, I knew, could live without me.

Ashby could not.

"Tell Phosey when she wakes up that I love her, and that I am sorry I failed her," I said. "And tell Sophie I am sorry I must miss her nuptials and that she was right about Thad. He will make her very happy. And tell Papa . . . tell Papa that he was right."

"Elina!"

"Goodbye, Tristan. I pray the next time we meet, it will be under happier circumstances."

I turned my back on him then, and slowly made my way up the causeway.

Once on board, I headed straight for the main cabin. At the door, I paused to quickly dash away my tears, wiping my nose savagely across my sleeve as I took a quick, fortifying breath.

I would take the time later to mourn my loss of Tristan. For now, I needed to be strong for what lay ahead.

Inside, I found Ashby alone with Gabrielle. Already stripped of his clothes, he lay stretched out on his bed, his color nearly as pale as the bleached linen sheet pulled up over his hips for modesty. Gabrielle sat in a chair next to him, her head bent down to her task as she rummaged through a large wooden box sitting on the table next to her. As I came closer, my eyes traveled from his face to the wound in his chest.

"Christ! What have you done?" I rushed over to his side.

The wound, when Gabrielle had tended it at the merchant's house, had been a round black hole about the size of a guinea. But now, it was a long gash of about six inches, the ragged skin in the middle revealing the place where the pistol ball had torn through him.

Gabrielle ignored me and continued with her task, only tearing her attention away when Hugh arrived holding a large black pot of steaming water.

"Move." Gabrielle spared me a distracted glance. "You are in Hugh's way."

Moving towards the foot of the bed, I watched in horror and fascination as Gabrielle spread Ashby's wound open while Hugh poured the water carefully into the gash.

Once Hugh had flushed the wound, and both Ashby and the bed were soaked, he took the empty pot and left us without a word. Gabrielle, meanwhile, picked up a large needle from her table, already strung with a kinky black length of catgut. She set to work sewing Ashby back up. This took some time, as she kept her stitches very small and close together. I knelt down and watched her, sufficiently convinced that she knew what she was doing.

Once she finished, she bit off a small length of the catgut and tied the last stitch firmly into place. Then she reached into her box and pulled out a jar of a thick black jelly-like substance that looked for all the world like congealed blood. This she smeared liberally over the wound, muttering something under her breath that I eventually realized were the Latin words to the Lord's Prayer, which greatly surprised me since I'd thought her to be a free-thinking Atheist. I allowed this to pass without comment, however, since I sensed in her the need for concentration.

Next, she drew out a small leather pouch from her box and gingerly withdrew an object wrapped carefully in a piece of very old brown leather. As she unwrapped the object, I saw that it was a very old coin or medallion of gold, worn down by the centuries to a dull burnished patina. With a pair of metal tongs, she warmed it over the candle burning on the table until it seemed to glow faintly. This she held over Ashby's chest, muttering a few unintelligible words as the glow slowly receded, then placed it into the jelly over the wound. Placing one hand over it, she picked up the small piece of leather which appeared to be parchment with strange letters written neatly in unbroken rows across it.

"*Dominus pascit me nihil mihi deerit,*" she intoned, "*super aquas refectionis e nutrivit me animam meam refecit duxit me per semitas iustitiae propter nomen suum . . . for though I should walk in the valley of the shadow of death, I will fear no evil, for thou art with me. Thy rod and thy staff, they comfort me. Thou hast prepared a table before me against them that afflict me. Thou hast anointed my head with oil; and my chalice runneth over. And thy mercy will follow me all the days of my life. And I will dwell in the house of the Lord forever."*

As the sound of her words faded into the shadows of the room, the atmosphere around us seemed to shift slightly, taking on a charged stillness. The hairs on the back of my neck lifted, and the air crackled like the moments just before a summer thunderstorm. I chided myself for my silly delusions, no doubt exacerbated by Bertram's wretched poison.

But when I glanced down at Ashby, I could have sworn that his expression seemed less pained, and his breathing appeared deeper and more regular.

I watched as Gabrielle folded the parchment into a small square, touched to forehead and heart, left shoulder then right, then placed it over the coin. Next, she pulled from her box several folded strips of flannel similar to the ones she'd used from my petticoat to dress Ashby's wound. She constructed another bandage and tied it securely into place over the coin and the parchment.

After a few gentle tugs to test the security of the bandage, she reached again into her box and pulled out what looked to be a small silver-gilt Chrismatory decorated with Christian and pagan symbols. Flipping open the lid, she dipped a long glass wand into the chrism and drizzled it liberally over the bandage, then set the wand aside and poured a small amount of the oil into her palm. As she briskly rubbed her hands together, the strong, musky scent of it reached my nose and made me sneeze.

Gabrielle placed both hands over Ashby's wound, closed her eyes, and began a third incantation in a strange, guttural language

I thought to be Old French. The words were too Germanic for me to understand, but I thought I recognized the name of the Saint Irene and what may have been an appeal to the Queen of Heaven, though this latter reference might have also been to a pagan goddess of the heavens.

"You are a witch," I said when it became clear she had finished.

She favored me with a measured look, then nodded as she stood and began to unwind her cravat. "I am a daughter from a long line of daughters skilled in the art of healing magic. And other magic."

I narrowed my eyes as she began to pull her shirt out of her breeches. "And now what are you doing?"

"You must leave," she said, pulling her shirt off over her head to reveal the twin swells of her breasts, the peaks of her rosebud nipples pebbling from their abrupt exposure to the cabin's chilly air.

"Absolutely not," I retorted as she turned her attention to the buttons of her falls.

I glanced down at Ashby, though in truth, if he'd opened his eyes at that moment—even if only to gaze upon the miracle of Gabrielle's naked body—I would have rejoiced. But he didn't stir; not even when Gabrielle slid her breeches down over the smooth curves of her hips.

"You must leave," she repeated, taking a seat so she could slide her stockings off her legs. "You will not like to see what I must do next, but I assure you it is necessary for the healing magic to work. You must leave us before I do it; you are very sick, and there is a chance that the magic will come to you instead of to Ashby."

She now sat before me completely naked, the candlelight lending her white skin a luminous glow as she poured almost half the remaining bottle of oil into her palm and began working it quickly and methodically over her body. She'd taken the pins out of her hair, so that now it streamed down over her shoulders to cover her breasts.

She had never appeared lovelier to my eyes.

I glanced back down to Ashby lying naked and helpless in the sheets. He was still so terribly pale, the warm undertones of his Portuguese heritage bleached from his skin.

"You will . . . make love to him then?" I asked, the words catching in my throat.

"No," she replied, her voice suddenly warmed with amusement. "I do not think even Ashby is up to the task just now, do you?"

"Then, what?"

"I have cleansed the wound as best I can," she said, slipping into the eloquence of her native tongue. "But he is still in very great danger from fever. And if fever does settle in, he will be too weak to fight it and he will certainly die. I must lie with him so that my skin touches his, so that his heart's weak beat will come to follow my own, and our breathing shall rise and fall together. I will draw the fever out of him, absorb it into my own body which is strong enough to fight it. I will do the same for you," she added softly, "when your withdrawal from the poison becomes too strong for you to defeat alone."

I glanced down at my arms crossed firmly under my breasts, my hands clamped tightly against my body to still their shaking. In the amount of time that had passed since Hugh had carried me up the stairs to the merchant's library, the shaking had already become much, much worse. It was a relief to know that when the drug's poison took me, Ashby would be in very competent hands until I recovered. And should the poison take me away from him forever, Gabrielle would be there to help him through his grief.

"Very well," I said, and turned to leave. But at the door, I stopped to look back at Ashby for what I feared might be the last time. "And Gabrielle?"

"*Oui?*" She paused to glance up at me, one knee already resting on the bed.

"Save him."

She held my gaze, and I saw in her eyes a flash of perfect understanding. "I will do what I can, but the rest will be up to you."

CHAPTER 41

I DO NOT REMEMBER MUCH from our voyage to Portugal. I was far, far too ill.

Hugh was with me for a great deal of the time, and I had periodic impressions of Gabrielle's presence. I believe I asked after Ashby a few times, though I could not remember ever receiving any sort of answer.

The first solid memory I have is of the soothing sounds of the seaside, with the surging thunder of the surf, pierced by the calls of the seabirds floating on the eddies above. There were other sounds, too, different from what I'd been hearing on board the ship; a woman humming a tune in another room, the excited bark of a dog somewhere in the distance. The air smelled different from anything I could remember; thick and verdant, like the inside of a hothouse or a conservatory with undercurrents of rosemary, thyme, and lavender, and brine from the sea.

I opened my eyes, immediately struggling to make sense of my surroundings. It seemed I was in a bed, but everywhere I looked, I could only see billows of diaphanous white clouds swirling softly around me. I blinked a few times, wondering if this was perhaps heaven, but then my eyes strengthened their focus and I found that I could see through the strange material.

I was in a bedchamber. With this small detail in place, every-thing around me began to make sense. The white clouds were, in fact, gossamer bed curtains blowing softly in the breeze from an open balcony.

With a tremendous sigh of relief, I sat up in bed and began to look for a way out. The silly bed curtains—and they were silly, for they couldn't possibly keep anyone warm in the winter—did not seem to have any beginning or end. Eventually I managed to escape by wadding them up from the floor and then pulling them over my head. I looked around at the thick walls of bright white plaster, the arched doorways and windows, the dusty red clay tile covering the floor, and the heavy, unfinished doors with iron strapping and studs like one would expect to find in a church or a monastery.

Portugal.

And there was a Portuguese man asleep in a chair next to my bed.

I knew Ashby immediately, though I doubt anyone else in England would have recognized in him the Earl of Ashenhurst. He was dressed simply in loose white linen breeches and shirt, no stockings, and sturdy canvas slipper-like shoes with soles made of rope. His hair was loose, falling forward over his down-turned face, and his skin looked to be several shades darker than I remembered. Gabrielle had bandaged him well, and his left arm lay cradled to his belly in a light cotton sling.

My relief at seeing him, sleeping so peacefully, was beyond the power of words. So too was the surge of emotion that left quiet tears streaming down my cheeks. Perhaps feeling the inten-sity of my gaze, he stirred with a soft flutter of his long lashes, then looked up at me and smiled.

"You are awake."

"I am."

"Why do you weep?"

HEATHER E. F. CARTER

"I thought I'd lost you."

"And I you," he said softly.

"I do not think I could survive it, Ashby, if I ever lost you again."

He watched me a moment as an immeasurable sadness slowly clouded his eyes. "Nor I you," he said.

⁓

Over the next several days, Ashby remained diligently by my side, helping me to regain my strength.

We wandered through his old house, named *Casa das Flores Escarlates* for the small star-shaped flowers that littered the grounds, and I listened as he told me the stories of his mother's family. He took me through the gardens, the olive grove, the terraced hillside of vines behind the house, and sometimes we took short rides on horseback along the blinding white sands of the beach. Sometimes, I would catch a glimpse of Gabrielle here or Hugh there, or even one of the servants who seemed as shy and elusive as fairy folk.

Except, of course, for Ângela, the voluble, highly opinionated, and lovably outrageous young girl Ashby assigned to be my lady's maid.

Still, despite all of the time we spent together, Ashby remained distant. We did not speak of Hull.

About a week after I woke, Ashby surprised me with a picnic in the orchard. We sat on a blanket in the shade of the orange trees, breathing in their tangy scent on the warm ocean breeze. As I leaned back to catch a few dappled rays of sunlight on my face, I felt relaxed and comfortable; Ashby had not included a corset along with my rather elaborate wardrobe of Spanish maja dresses, and I was not missing it. I tilted my head to the side with a contented sigh, and opened my eyes to find him watching me.

"I failed you," he said.

I sat up. "What?"

"In Hull. I failed you. In the brothel, and then later when you were kidnapped."

"Ashby, I love you."

"Well, you shouldn't!" he said, his tone suddenly bitter. "I left you in there, to be poisoned, to be tormented, to slowly be driven mad! I *left* you in there! I knew exactly where you were, I knew exactly how to get you out, but I *left* you there! Who knows the things they could have done to you! You, mercifully, were unconscious, so you wouldn't know. But it could have been anything."

"Is that it, then?" I asked, suddenly feeling cold. "You don't want me because I might be . . . soiled?"

"No!" he roared, startling me as he surged to his feet. "I want you so . . . so *desperately*. Every time I am near you, I want to die from not being able to touch you. But I don't deserve you, Elina. I *left* you in there. What kind of a man does that?"

"The kind who wants to save an innocent fifteen-year-old girl," I answered evenly. "A *good* man. A *heroic* man."

"What the devil do you know?" And then he spun around on his heel and stormed off, charging angrily through the grass as I watched.

Later that afternoon, he found me in the library contemplating the massive wooden crucifix his ancestor had brought back from a mission to the Americas two centuries before. He apologized for his behavior as I studied the graceful figure of the Christ nailed to the Cross, his haunted face and elongated limbs reminding me of a painting I had seen once by El Greco while on the Tour with Papa and Sophie.

I accepted Ashby's apology, realizing the extent to which he lived in two completely different and irreconcilable worlds. His father's family, his siblings whom he cared for in England, had nothing to do with this place.

Yet I sensed that Iberia had a far greater hold on Ashby's heart and soul than Ashenhurst Castle, that dreary pile of gray stone up in Northumberland with its barren estates. All unwanted like an albatross slung around the neck.

Ashby's mother had been a foolish woman to stray from her marriage vows and test the limits of her husband's honor by cuckolding him so publicly. But now, standing in this strange house built for coolness in this hot, exotic country, where even the radiant quality of the sunlight seemed to shimmer in the air like the iridescent wings of a dragonfly, I began to understand the desperation that must have motivated the lonely young woman's tragic course of action.

I already missed the country of my birth, but Estephânia, whose Latin blood sang to this romantic palette of burnished colors, most likely could never reconcile herself to England's misty grays and muted greens.

In the days that followed, matters between Ashby and myself did not improve. In fact, they deteriorated further.

He continued to spend all his time with me, though that time often passed in brooding silence. His constant, albeit unhappy, presence sparked in me the hope that things between us might not yet be past the point of no return.

One morning, about three weeks after I'd awakened to find myself on the western coast of Iberia, my maid Ângelica mentioned something that piqued my interest. As she plaited my hair in front of the dressing table, she told me in the midst of her usual barrage of chatter about a swimming hole nearby guarded by a Saint Benedita, who supposedly helped barren women to conceive. It was a lovely little spot beneath a waterfall, with a cave behind it that Ângelica claimed was good for exploring.

Later that day as I stood with Ashby on the veranda, squinting into the brilliant white light of the early afternoon, admiring the rolling hills of thick green vegetation tumbling down to the glittering waters of the Atlantic, I told him that I was in the mood for a swim.

"In the sea?" he asked dubiously, as he watched the surf thundering against the rocks below us.

"Oh, no," I replied. "I much prefer freshwater. It's cleaner and far less dangerous."

Ashby frowned, thinking a moment. "Yes," he said at length, "there is a place I know, not too far from here. Would you like to go tomorrow? After breakfast perhaps?"

"That would be perfect."

The following morning, we made a slow hike up into the hills. The day was hot, far hotter than it ever got in England this close to the sea, and Ashby was still a long way from being at his full strength.

The cloudless sky stretched endlessly above us, a dazzling azure, and a warm breeze blew in from the west, carrying with it the scent of the sea. I wore a white handkerchief tied over my hair, as well as a thick straw bonnet with a very broad brim, since my skin did not bronze in the sun the same way Ashby's did. He told me my freckles were charming, but nearly three decades of being trained to protect my porcelain white skin at all costs brought me close to tears one afternoon after I'd spent the morning out in the Portuguese sun with no bonnet.

After about ten minutes of walking steadily uphill, we crested the summit and left the Spanish heather, with their silly jester's hats of purple petals, and began our descent into thicker, leafier vegetation. Soon we reached a small wood, not unlike those one might find in England, full of birch trees, oaks, and maples. Lush green ferns covered the dark earth, growing thicker and more luxurious as the smell of fresh water grew stronger. We heard the musical splashing from the waterfall first, then felt the atmosphere around us shift slightly into a cool, dark hush. Finally we broke through the last line of protective trees, and came upon a small clearing scattered with the *Casa das Flores Escarlates'* namesake flowers in the tall grasses.

Nestled in the center, surrounded by large round rocks patterned brightly with lichen, was the sheltered grotto with its pool of crystal clear water. I could see the opening of Ângelica's cave just behind the sparkling downpour. I did not need to be Catholic to appreciate that this was a special, magical place.

"This place is guarded by a saint," Ashby said as though reading my mind. "See, over there you can see the offerings people have left for her help and intercession."

I followed the direction in which he pointed and indeed saw a small collection of candles and other small treasures to the side of the cave's opening.

Ashby walked over to the other side of the clearing and turned his back so that I could undress. It took me a few minutes of stretching and pulling to reach all my buttons and tapes. How much easier this would have been with his help. But I knew we were not yet healed enough for that kind of intimacy, and so I managed alone. Finally, I stood at the water's edge in just my chemise, hesitant for a moment as I deliberated, before finally pulling it off over my head, too.

The water was cooler than I expected. I lowered myself to the point where I could push off the rocks with my feet and glide into the middle. Then I turned my back and called out that I was safely in the pool. Ashby took longer than I expected, but then I remembered his bandages. He would need to take them off before taking a swim.

He joined me with a sudden splash, and I heard him come up out of the water, sputtering. I turned then and beheld my dark Incubus, water streaming off the bronzed muscles of his chest and arms, his bluish black hair slicked back from his face. I smiled when I saw that his eyelashes were clumped together, just as they'd been that night I'd interrupted his bath. But my smile faded when I beheld the wound just under his collarbone, the ugly place where the pistol ball had torn the hole through his body that had almost killed him. It was still black from dried blood, and I could see the small holes from Gabrielle's stitches. Suddenly I wanted to feel his wound, as though I could heal him just with the love in my touch. I began to make my way across the pool towards him.

"No, Elina," he said. "Please don't."

"There is something I need you to see, Ashby," I said, my voice firm.

Shaking his head, he backed away until the water came up only to his waist. Here he was trapped, for to retreat any further would be to compromise all modesty. And modesty, strangely enough, seemed very important to him just now.

As I walked towards him, I slowly rose from the water until it licked enticingly at my nipples. He watched me, transfixed, his face a distorted mask of pain. But I continued forward, merciless in my advance, until I came out of the pool before him like Venus out of the sea. Then I passed around him, moving until the water receded to just the tops of my thighs.

"Ashby," I murmured. "Turn around and look at me."

"No," he whispered. "I cannot. Please do not do this to me."

"Ashby," I repeated, my voice a little stronger. "You need to see this. Please turn and look."

Reluctantly, he turned around, though he kept his eyes carefully trained on the water.

"Ashby . . . " I pressed.

Slowly he looked up, his eyes taking in my thighs, my mound of dark red curls, my hips, belly, breasts, shoulders, throat, and then finally my face.

"Do you see?" I asked him gently. "Do you see me? No marks. No bruises. No wounds. I am the same woman you loved seven years ago. The same woman you loved at Scarcliff Towers. Hull has done nothing to me that cannot be washed away with a little clean water."

He reached out then, and tenderly cupped my breast. Tears shone in his eyes, and one spilled over to trickle down his cheek.

"It cannot be," he whispered, sliding his hand slowly down to the angle of my hip. "I left you in there. Alone. Defenseless."

"But I am strong, my love," I told him. "Far stronger than you realize. I am a survivor. It is what I do. I survive. They could not break me. And I will worship you for the rest of my life for saving my sister."

A sob escaped him. And then he was in my arms, his face cradled against my breast as he trembled violently from his grief. I held him, stroking his hair, murmuring gentle words against his temple. His heartbreaking sobs spoke of a damaged soul wracked with a guilt too great, too terrible, for any one man to bear. Those bastards in Hull had not broken me because, thanks to Ashby, I'd had a friend in the dark to hold me and protect me. But who had been there for him? Watching but not knowing what was transpiring down in the basement of that wretched house. Plagued by nightmares of torment, torture, and rape.

He held on to me desperately. But a broken man is not a ruined man; he can still be repaired; he can still be made whole. And I knew I was the only woman who could do it, just as certainly as I knew this act of healing would give to my barren womb Ashby's child.

His sobs quieted, and he stood with his head pressed against my heart, listening to the strength of its beat as I continued to stroke his hair. I sensed in him a shift, a readiness for what must come next as his body shed some of its burden of grief and began to come alive against me.

I pulled away from him and moved back into the water until we were standing together on level ground. Then I reached up, wrapped my hand around the back of his neck, and drew his mouth down to mine. His kiss was soft and tentative, reminding me suddenly of a time when I'd wondered what he must have been like as a virgin, hesitantly exploring a woman's body for the first time. I almost smiled at the memory, at how imagining him in such a way had seemed so impossible at the time.

But now as I kissed him, I could feel his innocence laid bare before me. With my other hand, I reached for his body beneath the water and tenderly cupped his testicles. He made a little noise deep down in his throat, moving closer to me until the hard tips of my nipples grazed his chest. I continued to stroke him beneath the water, feeling him growing hard and strong against my belly.

I shifted my attention to his erection, rubbing my hand up and down his shaft, feeling his pulse quickening just beneath the smooth skin. My core throbbed insistently between my legs, and I knew I was ready for him; had been ready for him for a very long time.

This would be no gentle lovemaking; his control had been shattered by grief, and his demons could only be exorcised through the hard use of my body. Then, and only then, could we begin the long task of picking up the broken pieces and building him back up again.

His erection pressed insistently against my belly, throbbing, aching, needing. He was ready, his mouth suddenly savage as it took mine, the tentative virgin forgotten as he drew blood from my lip. He had not yet touched me except to wrap his hands into my hair, but I didn't care.

This was not about me.

Abruptly, he broke away and spun me around so that I faced away from him. I instinctively parted my thighs and arched my back as the blunt tip of his cock nudged between my legs, hard and insistent as it blindly sought my opening. And then, with an abruptness that made me gasp, he pushed up hard and deep inside me until he slammed into my barrier. He grabbed roughly onto my hips, pulling me closer and immobilizing my body as he began to pump into me hard and fast.

With each stroke, he hammered against the wall of my womb until it seemed he would tear me apart, and my moans turned to cries as pleasure mingled beautifully with pain. He swept my hair away from my shoulders, sinking his teeth into the side of my neck hard enough to leave a mark.

Then, all at once, I felt him grow larger and harder inside of me and he was crying out, slamming into me again and again until his cries became indistinguishable from his sobs. I imagined the warmth of his seed shooting up inside of me - once, twice, three times. A shudder wracked him, and he thrust in one final push of release. Then he collapsed against me, the pulse of his cock fluttering, then slowing as he remained joined to me. I felt the most indescribable sense of tenderness towards him as I stood there, holding his weight while he nestled his face into the crook of my neck, his tears sliding down my shoulder.

Gradually his heartbeat slowed while his breathing returned to normal. I might have thought him asleep if not for the fact that he was standing up. Time passed as though we were in a dream, the sun moving across the sky, causing the shadows to shift in their orientation.

After a while he eased himself out of my tender body, and slowly turned me around to face him, stroking my bruised lip tenderly with his thumb. I took him instead by the hand and led him out of the cool water. We lay down on the soft grass, and I wrapped my body protectively around his, my arm across his chest, my knee drawn up over his hip, and my head resting on his shoulder.

I offered up a prayer of thanks to Saint Benedita, then joined Ashby in the drowsy space between waking and slumber as the warm afternoon sunlight dried our bodies.

The healing had begun.

EPILOGUE

THE NIGHTS WERE STILL chilly, though it was Spring. I hoisted myself out of bed and padded over to the hearth to place a new log on the fire. I stabbed at the embers meditatively, lost in thought as I urged them back to flame.

Another message had come for Ashby today. That made six now in the last month.

I turned and made my way over to the writing desk. Easing myself into the chair, I opened the drawer and pulled out a folded piece of paper. By the firelight, I read the following message.

The Dauphin is to be held in the Tower.

It was signed only with a small, star-shaped flower, drawn in scarlet ink: The Scarlet Pimpernel.

A soft creak in the floorboards at the door alerted me to her presence. She was always close these days, closer than usual.

It would soon be my time.

Two slender arms slid around my shoulders. "He needs you back in bed."

I turned and saw Ashby fast asleep in the bed I shared with him. "He doesn't even know I've left."

"*Non*," Gabrielle said, sliding her hand down to rest on my swollen belly. "*Le bébé*."

I couldn't help but smile. "How can you be so certain it's a boy?" I asked. But I already knew the answer. Gabrielle had a way of knowing things that none of us understood.

"Go," she said. "Back to bed. Now."

"Wait. What do you think this means?" I showed her the paper.

Gabrielle glanced over the note, though I knew she'd already seen it. Whatever Ashby was planning, Gabrielle was a part of it.

"I do not know," she lied, slipping into the familiarity of her own language. "These are not things for you to be worrying about just now. You need your sleep while you can still get it. He'll be coming soon."

I sighed. "Very well."

And I returned back to Ashby.

ACKNOWLEDGMENTS

A novel such as this is never written entirely alone. I am most thankful to:

Baroness Orczy, for the creation of The Scarlet Pimpernel, and for writing the books that played such a huge role in my adolescence.

Laura Taylor, my editor, my mentor and my friend. Thank you for your constant encouragement and advice. Without you, dear Laura, this book would not be in print.

Julia Bennet, my critique partner, for reading the entire manuscript, and providing priceless commentary and critiques and the occasional note of "my tea's gone cold," just to make me laugh while slogging through edits.

The Queens, my Twitter support group: CJ Noble, Catherine Matthews, C. D'Angelo, Sarah Elynn, and Beth Weg. I cannot summarize how much each of you mean to me, and the ways you have all helped me to grow as an author. I'm giving a special shout out to both CJ and Catherine for reading my manuscript, and loving Ashby and Elina's story almost as much as I do.

My Army of Beta Readers, with special mentions going to L.A. Myles and Ivy Blackwater. Thank you for reading my manuscript in its various stages. L.A., your suggestions helped shape Ashby in so many ways. Ann, your love for my manuscript helped me to realize that it was finally ready for the world.

To my beautiful husband Terry; my sister, and Elina's avatar, Adrienne; and to my dear friend Tava: You three are my trinity, my people. I wrote this story for you.

And finally to my parents, Lesley and Malcolm: Mom, you taught me to read, and introduced me to the world of The Scarlet Pimpernel. Dad, you taught me to love history, and to love Yorkshire almost as much as you do. Without the two of you, I literally would be nothing.

About the Author

Heather E. F. Carter is a former academic, with advanced degrees in Medieval Women's history and Early Modern European history. She wrote The Black Unicorn while a doctoral student in UCLA's history department, studying Eighteenth-Century England. Heather lives in San Diego with her husband, two children, and pet snake.